CAROL

ALSO BY DARIN KENNEDY

Fugue & Fable

The Mussorgsky Riddle

The Stravinsky Intrigue

The Tchaikovsky Finale

The Pawn Stratagem

Pawn's Gambit

Queen's Peril

King's Crisis

Other Titles

The April Sullivan Chronicles: Necromancer for Hire

The Sicilian Defense and Other Dark Tales

CAROL

DARIN KENNEDY

CAROL

Cover art and design by Natania Barron
Book design by Melissa McArthur

Printed in the United States of America
ebook ISBN: 978-1-943748-00-6
paperback ISBN: 978-1-943748-01-3
hardcover ISBN: 978-1-943748-02-0

Charlotte, NC

To my sister, Jill, and her daughters,
Katelyn and Olivia.
This one's for you.

PREFACE

I have endeavoured in this Ghostly little book, to raise the Ghost of an Idea, which shall not put my readers out of humour with themselves, with each other, with the season, or with me. May it haunt their houses pleasantly, and no one wish to lay it.

Their faithful Friend and Servant,
C.D.
December, 1843.

My thanks to Charles Dickens for giving us *A Christmas Carol*, a story for the ages. I have endeavored to honor his original idea while bringing something fresh to a story the entire world knows in their bones, heart, and soul. May it bring you both laughter and tears, and stick with you long after you've turned the last page.

Your faithful Friend and Servant,
D.K.
December, 2014

STAVE I

MARNIE'S GHOST

Wednesday, December 21st

CHAPTER ONE

Marnie is dead, to begin with. There is no doubt whatever about that.

So who the hell sent me this text?

A year ago tonight, I spent an hour in front of the mirror getting my hair perfect, slid into the prettiest black dress in my closet, and drove alone to the funeral home. The rest of the cheerleading squad showed up, of course, though I didn't have much to say to any of them. They all saw Marnie Jacobsen as an ideal to aspire to, perhaps even a legend, but as far as I was concerned, she was the only person on the planet who truly understood me, and she was gone.

Lying there in the casket, Marnie's skin shone as pale and fine as the white silk dress her mother chose as her final garment. Her lips were painted the same ruby red she wore to school every day, and her cheeks were brushed a subtle pink like the roses that surrounded the full-length portrait by her head. It seemed she could wake at any moment, but I knew in my heart those ice blue eyes of hers had closed forever. Could her death possibly have been as peaceful as she appeared in her cushioned metal box, what with her lungs full of water and her blood teeming with alcohol and Xanax?

A part of me wished it were me who drowned that day.

A part of me still does.

Instead, I'm left holding my breath, waiting for the welcome chill of fresh air on my face to let me know it's safe to exhale again.

"Excuse me." A high-pitched whine yanks me back to the present. "Do you work here?"

I look up from my phone. A petite girl, sophomore at best, gazes across the counter at me. I have no idea how she made it through the door without the bell sounding, but there's no doubt as to why she's here. Even soaked to the bone from the freezing rain outside, her eyes somehow still possess that glimmer of hopeful excitement I've been forced to endure a dozen times a day for the last week.

"No. I just like standing behind cash registers." I puff my chest up and glance down at my upside-down name below the "Philippe's Boutique" stenciled logo. "Thought I'd try out this name tag as a fashion statement."

"Sorry. I guess that was stupid." Blushing, the freckled girl glances down at my chest and does her best to smile prettily, though the mouth full of metal makes her grin look more like the grille of a car than anything a boy might be interested in kissing. And God help her, will someone please buy the poor thing some dental floss?

"Wait," she asks. "Carol. You're Carol Davis, aren't you?"

Fantastic. Here it comes. "That's what it says on my driver's license."

"*The* Carol Davis? The one who—"

I'm so not having this conversation tonight. "Look. Can I help you or not?"

She stiffens, her gaze dropping to the floor. "Umm, well, I

need a dress for the Christmas Eve Dance, and I'm on a bit of a budget."

Of course you are.

"I haven't seen you around school." I give her a quick up and down. Hand-me-down jeans. A top that was in fashion when I was a sophomore. Sneakers so worn they need to be tossed in the garbage. "I'm guessing you're a student at East?"

She nods. "Second year."

"Interesting. Sophomores don't usually get invited to the Christmas Eve Dance."

She blushes. "Jimmy Barnes asked me. He's a senior at East. You might have run into him. Academic team? Runs track?"

"Barnes. Barnes." I glance at the time on my phone. Still thirty minutes to closing. "Doesn't ring a bell." I motion to the nearly spent tear-off calendar on the counter, the date December 21st. "Cutting it pretty close, aren't you?"

The girl takes a deep breath. "I know Saturday is just three days away, but he just called this afternoon and..."

Her story fades into background noise as I wonder how it is Ms. Metalmouth has a date for Christmas Eve and I don't. The dance is the only good thing about this stupid season, and I've already been asked by pretty much every boy at West.

That is, except the one person I've actually got my eye on.

A tradition going back longer than I've been alive, the Christmas Eve Dance is in many ways bigger than prom in this town. As Aunt Valerie tells it, Havisham's two big high schools have had a friendly rivalry for as long as anyone can remember, but back in her day, it got a little less friendly. A particularly controversial football state championship—where I'm proud to say the West Havisham Lions squeaked out a victory over the rival Hedgehogs—led to some bad blood between the schools. We're not talking riots in the streets or anything, but it was enough for the town leaders to get involved. Their grand idea?

An emergency Christmas Eve Dance where the two schools could come together and return peace and harmony to our little town.

And wouldn't you know it, the teenagers of Havisham have made darn sure to keep that tradition alive ever since.

Silence. Guess she's finally stopped talking. Better tune back in.

"Sorry. It's been a long day." I slip into a practiced smile. "So, what kind of dress are you looking for?"

"Not sure exactly." She fumbles in her purse. "Jimmy already has his outfit all lined up and I was hoping to find something blue to match his vest." She produces a folded-up page from a tuxedo catalog. "Do you have anything that goes with this?"

Sucking air through my teeth, I shake my head with mock sadness. "Don't think so. Aqua's been out for about three years, but you might check our discount rack." I motion to the back of the store. "Lots of leftovers to pick through. You might get lucky."

"Discount rack?" Her brow furrows. "Look. I just need something pretty. Guys like Jimmy don't ask me to dances every day. Can you help me or not?"

My shoulders rise in a subtle shrug. "I'll do my best." The slight tremble of her lower lip sends me back to the last thing my boss told me before he left for the day.

Remember, Miss Davis. Philippe's voice washes across my thoughts, his flamboyant French accent punctuating every word. *The customer is always right.*

Fine.

"What's your name?" I ask, forcing a smile.

"Emily." She chokes on the word.

"All right, Emily. Let's see what we can do. What's your budget?"

She pulls a small wad of bills from her purse and spreads them on the counter. "Mom pulled together $150, and I've got a little extra to cover tax so—"

"Sorry. Philippe doesn't carry anything current in that price range. Like I said before, maybe the discount section?" I point to the large rack of last year's styles at the back of the store. "Let me know if you find anything in your size."

"But—"

"Look. I'm not sure what you want me to do. Pretty much everything new in the store is $350 and up." I lean in, and with a conspiratorial whisper ask, "Did you check Walmart?"

Emily's eyes narrow. She sweeps the money back into her purse and stomps toward the door. "I'm sorry I even came in here."

"Wait," I mutter under my breath. "Don't go."

The bell rings as the door slams shut behind the girl, her name already forgotten. The resultant icy gust sending my skin into goosebumps, I step into the back and pull out my phone. Taunted by the impossible text that waits there, I stare unblinking at the screen.

Hi, Care Bear.

Those three little words, dated December 21st, 8:26 p.m., from a phone number that hasn't been active in a year.

Exactly a year, in fact.

"It can't be. Marnie?" I glance around the room, nervous, as if speaking her name aloud on the anniversary of her death might somehow summon her like that urban legend Christopher always jokes about. The one where you stand before a mirror at midnight and say a dead girl's name three times.

Bloody Mary. Bloody Mary. Bloody Mary.

The doorbell chimes again, and I nearly jump out of my

skin. The phone tumbles from my fingers and lands on the carpet, the first piece of good luck I've had all night. Not sure if Valerie and Mike would be too keen on putting a third new screen on my little smartphone this year. I stoop to grab it and step back out to the counter to face this latest customer.

Wait. False alarm. Not a customer.

Roberta.

CHAPTER TWO

I put on as pleasant a face as I can muster. "Hiya, Bobbisox."

Her brown lips turn downward in a disapproving frown as she shakes out her umbrella by the door and slips out of her drenched raincoat. "Come on, Carol. I've told you a thousand times to leave that name in third grade where it belongs."

"And yet, a thousand times later, you keep walking through my door."

"Glutton for punishment, I guess." She waggles her thumb over her shoulder in the direction she came. "Curious. A minute ago, I passed some girl running up the sidewalk bawling her eyes out. Your handiwork?"

My arms instinctively cross as my face falls into a not-quite-practiced smirk. "Would you go into the nicest restaurant in town and expect to pay McDonald's prices? I just told her what we had available that fit her budget."

Roberta raises an eyebrow. "I suspect it had something to do with your delivery."

Ah, Roberta Oliver. A rare find indeed. Smart as a whip,

loyal to a fault, and nicer than any human being has a right to be. Girl's going to be valedictorian if she's not careful.

More than anything, though, the girl's defining characteristic remains her utter lack of fear about speaking whatever is on her mind.

A part of my life since kindergarten, I still remember when Roberta's mom and dad dropped her off the very first day at school and she sat next to me at our table in Ms. Burgess' room. At the time, the Olivers were one of the few Black families in Havisham. Our mothers became fast friends over wine and tapas, and our dads would drive the golf cart from green to green to get away from it all every few weekends. After the crash, the day the universe decided to kidney punch my existence with brass knuckles, Roberta was one of the few kids at school who would still talk to me. After Mr. Oliver passed away a few years later, we found something to truly bond over.

Back in the day, we were inseparable. Swim team. Summer camp. You name it. Nowadays, though, I can't quite seem to find the time for her. Which is strange.

Other than Marnie, who last time I checked was still resting in peace down at the First Baptist Church cemetery, I've never really cared much for anyone on the cheerleading squad though I see them all pretty much every day. Roberta, on the other hand, has come back no matter how many times I've kicked her to the curb, as down-to-earth and supportive as ever.

These days, she's the closest thing I've got to a best friend.

Not that I'd ever admit that to her. Don't want her to get a big head.

Also, it never hurts to have the smartest girl in school on your speed dial.

"Whatever. There are several dresses on our discount rack that would show off those hips of hers just fine."

"Wow." Roberta shakes her head. "Your kindness really knows no bounds."

"School's out, everyone else on the squad is enjoying their holiday break, and Valerie insists I keep this stupid job, knowing good and well what happens in four days." I cross my arms. "If I have to hear the whole 'learning the value of money' speech one more time..."

Roberta raises an eyebrow. "Your aunt has a point, you know."

"What?" My hand finds its way to my hip. "That working retail through the Christmas season will somehow make me a better person?"

"You know I'd never say that." She studies me for a moment. "It's just that...regardless of how much the circumstances behind it suck, you're about to come into more money than most people in this town can even imagine." Her gaze wanders around the shop. "A little grounding in reality may not be the worst thing that could happen to you."

"God, Bobbisox." I take a step back. "When did you turn forty?"

"Don't try to turn this around on me." Roberta fixes me with her trademark smirk. "This is *your* Hallmark movie life lesson, not mine."

"Fine." I check my phone. Twenty-four minutes to closing. "So, what brings you down here besides your intense need to play Jiminy Cricket?"

"With everything going on at home, I feel like we've barely spoken since Thanksgiving. I texted you a couple days ago, sent an email too, but never heard back on either. I thought I'd come by and see if you wanted to grab a hot chocolate." The pounding of the freezing rain hitting the roof doubles in volume. "I know this time of year can't be easy for you. The whole thing with

Marnie. Remembering your mom and dad." She tilts her head to one side, the compassion in her gaze palpable. "And Joy..."

My sister's name used to bring the waterworks as reliably as pressing a button, but those days are gone. *Toughen up*, the dead girl who texted me a few minutes ago told me once. *If you're the one who brings the tears, you never have to be the one who cries them.*

"So?" Roberta's insistent tone brings me back to the present. "Hot chocolate? My treat."

My head shakes before I've even decided what I want to do. "Can't tonight. Valerie wants me home right after work."

"S'okay. Maybe another time." Roberta's gaze drops.

I seem to be having that effect on people tonight.

My excuse is mostly the truth. It's no lie Valerie worries about me leaving work so late. I hear about it every night. What's really got my hackles up, though, is this stupid text. The more I think about it and whoever it is that's screwing with me, the more I want to get home, lock the door, and climb into bed. Am I angry? Absolutely. A little scared? Maybe.

"I appreciate the offer." I gesture at the ceiling where the volume of the downpour has gone up another notch. "Raincheck?"

"Sure." Roberta half-turns for the door. "I kind of needed to talk, but I guess we can catch up later."

"Sounds good." I turn my attention to the register, hoping Roberta picks up on my not so subtle cue.

She doesn't.

"You know, it's been really tough since we got the news about Tameka."

"I bet." And here we go. The conversation I've been avoiding for the last month. Surprise of the century, talking about dying family members makes me uncomfortable. "Any...news?"

"She's hanging on, but barely. The chemo has wiped out most of the cancer cells, but unless we find a bone marrow donor soon, the doctors aren't too optimistic she can survive more than a few weeks. All the different treatments have really taken a toll on her immune system. Even something like a simple cold could be all it takes."

"Your mom told you all that?"

"These days, it's just me, Mom, and Tameka." Roberta's eyebrows shoot up in exasperation. "I get to hear everything."

"What about Derrick?" A stony expression crosses Roberta's features, and I wish the words back into my mouth.

"As always, Mom knows how to pick 'em. Her latest knight in shining armor scooted two days after Tameka went to the hospital this last time. He and Mom were up late arguing that night and didn't know I was still awake." Roberta catches her breath. "Jerk said he didn't sign up to spend every minute of his life at a stupid hospital." She runs a sleeve across her eyes.

Awesome. Two crying girls in one night.

"I'm...sorry." I bite my lip so hard it hurts. "You liked him a lot, didn't you?"

"We all did. I sure didn't think it was going to end up this way. He and Mom had been together eight months." Roberta's sigh fills the room. "Wasn't meant to be, I guess."

"Different subject." I pull a medium-length black-and-white striped number from the rack and hold it up to her. "Do you have a dress for the dance yet?"

A quiet laugh cuts through her tears. "I need a date before I need a dress, don't you think?"

"No one's asked you? The Nubian Queen of the Fighting Lions Swim Team?"

"Very funny. Since everything with Tameka went south a few weeks back, I've barely made it to school, much less practice. Out of sight, out of mind, I suppose." Roberta takes the dress from me, drapes it across her body, and inspects herself in the mirror. "Hey, have you given any thought to coming back to swim? Coach still asks about you now and then."

"Not happening." I hand her a second dress, this one a long, purple gown with a scoop neck and silver trim. "Cheer, study, work, eat, sleep. Only so many hours in a day."

"Too bad." She holds the two dresses before her and then hands me back the black-and-white number. "The girl we've got on butterfly doesn't hold a candle to you."

"What can I say? I'm a woman of many talents. Still, like we talked about last year, swim and cheering just don't line up."

She steps away from the mirror and returns the second dress to the rack before shooting me a wink. "And how about you? Big plans this Saturday?" She leans in, her voice dropping to a low purr. "Christopher finally get up the nerve to ask you to go somewhere with him besides a comic book convention?"

It's my turn to laugh. "I swear. That boy and I spent one summer camp together between first and second grade and he's been Krazy-Glued to my life ever since."

"You know, he's actually looking pretty good these days. He's slimmed down a bit, and with those new glasses of his, he kind of has that whole Clark Kent thing going on."

I shake my head. "The only thing super under Christopher's clothes are those stupid t-shirts he wears. They get their own drawer, you know. It's kind of sad actually. So much wasted potential."

"So, you know where he keeps his underwear and you think he has potential to boot." Roberta's eyes take on a decidedly knowing gleam. "Interesting."

"Please." I make a point to roll my eyes. "In a *Pretty in Pink* world, Christopher Kellerman is and always will be the Ducky."

Shaking her head, Roberta dismisses me with a quiet laugh. "Call me when you've seen a movie filmed this century."

"Hey. The Eighties got Molly Ringwald. We got Miley Cyrus. Not a hard call."

"Whatever." Roberta picks the purple dress back up and holds it to her chest. "Actually, now that I think about it, if you're going to throw back a perfectly good fish like Christopher Kellerman, maybe I should cast a line and reel him in myself. As you were so kind to point out, I am short one date for the dance."

I feel my cheeks grow warm. "Sorry, sweetie. What's the First Rule of Date Club?"

Roberta's expression deflates as she returns the dress to the rack. "Sisters before misters."

"And the Second Rule of Date Club?"

She sighs. "Sisters before misters."

"Exactly. Now, feel free to fish all you want." I raise an eyebrow. "Just pick another pond, all right?"

"Happy to." She walks to the door, slips back into her raincoat, and grabs her umbrella. "Just proving a point."

"And what point is that?" I clamp my bottom lip between my teeth so hard, I'm afraid I'll draw blood. "Enlighten me."

Roberta opens the door and launches into her worst British accent. "Methinks the lady doth protest too much."

CHAPTER THREE

Before I can get out anything resembling a clever comeback, the door slams shut behind Roberta. The icy gust responsible sends a shiver straight through my core. I whip out my phone, ready to fire off some serious snark, when my eyes fall again on the unopened text.

Marnie Jacobsen, December 21st, 8:26 p.m.
Hi, Care Bear.

Who would do such a thing? And why target me? I may have been Marnie's best friend, but I'm nothing special. Just another high school cheerleader with halfway decent grades, a crappy job, and an "unsatisfying" home life.

Unless it all has something to do with the millions of dollars coming my way next week.

Great. The stalkers of the world are getting proactive.

"Let's get this over with." My pulse racing, I bite the bullet and thumb the screen, opening the message. My phone freezes for a moment, as if considering whether or not to comply with my request, and then the screen fills with white along with

Marnie's characteristic greeting above a website link spelled out in royal blue.

Click before midnight if you want
to experience the joy of Christmas!

"Like hell." I start to press the delete button, but decide on a better plan. A couple swipes across the screen bring the offending phone number front and center. "Get ready, jerk-face. Here I come."

I lose count of the number of rings, and with every cycle, I get more and more pissed off. I nearly give up on the call more than once, but letting this go is not an option. Nobody's going to scare the bejeezus out of me and get away with it.

Nobody.

Patience, however, has never been one of my virtues. In fact, I'm about to hurl my phone into the wall when someone finally picks up.

"Yes?" Scratchy and frayed, the voice on the other end comes across like someone's sick grandmother. "Virginia?" the woman asks when I don't answer.

"There's no Virginia here. I'm..." Wait a second, Carol. Remember what you're doing here. This is no time to play nice. "Hey. You sent me a text earlier. What's the deal?"

"A text?" The woman's grandmotherly smile all but beams across the cellular connection. "I'm sorry, honey. I don't know how to do that."

"But you already did." I feel my cheeks getting hot. "Earlier tonight, *you* sent *me* a text. What do you want?"

"Virginia?" A whiff of fear colors her words. "Is this you?"

I clench the phone so tight my fingertips tingle.

"Look, there's no one named Virginia here, but *your* number is showing up on *my* phone. Did you or did you not send me a text about twenty minutes ago?"

A new edge comes out in Grandma's voice. "Now see here, young lady. You're being very rude. As I said before, I don't have the first idea how to send a text or whatever it is you're going on about."

The heat in my cheeks rises again, this time from embarrassment rather than anger. "You don't, do you?"

"Not in the year or so I've had the phone. My granddaughter keeps offering to teach me how, but—"

My pulse ratchets up another notch. "You've had the phone a year?"

"Right at it." The kindness returns to her voice. "My daughter, Virginia, bought it for me last Christmas." An audible sigh comes across the connection. "First few months I got calls like this all the time. People looking for that Jacobsen girl who drowned. I almost had the phone company switch out the number, but around March or April the calls finally calmed down." She pauses. "Only Virginia calls me these days."

"So you didn't send the text."

"No, dear." The edge returns to her tone. "I didn't send the text."

"Sorry." I press *End* and place the phone face down on the counter. I half expect Grandma to call back and finish dressing me down—it's what I'd do—but no call comes. I glance at the time. 8:50. I consider wiping the counters down and cleaning the windows, but decide instead to close up a few minutes early and find out what vegetarian delight Valerie has waiting for me back at the house.

I lock up the cash drawer, stack all the credit card receipts for Philippe to process in the morning, and flip off the lights. The rain has finally let up by the time I step out into the cold darkness, but the weather isn't what chills me to the core.

Though the only living soul in sight is the zit-faced sophomore working the counter at the sandwich shop next door, I feel a set of eyes boring into me like a pair of lasers. I sprint to the hand-me-down Toyota Corolla Valerie bought sometime back in the Middle Ages and after a quick fumble of the keys, hop inside and lock all the doors.

After revving the engine a few times in an effort to get the heater working, I pull the phone from my pocket, open Marnie's text, and laugh. Though I know in my heart this has to be a stupid prank, it would almost make sense if she were the one who sent it. That girl had one sick sense of humor and knew exactly how I feel about December 25th.

Click before midnight if you want
to experience the joy of Christmas!

"Click this." And with that, I jam my thumb down on the *Delete* button. "Christmas? You can keep it."

CHAPTER FOUR

"Carol?"

Right on time. My nightly ritual with Valerie.

At least she doesn't just barge in like in the old days.

"Yeah?"

"You hungry?"

My stomach rumbles. I ignore it. "I'll get something after while."

Valerie's sigh isn't audible through the door, but I sense it all the same. "Promise?"

"Promise."

"All right."

The hardwood creaks as Valerie heads for the stairs leading down to the kitchen. I swear, you can't go anywhere in this rattrap without alerting the rest of the house. I know this used to be Grandma and Grandpa's place, but both Mike and Valerie make good money. They could live anywhere, but here we are stuck in a fifty-year-old split level with all the creaks and drafts that come with the territory.

Funny. Some people just can't let go of the past.

My computer chimes with a new email. My gaze drops to my laptop, and the blood in my veins turns to ice water. I scoot up the bed away from my laptop until my back collides with the unforgiving headboard, the light radiating from the screen flickering like a sputtering torch. There, above a work email from Philippe with the subject "We need to talk" and Roberta's message from earlier, the new email taunts me.

Subject line? *Hi, Care Bear.*

From a Gmail account that's been dead for a year.

At her mother's request, Christopher and I dismantled Marnie's entire online presence before school started back last spring. I thought we did a pretty good job at the time, but given the text from earlier and now this stupid email, I'm wondering if we really accomplished anything. If it had been me alone on the project, I'd just figure I screwed it up, but this is Christopher Kellerman we're talking about.

The boy bleeds microchips.

Wait.

Christopher.

Images from dozens of scary movies we've watched at each other's houses over the years flash across my memory with one story in particular crowding out the others.

And not for the first time tonight.

In far too graphic detail, the urban legend of Bloody Mary weighs on my thoughts. This time, though, there's nothing to distract me. The vision of the girl's blood-covered face grows in my mind until I can think of nothing else.

I rush to the bathroom, pull the door closed, and flip off the lights. As my eyes adjust to the near darkness, I turn and face the mirror. Lit only by the glow pouring from my phone where it rests next to the sink, my reflection in the glass looks like something from a B-horror flick. I imagine the face in the mirror covered in pig's blood beneath a prom queen's tiara...

"Bloody Marnie."

Climbing from a static-filled TV screen...

"Bloody Marnie."

Smiling wickedly from a second-story window...

"Bloody Marnie."

I stand in the darkness for over a minute, waiting for something—anything—to happen. Then, as I'm about to flip the lights back on, the phone buzzes with a text. Amplified by the stone countertop, the vibration echoes loudly in the tiny room and nearly sends my heart leaping out of my chest. I grab the phone and pull it up to my face, knowing good and well Marnie Jacobsen has sent me another message from beyond the grave.

Not so much.

It's Roberta.

See you tomorrow morning at the mall.

Second time tonight the girl has scared the crap out of me. I'll have to thank her later. Maybe shave off one of her eyebrows when she's sleeping. Or something worse.

"*Carol...*"

My eyes shoot back to the mirror, but where moments before my barely visible face looked back, I now stare into Marnie Jacobsen's ice blue eyes, her blood-red lips pursed as she studies me from beyond the glass. Breathless, I run to the door and throw it open, flip on all the lights, and look back, only to find the room empty.

My heart beating a hundred miles an hour, I rush from the bathroom and nearly go flying as I trip on the pile of damp towels by the door. I scramble to my feet and rush back to my bed, but not before flipping off the lights and slamming the door closed behind me. Leaping to the center of the mattress, I refuse to look back, though every instinct screams to at least glance and see if the dead girl from the mirror is drawing close. My fingers and toes tingle like they're covered in ants as I war with my hyperventilating lungs.

Breathe in.

This isn't happening.

Breathe out.

Marnie is dead.

Breathe in.

You just freaked yourself out with all this Bloody Mary crap.

Breathe out.

This is all in your mind.

Breathe in.

Except for one thing.

Afraid to even touch it, I sit staring at the open laptop. Its screen dark, the power light pulses like something alive. Eventually, I get brave enough to brush my fingers across the trackpad, and the screen returns to life. My eyes shoot to the top of my emails and there it is. Same as before. Taunting me like a bratty child.

MarnieJ@gmail.com. 9:26 p.m.

It's not possible, and yet...

I force my head and eyes to the left until I'm again staring at the bathroom.

The door stands wide open.

And I made damn sure it was closed.

Going against everything ingrained in me from the hundred or so post-horror-movie lectures Christopher has subjected me to over the years, I scoot off the bed and tiptoe to the open door. Reaching into the darkness, I stretch out my arm to pull the door closed, but reflexively jerk my hand away as my fingers brush the doorknob.

The metal is like ice.

"Carol?"

I nearly pee my pants at the voice from the hall.

"Are you okay?"

Nothing to fear. It's just Valerie.

"I'm fine," I grumble through the door.

"I thought I heard you yell."

"Just stepped on something." The exasperation in my voice is only partly intentional. "Sorry if I bothered you."

"No...no problem." An interminable pause. "Last chance for dinner. Mike and I both have to turn in early tonight."

"Be down in a minute." Woman's got a one-track mind. "All right?"

"Okay." No creaks this time. She's waiting on me.

After a minute, I can't hold my tongue any longer. "Anything else?"

"I guess not." She lets out a quiet sigh. "See you downstairs."

I wait until the creak of the hardwood floor fades away before returning to my task. Daring to touch the doorknob once more, I again find it cool to the touch, but the bone-numbing chill that emanated off the metal before is gone. I flip on every light in the bathroom and search the place from top to bottom. No ghosts. No dead girls. No hidden cameras. Nothing. Just a pile of towels that are going to be all moldy by morning if I don't hang them up.

What an idiot.

With God as my witness, I swear. From now on, only Sandra Bullock flicks for this girl.

CHAPTER FIVE

I return to my bed, take a few deep breaths, and pull the computer onto my lap. The underside is so hot I can almost smell the flesh of my thighs cooking, but I leave it there just the same. My fingers hover above the trackpad trembling like I'm about to rest my hand on some high-tech Ouija board. What happens if I open the email? Am I suddenly communicating with the dead? Or does it just unleash some computer virus that eats hard drives for breakfast? Remembering what Uncle Mike always says about discretion being the better part of valor, I close the computer, push it off my lap, and head down to get some food.

My thoughts wander as I trudge down the creaky stairs.

Fact. The messages aren't from Marnie. I watched them lower her casket into the ground. And last time I checked, the dead don't have email accounts on the other side.

Fact. Like Valerie's told me a hundred times over the years, especially after my countless movie nights with Christopher, there's no such thing as ghosts. Or monsters. Or goblins. Or any other creepy things that go bump in the night.

Fact. Whoever has hacked Marnie's old email account and

cell number is probably only the first of many. Monday morning is payday, and three million dollars is going to bring the weirdos out of the woodwork.

Looks like it's time for a new phone number and email address.

"And a new address," I mutter, glancing around the half-lit space at the dingy wallpaper that's been hanging since before anyone who lives in this house was born. "Definitely a new address."

As I hit the bottom of the stairs, it occurs to me I'm not the least bit hungry. Whatever appetite I had when I got home from work is a distant memory after all the fun of the last half hour. Collecting myself, I stroll into the kitchen and grab my usual seat by the window. Valerie stands facing the microwave, her finger poised to press the stop button, while Uncle Mike sits at the table perusing the paper. A smirk finds its way to my face. How anyone can stand to read something as mind numbing as the *Wall Street Journal* is beyond me, but it's Mike's nightly ritual. Hey, at least when he's distracted, he doesn't grill me with questions. A little peace and quiet at the dinner table is always a—

"Hiya, Carol." I hold in my sigh as Uncle Mike folds the paper and rests it on the table. "You look a little flushed. Everything all right?"

"I'm fine." My brain flips through lies like a Google search. "Was just getting in a few crunches before dinner."

"Really?" His bullshit meter about as sensitive as mine, Mike raises an eyebrow. "So. How was your day? Do anything fun?"

I take a deep breath. "Nothing much. Went shopping this afternoon. Umpteenth night shift in a row at the boutique. The usual." I glance over at Valerie who's watching from the corner of her eye. "I did find a cute pair of boots at the mall."

Mike lets out a quiet laugh. "At this rate, I'm going to have to put in another closet just to accommodate all your footwear."

"At least something around this house would be new."

"What was that?" Mike raises an eyebrow.

"Come on, honey," Valerie interrupts as she pulls a large plate of steaming tofu and snap peas from the microwave. "Carol can buy a pair of boots if she wants."

Mike glances over at me and shakes his head. "I suppose in four days, she'll be able to buy all the boots she wants, not to mention all the closet space she could ever need."

I fix him with squinted eyes. "As long as it's not under *this* roof, right?"

"What are you talking about?" Mike looks honestly shocked. "I never said that."

"You didn't have to."

"Now, Carol, calm down." Valerie rests a plate of reheated "tofu surprise" in front of me and joins us at the table. "Mike was just making a joke."

"My history teacher says every joke contains a kernel of truth." I glare at my uncle through slitted eyes. "Don't worry, Mike. A week from now I won't be underfoot anymore. You can count on it."

"Typical evening at the Frederick house." Mike's gaze shoots to Valerie. "Good old Uncle Mike can't say anything right."

I shoot out of my chair. "Know what? I'm not feeling too hungry. Can you just put this in the fridge for later?"

Valerie crosses her arms over her chest. "So you can lock yourself in your room for the third night this week?"

"I said I'm not hungry, but if it's really important to you that I sit here and pick at my food—"

"No," Valerie says. "I'll put it in the fridge."

So quiet, it's barely audible, Mike adds, "With all the other plates."

"Thanks." I shoot out of my chair, pretending I didn't hear the comment. "Shoot me a text if you need me for anything."

I'm halfway up the stairs before I hear Valerie's quiet "Okay," and in my room with the door shut before either of them can utter another word. Sometimes, I wait at the top of the stairs for Mike's inevitable commentary on my "unacceptable behavior" and Valerie's equally inevitable defense of her poor, orphaned niece, but not tonight. I used to give a crap about Mike's opinion, but those times are long past. In four short days, neither of us will have to put up with the other any longer.

As for Valerie, I can do no wrong in the woman's eyes, a simple fact I figured out years ago and have played to my advantage ever since. My Teflon coating has come in handy plenty of times over the years, although I've never been sure if it's that I remind Valerie of my mother, her only sister, or the fact that I'm about the closest thing to a daughter she will ever have.

I've heard it all a thousand times. Barring a surrogate or some kind of miracle, Mike and Valerie can't have kids. Courtesy of a tumor that left her doubled over in pain for six months, Valerie got to have a hysterectomy at the ripe old age of twenty-five, just a year after she and Mike got married. From what I've picked up over the dinner table through the years, they thought about adoption for a while, but all of that flew out the window when I got dumped in their laps ten years ago.

We don't owe her anything.

Mike's words echo in my skull like he spoke them five minutes ago.

As much as I wish it were different, we just can't take her.

I never told him I heard what he said.

Someone else will take her. She'll be fine.

The morning after the crash, and he all but turns me out on the street.

His "Welcome home, slugger" over breakfast that morning fell on deaf ears.

To their credit, Valerie and Mike have ensured I've never wanted for anything, but some things just can't be unheard.

Quiet footsteps creak the hardwood floor outside my door. "Are you okay in there?"

Valerie again.

"Do you need something?" I don't even try to keep the frustration from my voice.

"No. Just checking on you." I can almost hear the gears turning in her head in the thoughtful pause that follows, no doubt deciding whether or not to say what's on her mind. "We haven't seen each other much this week, but I know what tonight is. What it means. Do you want to talk?"

"Nothing to talk about."

"Okay." The hurt in that single word pretty much sums up our relationship these days. "Just let me know if I can do anything."

The boards sound again as she heads back downstairs, all a part of our nightly dance.

Now that she's gone, time to return to the matter at hand.

Despite all the warnings everywhere about viruses, phishing, and the like, I know myself well enough to understand I won't sleep tonight till I see what the email from Faux-Marnie says. I pop my laptop back open and after a deep breath, double-click on the subject line. The trackpad's burnished surface smooth as silk beneath my fingertips, I feel an almost electric jolt roll up my arm as the email opens. Not surprisingly, the same link as the one from the earlier text appears on my screen.

Click before midnight if you want

to experience the joy of Christmas!

"You must think I'm some kind of idiot." I may as well send a check to the next poor Nigerian prince who emails me. I move to delete the email like I did the text earlier, but change my mind at the last second. If this is just some creep trying to freak me out, it's probably not the best idea to get rid of all the evidence.

I close my email window and open up Instagram to see what's going on in the lives of my five hundred closest friends. A dozen messages wait for me at the top right of the screen.

Popularity has its price.

I scan through the various messages. Six are from the usual list of suspects jockeying for position in hopes of taking me to the Christmas Eve Dance—sorry guys, but I've got my sights set a little higher—while most of the others are from girls on the squad talking about what they'll be wearing Saturday night. And surprise of surprises, there in the middle of it all, a message from Christopher.

Dear Carol,

Hope your break is going well. I keep meaning to stop by the boutique and say hi, but Best Buy closes at 10 and Philippe's closes at 9. You do the math. Anyway, there's something I want to ask you. Maybe I'll come track you down tomorrow. Working your usual evening shift?

See you tomorrow!

Christopher

God. The boy even signs Instagram messages.

Oh well. Guess that's happening.

Not to mention I've got a pretty good idea what it is he wants to ask me.

I close my eyes, trying to decide what to say, or more likely, if I plan to return his message at all. I've already turned down half the football team's offensive line waiting for a certain basketball center to get off his butt and ask me out for Saturday. I'm sure as hell not showing up with the president of the Chess Club.

I open my eyes and find an additional message at the top of the screen. Before I can stop myself, my well-trained fingers click the Messages tab.

Click before midnight if you want
to experience the joy of Christmas!

From Marnie's Instagram. Fresh chills roll up my spine. Whoever this is, the bastard has access to all of Marnie's stuff: phone, email, social media.

God only knows what else.

I close the message, careful not to activate the link, and scoot away from the laptop. Pulling my stuffed panda bear, Mr. Shiners, to my chest, I stare at the screen and notice Christopher's message below Marnie's. A flash of inspiration flares to life in my mind. If anyone can track down this asshole who's tormenting me, I'm betting Christopher can. He's as tech-savvy as they come, and he's never been one to back down from a challenge. I speak from personal experience on that one. Guy's had a crush on me since we were six.

The lady doth protest too much, comes Roberta's taunting voice.

Hmm. She keeps up that crap, maybe I *will* fix her up with Christopher. They can go get crowned the brainiac King and Queen of the Christmas Eve Dance for all I care. I've got bigger fish to fry.

Like the fact a dead girl is doing everything in her power to get in touch with me.

I flop back on my bed and try to get my stomach to unknot as images from Marnie's funeral flit through my mind like some morbid highlight reel.

Marnie lying in her coffin as her mother looks on from the front pew of the church, all but oblivious to her surroundings as the same drugs that took her daughter's life course through her veins.

The pallbearers, six seniors from the football team, carrying Marnie to her final rest.

That first shovelful of dirt being hurled onto the metal box containing the empty husk that used to be my best friend.

The irony of how bothered I am by all this isn't lost on me. After all, Marnie was the one who taught me how not to care. Life's troubles always seemed to fall away from her like raindrops off her highly waxed BMW, a talent I coveted when we first met and learned to master over our two and a half years together. To this day, I can't believe the way she went out of this world.

Transferring into our school as a sophomore at the beginning of my freshman year, Marnie Jacobsen was all style. She made it onto the varsity cheerleading squad her first year, kept a solid 3.8 GPA, and had all the senior boys sniffing around from her first day. With Marnie, it was all about attitude. A former Army brat, she was forced to move every two to three years her entire life. She taught me right off the bat her strategy for success at a new school: take charge of the place before the place takes charge of you. By the time she was a senior, she might as well have worn a crown as she walked the scuffed hallways of our school. I've tried to prove a worthy successor to her legacy. I just wish she had told me before she died how empty being at the top would feel.

And how utterly alone.

CHAPTER SIX

I remember it like it was yesterday.

December 21st, one year ago almost to the minute. Valerie had asked me to come down and help her wrap presents, pretty much the most mind-numbing activity imaginable. I held out in my room for half an hour before going down, hoping she'd get a good head start on me. As I hit the bottom stair, I heard her sobbing. I glanced across Valerie's heaving shoulders at the old tube television they'd inherited from Mom and Dad.

"Valerie?" I asked. "Why is Marnie's house on the news?"

Valerie glanced across her shoulder at me, her face white and her eyes red and swollen. "Honey," she said, her voice a croaked whisper, "I need to tell you something."

"What is it?" I asked, my throat already growing tight as well. "What happened?"

"It's Marnie, Carol. They found her in the hot tub." She brought the sleeve of her tacky Christmas tree sweater across her eyes to wipe away the tears. "The newsman says they don't know how long she was under, but she's gone."

That's when the first text came in. From Nicole Van der Graaf.

The first of many.

"She...drowned?" I had spoken to Marnie earlier that day. She seemed fine. In fact, she was pretty sure her dad was actually going to make it home for Christmas for the first time in three years. "Are you sure?"

As if in answer, the newscast switched from an image of the Jacobsens' two-story house to a photo of Marnie in full cheerleading regalia. The trademark sparkle in those ice blue eyes came through, even on the ancient TV screen.

"But how?" I croaked. "Why?"

"We don't always get a why, Carol." Valerie rose from the couch and pulled me into a hug, one of the last I have ever allowed. "Sometimes things just are."

Valerie's clumsy attempt at softening the blow didn't help much.

And by not much, I mean not at all.

Still, I didn't shed a tear.

Not one.

That's how Marnie would have wanted it.

CHAPTER SEVEN

I awake hungry and cold in the dark. And not just "I've kicked off the blanket in my sleep" cold. Despite the flannel sheets, thermal blanket, and comforter pulled up to my neck, it feels like I'm lying in a walk-in freezer.

I glance over at my alarm clock. It's only 11:55. I rack my brain but don't remember flipping off the lights or pulling the covers up around me. Valerie must have checked on me before she went to bed, which leaves me all warm and fuzzy till I notice something else that's different.

My laptop rests open at the opposite corner of the bed from where I left it. And I know for a fact I closed the thing before I dozed off. Though the screensaver image swirls from one end of the spectrum to the other, the only color I see is red.

I swear, if Valerie was snooping around on my computer...

The clock flips to 11:56 as memories of the evening percolate through my skull. The various impossible messages from Marnie and their insistent references to midnight dance across my mind's eye. As I sit up to close the screen on my laptop, my phone buzzes on the nightstand. Ignoring the little voice inside telling me to leave it where it sits, I snatch it up only to drop it like a hot coal when I see the name on the screen.

Marnie Jacobsen, December 21, 11:57 p.m.

I slam the phone face down on the nightstand and for reasons I don't understand, rush immediately to the window. Somehow, a part of me is convinced some psycho in a clown mask and a blue jumpsuit will be standing in the grass staring up at me with an evil leer and a cell phone in his hand. Though the nearly full moon casts its silver blue light across the lawn, nothing out of the ordinary awaits me there. I scan the waterlogged yard for any sign of movement until a kaleidoscope of light fills the room and draws my attention back inside.

My laptop, previously lying dormant on the corner of the bed dreaming of swirling screensaver rainbows, has come to life. Photo after photo of Marnie and me together drifts across the screen, which wouldn't be particularly disturbing except for two things: most of the pictures aren't mine and at least half are of moments that were, as far as I know, never photographed.

"Stop it!" I half expect my scream to bring Valerie bolting down the hall, but utter silence reigns as the computer continues its guided tour of my two-and-a-half-year friendship with Marnie Jacobsen.

"Valerie?" I shout. Then, more timidly, "Mike?"

My breath steams in the frigid air as I rush to the door and grab the knob, but as with the bathroom before, the metal is like a hunk of ice. I jerk my hand away, leaving the top layer of skin behind, and grab a t-shirt from the floor to wrap around my hand before trying again. The knob turns easily, but the door won't budge an inch. I dash to the window for the second time in as many minutes, but as with the door, it's as if the stubborn thing has been nailed shut.

I fight back tears as I scream again for Valerie and Mike. I may as well be floating in the middle of the ocean for all the good it does me.

As the clock flips to 11:59, the stream of photos dancing across my laptop shrinks to a single dot before growing to form a sentence at the center of the screen.

Press any key to continue.
The joy of Christmas awaits.

I'm already terrified out of my mind. Not much you can put on a fifteen-inch screen that can scare me any worse than I already am. I take a deep breath and rest my trembling hand on the trackpad, and before I can give it another thought, something akin to electricity flows up my arm. Every muscle below my shoulder fires, sending my hand flailing into the keyboard so hard it hurts. Immediately, the screen goes black, and for a moment, I think everything is going to be all right.

A very short moment.

Like the cryptic messages that float in the green liquid of a Magic 8-Ball, Marnie Jacobsen's face forms from the murky light of the computer, peering out at me from the center of the screen as if she hasn't seen a living soul in centuries. Even paler than when I last saw her, her stare burns into my soul, her dead eyes filled with longing and sadness.

I leap back from the computer and end up on my rump on the floor. In response, her face grows bigger, closer, as if she means to follow me out of the screen. The red of her mouth the color of fresh blood, her lips spread in a dead girl's smile. A hand the color of raw fish reaches out from the screen and clutches the top of the computer like it's gripping the rung of a ladder. Slowly, deliberately, the ashen corpse of my best friend draws itself from the rectangle of darkness and onto my bed.

Her trademark blond locks obscure half her face, but I can still make out the hint of a grin.

After a coughing fit befitting a girl whose last moments were spent unconscious below the surface of a hot tub's frothy soup, the specter on my bed fixes me with a half-concealed gaze and greets me with two simple words.

"Hello, Carol."

CHAPTER EIGHT

My skin crawls as the pallid form in the spotless white dress stretches out across my queen-size mattress in a full yawn.

"God, it's cramped in there." Water leaks from her open mouth onto my comforter. "I've been trying to get your attention all day, but you've been ignoring me." She pulls her mouth to one side and studies me for a moment. "Hmm. Guess I taught you too well."

"Marnie?" The word nearly crystallizes in the frigid air. "Is that you?"

"In the flesh." She brushes the hair from her face. I wish she hadn't. "I'd give you 'live and in color,' but neither of those words really describe me anymore, wouldn't you agree?"

My mind races as I pull myself up from the floor. "Am I dreaming?"

"Nope. You're dead awake, sweetie."

"And you're just...dead?"

"Can't put anything past you, Care Bear." She shifts atop my down comforter, and for the first time, I notice the various cables linking the back of her head to the screen. She follows my gaze and grins. "Oh, don't worry. We'll get to those."

"Valerie!" I scream. "Mike!"

"They can't hear you, sweetie," she whispers. "No one can. Except, of course, me."

I'm halfway to the door before it dawns on me. I'm not going anywhere until the thing on my bed is good and ready to release me. I turn to face her, and it takes every ounce of will to keep my knees from knocking. "All right. You've been trying all day to get my attention. Well, here I am. What is it you want?"

"What do *I* want?" She strokes her chin, and a trail of water that comes from nowhere streams down her pallid forearm. "Seems like an eternity since anyone's asked me what *I* want." She rises from the bed and paces the room, still tethered to the screen. Her white silk dress drips on my carpet though she doesn't appear to be wet. "I suppose I'd like to be alive again." Another blink and her nose is an inch from mine, her smile replaced with an angry grimace, her fetid breath like rotting fish. "And not six feet in the ground with the worms and the vermin."

"I'm sorry," I stammer. My heart racing, I fight back tears even as I struggle to stay on my feet. "Really, but what I meant was, what is it you want with *me*?"

Her smile returns. "And that's the real question, isn't it, Care Bear?"

"You're going to kill me, aren't you?"

"Would that even bother you?" she asks. "Weren't you the one wishing yourself dead just a few hours ago?"

If possible, my stomach knots even tighter. "How could you possibly know that?"

"You're standing in your own bedroom chatting with a dead girl who just climbed out of your computer screen, and the fact that I know what you're thinking is what bothers you?

Seriously? You may want to take some time and reevaluate your priorities." Her expression turns pensive. "Not that time is something you have in abundance."

"I don't know what you want me to say." My entire body shivers from far more than the freezing temperature in the room. "Just tell me what you want."

Something like compassion flashes across her face. "What I want," she whispers, "is you."

"Me?"

Marnie looks away, her lifeless eyes almost wistful for a moment. The weight of her stare leaves me, and for the first time in several minutes, I can breathe.

"Let me put it in terms you can understand," she says. "One of the thousand things I've learned in my year away is that every person on the planet has a task put before them, something they must do before the end. Most complete their task during the course of their lifetime and at the moment of their death, simply move on to another place, be it a place they'd like to end up or... one not as much." Her gaze drifts back to me. "The rest of us are stuck wandering the earth, desperate for the chance to complete what we should have finished in life. Do you understand?"

"You said you're here for me." I cross my arms in front of my chest. "We saw each other almost every day for two and a half years. What more could you want from me?"

"Oh, sweetie. You don't get it." She reaches out with a pale hand. I shrink away as her cold fingers come to rest on my shoulder. "What we did in our short time together, the way we were. That was nothing to be proud of."

"Nothing to be proud of? How can you say that? We ruled that school."

"Ruled? None of us on this planet are put here to rule. We're put here to serve."

Despite my terror, I feel a faint smile break on my lips. "Are you sure you're *the* Marnie Jacobsen?"

"Don't mock, Care Bear. It's not good for your health." Marnie's ghost stretches her back, the popcorn sound as each vertebra snaps into place sending a chill up my own spine. "Not to mention, I've come a pretty good way to be with you tonight."

"Sorry. It's just the Marnie I know looked out for one person and one person only."

"And see where that left me?" She clutches the cables that connect her skull to my computer screen. "Bound to the very things I worshipped. The most expensive car, the finest jewelry, the newest gadgets. It was more important to be seen with the hottest guy and have a million followers on social media than to actually let anyone into my life. And now, here I am, talking to my one and only friend and she can barely stand to look at me."

"Excuse me, but you're kind of dead. Not to mention, we're sitting in a room that feels like it's somewhere in the Arctic Circle. It's not like we're hanging at Starbucks sharing a brownie and a hot chocolate like we used to back in the day."

"But I have sat with you. Many a night since my death. Watching you. Listening to you. As cold as I was when I was alive, you've grown even colder."

Another chill works its way down my spine, bringing an ironic truth to her words. "And you find that surprising?" A lone tear runs down my cheek, chilled before it can reach my chin. "You died, just like Mom, Dad...Joy." I wipe the crystallized tear away. "There's just no point."

Fascination blossoming in her dead gaze, Marnie draws near to me. "No point in what, Care Bear?"

"In getting close." I look up at her, and for a moment the anger flowing out of me eclipses anything coming from the ghost that used to be my best friend. "To anyone." I cock my head to one side. "So, Marnie. Why now? Why come to me tonight of all nights for your little intervention?"

Marnie's lips grow wide in a smile that would be almost pretty if it wasn't so terrifying. "Two reasons. First, the walls between this realm and where I've been spending my days seem especially thin this evening. No surprise there."

"The anniversary of your death."

"Not to mention the winter solstice."

"The longest night of the year." I bite my lip nervously. "And the other?"

She looks away. "Time grows short."

"Time?" I ask. "What time?"

"Time to give you a chance I never had, a chance to turn it all around, a chance I have spent the last year preparing for you." She again fidgets with the cables binding her to the computer screen. "There is still hope for you, Carol, if you will accept it. Otherwise, I wouldn't—no—*couldn't* be here."

"Thanks, I think, though I still have no idea what it is you want me to do."

I'm not sure if ghosts sigh, but Marnie seems to do just that. "All right. On to the tough part. I already know what you're going to say, but understand—"

"Just spit it out, already."

"Very well." Marnie takes a deep breath, as if a dead girl needs to breathe, and adopts a stance as if she's about to deliver a memorized speech. "Hear me, Carol Davis. You will be haunted these next nights by Three Spirits."

"Three Spirits?" My bullshit meter immediately goes off. "Wait a minute. Like *A Christmas Carol*? Now I know I'm dreaming." I turn my back on Marnie's ghost, but in the space of a blink, she is again before me, inescapable in her fury.

"DO. NOT. IGNORE. ME."

I scramble back from her, my pulse roaring in my ears as I

try not to puke from the stench billowing from her mouth. "I'm not ignoring anything," I say. "It's just...you're telling me I'm...Scrooge."

"Not Scrooge." Her enraged face shifts back to some semblance of a sheepish grin. "Well, not exactly."

"But that's just a stupid story Charles Dickens wrote like a million years ago. It's not real."

"Says the person talking to a dead girl." She glances at the mirror, a bloody tear forming at the corner of her eye when no reflection looks back. "Look, Carol. My time here is limited. As much as I'd like to stay and chat, I can't bring everything you need to the table. Believe me, I'd love to take all the credit for bringing you around, but I'm afraid without the assistance of the Spirits, your fate is sealed, and by association, mine. So, you will listen to what I have to say. What *they* have to say. For both our sakes."

"So I listen to these Three Spirits and then I magically wake up on Christmas morning all sentimental and run through the snow-driven streets like Jimmy Stewart screaming 'Merry Christmas' to anyone who will listen?"

"Would you rather spend eternity like this? Walking the world and yet not in it? Invisible to everyone you meet on the street?" She runs her hands down her dress, coaxing water from the wrinkled cloth. "You'd best be ready when they come. You won't get another opportunity."

"Can I get that in writing?"

She ignores my joke. "Expect the first of the Spirits tomorrow night at one, the second the next night at two, and the third on Christmas Eve at, well, whenever she feels good and ready."

"The Ghosts of Christmas Past, Present, and Future, just like in the movies."

Her face goes pensive. "The last prefers to be called 'Christmas Yet to Come,' but yes."

"And how do I know all of this isn't just some bad dream? A bit of indigestion or a hallucination from too much stress?"

"All will be made clear soon enough." Marnie's ghost turns back to the window. "You won't be seeing me again, but remember what we've talked about. Both our fates depend on it."

"One last question, Marnie?" I bite my lip. "Before you go?"

She studies me for a moment. "Shoot."

"Did you mean to do it?"

"Mean to do what?"

"You know. The hot tub last year. Did you mean to...well... you know?"

"Most important lesson of the night, sweetie." Her eyes burn through me. "You're not the only one with problems."

She backs away from me and takes the spot by the window where I stared out minutes before. I join her there as she directs my attention to Valerie and Mike's backyard.

A backyard that is suddenly anything but empty.

"Who are they?" I look out on what appears an ocean of lost souls.

"Others like me, each wandering the earth, desperate to finish one last task so they can move on."

The dozen or so specters closest to the window turn as one to face me. Some look newly dead, while others appear all but skeletal. The most terrifying, however, are the ones somewhere in between. At the center of the sea of spirits, the ghost of a girl no more than eight glares up at me, her jawbone hanging from one frayed piece of sinew. She looks a bit like...

No. I won't go there.

"They're coming closer." I back away from the window. "What do they want?"

"Face the Spirits or this will be your every moment for the rest of eternity."

The first of the specters passes the glass, an emaciated male form with half its skull missing. "Join us," it hisses as the temperature in the already chilly room plummets even further.

A second and third follow, the nearly jawless girl and a snaggle-toothed grandmother with a knitting needle in each hand like a pair of matched daggers. "Join us," the three of them growl together.

I turn to run for the door but stop in my tracks as another pair of ghosts pass through the adjoining wall. The one-legged postman and partly decomposed Doberman snarl at me as one.

Backing away from the onslaught of specters, I trip over a pair of discarded sneakers and fall backward onto my bed.

"Join us," the chorus of the dead repeats again and again. "Join us."

"Marnie?" I turn to find Marnie, her face now a glowing skull and the cables connecting her to my laptop screen glowing as if afire, standing above me.

"Remember what we discussed, Care Bear." Her icy fingers pass down my forehead and slide my eyelids shut. "But for now, sleep. You've got some long nights ahead of you."

STAVE II

THE FIRST OF THE THREE SPIRITS

Thursday, December 22nd

CHAPTER NINE

I stand poolside, the cool aroma of chlorine wafting off the water at once familiar and foreboding. Alone at the pool's edge, the staccato chirp of a whistle signals me to dive, and with instinct borne from years of practice, I comply. The freezing water hits me like an arctic flow. I glide below the surface for most of the first lap, the unbelievably frigid water stealing the warmth from my body with every stroke. I've traveled barely half the first length when my muscles begin to cramp. A few more strokes and my lungs burn like liquid fire. I pull to a stop and swim upward for the light, but though I fight for the surface with all I have, the open air always seems another arm's length away.

Even more disconcerting, I'm no longer alone.

Hovering above me, a blurred face stares down at me through the last few inches of water. I stretch out my hand for this stranger, but my fingers find nothing but open air. As if I'm a fish hitting the glass at the side of an aquarium, my fingertips trail along a transparent ceiling at the water's surface. My body quickly descends into panic mode, but though I beat at the barrier with every ounce of my strength, my struggles accomplish nothing but leaving my knuckles bloody and my chest burning all the more. A different, more primitive instinct kicks in and despite everything I've learned in years of swim practice, my lips part and I breathe in what feels like a gallon of ice water. Darkness encroaches on the periphery of my vision until all I see is the blurred face looking down at me from above, its features crystallizing in my mind into a smile I thought I'd never see again.

The innocence of her expression unchanged despite the years, Joy peers down at me through the six inches of water. Without a hint of anger, sadness, or judgment, her steady gaze emanates nothing but placid calm and fills me with a sense that's been missing from my life for the ten years since she was taken from me.

A sense of peace.

"Carol?" The voice cuts through the fog like a silver bell. "You okay?"

I jolt awake, my heart thumping, though I take some comfort in the fact the hand shaking my shoulder feels warm against my skin. My eyes open on Aunt Valerie leaning over me, a bit of flour or confectioner's sugar adorning her nose. Sunlight pours into the room, the sky beyond the window the blue-gray haze of late December.

Most importantly, we're alone.

"You were talking in your sleep," she says. "Bad dream?"

I wipe the sleep from my eyes and take a breath of sweet, sweet air. "You have no idea."

"Come on down when you're ready." Her voice rings with cautious excitement. "I made you breakfast."

"Breakfast?" I've been out for all of five minutes. "What time is it?"

"Quarter to nine. Why?"

"Crap." I leap from the bed. "I'm late."

"Late for what?" she asks as I tie my hair up in a ponytail and pull my winter uniform from the drawer.

"The squad has an event at the mall at nine." I check my phone. "Twelve minutes."

"You have another cheerleading event? It's three days before Christmas. Doesn't your coach understand the concept of holiday break?"

"Says the woman who insists I work the evening shift every night this week."

I check my face in the mirror. Never got out of my makeup last night. My face is far from perfect, but I look passable, and it's one less thing to do.

God, I must have slept like the dead.

The dead.

Marnie.

I do my best to shake off the chill creeping up my spine.

"It's funny," Valerie says. "All the shopping and other hubbub aside, the holidays used to be just that when I was growing up. A holiday."

A quiet laugh parts my lips. "Well, those days are over."

"Are you sure you want to go?" Valerie gives me a quick once over, her brow furrowing with worry. "You look exhausted."

"Thanks a lot." Truth is, after all the crazy dreams last night, I'd sleep another twelve hours if the universe would allow it. "Like Coach Spinnaker says, though, no rest for the cheery."

A flash of color catches my attention. The open laptop rests on the corner of my bed, the screen saver still performing its rainbow-colored gymnastics, and the floodgates of my memory open wide. Nightmares from last night play like some bizarre movie across my mind's eye. The ghost of Marnie Jacobsen, appearing first in my mirror before pulling herself from my laptop screen to lie on my bed. The disembodied spirits pouring into my room from every door, wall, and window, surrounding me. Marnie standing over me. Her blood-red lips. Her dress dripping the same water that filled her lungs the night she died.

Her dead hand on my face.

"Hey, Valerie?" I shudder as I slide out of the t-shirt I slept in last night and pull the blue and gold top over my head. "Random question. Did you hear anything strange last night?"

"Besides Mike's snoring?" She laughs for a second before concern again fills her features. The standard poker face I use for all things Mike and Valerie must not be firing on all cylinders this morning. "Why? Is something the matter?"

"I had the mother of all bad dreams last night. I was just wondering if you heard me scream out or...anything."

Valerie peers at me like a scientist studying a strange insect not found in any book. "What were you dreaming about?"

"I don't remember, exactly." My cheeks flush as I pull on my warm up pants and retrieve my shoes. "It's kind of already fading into the background."

"Must've been a bad one. Haven't seen you sleep with Mr. Shiners here in a long time." She retrieves the stuffed panda bear resting peacefully on my nightstand. "I had to all but pry him from your arms when I was trying to wake you up before." Her head tilts to one side as her expression shifts into full-on mom-face. "You sure you don't remember anything?"

Join us. Join us. Join us.

"I remember seeing...Marnie."

Valerie rests a hand on my knee. "I thought that might be on your mind. After all, yesterday was—"

I look up at her, my eyes as cold as I can make them. "I know what yesterday was."

She pulls her hand away as if stung. "Sorry, Carol. I'm just trying to help."

"Know what? Never mind. I'm already late and getting later by the minute."

"All right." Disappointment darkens her features. "Need a ride?"

"Nope. That Toyota of yours may be a death-trap, but I think it can still get me to the mall." I flash Valerie a mischievous smile. "Few more days, that won't be an issue."

"Still hell-bent on buying that German rocket on wheels?"

"It's a BMW Roadster, and yes." I rub at my chin and look thoughtfully at the ceiling. "Only question, I guess, is whether to buy one or two."

Valerie sighs. "Three million dollars is a lot of money, Carol. More than either of us can really wrap our brains around. I hope you don't get lost in all those zeros."

My eyes roll, almost instinctively at this point. "You really want to do this now? Round fifty-three of the great trust fund argument?"

"No." Valerie goes to the window. "I think we've covered that territory pretty well."

"I've already heard it all, Valerie. From you, Mike, Roberta. Last time I checked, though, my name was the only one at the top of the page."

"Fine." Valerie stares out the window, likely to avoid my eyes more than any other reason. "Be careful on the road. The weather's been okay so far this morning, but that Nor'easter is supposed to hit this afternoon and the roads are going to be crap for the next few days."

I give her my most winning smile and a quick double blink. "Yes ma'am."

"As for the stuff with Marnie, if you want to talk later, I'll be here."

"Thanks." I grab my keys from the bowl at the end of my dresser. "But I'll be fine."

"Hey, you never came back down and ate last night." Valerie rises from the bed. "I don't want to waste food. If you plan to skip dinner tonight, will you please call and let me know?"

"I'll do my best." I grab my bag and head for the door. "Catch you later."

I rush down the stairs past Mike and sprint out the door where the old Toyota sits in the driveway atop an ever-growing lake of oil. I hop into the torn vinyl driver's seat and am floored when the car starts on the first crank.

Though the mall is no more than ten miles from Valerie and Mike's house, the long train of traffic lights and four-way stops make it twenty minutes on a good day. The lawnmower motor in Valerie's old rice rocket does little to improve the situation. With each passing mile, I get more and more pissed off, a poster child for road rage if there ever was one.

I may be many things, but late isn't one of them.

Patient, either, I guess.

I'm finally making good time down the town's main stretch when some geriatric asshole in an old Chrysler with chipped black paint pulls out in front of me and proceeds down the highway about as fast as if he were stumbling behind his walker. I lay on the horn and regret it immediately. A blaring horn should sound obnoxious and command respect. The one on Valerie's car sounds like a castrated goat with lungs full of helium.

Just three more days till BMW Nirvana, Carol. Just three more days.

As I try unsuccessfully to get around old Ebenezer—God, did I just make a Scrooge joke?—my thoughts drift back to my chat with Valerie. I'm going to have to keep a lot of this stuff to myself. Val already thinks I'm a colossal pain in the ass half the time. I don't want her to think I'm certifiable as well. She'd send me back to Dr. Boyer, and I've already had more than a lifetime's share of therapy.

After all, the whole thing was just a nightmare, right? One too many times seeing the ad for George C. Scott's *A Christmas Carol*—the only one worth watching, in my humble opinion—coupled with the anniversary of Marnie's death. That's got to be all it is. Kind of like the time I got talked into seeing one of the *Paranormal Activity* movies and couldn't sleep for a week.

Except for one thing.

The texts.

I check my phone. The texts from Marnie's old phone number are gone. I flip over to my email account and find the email has disappeared as well. Keeping one eye on the road and the old Chrysler, which has accelerated up to a blistering 28 mph, I scroll through the Trash on the phone looking for the deleted messages. Nothing there either.

So, either I performed high level smartphone surgery in my sleep last night, or the texts and emails were as much a figment of my imagination as the ghosts themselves. Not sure if either of those options leaves me with a warm and fuzzy.

I'm still trying to figure it all out when the black Chrysler finally pulls off into a neighborhood and the road opens up—a whole mile before I get to the mall.

It's a Christmas miracle.

CHAPTER TEN

I'm fifteen minutes late and the parking lot is packed. Though the mall doesn't open for another forty-five minutes, the cold and damp has done little to deter all the last-minute shoppers hoping to get something for nothing. Vultures, all of them, ready to descend and strip the bones of this mall's bloated holiday carcass. Meanwhile, some poor grandpa playing Santa waits on his throne of holly for all the wet-bottomed screaming toddlers so he can make a bunch of promises their parents are going to have to keep.

A little melodramatic? Sure, but because of them, I'm stuck parking halfway across the lot, not to mention it's starting to drizzle and I'm pretty sure my umbrella is sitting by the back door at Valerie and Mike's place.

I pull the gold and blue pom-poms from my bag and rush through the falling mist for the door. If the squad got a late start, I may still be able to make it. Not likely though. Coach Spinnaker is nothing if not punctual, and she doesn't tolerate tardiness.

I try three doors before finally finding one that's unlocked. Sprinting past the Cinnabon and Orange Julius, I head for the big stage at the center of the mall. A small crowd surrounds the raised platform, and the rest of the squad has already taken their positions, including that bitch, Jamie Meadows, who for some reason is standing in *my* spot.

She's been gunning for me all year, and I'll be damned if some stupid nightmare and a malfunctioning alarm clock are going to give that silver-spoon-toting daddy's girl the upper hand. After a quick check for Coach Spinnaker, I leap onto the stage and head straight for my spot at the center of the formation.

"Hello, Jamie." I pour on the honey. "Thanks for keeping my spot warm."

She looks up from her hamstring stretch, a wide smile on her face. "Good morning, Carol. Sleep well?"

"Like a baby. Now, if you'll move along, I've got this." I crouch next to her and switch my voice to a coarse whisper. "Like Coach Spinnaker always says, stretching prevents injuries."

Jamie's eyes dart past me, and her wicked grin grows even wider. I turn to find our coach, Sally Spinnaker, glaring down at me.

"Good morning, Miss Davis."

"Morning, Coach."

Not even a hint of a smile. "Why are you bothering Miss Meadows?"

I offer an innocent shrug. "I need to get warmed up, and she's in my spot."

"Miss Meadows was on time." Both her eyebrows rise in accusation. "Unlike some others on the squad."

"But I'm co-captain."

"All the more reason to arrive on time. If you're going to be a leader, you're going to have to act like one."

My fingernails dig into my palms so hard, I'm afraid they're going to draw blood. "I overslept. Had a long day yesterday."

"Well, Miss Davis, you're not the only one with problems." I don't hear another word Coach Spinnaker says after the echo of Marnie's words from last night. I'm sure I'm getting the tongue lashing of my life, but I've got news for my favorite washed up ex-homecoming queen. Her trademark glare has nothing on the gleaming grin of a certain dead girl, and her angry rant sounds all but laughable after facing a mob of chanting ghosts.

I tell myself again the whole thing was all just a dream, but that doesn't stop the memory of being surrounded by the ever-encroaching dead from turning my stomach inside out.

Join us. Join us. Join us.

Great. I'd almost made it six months without a trip to the shrink.

Dr. Boyer, here I come.

"Are you listening to me, Miss Davis?"

Crap.

"Sorry, Coach Spinnaker." I tap my temple and try to dial back the pissed off a couple notches. "Lot on my mind."

"Clearly. You show up fifteen minutes late for warm up, climb onto my stage without checking with me first, and zone out when I'm talking to you."

I cut my eyes in Jamie's direction. "Come on, Coach. She's JV."

"*She* wasn't late. And this isn't an official school event. I think a little exposure might be good for her. Show her what it's like to be Varsity."

"I suppose." I feel my lips draw down to a tight circle. "If you think she can do the flip dismount at the end without killing herself..."

"Oh, don't worry, Carol." Jamie rises from the floor, puts her arms above her head, and stretches her lower back. "I've been practicing."

Coach Spinnaker looks her over dubiously. "I guess we'll see what you've got in a few, Miss Meadows." She turns to me. "As for you, Miss Davis, tardy is tardy and you know the rules." She motions to an empty chair on the front row. "You're welcome to watch from the audience if you like."

Jamie raises her hand to her mouth, but puts no effort into hiding her victory smirk.

"Fine." I give Jamie's ankle a nudge with my toe. "Break a leg, JV."

"Miss Davis!" Coach Spinnaker grunts.

"Just wishing her luck." I shoot Jamie a knowing wink. "You know. Theater style."

Before Coach Spinnaker can start into the same tired rant I've heard her spout a thousand times—the one about teamwork and school spirit and all that jazz—I leave the stage and head out to find a seat. It's funny. Every time there's any kind of squabble among the squad, she comes off so shocked, but I've seen the old yearbooks. Sally Spinnaker was Queen of the Fighting Lions Squad back in the day and has probably forgotten more about high school politics than most of us will ever learn. Not sure why she goes to so much trouble portraying herself as the Mother Teresa of the pom-pom set these days.

But like Dad used to say, whatever floats her boat.

I grab a spot near the back of the crowd and wait all of thirty seconds for the show to begin when a thought occurs to me. I don't owe Coach Spinnaker and Jamie the Wonder-Bitch anything. I'm at a mall three days before Christmas, and by God, I'm going to do some shopping. A little something for Valerie and Mike to avoid any awkwardness on the big day. Something with lots of words on pages for Roberta. And...

Hmm. That's about it.

Directly behind the stage is the entrance to Best Buy, and as I recall, they open an hour before the rest of the mall during the holidays. Maybe I can convince Valerie to finally replace the old tube set passed down from Mom and Dad—part of a package deal that included an eight-year-old girl with abandonment issues—and get one of those big flat-screens for the living room. If I butter up Christopher just right, maybe I can even get him to let us use his employee discount.

As if money is going to be much of an issue starting Monday morning.

I wait for the squad to get busy with one of our more complicated routines and sneak out the back. "Sleigh Ride" blares from the speakers as they get to work, their pom-poms shaking in time with the sleigh bells tinkling through the loudspeakers. Most are so involved, they have no idea I've gone. All, that is, except one. One last lingering glance back catches Jamie's petulant gaze tracing my every step. I can't help but laugh. Ghost, nightmare, or whatever, Marnie was right.

I'm not the only one with problems.

CHAPTER ELEVEN

Not quite fast enough to avoid the obligatory "Merry Christmas," I jet past the Best Buy greeter, shooting her a curt smile before adopting my strict "eyes forward" policy. Dodging several clerks along the way, all of them more than ready to chat up the cute cheerleader in their midst, I arrive at the back aisle where the TVs live. Lined up on either side of a wide carpeted aisle and arranged by size, the largest of them is nearly as wide as I am tall. The bank of screens all tuned to the same program, in this case *How the Grinch Stole Christmas*, leaves me feeling strange, as if I'm being watched.

Just my imagination playing tricks on me, I guess.

The Grinch. Most misunderstood character in TV history. Just wanted some peace and quiet. I get that. Everybody else can be all "Merry Christmas!" and "Happy Holidays!" to their heart's content. Me? I'd just like to shop for a TV without some loser with a name tag and a Santa hat trying to get my phone number under the guise of being helpful.

"Carol?"

Speak of the devil.

I turn on one heel to face the familiar voice. "Good morning, Christopher."

Dressed in the obligatory blue polo with yellow insignia, he's sporting a pair of those stupid antlers with blinking lights, flushing whatever good looks he might possess right down the toilet.

"What are you doing here?" He adjusts his glasses. "Shouldn't you be at your performance?"

"Actually, I should be *in* the performance, but that's an issue for another day."

"Oh." His eyebrows knit with confusion. "Can I help you with anything?"

"Thought I'd come in and check out your flat screens. I'm hoping I can talk Valerie into upgrading for Christmas."

"You've come to the right place." His lips turn up in that goofy smile of his. "Still watching that old tube set?"

"It's a dinosaur from another life." I draw my lips down to a tight line. "Time for something new."

"Well, I'm sure we have something here you'll like." More formal than he was seconds before, he turns and walks along the line of TVs. "Let me show you what we've got."

In true Christopher Kellerman fashion, he spends the next fifteen minutes explaining the latest advances in TV technology, half of which I don't understand and the other half I completely tune out. I wait till he finally stops running that nuclear-powered mouth of his before saying another word.

"Can you just tell me which one of these is the best?"

His cheeks growing a hot pink, he walks over to a Samsung in the corner. "From what I remember about your aunt's living room, this is the set I would recommend. Sixty-inch so you can watch Netflix from the kitchen, sharp picture, bright colors, deep blacks. Yep. This is the one."

"Sounds great. Can you put one on hold for me?"

"Umm..." Christopher's eyes drop. "Maybe."

"Is there a problem?"

"No." He glances up sheepishly. "It's just...it's three days before Christmas. We're not putting a whole lot on hold right now."

"Not even for an old friend?" I hit him with a few bats of the eyelashes. "It's just one TV."

"Okay." His voice downshifts into almost a groan. "I'll do it."

"One other thing." I bite my lip as I glance around the store for anyone who looks like they're with management. "Any chance you can help me out with your employee discount?"

"I'm not sure I can do that." His cheeks, already pink, go a shade closer to full crimson. "Anyway, this one's already on sale."

"Come on, Christopher." I draw close so he can smell the strawberry gum on my breath. "For old times' sake. You know, I wouldn't even know who John Hughes is if it wasn't for you."

"John Hughes is dead." Christopher turns from me and marches over to a nearby computer terminal. Muttering under his breath, he taps away at the keyboard, each keystroke like a hammer pounding nails into the coffin of what's left of our friendship. Before I can come up with any kind of response, he looks up from the monitor and fixes me with an exasperated half-smile.

"Why are you worried about a few hundred dollars, anyway? Don't you become a bazillionaire next week?"

It's my turn to have hot cheeks. "Know what? Forget the discount. Just put the set on hold. I'll be back with Valerie in a day or two to pick it up, all right?"

Christopher comes to attention and even pops me a little salute. "Yes, ma'am, Miss Davis. Will there be anything else?"

"No." His comment stings more than I'd like to admit. "That'll be all."

"I'll take care of it." Without another word, he disappears behind a doorway that no doubt leads down to the warehouse. A part of me wants to chase after him like the old days when we were kids and my big mouth inevitably left him with hurt feelings.

But who am I kidding? Things are different now. The day I go chasing after Christopher Kellerman again, I'll turn in my pom-poms and let them put braces back on my teeth.

As the entire bank of TVs continues with *How the Grinch Stole Christmas*, a new sound hits my ears. Somewhere between bells and piano, the opening bars of Tchaikovsky's "Dance of the Sugar Plum Fairy" echoes through the store, high-pitched enough to make my teeth ache. The music grows in volume with every passing second, the mysterious bell-like melody literally ringing in my ears. Strangest thing, I seem to be the only person who notices. Everyone else continues to shop as if nothing is happening. One guy even walks by humming "You're a mean one, Mr. Grinch" though I can barely hear the song over the blaring orchestral music.

Covering my ears, I walk a lap of the store, doing my best to locate the source of the music. Booming from everywhere and nowhere at once, it gets louder and louder with every step. A part of me fleetingly wonders if my nose is set to bleed from the onslaught of sound as my impromptu tour of the store brings me back around to the TV aisle.

And that's when I see her.

The bank of TVs continues to show the fifty or so identical Grinches, all slithering through the same pink house, stealing gifts and decorations. Their individual paths all in time with each other, it's like watching some bizarre yuletide display of synchronized swimming. One of the screens, however, contains an additional figure. Filling the foreground like she's a reporter giving her account of the devastating events in Whoville, this girl is anyone but Cindy Lou Who.

She's there for but a second before disappearing, only to reappear on another screen at the end of the aisle. I startle an older couple as I rush past them to get a closer look, but by the time I arrive at the TV in question, it too has returned to normal. My heart racing, I wait for the girl to make another appearance. I tell myself again and again she's just another figment of my imagination, but that does nothing to lessen the feeling—no—the certainty I'm being watched.

I linger for a couple minutes, vigilant for another appearance of the mysterious girl, until a static pop directly behind me reveals the one place I'm not looking. Too scared to even take a breath, I slowly turn to face the sixty-inch set filling the wall behind me.

And there she is.

Set against the cartoon that continues in the background, the girl appears as real as me, the 3D effect on this particular set beyond unnerving. Five years old at most, she looks out at me with knowing eyes of gold set off with dark circles as if she hasn't slept in years. Her hair hangs to the floor like strands of shining platinum. Her simple white dress is decorated with a single sprig of holly just below her left collarbone. The girl neither smiles nor frowns, but stares at me insistently as if I were the oddity who shouldn't be there. I briefly wonder if I'm a victim of one of those "Gotcha" shows that scare the crap out of you and catch it all on video before letting you in on the joke to a chorus of laughter.

Funny. After the last twenty-four hours, I seem to be fresh out of laughs.

I take a step toward the TV. The girl in the screen raises her hand, almost as if she can see me and is calling me to a halt. Before I can take another step, she motions to the set to her left.

Dr. Seuss vanishes from the screen only to be replaced by an image of a Christmas tree in a familiar living room, the two children at its base even more familiar.

An almost seven-year-old me sits on the floor beneath a fully decorated tree with the Christopher I remember from second grade. *Frosty the Snowman* is on the TV, and Christopher and I each hold a gift in our lap: his, an oblong container wrapped in gold and silver, and mine, a small box bundled in Sunday funnies. Calvin and Hobbes in all their four-color glory look up from my lap. Christopher is laughing, as is Joy, who sits in the corner with Mr. Shiners, her stuffed panda bear back then.

Most interesting? Neither of them is laughing as hard as the second-grade version of me.

It's easy to forget the three of us used to be pretty tight back in the day.

As Christopher tears into the paper, I remember what's inside the long rectangular box. What Mom and I spent an hour at the art store deliberating over. The perfect gift for my best friend at the time.

A part of me I thought had fallen away years ago brims with glee.

"No way!" Young Christopher pulls out a good half dozen professional grade paintbrushes and holds them before his face. "You remembered."

"They were the best ones at the store. The ones real painters use." The little girl that grew up to be me glances past the boy's shoulder, and then, like I'm watching a movie, the picture on the screen pans slowly to the right.

There. Exactly as I remember them.

Dad. Nodding at his little girl, his broad smile filled with energy, his eyes the kindest in history.

And Mom. Her slender arm around my father's waist,

pulling him close to her as the two of them motion for me to open my gift from Christopher.

I blink the tears away, and when my vision clears, the image is gone and the Grinch has returned to the screen. He's forcing his poor dog with the single tied-on antler to pull the sleigh full of Whoville booty up the side of the mountain. The deafening Tchaikovsky fades in seconds as I am quite literally returned to regularly scheduled programming.

"Found one." I nearly jump out of my skin, before I realize the voice is Christopher's.

I turn on him, more than a little pissed. "Found one what?"

"Your big flat screen. You're lucky. It was the last one in the store." Exasperation flashes across his features. "You've already changed your mind, haven't you?"

"No." I inhale, trying to get my heart rate back down. "That's the one."

"Good. I had to go into the bowels of the warehouse to find that thing." He hands me a slip of paper. "Here's your claim check in case I'm not around when you come to pick it up." His eyes narrow as his lips draw down into a tight circle. "Wait. Have you been crying?"

"No." I turn my head to the side and let out a fake cough. "Some guy just walked past a minute ago doused with half a bottle of cologne." I let out another forced cough. "Lucky I can still breathe."

"Really?" Christopher sniffs the air and scrutinizes my face for a moment before fading back into business mode. "Okay. So the set's on hold down in the warehouse. You're sure that's the one you want?"

An image of the younger version of Christopher flashes through my mind. The vision of his eyes lighting up as he opens the perfect gift echoes in the lanky teenager standing before me.

And those two little words.

You remembered.

"I'm sure." Without knowing why, I grab his hand and give it a vigorous shake. "Valerie and I will drop by today or tomorrow to pick it up."

His face screws up in mild bafflement. "Are you sure you're all right?"

"I'm fine. Promise."

Marnie's features replace Christopher's in my mind's eye.

You will be haunted these next nights by Three Spirits.

"Hmph," I mutter, peering toward the front of the store where pale December sunlight filters through the store windows. "Doesn't look like night to me."

"Night?" Christopher's confused expression drifts into one of concern. "What in the world are you talking about?"

"Nothing. Got to go." Without another word, I head for the door, trying not to make eye contact with the Salvation Army bell ringer as I head for the car.

Strangely enough, I'm not digging the sound of bells at the moment.

CHAPTER TWELVE

I crank the engine of Valerie's old Toyota and the radio blares the song "My Favorite Things" from *The Sound of Music*, though I punch the power button before Julie Andrews can so much as rhyme kittens and mittens.

Strange. I drove to the mall with the radio off. Wasn't quite in the mood for the one thousandth playing of "Grandma Got Run Over by a Reindeer" this season, and definitely wasn't ready for the good Fräulein Maria to deafen me with her dulcet tones.

Must have hit the volume button with my knee when I got out of the car.

Not important.

Dropping the car into reverse, I laugh despite myself as Uncle Mike's well-worn rant runs through my head.

It's not even a Christmas song, I've heard him complain countless times. *Just because it's got snowflakes and sleigh bells doesn't mean it should get played three times an hour every December for the rest of eternity...*

Then there's Valerie's counter rant about Dan Fogelberg's

"Same Auld Lang Syne" and how it makes her want to slit her wrists.

That stupid song gets as much airplay as "Silent Night" come every Christmas. What the hell are the radio stations going for playing that crap? It's supposed to be a happy season...

Heard it all a thousand times. Every December for a decade without fail.

I flip the radio back on, dropping the volume to a decibel level less than the space shuttle taking off, and start to look for another station when some douchebag rockets past in one of those tricked out Hondas and nearly takes off my front end.

"Asshole." Adding insult to injury, some auto-tuned Disney princess turned pop star begins to pipe through the car speakers. Roberta could name the artist in three notes, but not me. I can't stand that crap. Before I get sentenced to a full day with an earworm, I commence flipping stations. God, what I wouldn't give for satellite radio...

Ah, here's something.

"...your last two chances to see *The Nutcracker* until next year," the announcer proclaims in a deep rolling baritone. "Eight o'clock, Thursday and Friday night at the Civic Center. Come out and experience the enchantment of the Season." The advertisement fades into "Dance of the Sugar Plum Fairy," and my intestines twist into a knot.

"Oh, hell no."

I punch the power button on the radio before the bells of Tchaikovsky's ballet have a chance to haunt me a second time today. I'd rather listen to the windshield wipers. The silence, however, lasts all of three seconds before my phone begins to chirp. I root around blindly in my purse, strangely hoping the call is from Marnie.

Nope. Roberta.

I debate sending the call straight to voicemail, unsure if I can take another rehash of the Tameka situation so soon. After all the weirdness in the store, though, I could use a distraction.

"Morning, Bobbisox," I answer with as chipper a voice as I can manage. "What's up?"

"Carol? Where are you? I came to the mall to see the show and Coach Spinnaker has Jamie Meadows in your spot. Are you all right?"

I grit my teeth. "I'm fine. I overslept and our favorite drill sergeant in a tracksuit sidelined me for the day. Wanted to teach me a lesson, I guess."

"Where are you?"

"About to pull out of the parking lot." I glance out my windshield as the drizzle continues to pick up. "The weather is craptastic and no one seems to need me around here, so I thought I'd head back to the house."

"You want to grab a bite in the food court?" comes Roberta's hopeful voice.

I'm really not in the mood for small talk at the moment, but I had to skip breakfast this morning and the mere mention of food makes my stomach grumble to life.

"Sure," I breathe. "Meet you there in five."

I pull a U-turn and drive around to the other end of the mall where the rest of town has descended like a swarm of locusts. I circle the lot for a good ten minutes looking for a decent spot before giving up and parking at the Olive Garden across the street. Scanning the passenger seat for my umbrella, I remember again—I left it at home.

Fantastic. The cold mist falling from the sky should do wonders for my already frizzy hair.

I rush inside the food court after getting fairly well drenched and nearly getting hit by some jerk in a red Mini Cooper. The cool air joins forces with my wet clothes and skin to send a shiver from my toes to my teeth. Fortunately, waiting for me at a table between Sbarro and Cookie King, Roberta sits with two coffees and a bag that no doubt contains our favorite winter morning snack.

"Pumpkin muffin with cream cheese?" I ask with one eyebrow raised.

"But of course." She slips her hand into the bag and produces one of the little chunks of heaven. Giving me a quick once-over, she smirks. "You're soaked."

"Thanks for noticing." I take a bite of the muffin and wash it down with a sip of double-shot latte doctored just right. Girl knows me well.

"So, any change with Tameka?" I ask, deciding to both change the subject and climb on top of the elephant in the room.

Roberta raises one shoulder in a half-shrug. "Still about as weak as dishwater. She's really anemic from all the chemo treatments, but doctors don't want to give her any blood except as a last resort. Trying to avoid some kind of allergic reaction or something." Her face takes on a hopeful cast. "You should come by and see her sometime. She asks about you every day."

"Yeah." Her words fade into background noise as I notice a pair of eyes studying me from across the quickly crowding food court. In half a second, I become painfully aware that I probably look like a drowned rat with hair bows.

At six-foot-seven, Ryan King plays center for the Fighting Lions basketball team. Last year, he led us to the state championship and is well on his way to a repeat for his senior year. Most of the girls in school go for the muscular football types, but me? I'll take long and lean any day.

He shoots me a quick smile. I answer with a subtle wave.

But not quite subtle enough.

Roberta cranes her head around. "Girl, you making eyes at Ryan King?"

"Don't look at him!" I kick her under the table. "And so what if I am?"

She raises an eyebrow. "For starters, ow."

"Sorry." I chance another glance in his direction. "So, I'm into Ryan. What's the big deal?"

Roberta shoots me that look I know her kids are going to hate someday. "First, I'm sitting here spilling my guts about everything going on at home and I'm betting you haven't heard a word I've said. Second, any serious flirting on your part would mean you've forgotten what went down with him and Bethany Miller last year. And third and most important, you can do a whole lot better than Ryan King."

My head shakes almost instinctively. "I can't guess in a million years who you could be referring to."

Roberta takes a sip of her coffee. "Say what you want, but as far as I know, Christopher Kellerman has never dumped a girl the day after prom."

Ryan and Bethany, one of the guards on the girls' basketball team, dated for most of junior year, a relationship that reportedly ended over breakfast the morning after the dance.

Yes. Breakfast.

"He went out with that giraffe for like six months." I nibble at my muffin, the cream cheese sweet on my tongue. "I'm surprised he kept her around that long."

Roberta leans in close. "From what *I* understand, he kept her around just long enough."

"Wow." I laugh. "This is a switch."

And there's that look again. "I don't know what you're talking about."

"It's just you're the one who always gets on my case about gossip." My gaze shifts past Roberta and finds Ryan talking up some girl at the Cookie King. She's leaning across the counter, all smiles and giggles, and he's soaking it up like some jungle cat stretched out in a spot of sunlight.

"Just looking out for you," Roberta whispers. "Bethany used to think Ryan King was all 'Knight in Shining Armor' and you know how that worked out. Not to mention the fact he and Natalie Shepherd were still going out a few weeks back and he's over there chatting up some junior from East." She brushes my wrist. "Sorry to say it, Carol, but that burner is hot. You go touching it..."

"And I might get burned. Yeah, yeah, yeah." I glance past Roberta's shoulder again. The girl is tapping her number into Ryan's phone. "You're right about one thing. That burner is *definitely* hot."

"You haven't listened to a word I've said." Roberta peeks across her shoulder a second time and lets out a groan. "And now he's coming over."

Ryan leaves the girl at the cookie counter with a smile and a nod and strolls over to our table, stopping behind Roberta's chair.

"Hey."

"Hey," I parrot back at him.

"Hmph." Roberta scoots her chair a quarter turn and gives Ryan a look just this side of disgusted. "Well, well. If it isn't the King himself."

"At your service, ladies." His gaze shifts to me. "How's it going, Carol?"

"Can't complain." I take a sip of coffee. "You?"

"Doing pretty good." His hand goes to his neck like he's massaging out the mother of all kinks. Despite the weather, he's wearing nothing but a t-shirt, jeans, and loafers. His biceps are... impressive. "Haven't seen you around lately."

"School's out for Christmas, Ryan." Roberta gives him her

most motherly look. "You haven't been sitting in those empty classrooms all by yourself, have you?"

"What are you doing down here this early?" I ask Ryan, shooting Roberta a quick glare.

"Actually," he says, "I dropped by the mall this morning hoping I'd run into you."

"Me?" My cheeks get a little warmer.

Roberta rolls her eyes and mutters something so low I can't make it out.

"Thought I'd check out the cheerleading thing down at the main entrance," Ryan says. "When you weren't there, I decided to wander down here and grab a bite." His face breaks into a heart-melting grin. "Glad I did."

Roberta rises from her chair. "And that's about as much of this as I can stomach." She turns to me. "Don't forget what we were talking about, Carol."

I shoot her a jaunty salute. "Yes, Mother."

As Roberta stalks away, Ryan motions to her chair. "This seat taken?"

I incline my head and let a subtle smile briefly touch my features. "All yours, if you want it."

He takes a seat. "I figured that was a given."

"I've got to ask." I let out a purposeful chuckle. "What's it like?"

His brow furrows. "What are you talking about?"

"Walking around with the grand assumption that everybody is buying what you're selling."

His smile goes wider. "Never been given any evidence to the contrary."

"Wow. Someone thinks pretty highly of themselves." I bring my arms across my chest. "So, you came all the way down here just to watch the cheerleading squad do all the same stunts we do at every basketball game you've played the last two years?"

"Honestly, I'm usually too busy winning those games to pay much attention to anything else." For the first time since he sat down, his eyes drift from mine. "But if you want to know, I came by this morning to ask you something."

Interesting.

"You could have called, you know. My number isn't that hard to get."

"I wanted to do this in person." He smiles at me, his two-day growth of stubble turning up the heat on his patient gaze. "Do you have plans Saturday night?"

"Christmas Eve?" I pull out my phone and start to scroll through the calendar. "Let me check."

"The dance," he says, a hint of irritation invading his tone. "Are you going?"

There it is. "I don't know." I look up from my phone and fix Ryan with a playful stare. "Are you asking me?"

Before Ryan can answer, I catch a flash of blue out of the periphery of my vision. Walking as fast as his legs will carry him, Christopher is heading for the Starbucks at the far end of the food court. He doesn't make eye contact, but it's pretty clear he spotted us.

My cheeks flush hot, though I'm not sure exactly why.

"All right," Ryan says, interrupting my train of thought. "We'll do this all official like." He clears his throat in mock seriousness and takes my hand. "Carol Davis, would you like to go to the dance with me Saturday night?"

"Depends." I bring my full attention back to him. "What happened with you and Natalie? Last I heard, you two were hanging out."

"Natalie?" His lips curl into an incredulous smirk. "We've been over since October."

"Really?" I ask, putting just enough concern in my voice to sound legit. "What happened?"

He looks away, and for a moment, a crack appears in Ryan King's impenetrable shield of coolness. "We just weren't...right for each other."

"So sorry to hear it." I incline my head in the direction of the Cookie King counter. "And your friend over at Chocolate Chip Central?"

"One of my sister's friends." His hand returns to the knot in his neck. "I was just saying hi."

"You get digits from all your sister's friends?"

His cheeks go a shade pinker. "I didn't ask her to the dance. I asked you." He almost sounds earnest. Impressive. "So, what do you say? Saturday night? You and me?" He gives my fingers a gentle squeeze. "Music and mistletoe?"

My eyes flick right and I catch half a second of Christopher's pained gaze before he turns back to the barista making his coffee.

And just past him, another set of eyes. Almost like a reflection in the back of the espresso machine, the girl from the TV screen stares out at me shaking her head, her disappointed glare visible for just a second before her golden gaze fades into the burnished brass.

Taking a deep breath, I pull my eyes back to Ryan's and attempt to purge the girl's haunting glare from my mind, as well as Christopher's disappointed stare. Our fingers interlace and the electricity from his warm hands wars with the slow chill overtaking my body.

I suppress a shiver and summon up my best smile. "It's a date."

CHAPTER THIRTEEN

If looks could kill, I'd be taking my last breath right about now.

The girl from last night—what was her name? Anna? Emma?—storms out of Philippe's, her icy stare almost palpable as she nearly knocks me into the street. Behind her, a middle-aged woman with a haircut better suited for someone about twenty years younger carries a teal dress wrapped in plastic to protect it from the mist falling from the sky. She shoots me a stern glance before rushing up the wet sidewalk to catch up with the girl.

Great. Here it comes. Another lecture from Philippe. If there's one thing I've learned working here, it's that a tongue lashing always stings a little more when delivered with a French accent.

The bell rings as I open the door, and Philippe pops out from the back. The beaming smile he usually reserves for paying customers fades quickly into a frustrated glower when he sees who it is.

"Hi, Philippe."

"Miss Davis." Stroking his chin thoughtfully, he thinks for a moment before answering, "I suppose I must thank you for my early Christmas present."

I always know it's bad when I become "Miss Davis" instead of "Carol." This is not going to be fun. "Early Christmas present?"

"You know very well what I'm talking about." Philippe's eyes bulge in their sockets.

Playing dumb isn't going to help me this time.

"The girl and her mother that just left. They were waiting outside when I opened at ten, both of them already furious about the girl's treatment in *my* store last night, and on top of everything else, half-soaked from the morning drizzle. I had to practically give them that rather expensive dress to keep them from going online and trashing this place." His eyes roll up and to the right. "And there's no guarantee they won't go ahead and do it anyway."

"But—"

"No buts," he grumbles, refusing to meet my gaze. "I've fired people for far less than what that young lady said you put her through last night." He sighs. "You know how I feel about you, Carol, but when you pull stuff like this, you all but tie my hands."

"And if you and my dad hadn't been friends back in the day, we wouldn't even be having this conversation, right?"

Philippe surveys me with hard eyes. "You know good and well I've never said anything like that. You're a hard worker and a good employee, at least when you choose to be. But when you choose otherwise..." He holds his tongue for a moment. "Jack Davis was the best friend I ever had. Back when I was still drinking, your father saw me through more rough patches than I will likely ever remember. I owe him everything." He fixes me with a stern gaze. "That being said, this is a business, and the decisions I make here are just that. Business."

It's my turn to avoid Philippe's gaze. "I suppose you're thinking he'd be very disappointed in me right now."

A crack forms in Philippe's stony facade. "I've known you since before you could walk, Carol. What happened to the sweet little girl who used to sit with me at the park and feed the ducks?"

A block of ice forms in my chest. "Her parents and kid sister flew into the side of a mountain on their way home for Christmas a few years back. You may have heard about it. It was all over the news."

The anger in his expression deflates. "I miss them too, you know."

"So," I ask, "where does that leave us?"

"Well," he starts, thoughtfully, "regardless of how I feel about you and your family, I can't allow you to treat my customers this way. This store is my livelihood. My life."

I rub at my temple as a headache flirts with the edge of my consciousness. "Look, Philippe, if you're going to fire me, just do it. I've been dying to enjoy my Christmas break without being shackled to a cash register."

For the first time in our conversation, a hint of a smile appears on Philippe's face. "Oh, I'm not going to fire you. Not yet, at least. As your aunt and I discussed, this job is good for you, and just like your dad showed me, everyone deserves a second chance. Just know that for what remains of the Christmas season, I'll be staying in the store while we're open to ensure we avoid any further...unpleasantness. Is that fair?"

"I suppose." I sidle up to Philippe and shoot him my most innocent grin. "As long as we're on speaking terms again, I need your help."

An incredulous smirk flashes across his features. "My help?"

"Yes." I bury the nervousness in my gut beneath my beaming smile. "I need a dress. For the Christmas Eve dance."

His smirk blossoms into a knowing grin. "That smart young man from Best Buy finally got up the nerve to ask you, did he?"

My jaw locks. "Oh my God, if one more person tries to match me with Christopher Kellerman, I am going to tear out all my hair and join a convent."

Philippe steps back, abashed. "I'm sorry. I just assumed—"

"Assumed what?"

"It's just, you mention him often." His knowing eyes rile the butterflies trying to escape my belly. "I'm afraid I must have misunderstood."

I shake my head. "I'd tell you that ship has sailed, but the truth is, the U.S.S. *Carol and Christopher* was never even built, despite what the rest of the world evidently thinks." I let out a sigh. "On the other hand, I have had my eye on someone, and apparently, he's had his eye on me as well."

"Someone?"

"He asked me this morning. Came all the way down to the mall just to find me."

"And who is this young man of whom you speak?"

"His name is Ryan King. He's in my class."

"The basketball player?" Philippe strokes his chin. "Interesting."

Surprised, I let out a laugh. "You follow high school basketball?"

"But of course." A different type of affront appears in Philippe's gaze. "Just because a man owns a dress shop doesn't mean he doesn't like sports."

"Huh. I guess I always figured basketball was a little off your beaten path."

"I can see where you might think that." Philippe's exasperation fades into a knowing smirk. "Though you shouldn't pigeonhole people when you don't have all the facts, wouldn't you agree?"

"I suppose." Half afraid to say another word, I peer up at him through furrowed eyebrows. "So, Mr. Sports Center, are you going to help me pick out a kick-ass dress or not?"

Any residual anger remaining in Philippe's expression melts into the trademark excitement he brings to every customer who walks into his store. "I thought you'd never ask."

CHAPTER FOURTEEN

"You're home late." Though Valerie does her best to keep her tone level, fatigue and worry color her words, along with just a touch of anger.

Good God. I stay out late working at the job she's forcing me to keep and I'm still in trouble.

I just can't win around here.

"Sorry, Val. Been running late since I opened my eyes this morning. Coach Spinnaker didn't let me cheer at the mall, so I decided to go on to work. I stayed a little late straightening up the store."

And straightening things out with Philippe.

"*You* went to work early and stayed late?" Valerie asks. "Who are you and what have you done with my niece?"

"I may have had an ulterior motive." I shoot her a sheepish grin. "You see, I kind of need a dress...for the dance."

"Oh, really?" A grin peeks its way through her steely stare. "*Someone* finally broke through the ice?"

"The ice?" Rolling my eyes, I grab a seat at the dining room table and dig into the vegetarian lasagna Val has waiting for me. "Really. That's what you're going to say."

"Sorry." She raises her hands in mock surrender. "I'm just surprised to hear you actually decided to go." Valerie joins me at the table. "Tell me about the dress."

I let out a tired laugh. "Well, that's the thing. There are a couple of pretty ones I'm looking at, but we were so busy today with all the tuxes coming in and a few last-minute dress purchases, I didn't get a chance to try anything on. Not to mention I had to sell one of my favorites to some junior from East."

"I'm sure Philippe will find something you like that fits." Valerie brushes my hand with her fingers like she used to when I was younger and needed a little soothing. "And you'd make any dress look pretty."

"Thanks."

Valerie leans in. "So, this mysterious reversal about the big Christmas Eve Dance. I'm guessing there's a boy involved. Anybody I know?"

My cheeks get a little warmer. "More like someone you know...*of*."

"Oh." Something like concern flashes across her features. "Does this someone have a name?"

"His name is Ryan."

A knowing smile fills her face. "Ryan King?"

"Yeah. How'd you guess?"

Valerie laughs. "You know, Carol, your life isn't the top-secret spy novel you seem to think it is most of the time."

"And what's that supposed to mean?"

"Nothing. I just remember a certain twelfth grader who came home from her first day of school back in August mooning about this cute basketball player in her history class. Sound familiar?"

I bury my face in my hands. "God, I don't know why I tell you anything."

"Now, don't be mad. It's just exciting to see you looking forward to something for a change." She rests a hand on my knee. "It wouldn't hurt you to actually be happy for once."

I pull my leg away. "The last ten years of my life beg to differ."

"You can't live the rest of your life looking backward, Carol. If you're not careful, you'll run into something." Wounded, she rises from the table and heads into the kitchen. "I think I've got some stir fry left in the fridge if that lasagna isn't enough."

A series of beeps from the kitchen lets me know more food is on the way, and since I pretty much skipped lunch today, I'm not complaining. As I scarf down the leftover lasagna, a foreign sound hits my ears. Masked at first by the gentle hum of the microwave, a song begins to build in the room.

A particularly familiar song.

The bell-like tones of "Dance of the Sugar Plum Fairy" waft through the room. Quiet at first, the tune grows in intensity with every note. At first, I think it's merely my imagination, a flashback to my strange morning at Best Buy, but within seconds, there's no doubt.

Impossible as it seems, the song has followed me home.

"Valerie?"

No answer, though she's just in the next room.

"Mike?" I rise from the table. "Did you put on some music?"

I follow the sound into the den as the melody continues to crescendo. Though the old tube television appears to be switched off, music pours from the speakers on either side of the darkened screen.

"If this is some kind of joke, it's not funny." I grab the remote off the coffee table and jam my thumb down on the power button in vain hope an act so simple will somehow stop the music. Instead, the melody swells. Holding my hands over my ears to block out the sound, I do a quick sweep of the space. I almost hope I find Mike in the coat closet, my one and only uncle laughing as he gets me with another one of his stupid practical jokes, but there's no one in the room but me.

Just like in Best Buy this morning, the music grows louder with every note until my teeth start to shake in my head. A novel thought hits me: Just unplug the stupid thing. I rush to the wall outlet and grab the cord when, without warning, the lights dim throughout the house.

"That's it." I turn to dash for the front door. "I am outta here."

Something—A feeling? Or maybe a premonition?—halts my steps. Frozen to the spot, I can barely breathe. A strangely familiar shape from the fringe of my vision demands my attention. The screen empty no longer, the darkened tube is now populated by the strange, sad girl from the mall. Peering out at me as she did from the TV at Best Buy and again from the rear of the food court's espresso machine, she still neither smiles nor frowns, though this time the insistence in her eyes hits me with almost physical force.

"Who are you?" I ask, taking a step toward the set. "What do you want from me?"

"Who are you talking to, Carol?"

I gasp way louder than I'd like to admit at the sound of Mike's voice. The moment shattered, the lights return to normal and the music goes silent. The girl vanishes from the screen as though the set were flipped off.

I spin around and punch my uncle in the chest. "Thanks for the heart attack, Mike."

"Ow." He backs off, a grin creeping across his face. "Watch where you put those bony little fists of yours. You might hurt someone."

I don't even try to keep the exasperation from my voice. "Do you need something?"

"I just came down to watch a show, but if you and the TV are too busy talking..."

Valerie steps into the room. "Everything all right in here?"

Mike laughs. "I'm fine. I was just coming down to watch a show on the DVR and found Carol here having a one-sided chat with the old Panasonic there."

Valerie's attention shifts to me. "Carol?"

"You didn't hear it either?" I search for a hint of understanding in either of their faces, but find nothing but mystified stares.

"Hear what?" Mike glances around the room. "Wait. Did it sound like someone trying to break in?"

My toes curl in my shoes. "Not...exactly."

"Then what was it, Carol?" Valerie asks. "What did you hear?"

"I don't know." My gaze drops to the floor. "It sounded like...music."

Valerie's brow furrows. "Music?"

"Blaring out of the TV speakers. 'The Dance of the Sugar Plum Fairy' from *The Nutcracker*. You're both sure you didn't hear anything?"

"There's no music, honey," Valerie says, "and the TV isn't even on."

I flop down on the couch and bury my face in a pillow. "I know what I heard."

And what I saw.

Or do I?

"Are you sure it wasn't your phone?" Valerie asks. "A new ringtone or something?"

I drop the pillow to my lap. "It wasn't my phone. Are you listening to me?" Honestly, I wish it were something so simple, but even if that were the case, it wouldn't begin to explain the sad little girl who stared out at me from the TV just moments ago.

Valerie sits next to me on the couch and brushes her fingers across my brow. "Are you feeling well?"

"I'm fine." I brush her hand away. "And anyway, you two are the ones who need to get your hearing checked."

"Sorry. Didn't hear a peep other than you attempting to commune with the dead screen there." Mike chuckles. "Better check the deed on Monday, Val. Would hate to find out this house was built on an ancient burial ground or something."

I come off the couch as if struck. "Why would you say something like that?"

Mike's eyes go wide at my response. "Hey, it's a joke. You know. The old *Poltergeist* movie with the static-filled TV screen and the little girl..."

"I know the movie, Mike." My eyes drift over to the darkened TV screen. "You've made me watch it like a dozen times."

"You've got to be kidding me." Mike's eyes bore into me, his cheeks getting pinker by the second. "This whole thing is somehow my fault?"

"Mike," Valerie says. "Don't."

"Don't what? It's getting to where I can't even set foot in my own living room without getting swept up in some drama or another. Last month, I was the reason Carol couldn't study for finals. Month before that, I got booted from my own house so we could host a Homecoming party I'm pretty sure Her Majesty there didn't even want to attend." He motions to an empty corner of the room where one of the ceiling bulbs has burned out, casting the floor in shadow. "Now it's three days before Christmas, and I can't even put up a tree in my own house without being labeled an 'insensitive' jerk."

I turn so Mike can't see my tears. "I am so out of here."

Valerie intercepts me as I bolt for the stairs. "Carol, wait."

I don't bat away her fingers as she gently grasps my upper arm.

"Mike," Valerie whispers, "can you give us a little space?"

"Fine." He throws his hands in the air. "I'll just go work on some spreadsheets for tomorrow and hit the sack." He heads for the hall. "If anyone needs me, I'll be upstairs."

Mike huffs out of the room, and Valerie leads me back to the couch.

I let out a quiet laugh. "Wow. Someone needs some anger management training." One second of Valerie's laser beam glare and I decide against continuing down that path.

Valerie's eyes meet mine. "Carol, you are family, and that will never change, but a word of advice?"

"Do I have any choice?"

"Not really, so listen." Practiced patience keeps her voice even. "I'm begging you, please don't create a situation where I have to choose sides between my only niece and my husband."

My arms cross instinctively. "Or what? You'll kick me out?"

Valerie lets out an exhausted sigh. "Nobody is kicking anybody out. I'm just asking you to cut Mike a little slack, okay?"

"Cut *him* some slack?"

She smiles and slaps my knee. "At least as much as he cuts you, sweetie."

Whatever. "Message received."

"All right." She repositions herself on the couch to face me full on. It's a move I know well. It's what every therapist I've ever seen does right before they get ready to go into listening mode. A tell, if there ever was one. "So, what's this about music and sugar plum fairies?"

"I'm not crazy." I glance at the doorway leading to the hall. "No matter what Mike might think."

"Mike's just upset, but he'll get over it. He and I both know this time of year is hard for you, and after ten years, you know he'll get over it quick."

"It's not Mike that has me upset." I glance around the room. "Valerie, can I tell you something?"

She draws a hair closer. "Of course, honey."

"It's like this." I take a moment and decide telling the truth is worth the risk. "Tonight wasn't the first time I heard the music."

Her brow furrows. "What happened?"

"After Coach Spinnaker put the kibosh on me cheering today, I wandered over to Best Buy to do a little window shopping before heading to Philippe's." I glance at the still dark TV. "I heard it there first."

"The same song?"

"The same."

"Honey?" Valerie's expression tenses into that of reluctant inquisitor. "I have to ask you something."

"Shoot."

"Have you and your friends been experimenting with...you know...things?"

For the first time in hours, I laugh. "I'm not on drugs, if that's what you're getting at."

"Well." Valerie releases the death grip on her knee. "Good."

"There is something else, though."

"Okay," Valerie says. "What is it?"

I glance at the old Panasonic television, and before I can take in a breath to answer, a pair of sad eyes looks back from the darkened glass. Forlorn and imploring, the mysterious girl places a pale finger across her lips and shakes her head slowly from side to side, though her eyes never leave mine. I remember Marnie's words from last night, her warning of my fate if I didn't do as the Spirits required.

"Never mind." I rise from the couch. "It's been a really long day." I bite my lip before adding, "Tell Mike I'm sorry I upset him."

She stops me, her hand on my shoulder. "You know you can always talk to me, right?"

I nod and head up the stairs to my room where I shut and lock the door behind me.

"All right, little girl," I murmur. "I kept your little secret, so go ahead and bring it."

My hand still on the knob, I check the time. The clock says 10:17.

A memory of Marnie's words chills me to the bone.

Expect the first of the Spirits tomorrow night at one.

Before climbing into bed, I undo the lock and open the door a crack.

CHAPTER FIFTEEN

An overwhelming dread drags me from deepest sleep. A dread my groggy mind can neither define nor ignore. As I come awake, I find the air in my room frigid, just like the night before. My breath steams in the dim light of my alarm clock, and despite my down comforter and flannel sheets, my body shivers uncontrollably.

I check the clock. 12:57.

"Fantastic. Here it comes."

I slide from beneath the covers and slip on a sweatshirt to stave off the cold. It helps about as much as expected. Flipping on the lights, I creep about the room so I don't wake Mike and Valerie. Last thing I need is Mike scaring the crap out of me twice in one night. Truth be told, I think the ghost I'm about to meet should have that covered in spades.

The ghost I'm about to meet.

Guess I've decided to stop trying to convince myself this is all some kind of dream.

Wow. Life is so very different today.

I wait the last ninety seconds till the clock flips to one o'clock. Right on cue, it begins.

For the third time in twenty-four hours, the distinctive melody rings in my ears. Quiet at first, the sound builds with each successive note.

Tchaikovsky.

"Dammit." I climb back into bed and wrap a pillow around my head, trying to block out the sound. I may as well try to hold back a tsunami with an outstretched hand. I put my feet on the floor and shake my head. "Fine. You want me, you got me."

I step into the hallway, half expecting to find my aunt and uncle standing there, Mike with his hand on his forehead asking why I'm blasting *Nutcracker* at one o'clock in the morning. Half of me wants to wake them and prove I'm right, that I'm not just imagining things, but then Marnie's admonition hits me again, and I move toward the stairs, knowing all too well where I'm being led. In seconds, I stand in the darkened living room facing the television set. "Dance of the Sugar Plum Fairy" fills the room as if I stand before a live orchestra.

"All right. Where are you?" My words get no response other than the continuing crescendo of the music. My old swim coach's favorite saying echoes through my mind.

Fake bravado is better than no bravado at all.

I pull my arms tight around my body and glare at the TV. "Show yourself."

"Very well." A diminutive voice with a vaguely British accent rings out from behind me. I spin to find the little girl who has haunted me since this morning standing directly to my rear.

"Hello, Carol." Her ankle-length platinum blond hair shines in the darkness, surrounding her form in a halo of silvery light. Fashioned from ivory silk, her dress drags the floor as she takes a step back, the sprig of holly at her neck the only spot of color in her pale ensemble. Across her arm, she bears a dark cape complete with hood and a brass holly clasp, and I wonder for a moment if a ghost can experience cold. As with our two previous encounters, she neither smiles nor frowns, yet her expression is anything but indifferent. The opposite in fact.

Her eyes burn like twin fires in the darkness.

My fingers curl into trembling fists. "The Ghost of Christmas Past, I'm guessing?"

"Spirit, actually, though how you refer to me has little bearing on the many things we have to accomplish tonight."

If I expected her to be startled in any way by my naming of her, I am sorely disappointed.

"I have held many names over the centuries," she continues. "Midwinter, Nativity, Yule, Jól, Noel. I am the sum of all Christmases that have already come to pass." She takes a step toward me. "On this night in particular, however, I represent the various Christmases of *your* past." Her sad eyes wander over me, starting at my feet and rising till her gaze again meets mine. "Since you know my identity, Carol Davis, I must assume you also know why I am here."

"I've seen all the movies, if that helps." A thousand ants run up my back as I try to keep a semblance of cool. "I especially like the Muppet version." She doesn't say another word, so I continue. "I'm guessing you've come to show me some depressing reruns from my past to help me turn my life around?"

"Depressing reruns from your past?" She focuses on some point just across my shoulder. "You choose to refer to the unique memories of your life in such a way? I understand you've experienced much, but others have experienced far worse."

I take a step toward the Spirit. "What's so wrong with my life anyway? I'm near the top of my class in both grades and popularity, I just got asked to the Christmas dance by the hottest guy in school, and in a few days I inherit more money than God."

The Spirit's head tilts ever so slightly to the left as she looks on me with something approaching pity. "And does any of that bring you happiness?"

My turn to answer a question with silence.

"Do not judge until you have seen." Her gaze returns to mine, and despite my best efforts, I tremble. "I have come far to speak with you this evening and we only have so much time together before the dawn."

"Well, here I am." I turn up both my palms. "What is it you're supposed to show me?"

"The truth." Her lips grow even tighter. "A truth you currently ignore." She pulls in close, the radiance surrounding her ephemeral form warm against my skin. "Your truth."

"Whew." I let out a nervous laugh. "And here I thought you might get all cryptic on me."

Ignoring me, she stretches out a hand. "Shall we begin?"

I hesitate for a moment before taking her fingers in mine, her grasp both more solid and far warmer than I would have imagined. "So, are you going to tell me where we're going?"

"To wherever and whenever we need be." The girl pulls me toward the darkened television set. "Now, come."

As Tchaikovsky continues to blare from the speakers, she steps through the TV as if it isn't there and continues straight on through the wall. I follow close behind, the grip of her translucent fingers as strong as any man's. I inhale to scream in surprise as my body passes the wall, but before I can make a sound, the Spirit and I are standing outside. The precipitation has turned to sleet, yet despite the fact I'm dressed in nothing but my pajamas, sweatshirt, and slippers, I am warm in the silver light radiating from the Spirit's shining platinum locks.

"So." I make a visual sweep of our surroundings. "My own backyard. Sorry you came all this way, but I'm pretty familiar with the area. Believe it or not, back in the day, I'd even mow the grass from time to time."

Unfazed, the Spirit raises her arms, and the glow about her doubles in intensity. "This was merely a test. You have taken your first step in faith, and now we are ready to proceed."

"First step in faith? You're the one that dragged me out here. But faith? I don't think so."

"Really?" She almost smiles. "In case you missed it, Carol, you just walked through a perfectly good brick wall."

I'm getting the impression Ghosty McGhostypants here doesn't lose many arguments.

"Fine. So, now what? You take me back so I can watch myself sitting on Santa's lap when I was five? Back when everything was great and all of this holiday bullshit seemed to matter?"

"Actually, Carol," she whispers, folding her hands together as if in prayer, "I was thinking of an earlier Christmas."

CHAPTER SIXTEEN

The radiance pouring off the Spirit's floor-length hair doubles and redoubles until she appears as bright as the sun, and then in a blink, the space around me goes dark. As my eyes readjust to the dim light, a voice I never thought I'd hear again hits me like a wrecking ball.

"Push, sweetie!" Tears sting my eyes as my father's words, filled with confidence and no small amount of exhaustion, echo in the small room materializing around us. "Push!"

Detail by detail, the room takes shape. A table covered with surgical tools. My mother laid out on a hospital bed, her legs suspended in what look like a pair of vinyl saddles. A bright light from a swing-arm bulb beaming down on her midsection. My father, ever a tower of strength in my memory, wide-eyed and trembling as he squeezes my mother's hand.

"Okay, Holly." The doctor raises her head above the sheet to address my mother. "That's enough for now. Let's wait for the next contraction."

In the background, a rhythmic beeping from one of the machines gets slower and slower even as the tone goes deeper with every repetition. Both my father and I catch the worried glance shared between the doctor and the nurse.

"What's happening to the heart rate?" The confidence I always associated with my father's voice is gone. "Is the baby okay?"

"Your baby's going to be just fine, Mr. Davis," the doctor says, "but if we can't get her out in the next couple of pushes, we're looking at forceps or possibly C-section."

"Are you sure?" my father asks.

"It's okay, honey." Beads of sweat trickle down my mother's face as she locks gazes with the doctor. "Do whatever you have to do, Dr. Marigold. I'll be all right."

"We'll make sure of that," Dr. Marigold says.

My father clears his throat. "But Holly always made it clear she didn't want—"

My mother silences her husband with an upraised hand then returns her attention to the doctor. "Whatever it takes."

The slow beeping in the background starts to accelerate, and the tone returns to its previous pitch. Relief overtakes the nurse's face, and the doctor's bunched shoulders relax.

"All right," Dr. Marigold says. "Looks like we're out of the woods for a minute. Let's see what you can do with the next contraction." The doctor glances over at her table of instruments and eyes a pair of interlocking spoons the length of my forearm.

A strange pressure hits my temples, as if someone has put my head in a vise. I peer around the room looking for the Spirit and find her in the corner, partially obscured by the machinery tracking the baby's heart rate.

"You've brought me here to see my own birth?"

She peeks between the twisted cables. "Life. The greatest gift a person ever receives, though few remember the experience of coming into this world. I thought you might benefit from such a unique opportunity."

I turn back just in time to see my father check his watch before he leans in and kisses my mother's cheek. "It's 11:49. Looks like little Eve is going to make this a squeaker."

"Eve?" I look to the Spirit who places a finger across her lips and returns my attention to my mother.

"Wow." Mom's lips turn up in an exhausted smile. "Who knew nineteen hours of labor could be this much fun?" She inhales to say something else only to have the air driven from her lungs. "Here...it...comes..." she grunts between gritted teeth.

The heart rate begins to drop again almost immediately. Mom pushes with all her might as the contraction mounts. I chance a peek below the sheet and can just see the crown of a head. Covered with hair just like Mom always told me, I don't seem to be making much progress despite the fact the vein on my mother's forehead appears about to burst.

I glance over at the machines where the previously quick melody of the heartbeat has slowed to a frightening dirge. The ominous tone of each low-pitched beep hits me like a hammer strike.

"They've got to do something," I whisper to the Spirit. "The baby has to come now."

"Fear not, Carol. What you see is but a shadow of events that have long since passed into history."

"Tell that to her." The fear in my mother's eyes sends a dagger through my heart. Even more than my father, I don't remember ever seeing her afraid of anything.

Another few seconds and the contraction passes. The heartbeat returns to normal, though I know good and well another contraction is on its way.

"Holly," the doctor says, "the baby isn't liking the contractions, and the decelerations are getting worse every time. I think we can safely do one more set of pushes, but after that, we might be looking at a trip to the OR."

"But the baby's okay?" my mother asks. "Right?"

"She's not progressing. Next set of contractions, I'm going to put on the forceps and we're going to do our best to have a baby girl. Understand?"

"Is that absolutely necessary?" my father asks. "You said there were increased risks with forceps delivery."

"Forceps increase the risk of a tear to the mother and in some cases can cause complications with the newborn." Dr. Marigold raises her shoulders in apology. "Still, Little Eve's not coming any other way." She glances at the door. "At least not in here."

My mother considers for all of a second. "Just do it."

My father's eyes grow wide, but he doesn't say a word, his only response a silent nod.

Without hesitation, the doctor positions the two metal salad spoons, one on either side of the head, and interlocks the two handles. The pressure over my temples doubles. I try to catch the Spirit's gaze, but her focus is completely on my mother, as is everyone else's in the room.

A minute passes. Then another.

"What's wrong?" my father asks. "Where's the contraction?"

"She just had two in a row," the nurse answers. "Sometimes it takes a minute."

"Don't worry." The blood creeps back into my mother's face. "It's coming."

"Wait for it, Holly," Dr. Marigold says. "I'll tell you when."

The heartbeat begins to drop again, this time faster than before.

"All right." Dr. Marigold grasps the forceps handles with both hands and kicks one leg back for leverage. If I didn't know better, I'd swear she was preparing to rip the baby's head off. "Now, push."

Like before, my mother curls her chin into her chest and pushes like she was born for this moment. My father squeezes her hand, never once taking his eyes off his wife's face. The nurse, holding my mother's other hand, coaches her through the contraction, all the while keeping one eye on the digital read out on the monitor as the heart rate drops back down into the double digits again. Dr. Marigold, far calmer than I could imagine myself in the same position, pulls on the forceps handles like her life depended on it.

It's not her life, however, that hangs in the balance.

"Deep breath," Dr. Marigold says, "and push!" Though spoken at just above a whisper, the insistence of the doctor's tone comes through loud and clear. My mother obeys and with her second push, I see the head move.

"One more," Dr. Marigold says. "Deep breath...and push!" As one, my mother and her obstetrician contract what seems like every muscle in their bodies and together they deliver the head.

"Is that it?" my mother asks, her face drenched in sweat.

"The head is out, but the cord is wrapped around the neck." Dr. Marigold's fingers probe farther. "Twice." Tossing the forceps to the table, the doctor grabs a pair of what look like long metal pliers. Faster than I can imagine, she clamps the cord in two places and cuts through the blue-white tissue with the longest pair of scissors I've ever seen.

"Now..." Dr. Marigold whispers. "Just one more little push."

My mother pulls in a deep breath and curls into her stomach, grunting as she tries to hold her air. The doctor puts a hand on either side of the head and pulls down toward the floor. The pain from my temples moves down my neck and into my chest and back as Dr. Marigold delivers one shoulder, then the other, then the rest of the body. Resting in the crook of the doctor's arm, the baby is covered in a mix of blood and something that looks like cream cheese.

"That's me?"

The Spirit steps through the machinery and materializes by the bed. "All eight pounds, fourteen ounces of you."

As Dr. Marigold hands the baby off to the nurse, I notice the limp arms and legs, the pale coloring of the skin, the blue lips. I turn to the Spirit to ask what's wrong, but my mother beats me to the punch.

"Doctor, why isn't she crying?" The momentary relief passed, fear returns to my mother's eyes. "Is something wrong?"

"Give her a minute," the nurse says as she takes a towel to me like she's trying to rub off the top layer of my skin. "She just needs a little—"

And then, the most wonderful sound I've ever heard. A cry fills the space and the tension in the room melts like a snowball on the face of the sun. My lungs burn from breath long held, and as one, my father and I let out a long sigh of relief.

"Listen to her, Holly," my father says. "Little Eve is singing her first song." He wipes a tear from my mother's face. "She's going to be a songbird just like her mother."

"That's more than just a song, honey." My mother directs my father's attention to the clock hanging on the wall behind Dr. Marigold's head. "We're two minutes into Christmas Day. That's a Carol."

CHAPTER SEVENTEEN

"And the stupid pun that has followed me my entire life is born."

"Stupid pun..." The Spirit's expression becomes cross, her ghostly countenance shifting from sheer insistence for the first time since I met her haunted gaze. "You, Carol Davis, in all of humanity, are allowed the supreme privilege of seeing the love present in the room at the moment of your birth, and all you can speak of is the kernel of humor that went into your naming?"

"Hey. You put up with being an honest-to-God 'Christmas Carol' for the better part of eighteen years and get back to me." I pull myself nose to nose with the Spirit, my squinted eyes baking from the heat radiating off her. "The way I see it, all of this—you, Marnie, our little trip to the maternity ward—is nothing but the punchline to a joke told by someone dear to me who died ten years ago."

"Is that how you see yourself?" the Spirit asks. "A joke?"

"No." I feel my cheeks flush. "I was just talking about my name and all the other stuff that..." I turn from the Spirit and peer out the window at the snowflakes drifting gently past the glass. My hands ball into fists. "You know what I mean."

"Do I?" The Spirit touches my shoulder and directs my attention to the hospital bed where my mother cradles her newborn baby in her arms and my father stands over us as happy and proud as I've ever seen him. "Do you?"

"Take me away from here." I turn from the bed of my birth. "Seeing them again. So young. So happy. It's too much."

"Of course," the Spirit says. "Take my hand."

I clutch the girl's fingers and wince at the heat. "So my parents really loved me. Lesson learned. Can you please take me back to my house now?"

"I thought it was your aunt and uncle's house," the Spirit says with an all too familiar inflection. "Isn't that what you always say to them when they try to include you in decisions around the home?"

My arms instinctively fold across my chest. "I don't always say that."

"Perhaps." The silver light scintillating off the Spirit's platinum locks fills the space like a magnesium flare, and a moment later, we're standing in Mike and Valerie's front yard.

But something's wrong. Something's...different.

It takes no more than a moment to figure it out.

It's the lights.

They're everywhere.

I had forgotten how much Valerie liked to decorate for Christmas back in the day. Nothing like the simple electric candle in each window she has now, this house is lit up from stem to stern. Somehow, she's rigged up a scene of eight commando reindeer rappelling down the side of the chimney while a full-size Santa stands atop the roof, all decked out in red and white fatigues like some jolly old Army Sergeant. A miniature Rudolph floats above the front porch like a glowing red guided missile with legs and antlers. Most likely visible from space, the house is strangely beautiful, and more than that, familiar. In fact, it looks exactly the same as Valerie and Mike's first Christmas there, back when I was—

"Three years old." I spin around at the sound of Valerie's voice. My aunt, looking like she's barely out of high school, stands at the curb helping a little girl in a red velvet dress get out of my parents' old Volvo.

A velvet dress I remember well.

"Happy Birthday, Carol."

"My birthday's tomorrow, Aunt Valerie. Silly." The irrepressible excitement in my squeaky toddler voice makes my breath catch. "Did you get me something?"

"What do you think?" Valerie sweeps me up into a monster hug and spins my three-year-old form around in the chill December air.

"What is it?" Little Carol squeals. "A puppy?"

"Now, Carol. Don't be rude." Every bit of seven months pregnant, my mother sits with one foot on the curb, trying to pull herself out of the passenger side of the car. "Sorry we're late, Val. Had a little run of Braxton-Hicks contractions back on the freeway."

Valerie puts me down and goes to help my mom out of the car. "You okay?"

"Jack stopped at a gas station about twenty miles out of town. Got me some water and let me stretch my legs. They passed after a bit."

"Well, let me know if you need to lie down." Valerie heads to the hatchback and knocks on the glass.

My father pops the back and steps out of the car.

"Sorry," he says. "Almost to the end of the chapter."

"Another audiobook?" Valerie asks.

"The new Alex Cross." Dad pulls a stack of presents from the back of the car. "It's pretty fantastic."

"The man in the book said something bad." The toddler version of me crosses her arms and crinkles up her nose. "Mommy said not to say that word."

Mom sighs. "Jack couldn't stand one more verse of 'The Wheels on the Bus,' so James Patterson ended up whispering naughty words into my daughter's impressionable ears for the last hour or so."

"Nice." Valerie intercepts Mom as she moves to grab the rest of the wrapped boxes from the trunk. "Now, now, Mrs. Bun in the Oven. You take it easy. Jack and I have got this."

Mom's head tilts to one side. "You know I don't like being treated like an invalid."

Valerie's eyebrows shoot upward, her eyes flashing. "And you know I don't like it when you deliver babies in my living room. Now get inside and put your feet up. That's an order."

"Whatever you say, Sarge." Mom gives Valerie a quick salute and heads up the sidewalk with me in tow, all decked out in my velvet dress, white tights, and patent leather shoes.

"That everything?" Valerie asks my dad, as she grabs the other stack of gifts from the car.

"Just the bags and a couple things up front Holly insisted on bringing."

Valerie's eyes slide shut, her breath steaming. "You let her cook, didn't you?"

Dad lets out a chuckle. "You've known your sister a heck of a lot longer than I have. You ever try to convince her not to do something she's set her mind to?" He closes the hatchback with a free elbow. "Anyway, she just put together a pot of vegetable soup and some meatballs. Nothing too crazy."

Valerie shoots Dad a wink. "At least she let you drive."

"It's six hours." Dad heads up the sidewalk with Valerie close behind. "She was more than willing to let me handle that."

"Mike and I could've come to the beach."

"It's your first Christmas in Joy and Charlie's place, and Holly insisted we come." Dad shakes his head sadly. "Holly's really missed her mom these last few months. I wasn't sure about the whole Christmas homecoming thing, but here we are." He heads up the sidewalk. "Time to start new traditions, anyway. This time next year, we'll be living practically down the street."

"Oh, really?" Valerie brightens. "You got the job?"

"Nothing official yet, but everything is looking good so far. Holly is trying not to get her hopes up too much, but even the possibility of moving home has her beyond excited."

Dad and Valerie step onto the porch.

"So." Valerie inclines her head toward the front door. "Carol ready for the new addition?"

"I guess we'll see." My father's face settles into a worried smile. "Carol's one sweet child, but she always seems happiest when she's at the center of everything."

"What the hell?" I turn on the Spirit. "Why are you showing me all of this? I told you I didn't want to see them anymore."

No sooner do I turn away than the Spirit brings a warm finger to my chin and turns my gaze back on Dad and Valerie. "Has your life truly become so miserable that you can't enjoy reliving this moment when your family was still together?"

"And hear my dad call me a self-centered brat?" My fingernails dig into my palms. "I loved my sister more than anything, and she's dead. Dead and never coming back. Just like Mom and Dad. I can't even stand to watch the cabinet full of home videos Valerie has and you want me to sit here all smiles and relive all this?"

"You hold pain inside yourself like a lungful of poison gas." The Spirit comes eye to eye with me. "Can you not just let it out?" Before I can answer, she turns to the door. "Come. We are not yet finished here."

CHAPTER EIGHTEEN

Another flash of silver light and reality swirls around us anew, coalescing moments later into a version of Mike and Valerie's home that no longer exists. The orange Formica countertops in the kitchen that were there before Mike put in the granite and tile a few years back. The crazy wallpaper with which Grandma and Grandpa had covered every inch of wall space throughout the house. The plush carpet that left me with more than my share of rug burns over the years. All long since updated, seeing it like this makes it feel like...

"Home?" the Spirit asks.

"Great." I shoot the Spirit my most withering glare. "You can read my thoughts, too?"

"Perhaps, though I need no such talent to see what is spelled out all over your face."

I follow the Spirit from the kitchen and into the living room where Mom and Dad sit on either end of an old leather couch with the miniature version of me perched between them. My little legs are kicking so excitedly beneath the velvet dress, I'm afraid I might just take off.

"So." Valerie takes a sip of chamomile tea. "Any ideas about what you're going to name Carol's little sister?"

Mom strokes her belly and takes Dad's hand. "We're kind of partial to Joy."

Valerie nods. "Mom."

I glance at the Spirit, my breath catching in my throat. She doesn't look back, staring instead at the scene unfolding before us.

"I miss her." My mother pulls me close and strokes my long, flowing hair. "We all do."

Grandma Joy died not long after my second birthday. My memories of her are strangely fleeting yet quite specific. The jar of chocolate chip cookies she always had stashed on top of the refrigerator. The purse full of peppermints. The mouth-watering scents that filled her kitchen when she was cooking. Her infectious laugh. That ever-present smile, even on her last day.

Her passing was my first lesson in death and the never-ending cruelty of this stupid world. The most loving woman in the world, taken by something as random as a blood clot to the lung. She wasn't even fifty. Mike and Valerie ended up with the house, moving there from a two-bedroom apartment on the other side of town, and Mom, Dad, Joy, and I followed not long after. Grandma Joy's death was the first of many dominos to fall in my life, but I don't think I knew till my eighth birthday how much losing her affected me.

When all the other dominos fell.

Mike appears from upstairs. "Hiya, Jack, Holly." Tossing me a chocolate Santa Claus, he adds a deliberately silly, "Carol."

Three-year-old me snatches the candy from the air. "Thanks, Uncle Mike!"

"No sweat, slugger." Mike flashes that devilish grin that

always used to make me giggle when I was small. "See you've still got those lightning reflexes."

"Good to see you." Dad stands and shakes Mike's hand. "The house is really coming along."

"Any issues getting here?" Mike asks. "The weatherman said that last stretch of interstate is a bit icy tonight."

"Nothing I couldn't handle." Three-year-old Carol and I share an eye-roll as my dad's voice drops an octave into a fake baritone. "I was born to drive."

Mom laughs. "Says the man who was so enmeshed in his audio thriller half an hour back, he completely missed a pair of deer standing on the side of the highway."

Dad levels a half-vexed gaze at Mom. "We made it here in one piece, didn't we?"

Mom returns the look in spades. "Two seconds later, and we would've had a new hood ornament, complete with antlers."

"Aunt Valerie," Little Carol breaks in. "Do I get to open a present tonight like last year?"

My question cuts the tension in the room, and everyone shifts in their chair until I'm the center of attention.

Which is apparently, according to my father's own words, my favorite place to be.

"I don't know." Valerie winks at my mom. "Have you been good this year?"

"Yes!" Little Carol almost leaps out of her dress. "I'm always good."

"Always?" Mom asks, her face turned up in a practiced smirk.

Little Carol runs to her mother's side. "Tell her, Mommy. Tell her I've been good."

Mom lets out a quiet sigh. It's the most beautiful sound I've heard in years.

"Carol's been a little angel the whole way here." Mom

kneels and gives me—Little Carol—a quick peck on the cheek. "I think it would be more than fair to let her open one gift tonight."

"All right," Valerie says. "Just one."

"Yay!" My heart races as I remember even now fifteen years later what the little girl in the red velvet dress is going to find beneath the tree. Not the largest or prettiest wrapped of the selection, but without a doubt the one that I had to open that night.

I steel myself as this stupid holiday prepares yet again to kick me in the gut.

Little Carol rips into the paper, all red and green and covered with Christmas Cherubs dancing between wreaths and colored lights, and tears open the box. Inside rests a sweatshirt. Purple and pink, my two favorite colors, the words embroidered across the front still chill my heart, though for a very different reason than they did fifteen years ago.

"What does it say, Mommy?" Little Carol asks.

My mom looks away for a moment, her eyes shifting furtively from left to right. "It says '#1 Big Sister' just like you're going to be, right?"

"Oh." Little Carol's arms drop to her side, the excitement on her face evaporating like a drop of water in a frying pan. "Okay."

"What is it?" Valerie looks back and forth from me to my mother. "Is something wrong?"

"No, nothing's wrong." Hearing my mom's singsong conciliatory tone for the first time in a decade brings tears to my eyes. "Carol's just been having trouble adapting to the reality that we're about to become a foursome."

"Oh, Carol." Valerie kneels beside me. "You're going to be the best big sister ever, just like your mom was for me."

"Mommy?" Little Carol asks.

"We may be all grown up now," Valerie says, "but your mom and I were little once, just like you. She's four years older than me, just a few months older than you're going to be when your baby sister gets here."

Little Carol kicks the crumpled paper at her feet. "No one asked if I even wanted a baby sister."

"Honey." Gently, Valerie picks Little Carol's chin up off her chest and meets her hurt gaze. "Some of the best gifts in life are the ones we never asked for."

I turn to the Spirit short of breath, my heart about to beat out of my chest. "Please, Spirit. Take me away from here. I can't take another second of this."

The Spirit stares back at me without a hint of smile, though I find at least a trace of kindness in her stern expression. "You were selfish in this moment, like every other toddler that has ever walked the earth. But you learned something that day, did you not?"

"What do you mean?"

"To share. To care." The Spirit's eyes burn into me. "To love."

I look away, unable to stand the Spirit's fervent stare. "What other choice did I have?"

"It goes deeper than that, Carol, and you know it."

"What are you talking about?"

"Joy." An icy grip surrounds my heart at the name. "Your three-year-old self doesn't seem too keen on the idea of a sibling, but you and I both know that isn't the final word on the matter, don't we?"

"She was my sister." I wipe away the tear coursing down my left cheek. "I came around."

"And that's it?"

"That's it."

"Perhaps another Christmas, then?" Not a hint of emotion crosses the Spirit's resigned expression. "Maybe a year hence?"

"Don't."

"You know where we're going then?"

"Please." The tears flow freely this time. "Not there. Anywhere but there."

"If you refuse to remember on your own, you will be shown what you need to see."

I glance back once more at the petulant little girl in the corner, me a day shy of my third birthday, and wish I could take back everything I said that night. But as the Spirit said, these are just shadows, and as her phosphorescent hair fills the room once more with a silver glow, I have no doubt which shadow the light will cast next.

CHAPTER NINETEEN

Another hospital room, but this time it's not my mother beneath the cold, unfeeling lights.

Just shy of a year old, Joy lies on a small bed in pediatric intensive care holding on to life by a thread. Plastic tubing runs into both her arms, bringing life supporting fluids and medicine to her frail little body. Taped to the corner of her mouth, the tube in her throat is all that's keeping her breathing. Born a full eight weeks early and just three days after the Christmas we just left, her first year on the planet has been rough. Stuck in neonatal intensive care for the first month of her life, she's been in and out of the hospital ever since, this time with something the doctors call RSV.

The scene continues to materialize around me. A doctor and a nurse, both masked and gowned, gaze upon the helpless baby amid the nest of tubes and wires. My mother and father, only a year older than when I saw them moments before, appear to have aged a decade. And at their feet, decked out in the gown, gloves, and mask that was the only way the staff would let me come back and see my sister, a four-year-old me stands with tears streaming down her face.

"Can I see her?" Little Carol looks up at her mother. "Can I see Joy?"

Mom waits for the doctor's nod of assent before picking me up so I can see my baby sister lying in the hospital crib. As my younger self's face screws up with grief, I turn on the Spirit.

"You have no right to bring me here. You think I've forgotten this?"

The Spirit's expression doesn't change an iota. "Just...watch."

Fourteen years have passed since this night, and still I've never been able to expunge the image of my baby sister lying there helpless and fighting for her life, her little lungs pulling the skin of her chest tight across her ribs as if each breath might be her last. But if that's what it takes...

"Fine." I turn back to the small hospital bed where Little Carol's gaze flicks back and forth from her sister to her mother and father, the sadness in her face matched only by the confusion.

"Why doesn't Joy wake up, Mommy?" Little Carol's bottom lip quivers. "Why won't she just wake up?"

"Joy is really sick, honey." Mom brushes a lock of hair out of Little Carol's face. "The doctors are giving her medicine to keep her asleep while the machine breathes for her."

"She can't breathe without the machine? Is that the 'new-moan-ya'?"

"Yes, honey." She glances at my father, her lip trembling. "That's the pneumonia."

I look up into my father's worried eyes. "Why did Joy get the 'new-moan-ya' anyway?"

The doctor hands the nurse a small syringe and takes Little Carol's gloved hand. "Your sister came into the world a little early, sweetie. Even though she's a year old now, she still more likely to get sick than other kids. Just know we're taking good care of her and she's going to get better. Okay?"

Little Carol's gaze shoots from the doctor to my mother, and at Mom's subtle nod, the little girl I was a lifetime ago relaxes, though doubt flickers in her too-wise-for-her-years eyes.

"Okay, Doctor," she whispers. "Just help my sister. Please."

I still remember fragments of the day we brought Joy home after she was born, but the cold January morning a year later when she finally came home after a month in the hospital with the pneumonia that nearly took her from us remains as fresh as if it happened yesterday.

Before Joy, I didn't know what love was outside of what I felt for Mom and Dad.

That winter, I learned.

Did my sister and I have our fights? Did she annoy the crap out of me sometimes? Of course. We were sisters. Still, there's nothing I wouldn't have done for her.

And when the time came, that was all I could do. Nothing.

The scene surrounds us for another few seconds before reality swirls around us anew. In a moment, the Spirit and I stand alone in an empty gray space.

"That was cruel." I glare at the ephemeral little girl peering at me from between strands of her shining platinum hair. "Like I needed to be reminded of that day."

"And yet you show so little consideration for the less fortunate in your life today." The Spirit raises her hands in question. "When was the last time you did anything for someone who couldn't do something for you in return?" She turns from me and walks farther into the gray nothingness. "I could argue that a reminder is precisely what you needed this day."

"Whatever," I mutter under my breath. "Are we through yet?" I know the answer before I even ask the question. Based on our previous stops along Memory Lane, there is only one place the Spirit could be planning on taking me next.

"I can see in your eyes you know our next destination already." The Spirit turns away from me and holds out her arm. "Are you ready?"

"Does it matter?" I pause for a moment, as if I have a choice, before taking the Spirit's arm. "Let's get this over with."

She glances back at me, and for the first time, I find real emotion in her eyes. "I am sorry, Carol Davis, but these next shadows are the nearest to your heart. I hope you—"

"Just do it already."

"Very well." She turns from me and takes one hesitant step, then another, leading me through the gray nothingness until a darkened room begins to form around us. In one corner rests the old four-poster bed at Mike and Valerie's in what used to be their guest room, now my little corner of the universe. Cold mercury light filters through the frost on the windows and onto the sleeping form lying in the bed, her sprawling limbs somehow filling at least half the queen-sized mattress. She sleeps fitfully, shifting beneath the down comforter every few seconds as if she already knows the bad news that's about to fall in her lap.

Every person has that day, that hour, that moment that defines their life.

This is mine.

CHAPTER TWENTY

The door to the room cracks open, allowing a thin line of light to spill across my almost eight-year-old cheek. The barely audible sound of sobbing closes a fist of ice around my heart. I draw close to the half-open doorway and listen to the whispered conversation from the hall.

"I don't think we should wake her. Not till we've heard something definitive."

"She's got to know, Mike." Valerie's voice, crying. "She'll hate us if we wait till morning to tell her."

"She's going to hate us either way." A thoughtful pause. "At least for a while."

"Dammit, why did they have to fly tonight? The weather was for shit. That plane should never have left the airport."

"Come on, Val. You know as well as I do that Holly and Jack were set on making it back in time to spend Christmas morning with Carol." I step closer to the door and peek through the crack just as Mike takes Valerie's chin and pulls her despondent gaze up to his. "If nothing had happened, you'd be on the way to the airport to pick them up right now without a second thought."

Valerie pulls away, her eyes filled with anger, and for just a moment, a touch of hate. "I swear to God, Mike, if you come out with 'sometimes things happen' or some shit like that, you'll be hearing from my lawyer." She turns toward my invisible form and buries her forehead in the crook of her arm against the door frame. So close I can see every wrinkle in her grief-stricken face, I can't believe she can't see me. Her tear-filled eyes peer right through my body, staring at the sleeping girl who will never again see her parents alive.

"I'm sorry, babe." Mike steps in behind Valerie and, after a couple unsuccessful attempts, envelopes her in his arms. "I'm so sorry."

It's been a long ten years since that night, but as I stand there unseen watching a husband try to comfort his wife, I wonder if it ever dawned on my eight-year-old mind that I wasn't the only person who lost someone that day.

"I know what happens now, Spirit." I glance over at the form tucked beneath the covers and covet the last thirty seconds of innocence the girl will ever know. "I lived it." I turn to the Spirit, her incandescent hair pulsing in the darkness. "Any chance we can skip this next part?"

"That would be unwise," she answers. "Though it is true you have lived this moment before, it is possible you may learn a thing or two from experiencing it with the wisdom of a few more years."

Valerie and Mike steal into the darkened room and come to sit on either side of my younger self's sleeping form.

"Carol," Valerie whispers between barely contained sobs. "Carol. Wake up." It takes a bit of effort on Valerie's part to wake me up, a gentle shake of the shoulder the final prod causing Little Carol's eyes to flutter open.

"Aunt Valerie?" Sitting up and stretching, the girl that was once me lets out a yawn cut short by a series of barking coughs. She looks to the window. "What's going on? It's still dark."

"It's not morning yet, honey."

"Did Santa come?" Little Carol asks, her voice quiet and raspy.

Valerie shoots Mike a troubled glance.

"I don't think Santa's going to make it tonight," he whispers, resting a careful hand on his niece's shoulder.

"Is something wrong?" Little Carol asks after a second run of hacking coughs. "Is it Mommy and Daddy?"

Too choked up to answer, Valerie looks away.

Little Carol begins to tear up. "Uncle Mike?"

"Carol," he says after a few tense seconds. "There's something we need to tell you."

Little Carol's wide eyes shoot back and forth from Mike to Valerie. Before either can say another word, she scurries from beneath the covers and rushes to the window. Looking out at the mercury-lit back yard, she murmurs, "No, no, no, no, no, no, no..."

"Honey," Valerie starts, "it's—"

"Don't call me that." Little Carol spins to face her aunt and uncle, her eyes welling up even as my own vision blurs with tears. "It's something bad, isn't it?"

"Carol," Mike starts. "Your mom and dad—"

"No. Not from you." Little Carol descends into another bout of coughing, turning to Valerie when she can breathe again. "Tell me. Where are Mommy and Daddy?"

"Their plane never made it to the airport tonight." Valerie barely gets out the words before emotion takes her voice. "They're saying it...crashed."

"Crashed..." Little Carol turns back to the window. "But they're not sure, right?"

"We saw it on the news a few minutes ago," Mike says. "As

best they can tell, the plane carrying your mom and dad went down half an hour ago somewhere over eastern Tennessee."

Always the pragmatist, Mike was the one to deliver the knockout punch. At the time, I remember thinking he almost enjoyed doling out the news, but seeing it with fresh eyes, the pain etched in his features tells a far different story.

Valerie goes to the window and takes Little Carol's hand. "That's all we know right now, sweetie. We tried to call the airport, but we can't get through. The lines are swamped."

Little Carol stares out the window into the chilly night. "The firemen and fire trucks and ambulances are out looking for them, aren't they?"

"They're doing the best they can, I'm sure." Mike joins Valerie and Little Carol at the window. "Still, the news report said it'll probably be morning before we know anything for sure."

"They could still be okay, right?" Choked with emotion, Little Carol's voice is barely a whisper. "Like in that movie we watched last summer where the pilot crash-landed the plane and saved everybody?"

Valerie kneels behind my eight-year-old self. "Anything's possible, sweetheart."

Quiet for a moment, Little Carol rests her arm against the window. I can still remember the chill from the glass to this day.

"I was supposed to go with them," she says. "Grandpa Davis was going to take us to see the Alamo."

"You were too sick, honey." Valerie strokes Little Carol's back. "The doctor said flying with such a bad cold and an ear infection wasn't a good idea."

"But they...we...weren't even supposed to come back today." Little Carol barks into her sleeve. "Mommy told me this morning she changed the tickets. They were flying back early so they wouldn't miss my birthday."

"I know, Carol." Valerie's free hand curls into a fist. "I'm so sorry."

"Hey..." Little Carol turns and looks up at Valerie, her eyes wide as a new revelation hits her sleep-addled mind. "What about Joy?"

And here it comes. The last nail in the coffin.

"Joy was with your mom and dad." Mike's chin drops. "On the plane."

"No!" Little Carol runs from the room. Valerie chases after her leaving Mike alone in the guest bedroom staring out at an empty lawn covered in Christmas Eve frost.

"Enough!" I turn on the Spirit, the heat radiating off my cheeks like a small sun. "So I've had a lot of shitty stuff happen to me and become a shitty person because of it. Is that what you wanted to teach me? Is that the big revelation you've come all this way to shove down my throat? Because if that's the case, you've wasted your time. I already relive this shit-show every single day."

The Spirit looks on me with what could pass for pity on her otherwise placid face. "Memory is a strange thing, Carol Davis." Her stare bores into me. "Bear with me another moment, as there is a bit more here for you to see."

"Like I have a say in the matter."

In a blink, we're in the living room where Little Carol kneels at the fireplace, her head bowed beneath a green stocking emblazoned with Joy's name, the three capital letters spelled out in red and gold glitter. Eyes clenched shut, her lips move silently for what seems an eternity.

I can't believe it.

I'm praying.

Between the apparently never-ending runs of coughing, I'm actually praying.

The hardest thing to swallow?

That there was a time I actually believed somebody was listening.

Valerie appears in the doorway with Mike close behind. He takes his wife's hand and together they cross the room and kneel at either side of their only remaining niece, the fireplace cold for the first time in weeks in preparation for the arrival of good old Kris Cringle.

"Carol?" Valerie whispers. "Are you okay?"

"Am I supposed to be?" Little Carol asks.

"Of course not." Valerie pulls her in close. "But you will be."

"Don't forget, slugger." Mike puts his arm around both of them. "No matter what else, you've still got us."

Nestled between her aunt and uncle on the worst night of her life, I half expect this girl I was a decade ago to push them both away as the agony of her new reality sets in. Instead, she pulls them tight to her and utters seven words I had long forgotten ever left my lips.

"Mike. Valerie. Don't ever leave me. Okay?"

Valerie and Mike lock gazes and as clearly as if they'd spoken aloud, I see a decision pass between them.

"Don't worry." Valerie rests her chin amid Little Carol's curls. "You'll never be alone. That's a promise."

"From both of us." Mike kisses her pale forehead. "We're family, now more than ever, and we'll get through this together." He takes her chin and pulls her gaze to his just as he had Valerie's moments before.

I still remember what he said next.

"Do you believe me?"

As one, Little Carol and I nod.

I can't decide which of us is crying the hardest.

CHAPTER TWENTY-ONE

"Enlighten me, Carol Davis." The Spirit's stare burns through me, her outstretched arm directing my attention to the trio kneeling below the decorated mantel. "*These* are the people who receive the daily brunt of your sharp tongue and cutting eyes?"

"It's not like that." Mike runs his fingers through Little Carol's hair, and I turn away, too embarrassed to watch. "At least...not every day."

"Forget not to whom you speak," the Spirit intones. "If anyone in Creation knows intimately the past of a girl born on Christmas Day..."

"I suppose it would be you." New pain flares between my eyebrows. "Fine. I'll admit it. You have a point, but I'm not alone in all the snarky that flies around this place. Valerie's application for sainthood is pretty much all wrapped up, but my uncle Mike gives as good as he gets."

The Spirit's head shakes gently from side to side. "And yesterday, when you so gladly proclaimed your pending 'independence' from the couple that took in an orphaned eight-year-old girl without so much as a second thought, how exactly was he supposed to respond?"

A bitter laugh escapes my lips. "Like they had a choice in taking me in."

"You callow child." Her eyes blazing, the Spirit points again to the hearth. "Look at them."

I follow her fiery gaze and focus again on the trio huddled beneath the six mismatched stockings. Her head draped across Valerie's shoulder, my younger self has cried herself to sleep while Mike and Valerie continue to talk, their quiet conversation alternating between hushed whispers and resigned silence.

"This woman is your blood," the Spirit continues, "and far kinder than you deserve." Her gaze shifts to Mike whose strong arms encircle both his grief-stricken wife and the sleeping girl. "As for the man? He owed you nothing and yet gave you everything he had."

My cheeks flush hot. "He never lets me forget it, either."

"Michael Fredericks is as flawed as any man," the Spirit says, "but that has no bearing on his feelings for you." She takes a step in their direction. "Look at him, Carol Davis. See him in this moment."

"Oh, I see him."

His brave face. His self-sacrificing speech.

And all just a big fat lie.

"He sure talked a good game that night. Put on quite the show." My eyes draw down to slits until all I can see is their silhouette in front of the fireplace. "But I heard what he said."

"What he said?" The Spirit, her face teetering between befuddled and intrigued, comes closer. "Tell me, Carol Davis. Of what do you speak?"

"The next morning." I turn and step into the adjoining hall. "Standing right here. Eight hours later." The tears begin anew, though these tears are cold. "Some things you just can't take back."

"And so we come to the root of it." The Spirit draws close, her expression shifting even further from her usual complacent stare into something almost approaching compassion. "What is it you thought you heard?"

"Don't play games with me, Spirit." My teeth grind in my head. "I know what I heard."

"Do you?" The Spirit beckons me to again walk with her. "Are you quite sure?"

I hesitate for all of two seconds before taking her outstretched hand. "Fine. Show me."

Her hand warm against my clammy flesh, she raises her other arm, and the swirling gray from before returns, if only around our feet. Neither of us moves an inch, but time speeds up around us regardless. As if I'm watching a movie on fast forward, the remainder of the night plays out in seconds, the darkness outside shifting to dim light as dawn approaches. The Spirit lowers her arm, and the opaque mist recedes.

We stand, the Spirit and I, in the same hallway as before, but the remaining players have all moved. The first rays of sunlight peek through the east-facing blinds and illuminate the living room where Mike sits with Valerie, the two of them hunched over his old laptop. Neither appears to have slept, and it's hard to tell whose face carries more worry. Meanwhile, my younger self waits halfway down the stairs, her foot suspended just above the notoriously squeaky fourth step, listening.

"We don't owe her anything." Mike massages the bridge of his nose. "As much as it sucks, you know it's the truth."

Valerie's shoulders drop. "But we've made so many promises. So many plans."

"Plans?" he asks. "Promises?" Mike taps absently at his keyboard, though the gears in his head are clearly turning. "We have responsibilities right here, Val." Mike glances up from the computer. "You. Me. Carol. As much as I wish it were different, we just can't take her."

"But..."

"No buts." Mike's eyes return to the screen. "Someone else will take her. She'll be fine."

Little Carol quietly trudges up the stairs to her bedroom, her foot never hitting that telltale fourth step, and closes her bedroom door quietly behind her.

"See?" I turn on the Spirit, half-blinded by tears. "No matter what went down the night of the crash, this is what counts. The stuff that's said by the light of day."

Speechless for the first time this evening, the Spirit looks on me, dumbfounded.

"What?" I ask. "*What?*"

"You poor girl," she whispers eventually. "All these years..."

"What are you talking about?" I blot away the tears with the heel of my hand. "Mike wanted me to go. He couldn't have been any plainer."

"And yet, the next morning when you came down for breakfast, everything was fine."

My shoulders rise in an instinctive shrug. "Yeah?"

"For ten years, you've never come home to find your bags packed or the locks changed." The Spirit draws close, the heat wafting off her for once more comforting warmth than burning fire. "Did you never wonder why?"

"I suppose I always figured Valerie pleaded my case and got Mike to change his mind." I crane my neck to peer into the room where my long-suffering aunt sits with her head reclined across the back of the couch. "Or at least agree to let me stay. Woman should have gone to law school."

The Spirit raises an eyebrow. "What if I told you there was never a case to plead?"

In a blink, we're standing behind the couch. Mike is typing away at some document while Valerie looks on with rapt attention.

"What are we—"

The Spirit places a warm finger across my lips, silencing me. "Listen," she whispers, "and learn."

"And...done." Mike makes a few final keystrokes before retiring the laptop to the coffee table and taking Valerie's hand. "Now the big question. Should we go ahead and send it?"

"Can't we sleep on it tonight?" Valerie asks. "We might feel differently tomorrow."

Mike shakes his head. "It's only going to get harder the longer we wait."

"Fine." Valerie glances in the direction of the stairs where my younger self just retreated to her room. "Do it."

"Do what?" I ask.

Silent, the Spirit's knowing gaze seems even more maddening than usual.

"What are they talking about? Tell me, Spirit. I have to know."

"Very well."

Time freezes around us. Mike's fingers hover above the computer trackpad while Valerie looks on, a tear hanging from her chin like some salty stalactite.

"There." The Spirit points to the laptop screen. "Read."

I lean across the back of the couch so I can better make out the tiny letters of the email Mike has crafted. Short and to the point, the subject line reads, "*Re: Jong Yin.*"

"Jong Yin?" My eyes cut in the Spirit's direction. "What is this?"

"Keep reading," she whispers.

I return my attention to the screen.

Dear Mr. Chang:

It is with our sincerest apologies that my wife and I must withdraw from the adoption process for Jong Yin. Unforeseen circumstances have arisen in our lives and we are no longer capable of taking her on. We truly appreciate all you have done for our family and are beyond disappointed that we have to pull out so far along in the process. Please notify the orphanage of our regrets. We certainly wish Jong Yin all the best in finding a happy home.

Sincerely,

Michael Fredericks

"Who is...was Jong Yin?"

"A three-week-old girl." The Spirit steeples her fingers and brings them to her pale chin. "Born to a family in Beijing who didn't have the necessary finances to care for her, she very nearly became your adopted cousin."

"A baby." Though the rest of the room remains perfectly still, the tears coursing down Valerie's face resume their course.

Somehow, this doesn't strike me as strange at all.

"I knew Mike and Valerie were looking into adoption, but I never knew they'd gotten this far."

The Spirit's head tilts slightly to one side. "I suspect there are many things about your aunt and uncle you know little about."

"So, I kept them from having the baby Valerie always wanted. Fantastic." Mike's hand hangs in the air, his finger frozen half an inch above one of the biggest decisions of his life. "Wow. I didn't think it was possible to feel shittier about the last ten years of my life. Glad to know there's another whole layer of untapped excrement to explore."

Again, the Spirit shakes her head. "As always, Carol Davis, you focus on the loss."

I wave my hand in front of Valerie's face. "Why won't she stop crying?"

"She will eventually. The sadness of this day is nothing when compared with the joys of the years that follow. This day, the loss of potential weighed heavily on your aunt and uncle's souls, but consider what they gained." The Spirit directs my attention to Valerie's trembling hand. "Your aunt. She always wanted to have children of her own, did she not?"

"Yeah," I mutter, "but Valerie can't have kids."

The Spirit raises her eyebrows, incredulous. "Do you somehow believe her inability to bear a child would somehow lessen her desire to raise one?"

"I suppose I never really thought about it. Valerie and Mike have always been so busy keeping up with me, it's just...never come up."

"Ah, Carol Davis." The Spirit's eyes slide shut. "You've completely missed your own point."

"Then, please, almighty Spirit of Christmas Past, do enlighten me."

Exasperation flashes across the Spirit's pale face. "Your aunt lost a sister that night, but though she would give anything for it to be otherwise, she gained a daughter, a daughter of her own blood even, a daughter she otherwise would never have had."

"I'm not their daughter." The words sound false even as they fall from my mouth, but I utter them anyway, my jaw set in preparation for the Spirit's rebuttal.

Rather than the anger and frustration I expect to find, the Spirit's face fills with compassion. "Only because you do not allow yourself to be."

My gaze drops to the floor as the kernel of truth in her words sink in. "Are we done here?"

"Nearly." The Spirit waves her anemic hand, and time resumes its fateful march.

Mike presses the send button and the email vanishes from the screen. The swooshing sound from the computer speakers has a finality I've never appreciated before. After a moment, he closes the laptop down and pulls his wife tight to his side. "Done." He kisses her forehead. "We'll make this work. I promise."

She looks up at him, tears still flowing. "You're sure we can do it. Just the two of us?"

"That's just it." Mike rests a hand atop Valerie's and looks to the hallway where I stand rooted to the spot. "Now there are three of us."

The room swirls around us, and in a blink, we're back in the nowhere place where gray is the order of the day.

Dumbfounded, I circle the Spirit, pacing. "Mike said that?"

She answers with a silent nod.

"Why hasn't he ever said anything like that to me? I get that from Valerie all the time, but Mike always acts like I'm an imposition or a bother."

"And I suppose you've done nothing to earn either of those titles." The Spirit raises a questioning eyebrow. "After years of reaching out to you only to be pushed away or put down at every turn, he eventually stopped trying." She steps closer to me and gazes at me with knowing eyes. "Only the most foolish of gardeners continues to plant good seed in rocky ground."

"Great." My hands go to my hips. "Anything else, sensei?"

"I don't know," she says. "Do you finally understand the truth?"

"The truth that my life sucks and it's all my fault?"

"On the contrary." For the first time, the Spirit's face breaks into the slightest of smiles. "Your life has far more love in it than you recognize. There has been darkness and tragedy, but there has also been goodness and wonder and light. The only question is which you choose to let define you." She turns and steps into the returning gray. "Come. Our time grows short and we have one last walk to take before I must go."

I follow the Spirit through the ethereal darkness, colors swirling around us with each step, forming images, scenes, and faces, as the last ten years of my life play out around me.

The first Christmas after Mom, Dad, and Joy died. Valerie, Mike, and I took a trip to the Biltmore Estate to see all the holiday lights and decorations. A bittersweet memory, everything seemed so much bigger and brighter then, and for a moment, I see everything through nine-year-old eyes again.

My eleventh birthday. Our mountain trip with the Kellermans when Christopher broke his arm sledding with me. For a day that ended up being mostly spent in the ER, it was still one of the best days of my life.

Christmas Eve five years ago. I fell asleep on the couch watching some movie or other and woke the next morning all tucked in under the big homemade quilt that Mike's mom had sent for Christmas. Always figured Valerie was the culprit. Turns out it was Mike. Even brought me Mr. Shiners to keep me company.

Last year. Marnie's death was still weighing on me pretty hard, and Valerie took a few "mental health days" off from work. We spent the better part of Christmas Eve shopping at our favorite outlet mall and went through a lot of money she didn't have.

I may have said five words to her the entire day.

"All right, all right. I get it."

"Do you?" The Spirit appraises me with a skeptic's eye. "Do you really?"

"Look. If I just come out and admit my life hasn't been total crap, will you just take me home? Please."

"Very well." She lets out an exhausted sigh. "I suppose it's a start."

The Spirit's hair shines brighter than ever before, the silver glow blinding in its radiance. I clench my eyelids shut and raise a hand across my face, but the onslaught of brilliance continues, filling my mind with a warmth that for the briefest of moments washes away all the pain of the last eighteen years.

Then, nothing.

I open my eyes, and I'm back in my bedroom. Tucked beneath my covers, lights off, door cracked with just a hint of light coming from the hall.

"Spirit?" I sit up in bed and peer out the window at the mercury light filtering through the light rain outside. "Hello?" My room remains exactly as I left it, without a shred of evidence I ever left. Was it all a dream? Or a nightmare?

I inhale to call out, but think the better of it. One whiff of this to Valerie and she'd have me back in with Dr. Boyer in a hot second. She would have a field day with—

"It was no dream."

Nearly leaping out of my skin for the dozenth time that day, I trace the voice to the far corner of the room where the Spirit of Christmas Past stands all but invisible within her cape of darkness. Ever across her arm during our travels, the ebon fabric now flows past her shoulders to her feet and hides her gleaming locks beneath a voluminous hood.

"Take heed, Carol Davis. The Spirit of Christmas Present will come for you tomorrow night when the clock strikes two." She pulls the hood across her face and fades into the shadows, her voice dwindling to the barest whisper even as an inexorable drowsiness overtakes me. "Steel yourself for what she comes to show you, for the shadows of your past are nothing compared to what awaits you these next two nights."

STAVE III

THE SECOND OF THE THREE SPIRITS

Friday, December 23rd

CHAPTER TWENTY-TWO

Somewhere between a second and a century later, I awake, the hot air of my own breath threatening to suffocate me. I've subconsciously pulled a potent combination of flannel sheet, cotton blanket, and down comforter up over my head in defense against, I'm guessing, the frigidity filling my room. I sneak an arm from beneath the covers, grab my phone, and check the time.

"1:57? All of that in less than an hour?"

Wait. If the Spirit left, why isn't my room dark?

I fling the covers from my body and rush to the window where light as bright as midday pours between the pulled blinds. I pull the cord, revealing an overcast afternoon sky.

"Well," comes a voice that nearly sends me jumping out of my pajamas. "Look who's finally awake."

I turn to find Valerie standing in my doorway, arms crossed and leaning in the doorframe. Her pleasant smile at odds with her worried eyes, she's scrutinizing me like a doctor trying to make a difficult diagnosis.

"Is it really almost two?"

Valerie nods. "You were sleeping pretty hard. I popped my

head in to check on you a little after ten. Your phone was going off like crazy, but you didn't even move. I figured you could use the sleep, so I turned the blinds to keep the sun out of your face."

I pause for a moment, unsure if I want to ask the next question. "Did you hear anything strange last night?"

"The only thing I heard last night was your uncle's two nostril orchestra."

"That's it?"

"Yeah. Why? Did you hear some—"

"Wait a sec. It's two in the afternoon?" I kick my sleep-addled brain into gear. "Philippe!"

I rush to my phone and find seven unanswered calls, a couple with voicemail.

"Crap. Late two days in a row."

Valerie takes a step back into the hallway. "I'm sorry. If I'd known it was important..."

"Not your fault, Val. I just slept through two alarms and seven phone calls."

"Well, okay then." A hint of surprise hits Valerie's face as she steps back into the room. "Anything I can do to help?"

"Hang on and I'll tell you." I check the call list. Three from Philippe, two from Roberta, one from Christopher—wonder what that's about—and one from Ryan. Only Philippe and Roberta left messages. I listen to Philippe's first, his trademark biting wit in rare form today as he goes on a two-minute tirade on the many virtues of punctuality. Roberta's message is much shorter and far more cryptic.

Hey Carol, she says. *We need to talk. Call me.*

"Everything okay?" Valerie asks.

"After the mess yesterday, I promised Philippe I'd come in early today to help with some inventory and watch the shop over lunch so he could take care of some business." My scalp screams as I run a brush through my tangled hair. "He's going to kill me."

"If I had known you were going in early, I would have made sure you were up."

"Leave it alone, Val," I mutter as I rush around the room getting dressed for the second day in a row. "I'll take care of it, okay?"

"All right." Valerie shrugs off my words and raises a curious eyebrow. "So, any calls from the much sought-after Mr. Ryan King?"

I shoot her a mischievous sidelong glance. "Maybe."

"You want me to drop by later and help you and Philippe pick out a dress?"

"I'm hoping we can still make that happen, but if we're busy like yesterday..."

"Got it." Valerie checks her watch. "You better get a move on."

"I'm moving."

Her worried expression makes a return appearance. "You're sure everything is okay?"

"I'll know better when I get home." I finish sliding into my dress and grab my shoes. "See you tonight."

CHAPTER TWENTY-THREE

"I'd complain that you were late, Miss Davis, but that would be a smack in the face to late people everywhere, wouldn't you agree?"

"Sorry." I hurry from the front door and assume my spot behind the register. "I overslept."

"Overslept? Late night out with your three-point-suitor, I'm guessing?"

Despite the gravity in Philippe's tone, I can't help but laugh. "If only. Had the mother of all nightmares last night. Second night running, actually. Slept right through two alarms and half a dozen calls. I've been awake a grand total of"—I check my phone—"twenty-three minutes."

"Sorry to hear that." The ice in his expression melts a bit. "Everything all right?"

Other than the fact I've been visited the last two nights by my very dead friend and a holiday version of that ghost girl from *The Ring*?

"Nothing but the usual drama." I put on my winningest smile and lie through my pearly white teeth. "Besides, you know I wouldn't have missed what we had on tap for this morning for anything, right?"

"I suppose not." He allows a smile to peek through his gruff exterior. "The ice and rain have kept most everyone at home anyway. Lots of phone calls but very little traffic. Left me just enough time to work on our little project."

"Really?" All the fear and trepidation of last night's visitation evaporates as Philippe directs me over to a rack of dresses that appear custom-picked just for me. Every color, style, and fabric represented, I get a flash of what Cinderella must have felt when she met her fairy godmother. For a few minutes, there are no ghosts, no nightmares, no disbelieving glances from well-meaning relatives. Just me, Philippe, and a store full of some of the finest dresses in town.

"Let's take a look, shall we?" Philippe pulls the first candidate from the rack, a ball gown with a burgundy velvet bodice and a full skirt of black organza.

"Pretty."

"You hate it."

"I don't hate it." I give the dress another once over. "Just not the biggest fan of velvet."

"It'll keep you warm."

"For the five whole minutes I plan to be outside? No thanks." I flash a wicked grin. "Not to mention, I suspect Ryan will keep me warm just fine."

"Careful, Carol." Philippe laughs. "You'll bring out my paternal side."

"I'd hate to see that." I wave the dress away. "Bring out the next victim."

Philippe surveys the rack of dresses before pulling out a second candidate. "How about this one?" This new dress, a sleek, full-length number made of hunter green silk, sports a halter top and a ruffled fringe at the hemline.

"I like it, except..."

"The color, right?"

"Anything but green." I bite my lip. "Next?"

Philippe flips past a couple more dresses, giving each one a moment of careful thought before pulling out an electric blue gown with silver lines running from the right shoulder down to the feet. "I thought this might make a statement."

"Yeah." I try to pump some enthusiasm into my voice. "It's all right."

Philippe lets out a sigh. "Back to the rack with you as well, Blue."

We spend the next half hour looking at a good thirty dresses, all handpicked by Philippe and all exactly in my size. I've seen most before, but it's a bit different when you're shopping for yourself. I end up trying on about half, including the green silk number, yet none of them are quite what I'm looking for.

"Funny." Philippe shakes his head as he laughs. "Never would've pegged you as a tough sell."

"Sorry, Philippe." I glance around the shop. "I think I'm a little close to it all."

He strokes his chin, almost as if he's trying to read my mind. "Have you seen anything you've liked?"

"Not exactly." I glance down at my shoes. "But I do have an idea of what I'm looking for."

Philippe grabs a notepad and a pen and slides on his reader glasses. "Do tell."

"At Valerie and Mike's place, there's an old picture of my parents at a dance from their college days. Dad looks pretty sharp in his tux, but Mom's dress is what I always remember." I describe the dress as best I can from memory. The cut, the color, the material, even a few extras I'd like put on for a winter dance. Philippe alternates between dutifully jotting down every word and making rough sketches of the dress in the margins. When

I'm done talking, he works another minute or so and flips the pad around.

"Something like that?"

I forget sometimes that Philippe is an artiste. With an "e" and everything.

"Yeah." I laugh. "Something like that."

Philippe considers for a moment. "You know, I have a storage unit with a couple hundred dresses across town. I'll pop my head in on my way home and see if I can find anything remotely like what you're describing, though I'm not making any promises. Otherwise, we'll just have to find you something here, all right?"

"Sure." I feel my cheeks grow warm. "Thanks, Philippe. I don't know what to say."

"Say you'll be on time tomorrow. We're only open from ten to three, and if this year's dance is like all the others, the last-minute shoppers will be out in droves."

CHAPTER TWENTY-FOUR

"He *what*?" I don't even bother to keep the disbelief from my voice. "And slower this time. I want to make sure I hear you right."

Roberta sighs through the phone. "Christopher. Kellerman. Asked. Me. To. The. Dance."

"You're serious."

"You know it."

Girl knows my schedule better than me. Just getting off work, I was halfway to my car when my phone went off. Telling Roberta to hold on a second, I hop in, start the engine, and pump the gas a few times in an effort to get the heat coming. No blasting aria from Julie Andrews this time, thank God.

"Are you even listening to me?" Roberta's irritated tone brings me back to the present.

"Of course." I toss my head from side to side in an attempt to shake off the lingering weirdness of the last two days. "But would you mind...starting at the beginning?"

"Sure." She takes a breath. "Mom and I were shopping for a tablet computer for Tameka when Christopher came over. He asked who was taking me to the dance, and I told him I wasn't going. That's when he popped up and asked me. Said he knew I'd been really busy helping take care of Tameka and thought I could use a night out."

"What did your Mom say?"

"She practically accepted the invitation for me. Said you're only young once and that I had the rest of my life to sit home and worry about everything."

"But...it's Christopher Kellerman. What did you say?"

"I said yes, you big dummy. Just because you can't get past his Chess Club paint job doesn't mean the rest of us have to sit home on our duff while you're out with the Greek god of basketball."

My cheeks get hot for the second time that day. "I just wanted to know if you were going to be there or not."

"You're sure that's the only reason you were asking?"

"Oh my God, Bobbisox, if you start trying to fix me up with Christopher again, I will flat hang up on you."

"Hey, that's *my* date you're talking about." Roberta's quiet giggle sends my jaw into full clench.

"Whatever." I grind my teeth. "So, do you have a dress?"

"Nice subject change." She's silent for a moment, as if she's mustering up the courage to ask me something. "You want to know the truth? I was kind of hoping you might help me out with that. See if Philippe has anything decent on sale. Mom's put me on a budget, but that doesn't mean I want to go looking like last year's leftovers."

I laugh. "Philippe and I spent most of the day checking out half the dresses in the store. Several would look great on you. In fact, I think I may already know just the one."

"Ooh. Tell me about it."

"Just come by the store tomorrow around eleven. I'll take care of everything."

"Sounds good." Roberta's voice has a smile in it I haven't heard in months. It's good to hear. "You big tease."

"You know it, girl."

"That I do," she answers. "Question is, does Ryan King?"

And with that, the line goes dead.

A chuckle parts my lips. That little bitch.

I drop my hand onto the gear shift, slide the car into reverse, and check my rearview mirror before backing out. My heart flies up into my throat when a set of eyes looks back from what should be an empty back seat. With verdant green irises surrounding dilated pupils all set beneath a pair of bright red eyebrows, the woman's stare is warm, yet terrifying. Her full head of ginger hair spills past her shoulders like an orange waterfall and pools on the back seat around her. Her plump lips, painted a deep scarlet, turn up in a knowing smile as she raises a curious eyebrow.

I spin in the driver's seat to look on her with my own eyes only to find the back seat empty.

Empty, that is, save a small sprig of what can only be mistletoe.

I leap out of the car, the frigid air biting into me like a rabid wolf, and tear open the car's rear door. The mistletoe rests at the center of the back seat, three forked branches filled with tongue-shaped leaves of the deepest green and berries the color of bleached bone, all connected by a ribbon of red silk tied in a simple bow.

"What have I done to deserve this?" I grumble, wishing the words back into my mouth a moment later as it dawns on me the answer to that very question is likely coming in eight hours, wrapped in bright green paper and topped with a big red Christmas bow.

I climb back into the driver's seat, toss the mistletoe into the passenger seat, and pull out of the parking lot. I'm a couple miles down the road before I chance another glance at my rearview mirror. Though the back seat remains empty, I suspect I haven't seen the last of Miss Mistletoe.

CHAPTER TWENTY-FIVE

I pull up to Valerie and Mike's driveway and can't help but notice the car parked across the street. Jet black and so well cared for you could eat off the hood, Ryan King's Camaro sits not a hundred yards from where I sleep every night. He lives clear across town, and there's no one else on this street I imagine he'd be visiting. The sky is already dark, and with his tinted windows, I can't even tell if he's inside.

My breath catches at a gentle tap at my passenger side window. I glance over and see the lower half of a letterman's jacket filling most of the view. I slide the car into park and roll down the window. Ryan crouches until his face is even with mine, his face breaking into a winning smile that has likely opened a lot of doors for him.

Among other things.

"Hi, Carol."

"What are you doing here, Ryan?" I ask. "Besides, of course, scaring the crap out of me."

"It's a little before six, and I was on this side of town. Thought I'd say hi."

"Don't you have a phone?"

His smile grows wider. "I wanted to surprise you."

"Mission accomplished, then."

"Hey, it's cold out here." He glances down at the passenger seat. "Mind if I climb in?"

"Umm...sure." I roll up the window, whisking the mistletoe into the glovebox before unlocking the door and pushing it open. "Hop in."

Ryan slides out of his letterman's jacket and takes his time lowering himself into my wreck of a car. His torn jeans pull tight across his muscular thighs with just the top of a pair of plaid boxers peeking above his slim belt line. He reaches out with a not-overly-muscled arm and pulls the door closed behind him. Catching my gaze as the interior light dims to darkness, he raises an eyebrow. "Was that mistletoe in your seat?"

"Maybe." I have no desire to pursue this line of questioning, but I have a feeling it's coming for me anyway. Hey, maybe a girl will get lucky.

Mind out of the gutter, Carol. Not that kind of lucky.

"I found it in the parking lot at the store." Funny how lies just roll off my tongue these days. "Thought I'd hang it up inside. It is Christmastime, after all."

He raises an eyebrow. "And is there anyone in particular you're hoping to meet under the mistletoe this holiday season?"

I can't help but laugh at that one. "Dial it back a little there, Tex. I've already said I'd go to the dance with you."

"True." He puts the seat of Valerie's Hot Wheels car back a few inches in an effort to extract his knees from the dash. "Sorry if I scared you."

Apology accepted. Big time.

"I need to let you know," I blurt out before I can stop myself. "Valerie is pretty strict about boys."

He puffs up his chest and drops his voice an octave. "And is she just as strict about men?"

"Please." I roll my eyes, but the giggle that escapes my lips lets him know he won this round. "So, I'm guessing you didn't come all this way just to cram yourself into my tin can of a car and impress me with witty repartee."

"Honestly, I just dropped by to make sure I could find your house and, if you were here, discuss logistics for tomorrow night."

"Stop." I feel my mouth twist into a sarcastic grin. "You're going to make me blush."

He's quiet for a second, his wheels clearly turning. "The doors open tomorrow night at six-thirty, but everything gets going around eight or nine. I hear they're supposed to have a pretty good spread, but I was curious if you might want to grab a bite before the big event."

"Like...dinner?"

"Only if you want to." He rubs his neck and watches me like I might bolt at any second.

"Dinner would be nice." I glance at the front door of the house. "Anything but vegetarian."

"Done." Relief cascades across his features. "Pick you up at six?"

"Six it is." I inhale, half expecting him to lean in for a kiss, but instead, he grabs the door handle and lets himself out of the car.

"See you tomorrow night," he says, bending himself nearly in half to peer back inside. "I'll be the one in the powder blue tuxedo."

I bite my lip. "You're kidding, right?"

He smiles as he checks his watch. "You have just under twenty-four hours to find out."

I freeze in position as the door closes and don't move again until I hear the engine of Ryan's Camaro roar to life. Falling back into the seat, I whip my phone out of my pocket to call

Roberta only to catch a flash of movement in my rearview mirror. The woman who can only be the Spirit of Christmas Present sits in my back seat shaking her head, her eyes closed and her face colored with disappointment.

"What?" I jerk my head around to confront the Spirit, and this time she remains, her steady gaze piercing me straight through to my core. "What?" I repeat, a bit quieter this time.

She brings a delicate finger to her lips, her plump face containing not a bit of the mirth one would expect from a creature that's supposed to represent the "most wonderful time of the year," and points to the clock on the dash.

"Not yet," she whispers as the clock runs through the next eight hours in the space of a few seconds only to stop at 1:59. "We will speak soon enough."

CHAPTER TWENTY-SIX

The front door slams shut behind me as I race inside and up the stairs to my room. I climb to the center of my bed and try to stop hyperventilating when it hits me. I've just violated Rule #1: Whenever possible, don't let Mike and Valerie know when you get home.

A gentle knock at the door. Valerie. Right on schedule.

"Carol?"

All right. Let's try not to violate Rule #2: Never let 'em see you sweat. Showing any degree of emotional distress around Valerie is basically like dumping bloody chum in the shark tank.

"Yeah?"

"Everything okay?"

"Everything's fine." I put just enough of an edge in my voice to make it clear I want to be left alone.

"May I come in?" Her tone is hesitant, but unyielding.

Note to self. Next time, more edge.

"Sure."

Valerie pops her head in. Clearly dressed for a day where she didn't plan to leave the house, her Vanderbilt sweatshirt is covered in more than its fair share of flour, as is her face. Surprise, surprise, Val's been in the kitchen.

"What's going on?" she asks. "You stormed in like a herd of horses. You sure you're all right?"

"I said I was fine." I rattle through my brain for the right excuse and decide on something not too far from the truth. "I saw something on the way in that scared me and wanted to get inside."

"Would this thing be the black sports car that's been parked across the street for the last forty-five minutes?"

My arms cross instinctively. "Have you been spying on me?"

Valerie shakes her head and lets out a gentle sigh. "No, honey, but it's not my fault if your date for tomorrow night is about as subtle as a bulldozer in an art gallery."

My fingers dig into Mr. Shiners' chest. "What did he do?"

"Well, minus any cigarette I could see—thank God—he sat across the street for almost an hour, perched on the hood of his car like some latter-day James Dean, that is till the sun went down and the temperature dropped fifteen degrees."

"Really?" Another giggle pops out before I can stop it.

Valerie answers with an amused smile. "He even came up on the porch a couple times, which would have been fine if he would've just rung the doorbell like a normal human being."

My back stiffens, but I don't say a word.

"We could've invited him in," Valerie continues. "Kept him warm till you got home. It is winter, after all."

Ryan King. Alone with Valerie and Mike in my living room. I can see it now. The three of them discussing holiday plans. Swapping stories over hot chocolate. Laughing over baby pictures.

I realize I'm not breathing and let out the lungful of air I've been holding hostage. As insane as this week has been, at least *that* nightmare didn't happen.

"To answer your question, I did see Ryan, and he was a perfect gentleman." I drop my hands into my lap, forcing myself to relax. "He just dropped by to talk about tomorrow night."

"And?"

"He's picking me up for dinner at six, then on to the dance around eight or nine."

"And what time should we expect you in?"

My shoulders rise in an innocent shrug. "I guess that all depends."

Valerie's expression shifts into full-on mom-face. "I'm not sure I like that answer."

"Don't worry, Val. I've memorized the transcripts of the Fredericks' Birds and Bees lecture from cover to cover. Nothing like that to worry about."

"Then what?"

I don't dare tell her about the after party. That would be social suicide.

"I just want to keep my options open for the evening. This is my last chance to go, you know, since the whole thing got cancelled last year after the thing with...you know..." My gaze sneaks to the bathroom mirror, just visible from my perch atop my down comforter. The glass dark and empty, I finish my thought. "With Marnie."

I half expect Valerie to hit me with her patented "not on my watch" spiel, but instead, her lips part in a wistful smile.

"Okay," she whispers. "I trust you."

"Really?"

"Really." Her smile grows wider. "Hey. Did I ever tell you about the time I first knew Mike was the one for me?"

"Maybe." My initial fight-or-flight response nearly sends me racing from the room. Rule #8—or is it #9?—is never get Valerie started on the past. However, her reminiscing seems to be buying me an extended curfew, so I don't move a muscle.

"Didn't you two meet at some kind of band competition in college?"

"That's the story everybody knows." She stands and adopts an almost theatrical pose. "Two baritone players from opposing schools catch each other's eye across a crowded football field freshman year and end up commuting back and forth two hours almost every weekend for the last three years of college." She fixes me with a wicked half-grin. "But the first time I knew Mike was the one? That's a different story altogether. I can still remember that night like it was yesterday."

A morbid curiosity overpowers my usual inclination against having any knowledge of Valerie's personal life. Taking a deep breath, I whisper, "Let's hear it."

Valerie's eyes go out of focus even as her mind kicks into overdrive. "It was my sorority's spring formal our sophomore year. Mike and I had been planning for him to drive down for the weekend for over a month. Imagine my surprise when he called me out of the blue two days before and told me he couldn't make it."

"You're kidding, right?"

"One of his professors had pulled him aside after class and asked him to join a group of upperclassmen that Saturday night at a mixer. It was an opportunity to rub elbows with admissions officers from most of the medical schools in the state."

"Medical schools? Mike's not a doctor."

"This was back when Mike was still pre-med."

"Oh." I run my fingers through my hair and tie it up in a ponytail. "He said yes?"

"His professor told him it was a big opportunity and that he wasn't asking anyone else from the class. Mike felt like he had to go."

"Wow. That must have sucked."

Valerie shakes her head. "He was very apologetic, but I

wasn't hearing any of it. As you can imagine, the formal was a pretty big deal to me at the time." She dons a sheepish grin. "To say I didn't take the news well would be a bit of an understatement."

"Typical Mike," I mutter. "Business first."

"Hang on a minute, Carol. This story has a twist ending." She takes a breath. "So, there I was. Every person in my entire sorority has a date but me and the dance is in three days."

"What did you do?"

"What do you think I did? I went and found somebody to take me to the dance."

"Who?"

"Oh," her gaze drops to her lap, "this guy Patrick. We'd been hanging in the same circles since freshman orientation, and I knew he liked me. Nice enough guy. Poor thing had to bend over backward to get an outfit together in two days, but he did it. Tux, shoes, boutonniere, flowers, the whole shebang. Even got us last minute reservations at a pretty exclusive restaurant in town."

"Wow." I laugh. "Why didn't you marry *that* guy?"

"Well, that's the thing." She gets up and closes the door. "And this part's a secret, okay?"

"A secret?"

"Sort of. Mike knows about this part, but he doesn't know I know, do you understand?"

"I'm not sure."

"You will." She takes a deep breath. "So, it's around 6:45 the night of the formal and Patrick's running a little behind. I'm sitting in the common room of our house, pumping myself up to go out even though I can't stop thinking about Mike. Some nineties girl band is on the radio—Four Non Blondes, maybe?—when there's a knock at the door. A very distinctive knock."

"Who was it?"

"Mike and I always used a particular knock when we visited each other back in the day. I leaped out of my chair and was halfway to the door before I remembered I was still pissed at him and stopped dead in my tracks."

"You left him hanging?"

"I sure as hell wasn't going to give him the satisfaction of having me rush to the door after canceling on me last minute. I figured I'd let him knock a couple more times before I let him in."

"And did he?"

"Oh, another knock came. A few minutes later. I couldn't take it anymore, so I went to the door, good and ready to let Mike have it."

"And?"

"I opened the door all set to go nuclear only to find Patrick outside adjusting his bow tie."

"Patrick?"

"Yep. Only about fifteen minutes late, but ready to go. Shoes shined, smelling good, not a hair out of place. I grabbed my bag, and we headed out for the evening. He walked me to his car, opened the door, made sure my dress was in and everything."

"I sense a 'but' here."

"I couldn't stop thinking about Mike. No matter what Patrick did, my brain was stuck on one channel." She glances out the window. "And that was even before I saw it."

My brow furrows. "Saw what?"

"Mike's car. His dad's old yellow Saab. Kind of hard to miss."

"So he came? Blew off the whole med school thing and came for you?"

"I never saw him. At least not that night." Valerie lets out a deep sigh. "My best guess is he knocked, saw Patrick coming to pick me up, and took off. He called the next day asking if he could 'come down' for the day, and I said that would be fine. I never told him I knew he was there all along, and he never gave me an ounce of grief for going to the dance with another guy."

I squinch up my nose. "What about Patrick?"

Valerie lets out a quiet chuckle. "Poor boy never had a chance. Funny thing, I hear he made it big with some Internet start-up a few years after we graduated. Sold all his shares in the company for some ridiculous amount of money right before the dot-com bubble popped back in 2001."

"That's crazy." Unbidden, Christopher's face flits across my imagination. "Any regrets?"

"Not a one. That Sunday, the day after the formal, was one of the best days of my life. Mike really poured it on, trying to make it up to me. We never talked about it, but I think we both made a decision that day." Valerie puffs up her chest. "Me and him against the world."

"What's that like?" I ask, brushing away a tear.

"Like nothing else, sweetie." She rests a hand on my knee. "Like nothing else."

CHAPTER TWENTY-SEVEN

I stand beneath the shower, the water coursing down my body as hot as I can stand it, and try to scrub away any memory of the last two nights. Until this evening, I couldn't decide if I was going crazy or if somehow a bunch of ghosts from a hundred-and-fifty-year-old story had truly invaded my life. The sprig of mistletoe on my nightstand, however, tied up in its scarlet ribbon with berries like chaste little pearls, is anything but a figment of my imagination. Regardless of which is the truth, I have no doubt in five short hours the Spirit of Christmas Present, with her full cheeks, blood red lips, and knowing eyes will come. Whether or not she's an actual visitor from another place or just a delusion my neurotic brain has created doesn't really change a thing.

Another five minutes pass before I step out of the steaming shower, ready to rejoin the world. After half an hour of trying to boil the skin from my bones, the cool air from my bedroom hits me like I've opened a walk-in freezer. I towel off and slip into a thick terrycloth robe before grabbing the hair dryer. If tonight is anything like the last two nights, the temperature in here is going to drop in a few hours. Wouldn't do to go to bed with a wet head and catch my death.

Note to self. Never use *that* phrase again.

Hair dry, moisturizer applied, pajamas on, I check the clock. 10:45. A little over three hours till show time.

Can't wait.

I grab my phone to set my alarm to wake up before the Spirit arrives and find a couple of texts. One from Roberta and one from Christopher.

Our high school's new power couple.

For some reason, I'm not laughing.

Roberta's text is simple.

See you tomorrow at 11. Save me some hot dresses. LOL

Christopher's, not so much.

Hi Carol. I'd like to ask your advice.
Can you give me a call? I'll be up till midnight or so.

Wonder what that's about? Could he be calling for advice about his date with Roberta?

Wow. That would be weird.

Or maybe he's just calling to check in. That's probably it. After all, he did just spot me at the mall with Ryan yesterday. I'd blow him off, but history shows that just opens up a whole barrage of calls, messages, emails, smoke signals, carrier pigeons, you name it.

Say what you want about Christopher Kellerman, but the boy is no quitter.

I shoot a text to Roberta telling her I'll be on the lookout for her before staring at my phone for a long moment trying to decide whether or not I want to talk to Christopher tonight.

"Come on, Carol." I jab the call button. "Let's get this over with."

The phone rings twice before I hear a moment of static followed by Christopher's overly cheerful voice. "Hiya, Carol."

"Hey, Christopher." I attempt to inject at least a bit of enthusiasm into my voice. "What's up?"

"Thought I'd see you at work today."

"At work?"

"The big flat screen you put on hold yesterday? I figured you were going to pick it up."

"Oh yeah." Crap. Meant to grab Mike's truck and take care of that earlier. "Don't worry. Val and I will be in tomorrow."

"You know, that thing almost got sold out from under you twice today. Made it all the way up the conveyor belt one time. Had to pull seniority on the other guy to keep it from walking out the store."

"Umm...thanks."

"We close at five tomorrow. Just FYI."

"I said we'd be there." Neither of us speaks for a few seconds. I can hear Christopher breathing on the other end. He's nervous about something. Fantastic. "So, Christopher, you really just texted to remind me to pick up the TV?"

"Well, not exactly."

Here it comes. "Then what was it, *exactly*?"

Another pause. I swear I'm going to hang up on the boy.

"Christopher?"

"It's about Roberta." Yet another pause. "I...asked her to the dance."

"She told me."

"She did?"

"Of course she told me. She's like my best friend."

"Oh." I can almost hear his gears turning through the phone line. "Are you okay with that?"

Am I okay with that? Did Christopher Kellerman seriously just ask me such a thing?

"Of course I am." My words become very precise. "Why wouldn't I be?"

"It's just, neither of us had a date and I thought it would be fun and Roberta hasn't been able to do much lately because of her sister and—"

"Christopher, stop. You don't owe me any explanation. I just need to know one thing."

I swear I can hear him swallow through the phone. "What's that?"

"Tell me what it is you want."

"What I want?"

"You called me for advice. It's late, but here I am. What do you need?"

"I know it's kind of last minute, but do you think Philippe might have something at the formal shop for me? I have a couple of suits I wear to church for big occasions, but nothing I'd really like to wear for this thing." He clears his throat. "Maybe something a little more conducive to...dancing?"

"Dancing?" I laugh. "You?"

"You've never seen me dance." If I was expecting anything like embarrassment to come back across the line, I'm taken off guard by his tone. Christopher sounds—dare I say it—confident? "You might be surprised."

I smile despite myself. "You know, I just might."

"So, anything at your shop for someone who's all legs?"

"We'll see. Philippe is a bit of a wizard, but he doesn't keep a whole lot in stock, so no guarantees."

"You open at ten, right?"

"On the nose." And with God as my witness, I will *not* be late tomorrow. "Get there early, and Philippe and I will see what we can do. Okay?"

Before he can speak, the other line beeps in. It's Roberta.

"Sorry, Christopher. Emergency. Gotta run."

"Okay. See you tomorrow morn—"

As I flip to Roberta's call, it hits me. Tomorrow's going to be a busy day.

"Hey, Bobbisox. Just got off the phone with your knight in —" A couple of choked sobs come across the line. "Hey. Are you okay?"

"Not really." More croak than voice, Roberta barely sounds like herself.

"Did...something happen?"

"Tameka's temperature hit 102 a little bit ago. We just got to the ER, and they're already saying they're putting her back in the hospital for antibiotics and observation."

Crap.

"That sucks. Sorry."

"Just wanted to call and let you know I may not make it tomorrow."

"But, you have to come." My mind flashes on a Christmas Eve Dance with Ryan King and a dateless Christopher Kellerman in orbit. I shudder from head to toe. "Christopher is counting on you."

"Christopher is a big boy. He'll be all right. Tameka is my sister, though. She has to come first."

"If she needs you, I'm sure you'll be there, but don't you think you deserve a night? I mean, you've been by her side for months."

"By choice, Carol." Roberta sniffles over the phone line. "You wouldn't—"

"I wouldn't what?"

"Never mind." I can hear the trepidation in her voice. "It's nothing."

"I wouldn't understand. That's what you were going to say."

Roberta's voice is no longer the only one cracking. "Don't you think for a second that I don't get it. That I don't know what you're feeling. The way I see it, sick or not, at least you still *have* a sister." I swallow hard, trying to regain my composure. "They didn't even find enough of mine to bury."

"God, Carol. I'm sorry. I didn't mean—"

"Save it. I'll see you at the store tomorrow."

"Carol. I—"

I hang up the phone, the screen warm and slick with tears beneath my thumb. Roberta calls back once, twice, three times, but I just let all the calls go to voicemail.

I'm done for the night.

Except I'm not.

I lay my head down on the pillow and hope to get in at least three hours of sleep before some stupid ghost comes along to show me how much of a mess my life is.

Like I need any further lessons on that topic tonight.

CHAPTER TWENTY-EIGHT

Any concern I had about waking up in an icebox for a third night seems foolish as I kick the covers from my body, my skin damp with sweat. Moist heat cascades across my flesh like I'm sitting in a sauna. A part of me almost misses the cold.

The clock on my phone shows 1:58, the unheard alarm chirping like some obnoxious bird. Don't know why I bothered setting an alarm anyway.

As if the Spirit was planning to let me sleep through her visit.

It begins softly at first, but grows in volume with each line, a chorus of creepy children's voices filling the air with yet another song that gets played a gazillion times every Christmas season.

Last night, I was "treated" to Tchaikovsky; tonight, a chorus of creepy children's voices brings me a song of good cheer, assuring anyone listening beyond all shadow of a doubt that Christmas is indeed here.

"'Carol of the Bells,' huh?" I stare up at the ceiling. "Ironic much?"

Now that I think about it, though, as creeptastic as my

nightly serenades have been, at least the first two Spirits have let me know they're coming. If what I've seen in all the movies bears out, the hooded figure who comes for me tomorrow will likely not grant me such courtesy.

"Come on out," I say after taking a deep breath of the stifling air. "The sooner we get this started, the sooner you can get the hell out of here."

"Now, Carol." The whispered voice from my car, now robust and full, fills the room. "That's no way to talk to one who has come so far to speak with you and you alone."

My heart races. "Where are you, Spirit?"

"Where am I?" A deep, throaty laugh reverberates from wall to wall, ceiling to floor. "I am everywhere. Your homes, your shopping malls, your schools. Your very minds. I am Solstice. I am Yule. I am Christmas. Ignore me to your heart's content, but I and my brothers and sisters have been Present for millennia. Tonight, you are my charge."

"You showed yourself before." A tremor invades my voice. "In the car." Though I'm burning up, I pull my comforter around me, as if some down and fabric will protect me. "Come out into the open where I can see you."

"Very well." A feminine outline materializes at the foot of my bed as the clock on my phone flips to two o'clock. "'Tis the hour, after all."

In a burst of silver, the outline fills in, revealing a giant of a woman in green and white.

"I am the Spirit of Christmas Present. Look upon me."

A good two feet taller than me, the Spirit looks down on me with knowing eyes the color of pine boughs from beneath a head of orange-red hair that cascades across her shoulders, flows down her back, and kisses the floor. Her face plump, her breasts full, and her hips curvy, she's every bit what *Cosmo* would call "full-figured and fabulous" while continuing to fill its pages with twigs wearing lipstick and eyeliner. Her crimson lips contrast flawless porcelain skin that all but glows with an inner light. Lined with white fur at her neck, wrists and feet, her evening gown of green velvet accentuates her every curve while the mistletoe from my nightstand, all tied up in red ribbon, now rests pinned to her ample chest. A tiara fashioned to look like twin sprigs of holly sits atop her head, completing the look.

Philippe couldn't have accessorized her better.

"Come closer, Carol Davis," the Spirit says, her voice booming as if piped through a megaphone, "and know me better."

The flames from her torch—which looks an awful lot like the cornucopia Valerie uses as a table decoration at Thanksgiving—fill the room with nothing but the most flattering of light. A blink and the room is filled from corner to corner. Wherever the light of the torch can reach, I find presents wrapped in brightly colored papers and bows, mouthwatering food of every type, and decorations stacked from floor to ceiling: the horn of plenty held in the Spirit's hand made evident.

A glimmer in her eyes tells me she knows everything about me, even more perhaps than the Spirit of Christmas Past. I find it difficult to meet her gaze, choosing instead to focus on the buckled toe of one black boot peeking from beneath the white fur at her feet.

"I thought you were going to be some bearded guy in a bathrobe."

"Every Christmas is different, my dear, not to mention I didn't think it appropriate a bare chested ruffian appear mid-evening in the room of such a lovely young lady."

I let out a laugh.

"Did I say something amusing?" the Spirit asks.

"Not really." I glance at the door leading to the hall. "It's just I don't get called young lady very often unless I'm in trouble."

Her smile fades a bit. "Ah, dear Carol, how I wish I could tell you that weren't the case."

Any hint of wistfulness leaves my mind at her statement, replaced by a cold certainty at my core. "And what's that supposed to mean?"

The Spirit lets out a quiet sigh. "I've already said too much. All will be made more than clear by my associate tomorrow night. We have business enough this evening, you and I." She holds out her arm. "Now, Carol Davis, take my sleeve and let us be off."

Her raised arm reveals an empty scabbard at her side. The leather weathered and the silver at the throat and tip beyond tarnished, the ornately decorated sheath is an artifact from another time.

"Lose your sword?" I ask, hoping to get a rise out of the Spirit. Instead, I earn the most condescending of glares.

"And for what purpose would I carry a weapon? I am the very embodiment of Christmas, not some warrior who hides behind sharpened steel." She takes a step toward me. "Is the phrase 'Peace on Earth, goodwill toward men' so foreign to your ears?"

"Sorry, but you're the one wearing the scabbard."

"We will see many things this night, many that will be hard to accept and even a few you will likely wish you could unsee, but not one of them could you change with the edge of a blade." She offers me her arm a second time. "Now, take my sleeve so we can begin."

A big part of me wants to say no, to run, to hide, but deep inside, I know I can't hide from the Spirit or any of what she's come to show me.

"Fine." I grasp her sleeve, the green velvet warm in my fingertips. "Where do we start?"

As the room fades around us, the Spirit's voice fills the space. "With someone you have likely already forgotten, but who definitely hasn't forgotten you."

CHAPTER TWENTY-NINE

My bedroom, filled top to bottom with every yuletide item imaginable, fades from view, leaving this new Spirit and me alone in the gray limbo the Spirit of Christmas Past and I traveled last night.

"Your friend with the silver hair brought me here." I shudder at the surrounding nothingness. "What is this place?"

"The ether," the Spirit whispers, "the place between." She motions to the all-encompassing void around us. "It may be oppressive and dull, but it does serve its purpose. Contrary to what you learned in your geometry classes, the shortest distance between two points isn't always a straight line."

"You sound like my uncle, Mike." I stare out into the gray nothingness. "Man gets half his philosophy of life from *Star Trek* reruns and the rest from his *Lost* DVD boxed set."

"I would not be so fast to ridicule," the Spirit says. "Humankind depends upon its storytellers to retain its greatest truths. Modern man may believe everything boils down to numbers, but the fact remains that without story, those very numbers become meaningless." Her ghostly brow furrows. "And now, on to *your* story."

A gust of wind forces me to blink, and when I again open my eyes, I stand in a small room furnished meagerly with an old sofa, a second-hand loveseat, a couple of scratched up tables, and a dilapidated recliner facing an old tube set in the opposite corner. A decent collection of beer cans litters the coffee table while the man in the recliner—about four days out from his last shave and most likely his last shower—stares unblinking as a football game plays across the TV.

"Dad?" The voice, a girl's, and strangely familiar, echoes from the next room. "Do you want to see?"

The man crushes the beer can in his hand.

"Sure," he shouts, followed by an angry mutter. "Thing cost almost half a week's pay. You better wear the damn thing every day."

"Get ready, Al." A second voice. More mature. Female. "Here she comes."

A woman in her early forties, trying desperately to hold onto her twenties, pops around the corner, a hesitant smile on her face.

Suddenly, I know where I am.

"Spirit, get me out of here. These people have nothing to do with me."

"On the contrary," the Spirit whispers. "Everything you say or do, every smile or frown you offer, every life you touch. These all have everything to do with you."

"All I did was tell her the truth."

"No, Carol Davis. What you did was practice unnecessary cruelty."

Around the corner comes the girl from the dress store two nights ago wearing a sleeveless teal dress with a ruffled hem and silver sequins trailing down the skirt. She steps to the center of the room and does a clumsy spin, her mother's cautious smile echoed on her face.

I couldn't remember her name last night. Now, it's all but seared across my memory.

Emily.

Jimmy's girl.

In a two-year-old dress from Philippe's discount rack, the poor thing tries to look poised in her three-inch heels, though I can tell from her wobbly knees she's a lot more accustomed to sneakers.

"So, honey," the woman whispers. "What do you think?"

"What do I think?" He looks past his wife at the TV. "I think we just scored and I missed it because you're standing in the way. I think that dress is pretty flimsy for the $150 I spent two days slaving over a hot grill to earn." He turns his attention on Emily. "And most important, I think you should remember I never approved of you going to this stupid dance in the first place. Especially not with this new kid—what's his name —Billy?"

"His name is Jimmy, Al." Emily's mother rests a hand on her hip. "You know his name good and well."

"Jimmy, Johnny, Billy. All the same. Just a bunch of horny boys looking for a little action."

Emily runs from the room as her mother's face goes as purple as a beet.

"Albert Stockton!" Emily's mother fumes. "That is your daughter!"

Her husband glances over at her, his eyes half-closed with a mix of derision and inebriation. "Yes. That is my daughter. Excuse the hell out of me if I don't want her going out of the house dressed like a prostitute."

A door slams down the hall, and if possible, Mrs. Stockton's face goes a shade darker.

"Al, you're drunk."

Mr. Stockton shoots out of the chair and comes nose to nose

with his wife. I fully expect her to back down, but the brave woman holds her ground.

I'm guessing she's been through this before.

"Go ahead," she says. "Hit me."

"Don't think I won't." His face almost as red as hers, his hands ball into fists at his sides.

"Remember what the police said last time?" She plants her finger in her husband's chest. "How many second chances do you think you're going to get?"

Mr. Stockton backs off. All of half an inch.

"Whatever." He flops back into his chair in a huff and returns his attention to the game, his eyes boring a hole through his wife as he pretends she's not standing between him and the TV. Mrs. Stockton waits for another minute before leaving the room with an exaggerated sigh and wandering down the hall after her daughter.

I turn to the Spirit, who has watched impassive through the entire fight, and give her an incredulous shrug.

"This? This is what you brought me to see? Sure, she's got it bad, but I don't see what this has to do with me."

The Spirit frowns. "Does your lack of empathy know no bounds? Do you really not understand why you were brought here?"

Both hands go to my hips as my head falls to one side. "Look, your friend from last night took me on a fascinating tour of every shitty thing that's ever happened to me and tried to hold me accountable for most of it. Now you're telling me I'm responsible for this girl's life as well?"

"Every person on this planet is responsible for their actions and their actions alone. This much is true. Still, those actions and choices have repercussions on others." Her gaze shifts to the hallway, the girl's sobbing just audible in the pauses between TV commercials. "Emily Stockton lives this every day. All she wanted from you two days ago was a modicum of kindness. Would that have been so much to give?"

My gaze drops to the floor of the Stockton living room. "I didn't know any of this. Of course, I wouldn't have said those things if I knew she dealt with this crap every day."

"And there's the point."

I let out a sigh. "What point?"

"That you never know. Where someone's been. What they've seen. The things they've been through."

"What are you saying?" I rub at the bridge of my nose. "That I'm supposed to treat the whole world and every idiot in it with kid gloves?"

"No, but I might argue coming at everyone you meet with boxing gloves is more than a bit counterproductive and likely quite exhausting." She motions to the darkened hallway. "Not to mention you never know which of the people you're meeting have already taken a hit that day."

Marnie's voice echoes in my mind.

You're not the only one with problems.

"Fine. I need to be nice to people." I glance at the Spirit, knowing good and well the answer to the question I'm about to ask. "Is that it?"

"We're just getting started." She turns to leave and then corrects her course. Gliding to the center of the room, she waves her torch, illuminating Albert Stockton in a moment of golden light as a second ray of luminescence flies down the hallway after Emily and her mother.

"What are you doing?" I ask.

"You are not my only priority this evening, Carol Davis, and if any place could use a dash of Christmas cheer, it is this home."

The sobbing sounds from the hallway stop, at least for the moment.

"Is...is Emily going to be okay?" I ask.

"Only time will tell, my dear." The Spirit gazes at me quizzically for a moment before again holding out her arm. "Now, take my sleeve. We have many more places to visit before our evening together is over. Time is passing quicker than you can imagine."

"I don't know about that." I stare dubiously at the green-clad woman before me and question my sanity for the thousandth time in three days. "Apparently, I can imagine quite a bit."

CHAPTER THIRTY

I take the Spirit's sleeve and a few short steps later, we're back strolling through the ether. Barely audible above the rhythmic sound of my breathing, "Carol of the Bells" echoes through the gray as we walk, though the chorus of children has shifted into the bombastic guitars and synthesizers of Trans-Siberian Orchestra. Can't believe I know that, but I'd like to see someone live with Mike and Valerie for a decade and not come out of it with a PhD level of music trivia between their ears.

"Where to now?" My eyes slip half-closed as my lips curl into a sarcastic smirk. "If we're planning to visit all the customers I've somehow disrespected in the last year, you're going to need a couple more weeks."

"That won't be necessary," she says with a subtle wink. "And as you say, we would likely exhaust ourselves in such an endeavor."

"Wow, Spirit. I'm guessing you didn't win 'Most Sensitive' in your high school class."

She raises her eyebrows and with no hint of a smile answers,

"And you, Carol Davis, should be careful when speaking of pots and kettles."

"Fine." I don my best poker face, not wanting to give her the benefit of seeing me sulk. "Can we just get on with this?"

"Indeed we can." She waves an arm and we're standing in Philippe's Boutique, behind the register where I've stood for more hours than I care to remember.

"I thought you said we were done talking about work."

"Of the repercussions of your less than exemplary execution of your duties? Yes. But what of your employer himself? As the holidays approach this year, have you given the man so much as a second thought?"

"Philippe?"

"Yes." She peers around the empty-appearing store. "This uncommonly kind man has allowed you to remain employed when any sane businessperson would have shown you the door months ago."

"Like I need a job." I hold up three fingers. "You're the Spirit of Christmas Present. You, if anyone, should know what happens in three days."

My cockiness withers beneath the Spirit's knowing gaze. "Better than you, Carol Davis. More importantly, however, I know you. Believe me when I say that adding an infinite number of zeroes to the balance in your bank account would do little to increase what little happiness remains in your heart." She motions around the half-darkened store. "I also know that you get far more from this job than the few dollars Mr. Delacroix pays you."

"Philippe is a family friend from way back." I look away, unable to meet her gaze. "He knew my dad, you know, before."

"And so you take advantage of his sentimental lenience, all the while spitting in his eye and those of his customers with spite and impudence at every opportunity."

"So I don't let a bunch of brain-dead teenagers walk all over me. Big deal."

"But it's not your reputation alone that you are sullying. If it weren't for Mr. Delacroix's boundless compassion, he would have dismissed you the first week without a doubt." She fixes me with stern eyes. "Your words may be filled with bluster, but do you truly feel you've earned the meager wage this man has paid you for your slipshod work, much less his unfailing kindness?"

"Hey. I'm not some charity case Philippe brought in off the street. I do a good job at the Boutique. I put in a ton of hours, and I work pretty damn hard when I'm there."

"At sharpening your tongue, perhaps." Her withering gaze stings far more than her words. "Have you ever considered how much income you've cost your long-suffering benefactor over the last few months, sending girl after girl from your store in tears?"

"Philippe is doing just fine."

"Philippe," she says, enunciating each syllable, "is barely scraping by."

"That's not true." Heat rises in my cheeks. "He would've told me."

The Spirit's laugh is simultaneously kind and condescending. "You're a seventeen-year-old girl, Carol. No matter how close you may think you are, a grown man is not going to trouble you with his financial woes."

"But, if I'd known his business was having trouble, I wouldn't have..." Not sure how to complete the thought, I turn from the Spirit. "I'm not stupid, you know."

"Agreed." The Spirit lets out a solitary chuckle. "You are many things—self-centered, callous, unnecessarily cruel—but stupid you are not."

The heat across my face continues to rise. "I am not cruel."

"But you just admitted to treating his customers like dogs

because you thought he was well enough off that it didn't matter."

"Don't put words in my mouth, Spirit."

"I don't have to, dear Carol. You put more than enough there yourself."

Before my brain can form anything approaching a snappy comeback, I catch movement from the corner of my eye. Philippe, stumbling, steps into the room from the back. The clock behind his head shows 9:45.

"9:45." I turn to the Spirit. "When is this?"

"Christmas Eve, not twenty-four hours from now."

Philippe's usual smile absent, his furrowed brow shows more fret than I've ever seen on his face. A framed eight-by-ten of a figure in uniform hangs loosely in one hand while a half-filled glass of something I'm betting isn't ginger ale rests in the other. He takes a long slug from his drink and places the empty glass on the counter before sliding down the wall to sit on the floor.

"It's almost ten o'clock. What's he still doing at the boutique? We close at three on Christmas Eve."

"Where else does he have to go?" the Spirit asks. "Who does he have to go home to? You believe yourself so close to this man, but what do you really know about him?"

"I know he gave up drinking long before I was born." I step close to Philippe, amazed he can't see me despite his swollen eyes. "Or at least that's what he told me."

"Sometimes when storms threaten, people head for the most familiar ports, even ones they swore to never visit again."

"Who's the guy in the photograph?" I kneel at Philippe's side to take a closer look at the picture. "Tall, good looking. Someone from Philippe's family?"

The Spirit peers down at me. "In a manner of speaking, I suppose."

"Oh." My attempt to take a breath fails. "I take it they were...close?"

The Spirit nods. "Indeed they were."

I rise from the floor. "What happened to him?"

"What happens to everyone, eventually." The Spirit brushes her fingers down the empty scabbard at her side. "Not everyone who goes off to war comes back."

"I never knew."

"He knows how you feel, more than most, in fact." She brings her torch close to Philippe, allowing him to bask in the flame's light and warmth for a moment. "And not only in reference to the man in the photograph."

"How so?"

"On the day you lost your parents, Philippe Delacroix lost two friends who were, in essence, the only family he had left in the world." She lets out another laugh, though this one is sad and far from patronizing. "Why else, dear child, do you think you still have employment?"

"I guess I...figured he needed the help."

"But you have managed the store alone on many a night, albeit not to the best of your ability. As dire as his finances have been of late, would not Mr. Delacroix have been far smarter to let go his lone employee and manage the store himself?"

"Then, why didn't he?" Tears begin to roll down my face, a mirror of the twin rivers running down Philippe's cheeks. "Why?"

"Why, indeed?"

The Spirit offers her arm, and before I am even asked, I take her sleeve and we step through the wall and back into the dim.

CHAPTER THIRTY-ONE

The gray swirls around us, all but palpable as the Spirit and I stroll through nothingness. The eerie sound of children's voices singing of Christmas bells comes from every direction, a truly disorienting phenomenon in a place with no ceiling, walls, or floor.

"If your job was to come here and make me feel awful, you're definitely earning your pay."

"All you see is merely the way things are. As for my 'job'—if what we are doing can be defined as such—it is simply to open your eyes and illuminate that which you need to see." The Spirit raises her torch high above her head as we step from darkness and into the light of another home. A home I know almost as well as I know my own, though I haven't set foot inside the place in over a year.

The breakfast table is filled with unopened mail, the dishes sit in the kitchen sink unwashed and ignored, and the floor appears not to have been swept in months. In the next room, where I've watched more than my fair share of movies, the big flat screen on the wall is paused on the image of one of those reality show queens with no brain and even less of a reason to be famous. And there, just below the TV, picture after picture of Marnie Jacobsen: one of her in cheerleading gear, another in a formal gown, another in a pretty bikini as she rushes down the beach.

A quiet sob breaks the silence.

Seated alone and lit only by the TV, Marnie's mother clutches a glass of wine in one hand and the remote in the other.

"Why, God?" Her voice cracks as she drops the remote to the floor and buries her face in the crook of her arm. "Why?"

"Ms. Jacobsen looks awful."

"What you see is a mother in mourning. Christmas Eve is three days past the first anniversary of her daughter's death. Would you expect anything less?"

"But it's been a year." I take a step closer to Ms. Jacobsen, half-afraid I'm intruding, though I know she can't see me. "Shouldn't she be doing better by now?"

"Shouldn't you?" The Spirit's eyes flick to me. "An outsider might argue you stand here in the middle of the night speaking with a strange apparition all in an effort to work through issues stemming from your own bereavement."

Fantastic. The Spirit of Christmas Present is channeling my therapist. "But—"

"How many years, Carol Davis? Since you lost your mother? Your father? Your sister?"

"Point. Taken." I bite my lip, holding back a few things I probably shouldn't say to an omnipotent entity that holds my life in the palm of her hand as we wander through limbo. "It's just...I've seen her out and about. You know, at the mall. The coffee shop. She even makes it out to a cheerleading event from time to time."

"She puts on a brave face, but countless hours of therapy and the wonders of modern medicine are all that make such feats possible. Never forget, however, that this is a woman who pulled her only daughter's lifeless form from the frothy waters of a patio hot tub she never wanted to buy in the first place."

Scenes from the funeral fill my mind. Marnie's mother so doped up on the same meds that took her daughter she barely cried. Her father, who had flown in from Fort Something-Or-Other, trying to hold it all together. How the two of them barely spoke. How even then Marnie's mother seemed the loneliest person in the whole world.

"Did you not once call Marnie Jacobsen your best friend?" the Spirit asks.

I turn and glare at her through salty tears. "Marnie was the best friend I ever had."

"And in the last year of her life, did you not spend almost as much time in this home as you did your own?"

"Yeah." I try to swallow away the pineapple-sized lump in my throat. I know where she's leading, and I don't want to go there.

"This woman has prepared for you how many meals? Driven you to how many movies, sporting events, concerts?"

"More than I can remember," I somehow choke out.

"And dare I ask how many times you've visited her since her daughter's death?"

"Leave me alone." I turn from the Spirit and scan for any way out of the room, any doorway that will return me to the gray void of the ether. "I've seen enough."

"You will see what I have brought you here to see."

With a shaking hand, Ms. Jacobsen downs the last of her wine and drops the glass to the carpeted floor. Grasping a frame holding a picture of Marnie from years past, she holds it to her chest and begins to rock.

It's quiet, but I swear I can hear her humming a lullaby.

"Last year, you lost a friend. This woman lost her only

daughter." The Spirit passes her torch over Ms. Jacobsen, the golden glow erasing the sorrow from her face and allowing her to drift off to sleep. "Have you even spoken to her since?"

"When Marnie died, it was like losing Joy all over again." I pull nose to nose with the Spirit, the heat radiating off her face like a miniature sun. Fine lines now rest at the corners of her eyes and mouth, as if she's somehow aged in the last hour. "Sitting there at the funeral, all I saw when I looked at Ms. Jacobsen was myself the day Valerie and Mike told me about the crash. You think I'd volunteer to relive that?"

"You could have recognized a kindred soul and reached out. The two of you both loved Marnie Jacobsen in your own ways, did you not?" The Spirit peers down her nose at me. "Instead, you retreated into yourself, leaving her alone when she needed you most."

"Philippe's not the only one who heads to familiar ports when storms hit." I drop to the floor beside Marnie's mother. "And what's the big deal, anyway? I mean, I was best friends with her daughter and everything, but—"

"How many days have you spent in this house? How many nights? Weekends?" She motions to Ms. Jacobsen's sleeping form. "This woman lost more than one daughter that day."

"Why is she alone on Christmas Eve? I know she and her husband split, but doesn't she have family somewhere?"

"Kathleen Jacobsen, like her daughter, was an only child. With her divorce a few years ago and Marnie's passing, she is alone in this world."

"But Marnie still had grandparents, didn't she?"

"This poor woman's mother and father have reached out on numerous occasions." The Spirit shakes her head. "Each time she has turned them down, preferring to face the world alone."

"But I don't get it." I reach out for Ms. Jacobsen's cheek, but pull back, unsure if I should, or even can, touch her. "Surely she doesn't want to be alone at Christmas."

"Most of the time, people don't know what it is they want." She raises her arm and motions for me to take her sleeve, a glint of fire flashing in her visage. "Or, for that part, what they need."

CHAPTER THIRTY-TWO

"You've got to be kidding," I groan as the music fades and our new surroundings materialize around us. "Another hospital?"

"My apologies," says the Spirit, "but as a wise doctor once told me, this is where the sick people are."

"Ugh." My eyes roll before I can stop them. "Please tell me after all this drama you're not going to launch into some stupid stand-up routine."

"And what's wrong with a bit of laughter over the holidays?" She peers up and down the long hallway, her vision extending far beyond the confines of the gray walls and closed doors, and raises her "torch of plenty" above her head. A golden light fills the space, the glow warm on my face. "Now that you mention it, if anyone could use a bit of levity at Christmas, it is the unfortunate people found within these walls." The shimmering light surrounding us divides and divides again until countless swirls of radiance float in the air around us, orbiting the Spirit as if she is the sun and they a hundred tiny planets.

"Go," the Spirit intones.

The various spheres of light fly from her and pass the many

doors along the hospital hallway. The torch dims for a moment before roaring back with renewed brilliance. In this new light, the Spirit's face shows several wrinkles that weren't present before. Crow's feet mark the corners of her eyes and a shock of white hair trails down the side of her face.

"What happened to you?"

She looks at me quizzically for a moment. "Oh, you mean this?" Her half-smile shifts to one side as she runs her fingers through her newly lightened tresses. "This is but one of the first signs of my passing."

"You're dying?"

She raises her shoulders in a simple shrug. "I am the Spirit of Christmas Present. I exist for but this single season. When it is done, I shall evanesce, as each of my two thousand brothers and sisters have before me."

"You mean you don't live forever?"

"How touching. You're actually concerned." Her smile warms me like a ray of sunshine. "Fear not. Though this season will fade into memory like every Christmas that has come before, the idea of me will live on, as it always has."

"You know, for a Spirit of Christmas Present, our whole trip so far has been filled with nothing but doom and gloom, and now we're standing in a hospital. Where are all the scenes of children around the Christmas tree? The parades? The parties?"

The Spirit raises an eyebrow. "You seem quite enthusiastic about a holiday you profess to be the worst day of the year."

"Whatever." I peer up and down the sterile-appearing hallway. "I'm guessing this is the part where you parade a crowd of sick children past me to make me feel horrible? To make sure I do the right thing with all the dollar signs hitting my bank account next week? I've seen the movies, you know. The old miser Scrooge opens up his pocketbook and in doing so opens up his heart. Christmas miracles abound. The End."

"You speak of redemption like it's the worst thing that could happen to a soul." She fixes me with an impish gaze. "Truth be told, however, a bit of charity would likely unburden that stony heart of yours."

"I knew it. If that's what this is all about, I'll sign a check right now. Postdated and everything." I shoot her a wicked grin. "Charity of your choice."

"Your financial situation, Carol Davis, is the least of your problems, and near the bottom of my list of concerns. Allow me, however, to offer one piece of wisdom."

"Like I could stop you."

She continues as if I've said nothing. "Your belief that an infusion of money will make right everything that has gone wrong in your life could not be further from the truth."

"I'm not some stupid kid, you know." The warmth I felt from the Spirit moments before fades like the last rays of a winter sunset. "And you talk like I don't deserve that money." My hands ball into fists so tight, I fear my fingernails may draw blood. "I'd give it all away in a second if I could just have my family back."

The Spirit shakes her head sadly. "Even now you have more family than many who walk this world."

"Valerie and Mike? That's not...the same thing."

"Only because you insist on keeping them at arm's length." The Spirit pulls close. "Do you really think your aunt could love you any more if she *were* your mother?"

My cheeks erupt with fresh heat. "My mother is dead."

"And you make certain every person you meet knows that fact, don't you?"

"Everyone's life has a defining moment." A wave of nausea passes through me as a mantra I've said a thousand times hits my ears like I've never spoken the words before. "If the crash isn't mine, I don't know what is."

"You and every other person on the planet redefine yourselves every moment that you take breath. An infinite number of 'defining moments' awaits you, Carol Davis." She takes my arm in her warm hand and captures me with a knowing stare. "Some loom closer than you might guess."

A shiver trails up my spine. "What's that supposed to mean?"

Ignoring my question, the Spirit releases me and proceeds down the hospital hallway with me close on her heels. "What defines you isn't your past, your appearance, your possessions, or the number of dollar signs in your bank account." She turns on me. "It's your choices."

"You sound like Valerie."

"A high compliment." The Spirit's smile fades quickly. "A question, Carol Davis?"

"This should be good."

"Your every moment seems devoted to what's missing from your life, with no appreciation for what you have. Have you ever given any thought to what it is you actually want?"

"What I want?"

"It is a question that has baffled men and women, kings and peasants, philosophers and fools, for all of time." The Spirit clasps her hands together at her waist. "What is it, Carol, that you truly want?"

I run both hands through my hair and laugh. "That's an easy one. I want this stupid week to be over. I want to finally get what's coming to me so I can start putting the last ten years behind me. But most of all, I want you and every other Dickens reject in the tri-state area to go away and leave me the hell alone."

"Careful what you wish for." The Spirit bows her head and

sighs. "Without my sisters and I, your first two wishes will no doubt come to pass, much to your detriment."

I cross my arms. "Again with the mysterious."

She peers at me from beneath her strawberry-red eyebrows. "There are many specifics about your life I am at liberty to reveal, but the most important truths you must learn for yourself if they are to matter to you at all."

"Blah, blah, blah. If you've really 'come so far' to help save me from myself, then do it." I try with little success to keep my voice from cracking. "Help me."

"Very well." Her eyes go up and to the left as if she is struggling to remember something important. "To begin with, you should reconsider your first wish that this week be over more quickly. Christmas Day, for good or ill, already comes for you on hooves of fire." Her gaze bores into me with almost physical force. "Even more ill-advised is your second wish. Asking to receive 'what's coming to you' can be a dangerous request indeed."

"But it's three million dollars." I hold my hands before me, incredulous. "If I'm smart about it, I'll never want for anything."

She smiles sadly. "And tell me, dear Carol, what is it you want for now?"

"Come Monday, nothing. I can live wherever I want. Buy anything I need. I certainly won't be needing any stupid job."

"Are you quite certain?" The Spirit's head lolls to one side. "Many among the world find joy in their labors." She motions to a young nurse walking by carrying one of those little plastic medicine cups and a pitcher of water, a thoughtful smile of accomplishment on the woman's face. "Perhaps even a sense of purpose and meaning for their lives."

"Maybe." My teeth clench so tight my head begins to throb. "But don't you get it? Once my birthday hits, I won't have to worry about anything ever again."

The Spirit shakes her head. "There is more truth in that statement than you know."

"Good God, if you just come out and say something, do they revoke your Cryptic Club membership card?"

"Even the wealthiest of this world cannot buy their way past the troubles of life. In fact, money has the potential to cause as many problems as it fixes." Her eyes burn into me. "Or more."

"The root of all evil." I shift uncomfortably in my shoes. "Isn't that what they always say?"

"The love of money, at least. Timothy wrote that bit of wisdom centuries ago, and I would argue it's truer today than ever before in history." Her eyebrows knit with concern. "And we still have yet to discuss your most fatal assumption."

"And what might that be?" I ask, not really wanting to know the answer.

The Spirit looks away. "That the money from the airline settlement is all that is coming for you."

Another chill begins a slow tap dance up my spine.

"Wait. You've brought me to a hospital." I try to take a deep breath, but my body rebels. "Is there someone here I'm supposed to see?"

"Indeed. Someone with whom you're quite familiar."

My stomach knots. "Is it me?"

The Spirit's face breaks into yet another sad smile, her gaze shifting to peer across my shoulder. "And here she is. Right on time."

I twirl just in time to catch a glimpse of Roberta's worried features as she disappears into a room down the hall.

"Roberta?"

The Spirit heads down the hallway, motioning me to join her.

"Shall we?"

CHAPTER THIRTY-THREE

As we come to the door, I crane my neck so I can see past the Spirit's green-clad form.

"Do I have to go in there?"

The Spirit steps to one side. "It is important you see what lies beyond this door."

"Please." The trembling in my lip is anything but intentional. "I...can't."

The Spirit raises her arm and points, the nail of her lone finger painted blood red. "Go."

I hesitate another moment before forcing myself to take the last few steps into the room.

From the shallow alcove beyond the door, the lower half of a hospital bed is just visible in the glow of the monitors and the dim sunlight peeking through the drawn curtains. Roberta stands at the foot of the bed covered in a yellow hospital gown, gloves, and surgical mask, and is stroking the pair of feet just visible beneath the blanket. In the corner, a sleeping form rests in the lone recliner chair, wrapped in a blanket and masked as well. Another step and the identity of this second person becomes clear.

It's Ms. Oliver, Roberta's mother.

This isn't my room at all, but Tameka's.

I can't decide which hits me harder, my relief at this realization, or the guilt that accompanies it.

"She has a strong heart for one so small." The Spirit appears beside me. "Still, there is only so much one little body can withstand."

Roberta steps around the bed and sits at her sister's side, dabbing at her forehead with a damp cloth. Waking, Tameka looks up at her older sister with weak, sunken eyes that somehow retain some small fragment of the youthful exuberance I remember. Visions of Joy, her little body emaciated beneath the hospital lights all those years ago, hit me like a tsunami of remembrance. Roberta does her best not to let the concern show in her eyes, but with every shaking chill that runs through Tameka's body, another piece of her soul gets chipped away.

I would know.

"She's so...thin," I whisper.

"Leukemia is a horrible disease," the Spirit says, appearing at my side, "and the treatment is in many ways even worse."

"She keeps shaking." My breathing quickens. "What's wrong with her?"

"What isn't?" The Spirit steps to the bedside opposite Roberta. "Cancer fills her blood, as do the doctor's medicines in hope they will poison the problem more than the patient. On top of that, infection fills one of her lungs and has spread to her blood as well."

An icy fist grips my heart. "Pneumonia."

"Indeed." The Spirit slowly waves her torch over Tameka's trembling form, and for a moment, the chills stop. "She has a long night ahead of her."

"Wait. What day is this we're seeing?"

"The very night I came for you. These events occurred just a few hours ago."

Before I can ask another question, the blanketed form in the corner stirs.

"Roberta?" Ms. Oliver's voice creaks from behind her mask. "Is that you?"

"It's me, Mama."

"I thought you went home."

"I called the nursing station half an hour ago to check on Tameka. They told me about the fever."

"They just hung a new antibiotic." Ms. Oliver emerges from her blanket cocoon, a dusky moth too exhausted to take flight. "They think they're getting ahead of the pneumonia and the infection in her blood, but she's not going anywhere anytime soon."

"So, we'll be here for Christmas Eve?"

"Tameka and I will be here." Ms. Oliver's eyes reveal the kindly smile hidden behind her mask. "You, Roberta Oliver, have a dance to attend."

Roberta crosses her arms. "I'm not going."

"But you have to go." Tameka's voice, a low croak, surprises me as much as it does Roberta and her mother. "It's the Christmas Eve Dance. You've been talking about it for a year."

"Your sister's right." Ms. Oliver rests a hand on her older daughter's shoulder. "The doctors say Tameka is stable. Your sister and I will be okay for the few hours you're gone."

Tameka pulls herself up in the bed. "Plus, if you don't go, who's going to tell me all about it?"

"But—"

"No buts." Ms. Oliver squeezes Roberta's shoulder. "You only get to be a senior in high school once."

"If they let me graduate after all the days I've missed."

Roberta laughs sadly. "Do you think anyone at the dance will even recognize me?"

"Of course they will, honey." Ms. Oliver's eyes grow wistful. "I still remember going to the Christmas Eve Dance when I was your age."

"You and Dad?"

"Your father and I had only been dating a few months." Ms. Oliver's lips spread into a wide smile. "He looked so handsome that night."

Roberta takes her mother's hand and inspects the diamond engagement ring and wedding band that encircle her finger. "That was the night he asked you to marry him?"

"No. He waited till spring. Said he wanted us to be surrounded by flowers and green and life." Ms. Oliver sits on the bed and runs her hand through Tameka's braids. "But that night? That was the night I knew. The night he told me it was going to be me and him forever."

Tears form in the corner of Roberta's eyes. "I guess forever doesn't always come with a guarantee."

"He fought it, baby, just like your sister here." She brushes Roberta's knee. "He's still here in spirit, though."

"Is that true?" I glance up at the Spirit's face, but she is completely engrossed in the drama unfolding around us. "Never mind," I grumble as I turn my attention back to the Oliver family.

Roberta's nose crinkles. "Life sucks sometimes, doesn't it?"

"Life is life, honey. We're all here on borrowed time. You love the people in your life while they're here and remember them after they're gone. That's just the way it is."

Roberta rubs at the bridge of her nose. "I don't even have a dress yet, you know."

"I thought you were going to ask Carol," Tameka whispers.

"Carol's been a little...busy lately."

"Lately?" Ms. Oliver asks.

"Mom." Roberta shoots her mother a wicked frown and turns back to her sister. "Carol agreed to help me find a dress in the morning." She takes Tameka's hand in her gloved fingers and squeezes gently. "She told me to tell you hello."

Tameka's eyes light up. "Tell her to come see me if she can. I won't get her sick. I promise."

Roberta turns her head and tries to blink away the tears forming at the corners of her eyes. "I'll tell her." She and her mother share a downcast glance. "You know, Tam-Tam, between working at the shop and cheering and everything else, she's just had a lot on her plate."

Ms. Oliver takes Tameka's other hand. "Just like your daddy, she'd be here if she could."

It's my turn to swallow away the lump in my throat. I turn to the Spirit and wipe the tears from my eyes. "She's been asking for me?"

The Spirit scowls, as angry as I've seen her. "Your friend has all but begged you for weeks to come visit her sister, and while Roberta is old enough to recognize when she's being spurned, little Tameka is not." An all too familiar fire flares in her eyes. "Who exactly did you think it was asking for you all this time?"

"But why is a visit from me so important to her? I'm just her sister's friend from swim team."

"Do you even hear the words coming out of your mouth?" the Spirit asks. "Have you divorced yourself so far from reality that you can't understand the most basic of human emotions?"

I pull in a deep breath. "Enlighten me, then."

"Until you met Marnie Jacobsen, it was you and your best friend Roberta against the world, all but inseparable despite your endless sourness. After-school trips to the mall. Swim meets. Sleep overs."

"So?" I peer at the Spirit. "Things change."

"They do. But what you have forgotten is that little Tameka was right there in the mix from the beginning. Whether you meant to or not, you became a second big sister in that little girl's eyes. She hasn't forgotten that." The Spirit's eyes narrow. "Have you?"

CHAPTER THIRTY-FOUR

A legion of invisible handbell players brings the music this time as "Carol of the Bells" echoes through the ether and threatens to deafen me with each ear-splitting clang.

"I'll go see her," I shout above the din. "I swear."

"I have no doubt about that." The bells quiet in deference to the Spirit's authority. "But for tonight, we still have a few stops to make."

"Of course we do." I clutch the Spirit's sleeve, the velvet of her dress soft beneath my fingers. "Where to next, Spirit? You going to show me some puppies getting beaten because of something I did when I was six?" I fight to keep myself from digging my fingernails into her arm. "Or how I'm responsible for all the starving children in Africa?"

"All the woes of the world do not fall upon your shoulders, Carol Davis, though changes that sweep the world almost always start with one small voice."

I shake my head. "You know, if you weren't 'fading' or whatever after Christmas, you could totally apply for a job at Hallmark with material like that."

"Is it possible for you to speak in anything but sarcastic drivel?"

"I don't know. Is it possible for you to speak in anything but riddles?" I get no response to my little jab, and decide against prodding a ghost, or angel, or whatever a Spirit of Christmas is. "So, where *are* we going now?"

"Our penultimate call of the evening." She picks up her stride. "A soul you have dismissed on so many occasions it's a miracle he still holds any emotion for you, good or ill, in his big heart."

Somehow I knew we'd end up here.

"Christopher," I mutter as a room I've spent countless evenings watching reruns of everything from *Aliens* to *Xena* materializes around us. A place where I received a cinematic education on the differences between *Star Trek* and *Star Wars*, old and new *Doctor Who*, and even mastered the fine distinction between elves, dwarves, and hobbits. The space appears to have grown up a bit in the years since I set foot in this house. Though the three-foot high blue police box still rests in the corner, most of the posters covering the walls have been replaced with various pieces of artwork, some pencil and ink and some painted, no doubt from the many fan conventions Christopher hits every year.

A fantastically detailed black-and-white drawing of a pair of knights fighting an ogre, a beautifully rendered oil painting of a blue dragon, and dozens of other staples from Christopher's obsession with science-fiction and fantasy cover nearly every inch of his walls. A few have been taped up, but most are framed and hung with the precision that is Christopher's trademark. An impressive collection, there are characters from almost every movie I remember watching with him from the foot of his old queen-sized four-poster bed.

"Christopher must have spent a fortune on these." I peer

around the room. "Every one of them signed and framed. It's like he's hit up every artist on the planet."

The Spirit chuckles. "I'm afraid, dear Carol, that you're missing something."

"What?" I peer around the room. "What is it?"

"Take a closer look. Each of these drawings is indeed signed, but not, perhaps, in the way you imagine."

I release the Spirit's sleeve and step closer to the wall. A triptych of a familiar ranger, elf, and dwarf occupy the center of the wall, and though done in black and white ink, the likeness to the movie actors is uncanny. Real enough they appear about to leap off the wall and speak, I'm transported back to my first viewing of the *Lord of the Rings* movies. A fourteen-hour marathon one Saturday an eternity ago, I ate enough popcorn that day to give me a bellyache for three days. I actually slept over that night—Mike and Valerie were enjoying a rare weekend away and the Kellerman's had let me stay the weekend.

Times were so much simpler then.

I take a step closer and find the same calligrapher's signature at the bottom of each drawing. A swoopier version of a signature I've seen at the bottom of countless notes passed me in class over the years, and most recently at the bottom of a claim check for a flat screen TV.

"These are all Christopher's?" I pull in close to an almost photorealistic drawing of Liv Tyler in full elven regalia. "They're...fantastic. I knew he liked to draw and paint, but I didn't know he was capable of anything like this."

"And when was the last time you asked?" She motions to the wall of art. "In fact, when was the last time you thought of this talented young man as anything other than a burr in your saddle? Was his friendship such a burden to you? His willingness to accept the scraps left for him so off-putting?"

"We've just...grown apart over the years. That's all."

"No. You've pulled away. From him. From Roberta. Your aunt and uncle. In fact, you chose to pour all your energy into the one person in your world that was even more self-absorbed than you. And when she was gone—"

"Stop it!" I bury my face in my hands. "Don't you think I know all this? Don't you know how alone I feel every minute of every day?"

"You hang by your fingertips at the edge of a cliff and bite at any hand that reaches down to pull you up." She rests her hands on her hip. "This boy, for instance. What has he ever done to deserve such disdain? You were once the closest of friends, and though you have indeed grown apart over the years, he has shown you nothing but kindness."

"Leave me alone."

"But you just said you didn't wish to be alone anymore."

I squint my eyes at her. "You know what I mean."

"I do." The Spirit studies me. "Do you?"

Something approaching a growl comes from deep inside me. "Have we seen enough here?"

"Nearly." She motions to a draped easel in the corner, one I've been trying to ignore since we arrived. "You should take a moment to peruse Christopher's latest work. I think you may find an even more familiar face under that cloth."

"Fine." Fear and curiosity war within me with each step toward whatever lies beneath the draped sheet. An almost electric shock runs up my arms as I grasp the edge of the cloth and reveal the hidden canvas.

"It's...me." No swords, no blasters, no magic wands. Just a nearly completed oil portrait of me leaning against a tree in my favorite sundress.

A moment is all it takes to remember when Christopher took the photo clipped to the top of the frame.

A wet afternoon last spring. Four months after Marnie's death. The winter had lasted longer than any of the weathermen had predicted. Mike joked that Punxsutawney Phil must have seen his shadow two or three times before running back to his hole. The day of the picture was the first morning it had been warm enough to go outside without a coat, and though Valerie fussed about it until I shut the car door, I was wearing that stupid flower print dress no matter what she said.

It rained that day.

God, did it rain.

And I couldn't have cared less.

The scene plays out in my mind. It's right after school and I'm heading out to the car, soaked to the bone with hair hanging all down in my face. Christopher is standing in the parking lot in his rain gear trying to capture a photograph of a rainbow arching across the school.

"Better hurry," I told him. "Something that pretty won't last."

"Why do you think I'm standing out here in this stupid poncho?" He snaps a dozen or so pictures and lets the camera drop to his chest. "And speaking of pretty," he asked, "mind if I take your picture?" He bites his lip. "You know, for the yearbook."

"You've got to be kidding." I brush the hair from my face. "I look like a drowned rat."

"You look great." He raises an eyebrow, his mouth turning to one side the way it always does when he's about to let loose one of those smart ass jokes that stand as his dubious claim to fame. "Besides, with this picture, you'll have a lock on 'Most Likely to Die of Pneumonia' next year when we do senior superlatives."

I can still taste the bile in my mouth at the word.

Pneumonia.

"Not funny, Christopher."

"Come on, Carol. I'm just playing." He raises his camera, adjusting the focus. "Let me take your picture. We'll put it with a caption about 'April showers and May flowers' or something."

"Fine." I lean against the old walnut tree that overhangs the far end of the school parking lot and put on my most winsome smile. "But you better make it a good one."

He smiles. "I don't think you could take a bad one."

Surprised by this new and almost confident side of Christopher, my practiced smile fades into one more real. The camera flashes. The shutter releases. Christopher lowers the camera and checks out the screen.

"Don't you want to take a couple extra?" I ask. "So you can pick out the best one?"

Distracted, Christopher pauses for a moment before glancing up at me. "What? Oh. No. Don't worry. I've got what I need."

"You sure?" I step toward him. "Let me see."

"That's all right. It's a good shot. Trust me." Christopher flips the camera off and heads back toward the school. "I'll send you the file when I've got it all perfect, okay?"

I'd seen Christopher's work with Photoshop and knew he was good, so I didn't push the issue at the time. He never showed me the picture, and quite frankly, I'd forgotten he'd taken it till today. Christopher and I talked less and less the rest of that semester, and once I set foot in school the first day of senior year, any conversations beyond a quick nod in the hall became few and far between.

"Hmm," comes a voice from the door. "Thought I left that covered up." Christopher steps into the room and stands by my invisible form. I study his face as he, in turn, studies the painting. With a resigned sigh, he touches the corner of the portrait. "Be seeing you in the morning, Carol."

He pulls the sheet back over the painting and accidentally knocks a paintbrush to the floor.

A quite familiar paintbrush.

I glance in the Spirit's direction. "Is that what I think it is?"

"You recognize it, don't you?"

Christopher picks up the brush from the ground, returns it to the easel, and leaves the room. His hand snakes back in through the half-closed door and flips off the light, leaving the Spirit and me in near darkness.

I sit on the bed and look up at the Spirit, the two of us only visible by the somewhat dimmer light of her torch. "He kept the brushes after all these years?"

"They were good brushes, from a good friend." She sits next to me. "Do you even remember what he gave you that Christmas?"

The bottom of my jewelry box. Wrapped in tissue. Still on its original chain.

"Maybe." My gaze drops to the floor. "That day seems like a lifetime ago."

The Spirit peers at me, her accusatory glance daring me to spill my guts, but I hold my tongue, and though I have no doubt she knows I'm holding back, she holds hers as well. The two of us sit on Christopher Kellerman's bed for a moment, neither of us saying a word.

Eventually, it's me that breaks the silence.

"We've been at this a while." A yawn overtakes me before I can stop it. "Any more stops on this little tour of my life?"

"Just one."

"Then let's get on with it." I take her sleeve before we even stand. "I'm about to hit a wall."

"From your mouth to God's ears," the Spirit whispers as the room around us fades to gray. "Mind your words, Carol Davis. The universe is always listening."

CHAPTER THIRTY-FIVE

The Spirit and I walk the ether side by side. The music is notably absent this time, and neither of us makes a sound other than the quiet swishing of the Spirit's green velvet dress. Though another streak of white has appeared in her hair, she doesn't show any signs of slowing down. My eyes, on the other hand, grow heavier with each step.

"Where else could you possibly be taking me tonight?" I mutter so low I barely hear my own words.

Responding as if I'd asked her outright, the Spirit states plainly, "We return now to the place we started our journey." She waves an arm, and the surrounding nothingness lightens a shade. "Your home."

I clutch her arm tighter. "But...I thought you said we had one more stop." I don't know who is more surprised by the half-disappointment in my voice, her or me.

"And indeed we do," the Spirit answers without missing a beat. She raises her torch and the gray surrounding us settles to the ground like so much dust. In a blink we're standing in Mike and Valerie's kitchen. "Home is, after all, where the heart is."

"But I live here. Every day. What could you possibly have to show me I haven't already seen a thousand times?"

"You may live here, Carol Davis, but so do two other people."

As if on cue, Mike walks into the kitchen in a huff. Wearing an old Counting Crows concert t-shirt and striped pajama pants, he's a little off from even his normal not-quite-chipper self. Not far behind him, Valerie storms into the room. Her face is red and her cheeks are streaked with tears.

I've seen that face before. She's mad. Full on crying mad.

"Carol can stay here as long as she wants." Valerie throws her hands in the air as if she's afraid of what they'd do if left to their own designs. "And that's that."

Mike stands facing the corner, both fists pressed into the kitchen counter. Without turning around, he takes a deep breath and grumbles, "I never said I wanted her to go."

"You might as well have. It's written all over your face."

"All over my..." Mike spins around. "Come on, Val. All I've heard for three months now is your niece shooting off at the mouth about how she's leaving after the New Year. No 'Thanks for all you've done for me' or anything. Just a big 'I'm outta here' like we've had her locked up in prison for the last decade."

"Now, Mike."

"Don't 'Now, Mike' me." He pinches the bridge of his nose. "You know what? It's fine." Mike goes to the fridge and starts rooting around for something to eat. "If she's so hell-bent on getting away from here and us, that's great with me. I'll even help her pack."

"She's a teenager, Mike. She doesn't have the first clue what she wants." Valerie claws at her forehead. "Hell, when I was her age, I screamed at my mother every day, dyed my hair purple, and wouldn't date a guy unless he had a soul patch and a guitar."

"And you know I get that, right?" Mike pulls a half-eaten pumpkin loaf from the refrigerator and cuts himself a slice. "We were all young and stupid once, but that doesn't mean she gets a blank check to talk crap about the roof we've put over her head the last ten years." He takes a bite. "And definitely not while she's still sleeping under it." Crumbs fly from between his lips with those last few words.

Valerie looks away. "She's not like that all the time."

"Not with you." Mike pulls out one of the stools from the island and continues to devour the slice of pumpkin bread. "On her worst day, you're still her mother's sister. I'm just some guy she uses for target practice."

"Is that what he really thinks?" I ask. "It's not like I always—"

The Spirit shushes me and directs my attention back to Mike and Valerie.

"She may not say it much, but—" Valerie course corrects at Mike's raised eyebrow. "All right, so she never says it, but you've got to know how much she appreciates you."

Mike looks up from his plate, his head shaking as a half-exasperated smile appears on his face. "Does she have any idea how many second chances you've given her over the years?"

"Mike, Carol is family. No matter what she says or does, that's not going away. We're all she has, and I won't abandon her." She pulls around behind Mike and rubs at his shoulders. "I know this isn't what you expected when Jack and Holly asked us to be godparents for the girls all those years ago, but has it really been all that bad?"

"You know it hasn't. It's just...we talked for years about having kids, and as horrible as the circumstances were behind Carol coming to be with us, for all practical purposes, she's our child." Mike shoves the remaining crust of bread into his mouth and rests his face in his hands. "When I see her now, I feel like such a failure."

"What?" Valerie and I say simultaneously.

"I talked a big game my whole life about how I was going to be the best dad, provide for my family, bring up my kids right. And look what I've got to show for it. I've spent ten years raising a teenager who can't stand to look in my direction and is biting at the bit to get the hell away from me. My wife is so stressed out she hasn't slept a full night in weeks. I'm stuck in a job that could evaporate at a moment's notice if my boss decides on a whim to 'go another way.' And to top it all off, I can't even decorate my own house and celebrate Christmas without throwing a match into my powder keg of a home."

"It's okay, baby." Valerie's hands move up to Mike's neck. "Everything's going to be okay. We'll just celebrate the way we always do."

I turn to the Spirit as Valerie and Mike both disappear to separate ends of the house. "What are they talking about? We've always just skipped Christmas since I came to live with them."

The Spirit shakes her head, laughing sadly. "Tell me, Carol Davis. What would you do if your goddaughter fell out in a screaming fit two weeks before her ninth birthday simply because you had the audacity to bring a Christmas tree into the house?"

Mike and Valerie reappear at either end of the kitchen. Mike carries a package wrapped in turquoise paper and a big silver bow in one hand and a miniature Christmas tree in the other. Valerie has changed into a long hockey jersey and a Santa hat and holds a red-and-gold-striped gift bag. Mike sets up the Christmas tree on the kitchen island and plugs it in while Valerie flips off the lights. Soon, the two of them are lit solely by the soft glow of the tiny tree. Mike hands Valerie her present.

She shakes it gently and places it beneath the tinsel covered branches.

"Why don't you open mine first," she says, handing Mike the gift bag.

Mike reaches inside and pulls out a sprig of mistletoe that bears a striking resemblance to the one decorating the Spirit's collar. He smiles. "And whatever am I supposed to do with this?"

"What you always do with mistletoe at Christmas." She offers him a wink. "Hang it."

Mike lets out an amused chuckle. "Do you have any particular place in mind?"

She raises an eyebrow. "Wherever you want it, baby."

"How about right here?" Mike rises up on his tiptoes and hangs the mistletoe from the nearest blade of the kitchen ceiling fan. "Will this do?"

Valerie pulls close to Mike, their lips a hairsbreadth apart. "That'll do just fine, sir." She interlaces her fingers behind Mike's neck and pulls his mouth onto hers. There they stand for what seems the longest minute of my life, wrapped in a fervent embrace and enjoying the kiss with something I can only describe as hunger.

"Maybe you can help with all this stress I've been under lately," Valerie breathes when they come up for air.

"You know," Mike whispers. "I'd forgotten that purple hair of yours." He picks Valerie up and sets her on the kitchen island. She shivers as his series of kisses trails down her neck and onto her shoulder. Any disgust I feel at seeing my aunt and uncle making out is more than eclipsed by my fascination at the moment. A peck on the cheek or a quick hug is the most affection they've shown in front of me since I can remember. To know they still have this kind of passion punctuates a realization that hit me moments before when Mike plugged in the tree.

My aunt and uncle have been holding their breath for the last ten years.

Just like their niece.

And that's not all.

We're all holding our breath. Spinning our wheels. Me. Valerie. Mike. Roberta. Phillipe.

Christopher.

And for what? For everything to magically get better? For the sun not to rise the next day?

Mike's hands trail down Valerie's back, and the fire in my cheeks goes nuclear. As if in answer, the room fades back to gray until all that remains of the kitchen scene is the little plastic and wire Christmas tree, its dim light barely visible through the gray ether.

"My apologies, Carol Davis, if I allowed that to go on a bit long." Her lips are pulled to one side as if she is prudishly trying to conceal a grin. "There are things you are meant to see and things you probably shouldn't."

"Thanks." I shudder through a quiet chuckle. "Really didn't want to have to gouge out my eyes tonight."

"And since you asked about the lighter side of Christmas..." The Spirit waves her torch across the little blinking tree that floats in the space between us. The triangle of plastic and wire and artificial needles transforms from some cheap Walmart throwaway into a miniature representation of the most perfect evergreen in existence. The lights along every branch shine like celestial bodies in the night sky while the gold star at the top blazes like the midday sun.

"And now, dear Carol, our time draws to a close." The Spirit steps around the tree, which grows larger with each beat of my heart. "I hope you have seen all that you need to help you on your way."

"To help me on my way? All I've seen is that pretty much

everyone in my life is just as messed up as me. Just as sad. Just as angry. Just as numb."

"Sad and angry, perhaps," the Spirit says. "But numb? You are nothing of the sort." She pulls me aside as the Christmas tree's trunk reaches the ground and its upper boughs grow past my head. "In fact, you feel everything so acutely that you have walled yourself away from the world so you never have to feel anything again." Her eyes trail up and to one side, as if she is pondering some grand philosophical question. "The great irony of this is that you've convinced yourself you truly care about nothing and no one. It is clear from our brief time together, however, that nothing could be further from the truth."

Before I can formulate an answer, the Spirit's dress parts below her waist like green velvet theater curtains. Beneath her ample hips where her legs should fall lies only darkness and one lone little girl. Her hair is bedraggled, her eyes sunken, her limbs all but skeletal. She stares out at me like a starving man stares at a steak.

"I thought there were two of them." I try to sound smug, but it's all I can do to keep my knees from knocking. "Like I said before, I've seen this movie a few times." I cross my arms before me and focus on the Spirit's face, anything to keep from meeting the gaze of the apparition that glares from beneath her gown.

"Fear not, Carol Davis." The Spirit laughs. "Ignorance and Want haven't gone anywhere, but as Cro Magnon replaced Neanderthal, so too has this child replaced those twin evils of humanity." She inclines her head and looks at me with smug superiority. "And in your soul in particular."

"And what child is this, oh great Spirit of Christmas Present?"

The Spirit's face twists into something ugly. "Don't be clever with me, little girl. I can see your heart as plainly as I see your face. This child was born in you ten years ago and has grown stronger every day since. You've heard the parable. It's the wolf you feed that grows."

The thing beneath the Spirit's waist stares at me, all but snarling in the glow of the still growing Christmas tree.

"What...is she?"

"This, Carol Davis, is Apathy," she whispers, though her voice echoes through the ether like a shout. "Worse than Ignorance, as the absence of knowledge is far less an offense than indifference, and all but the root cause of Want. Tell me, were it not for Apathy, could Want even survive?"

"This girl, Apathy. That's not me. Just a moment ago, you said I cared more than anyone."

"No," the Spirit counters. "I said you *feel* more than anyone. A person can't help what they feel. Whether or not to care, though? That is the choice I spoke of before. A pivotal choice of which you have fallen on the wrong side for far too long."

"I've helped people." I start to hyperventilate. "Dozens of times. At the shop, at school, at home."

"You help others when it serves you." The Spirit crinkles her nose while the girl beneath her dress picks at her teeth with a ragged fingernail.

I hold back the vomit brimming at the back of my throat. "That's not true."

"Tell me, then. When was the last time you did something for someone that didn't benefit you in some way? Tell me and I will hide this child from your eyes."

I rack my brain, desperate to prove the Spirit wrong, but in the end, all I can do is bow my head in embarrassment.

"I...can't."

The Spirit smiles proudly. "Before you can solve a problem, you have to recognize one exists." Her dress falls together, and the withered girl disappears from view. "Congratulations,

Carol. You've taken your first step toward becoming a better person."

"Fantastic. You're channeling my therapist again." A long yawn escapes my lips. "So, what now?"

"You should get some sleep. You have a long day tomorrow."

The Spirit holds aloft her torch, and the gray around us dissipates. We stand in my room on either side of my bed. The stacks of gifts, tables of food, and lavish decorations from before have all vanished, leaving only the Spirit and the now enormous Christmas tree in the corner to show that anything is out of the ordinary.

"To bed with you," the Spirit says. "We have accomplished all we can this night, and I must take my leave. Farewell, Carol Davis. Remember what you've seen and heard this evening."

And that's when it hits me. What's been bothering me all night. Since our second stop, a nagging realization has grown more and more glaring with each place the Spirit has taken me, and no more so than when we visited my own home.

"Excuse me," I whisper. "One last question?"

The Spirit, already turned away, glances back across her shoulder. Her hair is finally a full shock of white, and her face is lined with new wrinkles. "One."

Her voice, once robust, is a quiet rasp.

"Like I said before, I've seen the movies. Even read the story in English class a few years back." I take a breath. "In the original, the Spirit of Christmas Present takes Scrooge on a tour of Christmas Day to show him the error of his ways."

"What of it?" the Spirit asks, turning back to face me.

"You've only shown me events from this evening or Christmas Eve. Why don't I get to see Christmas? Isn't that the big day?"

The Spirit stares at me for a long moment, either unsure of how to answer or bound from doing so. As I inhale to speak again, the Spirit steps forward, raises her wrinkled index finger, and places it across my lips.

"Do not ask again, dear Carol. Believe me when I tell you that I understand your question, but the answer you seek lies with my dark sister who comes for you tomorrow night."

"But—"

"That is all I can say." The Spirit's brusque answer echoes in my mind as she steps behind the still glowing Christmas tree and vanishes from sight. I try to look away, but I'm mesmerized by the many lights, my breath catching as they begin to go out one by one.

"Spirit?"

Faster and faster the lights of the tree are doused until only two remain.

"I'm scared." I backpedal till my calves hit the footboard of my bed. "Spirit?"

Near the base of the tree, side by side, the pair of lights grows brighter with each passing second.

Like the headlights of an oncoming car.

Before I can take another breath, the two lights converge in my vision, drowning out all else in the room with their unyielding radiance until all I see is white.

Blinding inescapable white.

STAVE IV

THE LAST OF THE THREE SPIRITS

Saturday, December 24th

CHAPTER THIRTY-SIX

"This has to be what a hangover feels like," I mutter as I unlock the door to the boutique and step inside to escape the chill. I head immediately to the back office and turn the heat up to 75 from the arctic 62 where Philippe leaves the thermostat set every night. "Hell, at least it's not raining."

I'm here a full thirty minutes before the shop opens. No matter how punched in the gut last night left me, there was no way I was going to be late today. Not after Philippe went all fairy godmother on me yesterday despite me missing half my shift. Also, Christopher is due here at ten to shop for tuxes and Roberta is dropping by at eleven to pick out a dress.

That is, if we're still speaking.

A twinge of pain flares behind my eye, worsening the fog around my thoughts. Valerie came and got me up right at eight like I asked her to. She said it was like trying to wake the dead, not exactly what I wanted to hear first thing after spending all evening with a ghost, but whatever. Explaining why she found me passed out on the floor was a colossal pain, but it was worth it. Today is a big day, and one I can't afford to sleep away.

Unable to quell my curiosity, I do a quick sweep of the store. Nothing resembling the project Philippe and I discussed yesterday is to be found on any of the racks or in any of the nooks and crannies only he and I know about.

What if he got too busy?

Or worse, what if he forgot?

Maybe I'll be wearing that hunter green halter top later tonight after all.

A series of four knocks at the door brings me out from the back.

"Come back later," I shout. "We open at—" The word "ten" catches in my throat as I catch sight of the hooded figure just visible through the fogged-over glass door.

Knock, knock, knock, knock.

"God." I can barely breathe. "Not already."

Knock, knock, knock, knock.

I'm starting to hyperventilate when a familiar voice calls my name.

"Carol?"

My eyes narrow.

"Thanks a lot, Christopher," I grunt to myself. "Just shaved another year off my life."

"Come on, Carol," he shouts through chattering teeth. "I can see you. Let me in. I'm getting frostbite out here."

"Coming," I half-sing, half-shout.

I turn the latch and open the door on Christopher's shivering form. Once inside, he slips out of the big duster he's worn the last couple winters and pulls back his sweatshirt hood. His cheeks and nose a bright red, his teeth chatter like one of those wind up skulls you see at Halloween.

"How long have you been standing out there?" I ask.

"Just pulled in, actually."

"Then why are you all bundled up like Nanook of the North?"

Christopher runs his fingers through his almost stylishly mussed hair. "Heat's out in the truck. Have to get it looked at next week."

I cross my arms. "You're early. Wasn't expecting you till ten."

"I had to go in at five to help stock shelves. My relief just got in so my boss freed me up for a bit so I could get this taken care of. I don't have much time, but here I am."

"You big dummy. We don't open for half an hour and Philippe is the only one who knows what men's wear we have on hand."

"Fortunately for you, Mr. Kellerman," comes a familiar French voice from outside, "I awoke early this morning and couldn't get back to sleep." Philippe pulls the door closed behind him, turns the deadbolt, and fixes Christopher with an appraising stare. "I take it you're here to find something to wear this evening?"

"Yes, sir." Christopher shoves his hands in his pockets. "Hope it won't take too long. This little block of time is all my boss would let me have today. He needs me back by ten."

Philippe checks his watch. "Not a problem. It's only 9:35. We'll get you taken care of and back to work before the first soul sets foot in the boutique today." He steps past me and motions for Christopher to follow. "Step into my office, Mr. Kellerman. Let's see if we have anything in your size."

The two of them head to the back of the store, leaving me alone with my thoughts. I stare at the glass doorway where something as harmless as Christopher Kellerman's silhouette almost had me peeing in my pants moments before. Marnie's words from three nights ago echo through my head.

Expect the first of the Spirits tomorrow night at one, the second the next night at two, and the third on Christmas Eve at, well, whenever she feels good and ready.

"Fantastic."

I tidy up the desk, sort some receipts, alphabetize the few remaining tuxes and dresses that haven't been picked up, all in an effort to ignore the fact that at some point in the next few hours, a shrouded form waits for me that is anything but an old friend in a ridiculous coat.

Twenty minutes pass before Christopher and Philippe rejoin me at the register.

"Your friend is lucky," Philippe says. "This other young man cancelled at the last minute." He hands Christopher a black zipper bag. "The jacket fits well, and if anyone asks about the pants, he can tell them high-waters are in style."

Christopher steps up with the tuxedo draped across his arm. "Thanks, Carol. You and Philippe are life savers."

"That's what I do." I let out a sarcastic laugh. "Save lives every chance I get."

Christopher's eyes drop even as Philippe's fasten on me like a pair of vice grips.

"Well," Christopher says, "drop by the store later if you can. I still have your TV on hold."

"Oh. Yeah." It's my turn to look away. "Sorry. Didn't make it by yesterday."

"Don't worry. Christopher Kellerman is on the job." Christopher's lips turn up in a goofy grin. "It almost got sold out from under you again last night, so I hid it down in the bowels of the warehouse where no one but me can find it."

"Umm...thanks." I bite my lip. "Valerie and I will try to get by later today."

"Sounds good." Christopher turns to Philippe. "Thanks for everything, Mr. Delacroix."

"Not a problem." Philippe glances at me and shoots Christopher a wink. "Any friend of Carol's is a friend of mine."

Philippe lets Christopher out the front and locks the door behind him before turning on me like a trained interrogator.

"I swear, Carol, I have no idea why you aren't the one he's taking to the dance." At my clearly dumbfounded gaze, he adds, "Can't you see it?"

"What?" I groan. "What is it I'm not seeing?"

"You can't, can you?" Philippe studies me for a moment. "A pity, really. In my experience, everyone figures it out eventually." He turns and marches around the counter. "I hope in your case it isn't too late."

CHAPTER THIRTY-SEVEN

"So," I ask, desperate to change the subject. "Did you...find anything?"

Philippe raises an eyebrow. "Find?"

"You know. The storage unit?"

"Oh." A mischievous smile breaks across his face. "You're asking about the dress." He wanders behind the counter and slowly sifts through the receipts I just sorted.

"Well?"

"Hang on a minute. Just making certain all is ready for the day."

He goes back over everything I just did, not saying a word or even shooting me a glance to acknowledge my agony. I manage to hold my tongue until he starts straightening the twenties in the register.

"Come on, Philippe. You're killing me." I sidle up to the desk and put on the most fragile face I can muster. "Did you find me a dress or not?"

"Did I find you a dress? No."

"Oh." My shoulders slump. "That's okay. I—"

Philippe cuts me off with a quick finger to the lips, reminiscent of a certain ghost I met recently. "Did I painstakingly assemble you the loveliest dress I've seen this holiday season at the cost of a good night's sleep? Yes." Stroking his chin, he again checks his watch. "We still have a few minutes before any customers should arrive." He tilts his head to one side and grins. "Unless, of course, you have any more early morning patrons heading our way that you haven't told me about."

"He came a half hour early. Sorry about that."

"Sorry?" Philippe laughs. "Truth be told, I was rather hoping I was interrupting something."

I shake my head. "How many times do I have to tell you and the rest of the world there's nothing going on between Christopher and me?"

Philippe lets out a long sigh. "All I can say is that the young man I just fitted was far more concerned about what *you* would think of his tuxedo than he was of his date's thoughts on the matter."

My cheeks grow a couple degrees hotter. "Poor boy has had a crush on me for years. I've done everything I can to let him down easy, but he just keeps coming."

"Maybe that should tell you something." A subtle rise in Philippe's eyebrow accompanies his not-so-subtle proclamation.

Before I can respond, Philippe heads for the door and disappears into the morning chill. I slip into the back and think about what he said. Christopher and I used to be close. The best of friends, really. But that all changed at some point. I'm not sure exactly when or why. But everything is different now.

The sound of a trunk slamming shut brings me back to the present. A moment later, Philippe steps back inside with a brown zipper bag folded across his arm.

"I'm not even going to tell you how many favors I had to call in to get this ready in time."

"Favors?"

"I may have impeccable taste and the best selection of formal wear in a hundred miles, but I am no dressmaker."

"Then who?" I ask. "How?"

"Another time, Miss Davis." He holds the brown zipper bag out to me. "Would you like to see it?"

My heart leaps in my chest. "You have to ask?"

Philippe pulls around one of the rolling hanging bars and hangs up the dress. Grasping the zipper, he turns to me and with the panache of a trained game show host, asks, "Are you ready?"

I take a breath. "Ready."

He smiles. "Close your eyes."

"Seriously?"

"A couple of friends who know their way around a sewing machine slept a total of six hours getting this right last night, which is a couple more than I got myself." Philippe's smile is tired, but insistent. "Humor me."

"Fine." My eyes slide shut, and I'm immediately aware that Philippe isn't the only one who didn't get much sleep last night. Visions of my last three evenings dance through my memories. Marnie's blood red lips. The Spirit of Christmas Past's forlorn face. The knowing glances of the Spirit of Christmas Present.

And her assurance that tonight the last Spirit will provide the answer to a question I wish I'd never asked.

"Okay," comes Philippe's thick baritone. "Open your eyes."

I blink the bad memories away as my eyes focus on a garment that less than twenty-four hours before was nothing but an idea. A scoop necked, sleeveless A-line with an empire cut, the dress's wine red chiffon stretches to the floor. Every detail is as we discussed: the beaded cap straps, the ruffle at the hem, even the trio of golden snowflakes drifting across the bodice. If Philippe had pulled the dress straight from my mind and held it before me, it couldn't have been any more perfect.

"It's beautiful," I whisper. "Can I try it on?"

"You'd better," Philippe says. "As many dresses as you've modeled for me over the years, I know your measurements like the back of my hand, but we've got about eight hours if this beauty needs alterations. Now, scoot. To the dressing room with you before the customers start pouring in."

"I don't think we're going to be—"

"Scoot."

I give Philippe a jaunty faux salute. "Yes, sir."

"One more thing." He pulls a pair of matching red leather pumps with three-inch heels adorned with satin bows on the toes from the bottom of the bag. "Don't forget the shoes."

"Philippe." Before I can stop myself, I wrap my arms around Philippe and squeeze him tight.

Clearly taken aback, it takes a couple of seconds before he hugs me back.

"Thank you," I whisper. "Thank you so much."

Any hint of his usual sardonic tone absent, he answers simply, "It was...my pleasure."

I collect myself and head for one of the three dressing rooms at the back of the store. There's still a slight nip in the air, so I make short work of my sweater and slacks and slide into the dress as quickly as possible. The chiffon is cool against my skin at first, but warms quickly around my chest and hips. I pull on the shoes and turn to look in the mirror and see one thing and one thing only in the eyes that look back.

My mother.

My beautiful, funny, brilliant, perfect mother.

I pull my arm across my eyes to wipe away the tears.

When my vision again clears, another figure has joined my

reflection in the mirror. The same height as me, if slightly hunched, the form is draped in a black cloak. The broad cowl and flowing fabric hide any clue of gender save the bony hand half hidden in the voluminous sleeve. A girl's wasted fingers caress the trio of pine cones fastened over where her heart would lie, if a dark phantom such as this can claim such a thing.

I spin around and am barely surprised to find myself alone in the changing space. I turn back to the mirror, fully expecting the form to have vanished like the three ghosts that have come before. Instead, my reflection is what has disappeared. The Spirit's form now fills the mirror, a low mist playing about the bottom of her cloak, her emaciated index finger motioning me to come closer.

Ever closer.

"The Spirit of Christmas Yet to Come, I'm guessing?"

A slight inclination of the hood is the only answer I receive.

"My apologies, Spirit." I try not to stammer. I fail miserably. "It's just...I wasn't expecting you so early in the day."

The crooked finger continues to beckon with steady insistence.

"You've come to show me the future." I know the Spirit is studying me, though her eyes remain hidden. "Things that haven't happened yet. Is that right?"

Another tilt of her dark cowl.

"But unlike your sisters, you're taking me in broad daylight."

The Spirit floats away from me and deeper into the space behind the mirror.

"You want me to follow you?" I run my fingers down the dress. "In this?"

Surrounded by the mirror reflection of the changing room, the Spirit turns to one side and points to something beyond the metal at the edge of the glass.

"What is it?" I ask. "What do you want me to see?"

No answer. Not even a movement.

I step to the mirror and touch it, or at least try. My fingers pass the surface, the glass like a sheet of warm honey. Taking a breath, I step into the mirror, and impossibly, out of the mirror at the same time. My feet come to rest in the same little changing room, but things are different. Only the emergency lights are lit, leaving the room in an eerie twilight state.

I crack the door and peer out. The digital clock hanging on the wall reveals the time and date: 10:35 p.m. on December 25th. Opening the door the rest of the way, I find the Spirit waiting for me. After letting out one terrified squeak, I follow her outstretched finger to the front of the store where the quiet sound of mumbled singing gets louder with every step. There, in a pile of crumpled dresses and tuxedos, lies Philippe in a state the likes of which I've never seen.

Unshaven and unkempt, he's nothing like the impeccably groomed businessman I've known for as long as I can remember. Dressed in the same clothes I just left him in, he stares with bloodshot eyes into the business end of a half-empty bottle of Merlot. The picture he held in my previous vision rests askew, leaning against his foot. Beside it, a picture of me with my mother and father taken just a few weeks before the crash rests far from its usual home on Philippe's desk. The spiderweb cracks of the glass indicate the frame has been thrown.

Philippe whimpers and turns up the bottle between each broken chorus of "Joy to the World," alternating between studying the picture of the young soldier and my family. Mike and Valerie filled me in a few years ago about Philippe's bad history with alcohol, but seeing it up close and personal is another matter entirely.

"*No more let sins and sorrows grow,*" he sings in a drunken baritone, "*nor thorns infest the ground.*"

"Spirit," I beg. "Get me out of here. I can't stand to see him this way."

"*He comes to make His blessings flow...*" Philippe stops long enough to take a long drink of wine and wipe his mouth on his sleeve.

"Spirit, please." I glance at her from the corner of my eye, her only answer the lone bony finger pointed at the shell of my friend lying on the ground.

"*Far as the curse is found.*" Philippe spits the word curse as if that were what it was. "*Far as the curse is found.*" The remainder of the chorus descends into half-incoherent mumbles before turning into nothing but drunken sobs.

"What did this to him?" I turn back to the Spirit, my stomach in knots. "Philippe has been sober for years."

The Spirit's hand retreats inside her cloak as she floats toward the back of the store.

"Hey," I shout after her. "I'm talking to you." I rush to catch up to the Spirit. I draw close and reach out a clawing hand to catch the edge of her cloak only to have my fingers land on the handle to the changing room door. Fully lit again, only my work clothes and boots litter the floor. I turn back to the mirror, and other than the tears coursing down my cheeks, everything appears as it did before. I turn the handle and step back out into the store.

Behind the register, Philippe stands in his usual crisply pressed shirt and slacks, no different than when I left him moments before. He glances up from behind his reader glasses, his surprised expression breaking into a grand grin.

"Dear Carol," he says, biting his lip and eyeing me—I can't believe I'm saying this—like he's seen a ghost. "Do you have any idea who you remind me of in that dress?"

"My mother." I wipe away the tears and do my best to mirror his smile. "Even I can see it."

"But even more beautiful, if that's possible." Philippe slips off his glasses and comes over to me. "Give me a spin. Like I said, I'm good, but I still want to make sure our little eleventh hour project fits you just right."

I perform a quick pirouette and come to rest facing Philippe, doing my best to mirror the exuberant grin on his face despite what the Spirit just showed me.

"Thank you, Philippe," I choke out. "It's perfect."

His nose wrinkles on one side. "Not quite." He draws close and fiddles with the cap strap at my left shoulder. "Just as I suspected. The stitching here isn't holding." He checks the other side. "Nope. Just the left."

"Will it hold?"

Philippe grabs a safety pin from a bowl by the register and pins the strap to the top of the dress. "It will now." He steps back and inspects the dress one last time. "No doubt, some of my finest work. Only had to tear apart four other dresses to put this masterpiece together."

"Four dresses? But—"

Philippe silences me with an insistent stare. "Just stay and help through the lunch hour and we'll call it even." He smiles, though the fatigue shows in the dark circles beneath his eyes.

"Philippe?"

He glances up into my face. "Yes?"

"Are you...okay?"

"Of course I am." His expression shifts from happiness to concern. "Why do you ask?"

"I don't know." I want so bad to tell him the truth. That I know about the soldier in the photo. That his past issues with alcohol appear poised to make an encore appearance. That something horrible is rolling down the hill for him that neither of us expects or comprehends. "I just worry about you sometimes, all alone at Christmas."

"I'm not alone, Carol." He laughs wearily. "I've got you, don't I?"

"I guess you do." I glance over at the store's front window and where before I saw my mother's face in my reflection, I now see only one thing.

Fear.

CHAPTER THIRTY-EIGHT

I work till one in the afternoon, looking up every time the bell rings hoping to see Roberta's quirky smile. I even shoot her a text, a text that remains unanswered.

She never comes. Not that I blame her. I wouldn't have come either.

"Philippe," I call out. "I'm heading out, all right?"

"Is it one already?" he shouts from the back.

"Quarter past. I've got to get home and get ready for the dance. Ryan's picking me up at six."

"Less than five hours to get ready?" His voice takes on the sarcastic flare that is honestly one of my favorite things about the man. "Ridiculous," he says with a laugh. "What Scrooge kept you at work so late on Christmas Eve when you had a dance to attend?"

My heart freezes in my chest at the words.

I lay the dress across the counter and go to the back where I find Philippe perusing through the last couple of dresses and tuxes that haven't been picked up yet, the purple velvet number I set aside for Roberta at the top of the bunch. With his reading glasses perched on his nose, Philippe appears every bit the studious scholar of life I know him to be. So much more than a man who owns a dress shop.

"You, sir," I give his shoulder a soft punch, "are anything but a Scrooge."

He glances up from his ledger, concern returning to his features. "My turn to ask, Carol. Are you okay? You seem quite...sentimental today."

I take a deep breath. "It's just Christmas." Uncomfortable, I let my eyes drop, unable to meet Philippe's gaze after seeing him so differently in the Spirit's vision. "Hitting me harder than usual this year."

Philippe takes my hand. "Anything I can do?"

"Actually, there is." I hold up my phone. "Call me tomorrow. It would be good to hear from you."

"You want a call from your boss on Christmas Day?"

"You're not just my boss and you know it."

Philippe adjusts his glasses and swallows. "I'll call you tomorrow afternoon." He waves me toward the door. "Now get out of here. Three people stayed up most of last night to put that dress together. You'd better show up looking resplendent or we're going to have words."

"Understood." I turn for the door and glance across my shoulder. "I'll take pictures, okay?"

"Go."

I'm barely around the corner when the doorbell rings.

And there she is.

Roberta.

An hour and a half late.

Her eyes suggest that, like everyone else in the store, she didn't sleep well last night.

"Hi." It's all I can do to look her in the eye.

"Hi," she says back. "Sorry I'm late. Tameka had a bad night."

Crap. Of course, that's it. "Sorry to hear that."

"Do you still have time to help me?"

"Actually, I was just heading out." I motion to the back. "There are quite a few dresses left in your size, but I picked out one that would look fantastic on you. Philippe has it in the back."

"Thanks." She steps toward me. "Look, Carol. I'm really sorry about—"

"Don't worry about it." I gather up my dress and head for the door.

"Carol, wait." She tries to catch my arm as I dodge around her. "You have to know I didn't mean anything last night."

"I know." I grab the doorknob. "See you tonight?"

Roberta sighs. "See you tonight."

I step out of the boutique and pull the door closed behind me. Unsure if what I'm feeling is anger, embarrassment, or something in between, I rush to the car, stow the dress in the back seat, and hop in to think. A good five minutes pass as I sit in the frigid air before I decide to bite the bullet and go back inside. I pull the handle and step back onto the asphalt only to feel an unnatural chill wash across my feet.

"Not again."

My pulse races as black fog pours from beneath the car, across my feet, and up my legs. Soon, the entire parking lot is held in its murky embrace, and I am alone.

Well, nearly alone.

Across the street, beneath the awning of the corner coffee shop, the Spirit watches me, her crooked finger bidding me join her. For a moment, I consider running, but the inky black at my feet goes in all directions as far as the eye can see.

There's no escaping what she wants to show me.

"Fine." I stroll through the dark fog, trying to keep my knees from knocking, and join the Spirit at the coffee shop entrance.

She raises her arm and points a gnarled finger at the door.

"You want me to go in there?"

The Spirit's hood shifts slightly. I peer through the glass doorway. There, in our favorite comfy chairs in the corner sit Roberta and I, a pair of mochas resting on the table between us. We're laughing like nothing has gone wrong between us.

No. It's more than that.

Watching the two of us together, it's like the last year and a half never happened. Like I never left the swim team. Never started cheering.

Never left my best friend in the rearview mirror.

"This is the future?" I ask the Spirit.

The Spirit remains perfectly still, the trio of pine cones at her chest hanging motionless, her crooked finger pointed unerringly at the door.

"Okay, okay." I grasp the cold metal of the handle and pull. Neither warmth nor cold pour from the open doorway, but rather a profound sensation of loss.

Where moments before she and I sat laughing, Roberta now sits alone. Her features aglow in the light of the Christmas tree in the corner, she looks basically the same as the girl I just left. Her face, however, is older somehow. Harder. She alternates between swiping her thumb across the face of her phone and staring catatonic at whatever images fill the small touchscreen. In a blink, the Spirit is behind her chair, her crooked finger pointing at the glowing phone.

Stepping carefully through the opaque fog that has covered the coffee shop's hardwood floors, I slip behind the chair and peer over my friend's shoulder. The image on the phone screen is anything but surprising.

Tameka, a year or so before her diagnosis, blowing out the candles at a birthday party.

Flip.

Tameka, from last Christmas, an enormous bow from one of her presents stuck in her hair, her eyes crossed and her lips pursed like some extra from *Finding Nemo*.

Flip.

Tameka and Roberta in the hospital. Roberta lies next to her sister in the hospital bed, her arms wrapped around the little girl. The oxygen tubing draped across Tameka's exhausted little face summons images of Joy from all those years ago. Roberta lingers on this one for a while, before swiping her thumb across the screen again.

Flip.

Roberta and I in our old red swim team suits, swim caps over our hair and goggles pulled up on our foreheads. Little Tameka stands between us grinning so wide I'm afraid the top half of her head might fall off.

It's at this one Roberta stops flipping pictures and starts to well up.

"You okay?" comes a voice with a bit of Southern twang.

Roberta and I both look up simultaneously to find one of the baristas staring at her.

"I'm fine," Roberta says.

"You don't look fine." The barista takes a step closer. "Anything I can do?"

"No," Roberta says. "Just sitting here remembering. It's been one hell of a year."

"Well, if there's anything I can do, just let me—"

"I said I was fine." Roberta looks up at him with cold anger in her eyes. "Don't you have some crumbs to sweep up or something?"

"Sorry." His expression quickly shifting from shock to hurt and on through to pissed off, the barista does a quick about face and retreats to the opposite corner of the café. The resolve in Roberta's face begins to melt for all of half a second before her features harden again. She rests the phone on the table and picks up her coffee, taking an occasional sip as she stares expressionless out the window.

"What the hell was that?" I shout at the Spirit. "I've never heard Roberta raise her voice to another soul, not even me when I was being a total—" And that's when it hits me.

"She's turning out just like...me." I spin to face the Spirit. "She loses her sister, just like I did, and ends up exactly the same."

Subtly, the Spirit shakes her head from side to side and again points at the phone. There, the same three faces stare back at me.

Tameka's.

Roberta's.

Mine.

"Wait." I look up from the table and find the Spirit gone and the ink-like fog returned to wherever it came from. "What does it all mean?" A blink and I'm back in my car. The keys rest in the ignition, but the engine is silent.

I grab the keys and rush back inside. "Philippe! Philippe!"

"What is it?" Philippe runs out of the back. "Carol? What are you still doing here? You left like half an hour ago."

I check my phone. It's after two. "I, um, forgot something." I look around the store. "Is Roberta still here?"

"She just left." Philippe leans against the wall. "She really liked the dress you picked out."

"But...she's gone?"

"Yes, Carol. She's gone." He strides over and rests the back of his hand on my forehead. "You sure you're feeling all right?"

"Not really, but it's nothing you can fix with a shot." An image of Philippe, lying drunk on the floor filters through my imagination. "You know, like in the doctor's office."

"You're acting very strangely." Philippe picks up the phone. "Let me call your aunt."

I grab the phone from him and rest it back in its cradle. "Valerie's very busy today and I'm headed straight home. I promised to check in with her when I get there, okay?"

Philippe studies me dubiously. "Okay."

I raise a finger. "No calls. I'm already on thin ice at home this week. Wouldn't want to get me grounded from going to the dance after all the trouble you and your friends went through, would you?"

"No calls," he says, "but I will be calling you tomorrow." His brow furrows. "As requested."

"Done." I rush for the door. "Talk to you tomorrow."

CHAPTER THIRTY-NINE

I race home and pull into the driveway just before 2:30. An hour later than planned. I hate to think of myself as that girl who takes all day to get ready for a date, but tonight, three hours and change seems like the blink of an eye.

I charge inside and head for my room. Valerie is waiting for me at the top of the stairs.

"You're a bit late. Something happen at work?" she asks. "I didn't want to bother you, but I wanted to make sure—"

"It's okay. Got held up trying to get out of the shop, but everything's fine." Strangely happy that the lies continue to roll off my tongue with ease, I head into my room and toss the garment bag onto the end of the bed before crashing into my mountain of pillows.

"You sure?" Valerie follows me into the room. "Looks to me like you've been crying."

"Didn't sleep well again last night," I grumble from the corner of my mouth not buried in pillow. "Guess it's starting to show."

"That's three nights in a row. Do you need to see the doctor? He might be able to—"

"Give me something to help me sleep?" I roll over on my back and pull my head up to glare at Valerie. "No more pills. You promised."

"You're right, you're right. No more pills. How could I forget?" Her gaze shifts to the brown zipper bag on the bed. "So," she asks, "may I see the dress?"

"Of course. In fact, I'm pretty sure you'll like it." I hang the dress from the top of the closet door and let the zipper bag fall to the floor. Valerie stares quizzically for a moment before the telltale flash of recognition.

"Holly's dress. The one she wore to her junior formal." Valerie runs into the hall only to return a moment later with the picture of my parents in hand. Holding the framed photo up before her, her eyes dart back and forth between the picture and the dress. "You know this is what she was wearing the night your father proposed, right?"

"Mom looks so beautiful in that picture. So happy."

I take the picture and study Mom's face. The pair of dimples I inherited. The flowing dark locks. The slightly crooked smile. It's like looking into a mirror.

"This dress is amazing." Valerie caresses one of the golden snowflakes along the dress's bodice and runs her fingers down the wine red fabric. "How did you possibly get something so perfect with basically a day's notice?"

"What can I say?" I pull down the dress, hold it to my chest, and spin around. "Philippe is a magician."

Valerie regards me with an amused glance. "Apparently."

"And what's that supposed to mean?"

"It's just, you actually seem happy for a change. It's a good look on you." Before I can say another word, Valerie glances at her watch. "But enough chit-chat. We've got just over three hours to get you ready for tall, dark, and broody."

My lips draw into a tight circle. "You have to be promise to be nice when he gets here."

"Oh, I'll be nice." Valerie's mouth curls into a wicked grin. "Besides, Mike's the one on shotgun duty this evening."

I feel my brows knit. "Shotgun..."

"Just joking, Carol. Boy, you *have* had a long day." Valerie heads for the door. "Now, hit the showers and I'll be up in half an hour to help you with your hair." She steps out into the hallway, careful to pull the door closed behind her, a trained reflex I've never really given much thought to till now.

My life seems to have more than its fair share of closed doors.

Time for deep thoughts later. I have a date.

My first thought as I venture into the bathroom is whether I'll ever look at a mirror the same way again. Fortunately, no dead girls, random ghosts, or dark-cloaked phantoms await me in the reflective glass.

Just a girl on the eve of her eighteenth birthday with enough bags under her eyes to pass for fifty.

Fantastic.

I slip out of my work clothes and turn the shower as hot as it will go before hopping in. I spend a few extra minutes beneath the stream of scalding water in an attempt to wash away the morning chill, both natural and otherwise. My hands are just starting to prune when I turn off the water and step out onto the cool linoleum.

No.

More than cool.

Freezing.

Instinctively, my eyes go to the mirror. There, written in the fogged glass in elegant script, three simple words demand my attention.

Don your robe.

A shiver overtakes me as an image of the emaciated finger that left me the not-so-subtle message flits across my imagination. A moment later, all warmth leaves my body as the temperature in the room plummets. The fog on the mirror turns to ice, crystallizing the steamy calligraphy. I quickly dry off, wrap my hair in the towel, and slide into the green terrycloth robe hanging on the back of the door.

"This Spirit means business," I mutter through chattering teeth as I tie the robe closed. "All right. Ready or not, here I come."

I step out onto the plush carpet of my bedroom. The room remains empty and the door closed, but someone has turned off the lights, leaving only the gray December daylight filtering between the blinds to illuminate the room. I creep to the door and flip on the overhead light and find that everything is exactly the way I left it, more or less. The covers on my bed have been straightened, and the laundry is off the floor, clearly Valerie's handiwork. But that's not the change that bothers me.

A fine layer of dust covers every stick of furniture, every framed picture, every knick-knack.

It's like no one has set foot in the room in months.

"Hello?" No answer. "Spirit?"

Not that the Spirit of Christmas Yet to Come has proven particularly talkative to this point, but the eerie quiet, not to mention the freezing temperature, has every inch of me in goosebumps.

"Come on," I shout. "Show me. What do you want me to do?"

Silence reigns. No air running through the vents. No blaring TV from downstairs. No wind whistling through the gutters by my window. Just silence. And then, I hear it. A scratching at my bedroom door. A lone fingernail on hollow wood.

Pulling the damp terrycloth close about me, I go to the door and grasp the doorknob. Neither cold nor hot, the metal turns easily in my hand, though the hinges creak as I pull the door open.

As if the door hasn't been opened in a while.

Finding the hallway empty, I sneak down to Mike and Valerie's bedroom only to find no one there. The same with Mike's home office across the hall.

"When is this, Spirit?" When I get no answer, I step into the office and take a look at the *Wall Street Journal* resting on Mike's desk. Dated exactly one year from now, it lies askew as if thrown there in passing.

"Well, that answers that."

I creep down the stairs, feeling almost like an intruder in a stranger's home. The main floor is dark except for the fluorescent light streaming from the kitchen. Half afraid of what I might find, I wander up the short hallway and find Valerie and Mike eating silently, he a bowl of oatmeal and she a cup of yogurt. Each in their own little world, they barely acknowledge each other. Valerie looks up from her breakfast every few seconds to check on him but doesn't say a word.

After what seems an eternity of this apparent game of who can ignore the other longest, Mike is the one who finally breaks the silence.

"What?" He doesn't even look up from his steaming bowl of oatmeal.

"Hmm?" Valerie glances over at him, as if she hadn't noticed him till that moment.

"You keep looking over at me," Mike says. "If you've got something to say, just say it."

Valerie takes a deep breath, gathering the courage to speak. I would know. It's something I've seen her do a thousand times when getting ready to talk to me.

"It's Christmas morning," she finally says. "Are we really just going to sit here and not talk to each other?" She pauses a moment before adding, "Again?"

"Of course not." Mike puts down the paper. "What do you want to talk about?"

Valerie sighs, her gaze falling to the floor. "Look. I put up the tree, the lights, the whole shebang. I thought this was what you wanted."

Mike simmers for a moment, a teapot about to whistle. Or maybe explode.

"What I want," he says through gritted teeth, "is to have my wife back." He drops the spoon into the bowl and storms into the living room. Valerie rubs at the bridge of her nose before eventually following him into the darkness beyond the doorway.

"Stop it, Spirit." I search the room for any hint of my mysterious tour guide. "If I wanted to see Mike and Valerie fight about me for the hundredth time, I wouldn't be moving out."

That's when it hits me.

"Ah, I get it. This is what happens if I move out next week. You're hoping a big, fat guilt trip will get me to change my mind and stay with my loving aunt and uncle."

No response.

"Look." My arms cross my chest almost of their own accord. "I've got a dance tonight and about three hours to get myself perfect before the hottest guy in school shows up on my doorstep."

Still nothing.

"And you couldn't care less." I take a step toward the hall. "Well, if all you've got to show me is Mike and Valerie having another snit, I'll be upstairs in my room."

I step through the doorway leading back to the stairs and my room only to find the Spirit waiting for me, her gnarled finger pointing in the direction of the living room.

"Why is it so important I see this?" I grumble.

The Spirit doesn't move an inch. Regardless, the insistence of her silent demand hits me like a flying brick.

"Whatever," I grumble. "You're the boss."

I stride past the silent phantom, recoiling when my elbow brushes her shadowy cloak. It's odd. I held tight to each of the other two Spirits without so much as a second thought, but just the notion of touching the dark shroud that hides my future makes my heart do somersaults.

As I step into the living room, I find Valerie on all fours, the cord for the Christmas tree lights in her hand. She jams the plug into the wall socket and then stands and brushes the shed pine needles from her knees.

"There," she says. "Tree's lit. Presents are wrapped. Everything's perfect."

"This?" Mike actually rolls his eyes. "This is perfect?"

"Ten years, Mike. Ten years of 'Why can't I have Christmas?' Ten years of 'Why can't things be the way they were before.' Well, Mike. Here it is. Just like before. Just the two of us. No Carol. And you've finally got your Christmas tree."

"*My* Christmas tree." Mike runs a shaking hand along his scalp. "Come on, Val. You know I don't care about any of this." He takes a cautious step toward her. "None of it. Not if I don't have you."

Valerie crosses her arms and looks away, her lips drawing down to a thin fine line. "What was the one thing I asked for last Christmas?"

"Valerie..."

"When everything was going to hell. What was it?"

Mike looks away. "To take it easy on Carol."

"You knew better than anyone how much she was hurting. How vulnerable she truly was."

"So, we've finally come to this." Mike's jaw muscles tense.

"It's my fault she's gone. That's what you want to say, isn't it? What you want me to say?"

"No." Valerie's eyes fasten on a picture of the three of us hanging on the opposite wall. "But things could've been different."

"You know what? That's it. You can say what you want, but I took that girl in when she needed a home, and all I ever heard from either of you was how nothing I ever did was enough."

"Mike—"

"No. I'm not done. Carol's been gone for a year now. I've done everything I can think of to rebuild our lives and make it all better, and I still can't do anything right." Mike heads back for the kitchen with Valerie hot on his heels and me bringing up the rear. He fishes his keys out of the basket by the microwave and heads for the door.

"Where are you going?" Valerie shouts after him.

"Out." The door slams. Valerie collapses into one of the stools around the island.

"So, my moving out causes problems. I get it." I glance back one last time at Valerie, now sitting up straight in her chair and staring blankly out the window, before joining the Spirit in the hall. "But what's the big deal? I've seen them fight worse than that half a dozen times when I was still living there."

The Spirit's cowl shifts to one side as her skeletal hand rises from the darkness of her robes and points to the stairs.

"What now?"

Nothing. No answer.

"Something else for me to see? One more dropkick to the gut before we head back?"

Silence. Finger. Stairs.

"All right, all right. I can take a hint."

I cruise up the stairs, barely surprised to find the Spirit awaiting me at the top, directing me back to my room.

"Back where we started, huh?" I follow her direction, closing the door behind me, and sit on the bed. The Spirit doesn't joint me.

"Where now?" I wait for an answer. An appearance. Anything. "Spirit?"

I pace the room waiting for something—anything—to happen, all the while trying to figure out how my aunt, who is so particular about her house she might as well open up a Molly Maid franchise, can possibly stand knowing there's so much dust in here, even if it's a room she never goes in anymore.

"Spirit?"

I check every corner of the room.

"Spirit?"

I walk over to the dresser where my favorite picture of Mom, Dad, Joy, and me rests. I wipe the fine layer of residue from the glass and study the picture. It's of the four of us at the beach the summer before the crash. Dad's got just the beginning of a belly and is trying to suck it in. Mom is, well, as gorgeous as she is in every picture I've ever seen. And there stands Joy, covered in wet sand from the neck down. And me in a similar state, smiling to beat the band. We'd begged Dad to bury us up to our chins, and after a lot of groaning and moaning, he'd done it. It seemed like the most important thing in the world at the time, and this picture is one of the few I have of that trip. Our last big trip together.

No matter where I went, no way I would have left it here.

A chill passes through me like an electric shock. I fumble with the frame, nearly dropping it to the floor.

I glance up, and the Spirit stands before me, her gnarled finger pointing at the picture.

"I don't get it, Spirit." I look down at the photo held in my trembling fingers. "If I moved out a year ago, why is all my stuff still here?"

The Spirit remains still, her withered hand stroking the trio of pine cones hanging at her chest for what seems like hours before pointing across my shoulder.

"The window?" I ask. "Is there something outside you want me to see?"

I step to the window and pull up the blinds. There's no rain or snow. Just hard frozen ground and nothing else to speak of. Valerie's garden has died back, but that's pretty standard for winter around here. All the yard and lawn equipment is put away. Not a thing is out of place. I haven't the first clue what the Spirit is getting at.

"Spirit, I—" Before I can get out another syllable, a snowbird flies full tilt into the glass. The impact is so loud, my hands fly up to protect my face.

"Carol?"

Valerie's voice. Insistent. Worried. And a little annoyed.

I open my eyes and look out on the same dreary day from which the Spirit of Christmas Yet to Come has taken me three times now. In a room no longer laden with dust, my clothes lay once again strewn across the floor and I stand by the window in my robe and towel. Though the Spirit has once again vanished, my heart still pounds, the image of the bird's body smacking into the glass replaying in my mind on what seems an endless loop.

"Carol?" A touch of annoyance creeps into Valerie's tone.

"What?" I shout, my vocal cords threatening to rebel.

"It's almost four. You've been in there for over an hour. I've got other things to do today, so if you want my help with your hair, it's now or never, understand?"

Now or never.

"Understand?" she asks again.

"I'm not sure," I mutter as an all too familiar chill creeps up my spine, "but I think I'm beginning to."

CHAPTER FORTY

"Ow," I grunt as Valerie tags my ear with the flat iron. "Watch it."

"Sorry." Valerie soaks a washcloth in cold water and presses it to my earlobe. "I'm having to hurry a bit."

"It's okay." I bite my lip, choosing my words carefully. "It's my fault you're having to rush, anyway."

Valerie and I lock eyes in the mirror, surprise blossoming on her face. She tries to pawn it off with a quick, "Who are you and what have you done with my niece?" but I know all too well what that look means.

She expected me to bite her head off.

Hell. So did I.

"So," Valerie says, "Ryan is picking you up around six, and it's almost 4:45. Just enough time for makeup and last-minute preparations before your knight in shining armor pulls up at the castle gate."

"Ugh. Can you keep the metaphors to yourself? It's just a date."

"You know, it's okay to get excited every once in a while, Carol. A cute boy has asked you out. He's coming to pick you up in a big, shiny sports car. You're wearing the prettiest dress I've seen this year. Honestly, I don't know how you're keeping it together."

My eyes drift closed. "I've got a lot on my mind."

Valerie's face shifts into Mom mode. "Well, since we're on serious topics, let's talk about rules for tonight."

Great. Here we go. "Shoot."

"First, I want you in by one o'clock."

"One?" I try to keep my voice even and calm, but I have trouble keeping the indignation out. "You're kidding, right?"

"Party only lasts till eleven, sweetie. I think an hour or so at the after party is more than enough."

"After party?"

One of Valerie's eyebrows disappears behind her bangs. "Never forget, it wasn't that many years ago that I was the one going to this little shindig. And yes, even back in the Stone Age, the Christmas Eve after party was the event of the year." She glances down at the floor. "Tell you what. How about 1:30?"

That's...perfectly reasonable.

"I suppose." I stare at her in the mirror, lips pursed as she continues to work at my hair with the flat iron. "What else?"

"No alcohol," she whispers. "And no getting in a car with anyone who's been drinking. Nonnegotiable, got it?"

"Come on, Valerie. You know I don't touch that stuff."

"That doesn't change the fact that there will be alcohol at that party." She does her best to busy herself getting the last bit of curl out of my hair, but I know she's avoiding my eyes. "I guess I'd like to know you'd thought about what you'd say before someone asks."

"Have you ever thought about writing for afterschool specials? You'd be fantastic."

"Snark away, young lady. I've been in your shoes before, and I haven't always made the smartest decisions."

I shoot her my wickedest grin. "So... I should do as you say and not as you do?"

"You should listen to someone who has navigated shark-infested waters and come out the other side with ten fingers and ten toes."

"I'm guessing I know Rule #3 then."

Valerie shrugs. "Mr. King may be a legend on the basketball court, but if he's thinking of going for a home run his first time at bat tonight, I hope you're ready."

"Don't worry." Now it's me who can't look Valerie in the eye. "Ryan's not that kind of guy."

Valerie doesn't say anything for a moment. I wonder briefly how much she actually knows about Ryan King, particularly regarding prom last year. It takes half a second to decide it's in my best interest to just let it drop, that is if I want to continue to have plans for the evening. In the end, all she adds to the discussion is, "I just want you to be careful."

"Don't worry." I rise from the chair, my hair about as perfect as it's going to get. "Home by 1:30, no booze, keep my clothes on. Got it." I turn and catch Valerie blotting a tear from the corner of her eye. "Anything else?"

She pulls me into a bear hug and whispers in my ear, "Have a great time."

Unbidden, a specter in black flits across my mind's eye. Silent as the night. Her unseen eyes studying my every moment from beneath her voluminous hood. Her emaciated finger pointing at me from within her dark shroud.

Always pointing.

"I wouldn't worry about that either." I return Valerie's hug and hope she doesn't feel me tremble against her. "I have a feeling tonight's going to be one memorable evening."

CHAPTER FORTY-ONE

The doorbell echoes through the house, and despite my ghostly interruption, I'm actually ready on time. I know better than to think I'll get out of the house without Valerie snapping a picture or two, so I wait on the corner of my bed and let her answer the door. A lone piece of Marnie's litany of advice on boys runs through my head.

Either they're waiting on you or you're waiting on them, Care Bear. You pick.

Mike had to run some errand right around the time the rain picked back up, so it's just me and Valerie in the house. I've seen how Mike deals with boys who come nosing around, so I'm kind of glad he's not here. Valerie's little shotgun comment before wasn't quite a joke.

"Carol?" Valerie's quiet voice sounds from beyond the door. "Ryan is here."

I pop open the door. "His tux. It's not powder blue, is it?"

She grins. "You'll just have to come downstairs and see, now won't you?"

"Tell him I'll be right down."

As Valerie heads back down the hall, I turn and look at myself in the mirror one last time.

Hair, makeup, dress: all perfect.

And more importantly, the only face looking back from the glass is me.

Still, something isn't right.

The chain at my neck. One of my favorites, Marnie and I picked it out for me to wear to the Christmas Eve Dance last year. Obviously, that didn't happen, so I thought I'd wear it this year instead. A silver chain terminating on a crystal icicle, I'm suddenly not liking it. The color of the metal just doesn't match the golden snowflakes on my dress.

I dig through the mahogany jewelry box that once belonged to my mother. Necklace after necklace, a multi-stranded collar of faux pearls, a lace choker, a long string of costume jewelry. Nothing seems quite right.

Then I come to it. The carefully folded tissue resting at the bottom of the box.

I pull the tissue from its felt cocoon and reveal the necklace Christopher gave me all those years ago. Letting the thin gold chain drape across my fingers, I lay the garnet charm at my left collarbone.

"Perfect."

Well, almost perfect. After all, Christopher is going to be there. What would he think if—

"Carol?" comes Valerie's voice from below. "Is everything all right?"

I crack the door, and with as pleasant a lilt as I can manage, call out, "I'll be right down."

Fastening the necklace behind my neck, I gather the clutch Valerie let me borrow for the evening, drape the wrap Philippe gave me around my arms, and head for the stairs. Funny. I've never cared much for heels, but between Marnie's insistence on me embracing my more fashionable side and Valerie's endless encouragement, I've mastered the stupid ankle breakers. Still, the rain hitting the roof sounds like someone needs to build an ark, and I find myself wishing for my favorite pair of boots instead.

I'm halfway down the stairs when I catch my first glimpse of Ryan. His shoes, jet black, are shined to perfection. Each step reveals a bit more. Carefully pressed pants. Black jacket. Wine red waistcoat to match my dress. Matching tie. And finally, his face. A subtle smile and amused eyes beneath hair styled so perfectly, the boy could have just stepped off a magazine cover.

"Hi." Ryan raises a hand, his eyes flicking from me to Valerie and back.

"Hi, yourself." I somehow make it to the bottom of the stairs without becoming an avalanche of wine red chiffon and glide over to Ryan. First Christmas Eve disaster averted. "Not quite what I was expecting, but I must say, I like the red." I take his tie between my fingers and thumb. "But I don't remember telling you about my dress. How did you...do this?"

"Got a call yesterday." He shoots me a wink. "Something about how powder blue probably wasn't the right choice for the evening after all."

I glance at Valerie.

"Don't look at me," she says with a grin. "I just work here."

"But if it wasn't you..."

It takes just a moment.

Philippe.

"Hm." I hold back a laugh. "Looks like I owe a little bird somewhere a favor."

"And while we're on the subject of your dress," Ryan says, keeping his gaze at a respectable height, "you look *fantastic*."

Hearing my pet word used for once without even a hint of

irony brings a strange heat to my cheeks. Fortunately, Valerie chooses that moment to step in.

"All right, you two. You know the drill. Get together so I can get your picture." She grabs her phone and fiddles with it a few seconds before resting it back on the table. "On second thought, let me get the big camera. I want this to look good."

As Valerie exits, I turn to Ryan. "Wow. On time, dressed to the nines, perfect hair. If I didn't know better, I'd say you were trying to impress someone."

"Hey, I'm taking the prettiest girl in school to the dance. Just wanted to make sure I measured up."

"Oh, you measure up all right."

Ryan certainly fills out a tuxedo. My cheeks go a couple degrees hotter and I'm struggling to come up with something clever to say when Valerie steps back into the room. She peers at me for a second, no doubt puzzled by the fact my face now matches my dress, before holding up her camera.

"Smile, you two," she says. "This is one for the books."

As she snaps the shot, I hear a key in the door. A moment later, Mike steps into the room, dripping wet with a couple grocery bags in each arm. He does a quick survey of the room, his eyes pausing on me as if he's run into an old friend in an unexpected place.

"You're right, Val." Staring at me, he takes a step closer, his face filled with wonder. "It's uncanny."

"I told you," Valerie says with a big smile.

"Told him what?" Ryan asks.

"My mom had a dress just like this when she was in college." I pass my hands down the bodice of my dress. "Want to know what my mom looked like back in the day? You're looking at her."

"And Ms. Fredericks," Ryan says to Valerie. "Carol's mom was your sister?"

"That's right." Valerie's eyes go to the floor. "Just me and Holly growing up."

"Well, I can definitely see where Carol gets those pretty eyes of hers."

And it's Valerie's turn to blush. "Flattery will get you everywhere, Mr. King."

"Not everywhere," Mike adds as he extends a hand to Ryan. "Mike Fredericks."

"Ryan King." Ryan gives Mike's hand a firm shake. "Good to meet you."

"You take good care of my niece tonight," Mike says. "She's all we've got."

A quiet groan escapes my lips. "Really?"

Mike glances over at me with a subtle half-smile. "Just setting the ground rules." He turns back to Ryan. "You'll have her home by one?"

"Carol and I already went over all the rules." Valerie steps up and takes Mike's arm. "And I told her 1:30."

Mike's eyes shift to Valerie's fingers at his wrist, then back to Ryan. "Fine. 1:30. And not a second later."

"Not a problem, Mr. Fredericks." Ryan gives Mike his winningest smile. "I'll have her back before curfew."

"Good." Mike turns to me. "As for you, young lady..."

"Valerie just told you," I whisper harshly. "We already went over everything, okay?"

Mike pauses for a moment, wounded, before finally saying, "I was just going to say have an awesome time." He gives me a quick half hug to keep me from getting wet. "Okay?"

"You too, Uncle Mike." I remember what the Spirit of Christmas Present showed me about tonight. About how Mike and Valerie celebrate Christmas when it's just the two of them. "We'll be back by 1:30." I hit him with a barrage of fluttering eyelashes and barely suppress a smile as I pull away. "And not a second before."

"Stay warm out there." His brow furrowed in a confused stare, Mike heads for the stairs, turning back only to say, "And be safe on the roads tonight. The rain's not supposed to let up till morning."

Valerie rummages through the hall closet and pulls out our giant blue and white golf umbrella. "Take this, Ryan." She motions to his compact umbrella lying in a puddle at the door. "Don't think that one's going to cut it tonight."

"Thanks, Ms. Fredericks." Ryan takes the tent-sized umbrella and offers me his arm. "Shall we?"

I pull my wrap tight around me and slip my fingers into the crook of Ryan's elbow. Looking up into his placid blue eyes, I allow myself a grin, even as a sure realization falls across my thoughts like a cool shadow.

A certain Spirit, her face too terrible to behold, is far from through with me.

CHAPTER FORTY-TWO

"I never would have pegged you as a sushi guy."

Ryan looks up from his menu. "Till this week, we haven't said much more than two words to each other." His lips part in that devil-may-care smile that melts me every time. "I'm betting there's a lot you don't know about me."

I glance toward the rear of the dining area where the restroom sign glows a muted amber. "Like what?"

"I don't know." Ryan thinks for a second. "I play a little guitar when I'm bored."

I raise an eyebrow. "Are you good?"

"I took lessons when I was a kid, but I mostly just strum a few tunes when I need a break from homework." He smiles. "Mom hasn't thrown it out, so I guess that's a good sign."

"You'll have to play me a song some time." I lean across the table. "What else? Favorite movie?"

Ryan laughs. "I like a good action flick as well as the next guy, but I guess my favorite has always been *A Few Good Men*. Me and Dad always watch it anytime it comes on TV."

A Few Good Men? Be still my heart. "A classic."

The waiter drops by the shrimp dumplings, we ordered and

Ryan spears one with a lone chopstick. "You?" he asks, before devouring the dumpling in one bite.

My eyes drop to my lap. "You'll laugh."

"Try me."

"Promise you won't run?"

He raises his right hand and places his left on the menu. "So help me, oh god of raw fish."

"Okay." A quiet giggle bubbles up from deep inside. "I don't usually admit it, but I love *Sixteen Candles. Pretty in Pink,* too. And *The Breakfast Club*." Again, I glance in the direction of the restrooms. "Brat pack all the way."

"The awesome eighties." Ryan laughs, but not in the way I expected. "Looks like we were both born a generation late."

"I don't know." My lips encircle my straw and I take a slow sip of water. "At the moment, I'd like to think we're both right on time."

Before Ryan can respond, the waiter comes to take our order. Ryan orders a couple things I've never heard of while I order my usual standby, the spicy tuna roll and a small order of shrimp tempura.

As the waiter heads off toward the kitchen, I snag a dumpling and wash it down with a gulp of cool H_2O. In response, my stomach rumbles to life. I had no idea how hungry I was and debate calling the waiter back to order another roll.

"So," I ask, "what's *unagi*?"

Ryan chuckles. "You really want to know?"

"I just ordered a plate of raw fish wrapped in seaweed." I fold my arms together and lean across the table. "I think I can take it."

"Okay." Ryan leans back in his chair. "It's eel."

"Eel." I try to keep any reaction from my face, but Ryan picks up on the faint crinkle of my nose.

"Believe it or not, it tastes just like chicken."

"Maybe we can trade a bite. I'm always up for trying something new."

Ryan catches my eye, a mischievous look behind those baby blues of his, and the hair on my neck stands on end.

"Will do." He devours another dumpling. "Just do yourself a favor and don't look up how they make eel sauce."

"Noted." I look around. "So, I kind of figured we'd be doing some kind of group thing. Weren't the rest of your buddies all hitting the Italian place two blocks over?"

"That was the plan, but I heard you liked this place."

"I do, or did, I guess..." Marnie and I used to come here all the time, but it's been over a year since I set foot inside. "Who told you?"

"Same little bird that told me red was your color."

"Ah. My fairy godfather strikes again."

An image of a photograph I've never actually seen with my own eyes flashes across my memory. A handsome soldier who, no doubt, carried the biggest secret of his life right up to the day he died.

Fairy godfather.

Note to self. Never say those words again.

Still, nice to have a little *Cinderella* mixed in with my week of Dickens.

I glance around the place. The restaurant is pretty full for Christmas Eve. Mostly adults, there is only one other couple I recognize from school. Some guy from the academic team in a hand-me-down suit and his date—I think she's in my AP History class—wearing a midnight-blue velvet dress that used to hang in the window at the boutique. Her name is Debbie? Denise? Something like that.

"You didn't want to hang out with your friends?" I ask.

"We'll see them all later." Ryan's eyes shift left and right. "There's a method to my madness anyway."

"Oh, really?"

"Confession?" Ryan takes deep breath. "I heard there was someone going with the big group you're not particularly fond of."

"Ah." I bite my lip. Hard. "Wonder who that could be."

Truth be told, there's not a doubt in my mind. It's got to be Jamie Meadows, my favorite social climber pain in the ass. This once, however, she may have done me a solid. A big group date would have been fun, but for two hours, I've got Ryan King all to myself. On a real live, old school, one-on-one date.

Have to remember to send her a thank you note.

"So." My eyes drift once more to the back of the restaurant. "What are you thinking?"

"I was about to ask you the same thing." Ryan's eyes shoot in the direction of the restrooms. "You keep looking back there. Everything okay?"

"Everything's fine." Other than the fact I have to pee so bad, I'm starting to squirm. After the week I've had, the thought of entering that restroom alone terrifies me, but another few minutes and the decision is going to be taken out of my hands.

Seriously, do none of the women in this place need to at least wash their hands?

"So," Ryan asks, "what are you and your aunt and uncle doing for Christmas tomorrow?"

"What?" I ask, jolted back to the present.

"Tomorrow. Christmas. It's your birthday, right?"

"Oh. Don't know exactly. We'll probably do a little dinner at the house. Valerie usually cooks all day." My chest grows tight. "Sometimes she'll even cook me something a respectable carnivore can eat."

Ryan's brows knit together. "No party?"

And here comes the explaining. "That's the problem with

having a birthday on December 25th. Most people usually have other plans."

"So, just you and them, then?"

"Roberta usually swings by at some point in the afternoon, though I'm not counting on seeing her this year."

Ryan's lips quirk to the right. "She's coming tonight, right?"

The tightness in my lungs ratchets up another notch. "As far as I know."

"What about Christmas?" Ryan leans across the table. "I didn't even see a tree up at your house."

My eyes slip closed. "You can't be the only person in town who doesn't know."

"About what happened to your family?" Ryan answers without missing a beat. "Of course I know." He leans in. "Still, Christmas is...Christmas."

"Maybe in your world. To me, December 25th is nothing but an annual sucker punch to the gut and a reminder of how quickly you can lose everything you love."

In a surprisingly tender move, Ryan reaches across the table and takes my hand. "Sorry. Didn't mean to upset you." He squeezes my fingers gently, and I let him...for all of two seconds.

"Excuse me," I mutter, pulling my fingers free and rising from the booth. "I need to go wash up before our food arrives."

"Okay." Ryan's hand retracts as if I slapped his knuckles with a ruler. "See you in a minute."

"Be right back." I spin on my heels and head for the bathroom, trying to decide which is tying my intestines more in knots, the shrouded Spirit likely waiting beyond the door or the hurt flashing in Ryan King's electric blue eyes.

I step into the ladies' room and take care of business, expecting all the while to get whisked right out of the stall by my friend in black, and then head for the sink to wash up. The warm water feels good, washing away my anxiety even as it cleanses my hands, that is until I glance up and catch my reflection in the mirror. Ryan hasn't said a word, but even after both my and Valerie's best efforts, it's obvious at a glance I haven't slept in days. The bags under my eyes, the drawn face, the trembling lip—they all tell a story. The hair, makeup, and dress may create a pretty facade, but I know the truth.

What lies beneath.

But that's not what's really bothering me.

"What the hell is wrong with you?" I ask my haggard reflection. "He was just trying to be nice."

And you ran.

Like you always do.

"Stupid, stupid, stupid." I fan my face for a moment and then rest both palms on the cold stone countertop.

"Hi, Ryan," I mutter, letting my voice lilt like some valley girl in one of my eighties high school flicks. "In case you're wondering, yes. You're out with a complete psycho that hates Christmas, the holiday the rest of the world loves and waits for all year long." Might as well tell him I hate babies and puppies while I'm at it. Wouldn't want him to have any second thoughts about running screaming from the restaurant.

I check myself over in the mirror one last time, half-surprised to find no one but me looking back from the glass, and head back for the dining area. Above the door, a framed piece of traditional Japanese art depicts two women conversing on a low couch, one in a bright red kimono, the other in black, her face hidden. My heart racing, I rush for the door and yank the handle.

It won't open.

And this door doesn't have a lock.

I pull on the handle with all my strength.

Nothing.

"Help," I shout. "Let me out of here."

No response.

"What now, Spirit?" My eyes dart left and right. "Show yourself."

Still nothing.

"Look. I'm right in the middle of the biggest date of my life. Do we have to do this now?"

Silence.

"Please." I step back from the door. "Just open the door."

A heartbeat passes, then another, before the Japanese characters in the painting swirl into letters far more familiar.

Very well.

As if pushed by unseen hands, the door opens, though what lies beyond is anything but the quiet restaurant I left minutes before.

CHAPTER FORTY-THREE

The echoing thunder of applause fills my ears as I step out onto the concourse of some ginormous arena. I'm reminded of the time Mike and Valerie dragged me two states away to see U2 a couple years back. People everywhere wait in lines for bathrooms, beverages, snacks. The smell of buttered popcorn and beer fills the air. Somewhere, an ear-shattering buzzer sounds and the crowd goes quiet. At that moment, a man and his two middle school boys hurry by, all of them wearing Miami Heat t-shirts and ball caps, the younger sporting one of those big foam fingers proclaiming, "Heat #1."

"A basketball game? Seriously?"

I follow the man and his boys, scooting past the green-jacketed ticket checkers and down to an open seat not too far from the floor. Looks like Spurs vs. Heat, one of my favorite match ups. I may not be an expert when it comes to the NBA, but I've logged enough hours on the couch beside Mike Fredericks to know who I like and who I don't.

It's the end of a timeout, and the Spurs cheerleaders fill the court. Dressed in sexy Santa uniforms and knee-high black boots, they're rocking out to a techno dance mix of "Jingle Bell

Rock" and kicking it. The choreography isn't all that different from routines I've done a thousand times, and I search for my own face among the squad. It isn't me, however, that I've been brought to see.

As the Spurs take the court, Ryan King heads for the top of the key and waits for the buzzer to sound. A good ten years older and even more muscular than the high school senior I just left sitting at our booth, he strides the hardwood floor of the arena like he owns the place.

The buzzer shatters my eardrums as the last few seconds of the first half begin to tick away. The Heat inbounds and makes it just past half court before Ryan leaps in with a steal and sprints for the opposite end. The buzzer goes off as Ryan's layup ties the game at fifty-two points. Both teams exit the court while the Heat cheerleaders hit the floor and start the halftime show.

"So, Ryan King ends up going pro." I glance around as half the crowd heads for the main concourse. "Not a big shocker there."

A blink and I'm standing in the aisle of the first-class section of a plane. Through the dim light, I can just discriminate the impressive outlines of professional athlete after professional athlete. Most of the players are either dead to the world or fighting sleep, but not Ryan. He sits in his posh seat on the aisle, barely blinking, staring straight ahead. He doesn't read, check out the movie, or even put his seat back. He just...stares.

I pull closer and notice the phone in his hand, the subtle glow lighting up his tired face. As if on cue, he glances down at the screen and begins to flip through his hundreds of contacts. Most of the names female, no two area codes are the same. I half expect a smile or at least a twinkle in his eye as he passes through more than his fair share of Megans and Melissas, but Ryan's only reaction as he hits the second half of the alphabet is a single, exhausted sigh. Once finished with his

A to Z review, he puts his phone to sleep and attempts to do the same.

Another blink and I'm standing at the window of a swank apartment at least thirty floors above ground level. Urban sprawl extends in every direction, and the Tower of the Americas sits in all its glory just a few blocks away. Though five or six years have passed since Valerie and Mike dragged me along on their trip to Texas, I still remember the Alamo and visiting the Tower like it was yesterday.

I turn to find Ryan reclined on a couch while some young blonde wearing a skirt that barely qualifies as a napkin nibbles on his ear like a gerbil at its water bottle. Ryan's hands on her body are all passion, but his distant eyes tell another story altogether. I'm guessing she senses it too as a moment later she lays off his ear and flips a leg across his lap. As she moves to pull her postage stamp of a dress over her head, I step into the next room.

Regardless of the lesson I'm supposed to learn tonight, I'm not watching that.

Another blink and I'm in Ryan's bedroom, the space lit by the flickering glow of the silenced big-screen TV on the far wall. The blonde lets out a quiet snore every couple of seconds, her barely covered body curled into a ball just below the king-size headboard, while Ryan's six-foot-seven form lies stretched out beneath the covers. Propped up on more pillows than we have in our whole house, he stares at the screen as an infomercial advertising an exercise machine he doesn't need plays across the screen. He reaches for the girl's shoulder, her chest rising and falling with each raspy breath, but his fingers stop short. Quietly, he steals from the bed and stands in his boxers by the enormous plate glass window overlooking the city. Clearly at the height of his career, with muscles carved by some Renaissance sculptor and, no doubt, a woman in every city, a lone emotion emanates from the high and mighty Ryan King.

"Sadness." I walk over to him, pulling so close I could stand on my toes and kiss him if I were actually standing in the room. "Why is he so down? Looks to me like he has everything."

I sense her before I see her. A haze at the edge of my consciousness. A chill that comes from deep inside and radiates from every pore. I turn, and as expected, find the Spirit of Christmas Yet to Come standing over the girl's sleeping form, her arms spread wide as if she is offering to embrace. Slowly, deliberately, her cachectic hand motions to the girl and the cascade of her blond hair spilling across the pillow. The enormous TV that takes up the better part of the wall. The shelf of trophies placed above the bed.

"So... Ryan King ends up a bazillionaire with supermodels climbing into his bed." My hands go to my hips. "I've got news for you. If this is your way of warning me off, you're doing a pretty crappy job. Good looking, successful, and rich. That's pretty much the trifecta."

The Spirit stands impassive, her fingers caressing the lowest of the three pine cones at her chest. I feel her concealed eyes on me and wonder again what horrible face she hides behind that hood.

"I don't get it, though."

Ryan leans against the window, his well-muscled forearm serving as a cushion between the cold glass and his forehead.

"He's got it all and yet he seems so unhappy. What am I missing?"

Another blink and the Spirit and I are standing roadside. Cars rush past and I step away instinctively, though I know at some level the Spirit's power would allow me to skip across all four lanes of traffic without a scratch. One thing is clear: we're back home from our little jaunt to Texas. Across the street, the parking lot of a familiar steakhouse lies all but empty. The one on the southeast end of town that Mike likes to hit when Valerie is away, it's right across the street from...

"Not funny." Refusing to grace the Spirit with so much as a glance, I turn on one heel to confirm what I already know. My dress brushes the front wheel well of the BMW Z4 Roadster I've been lusting after the last few months. A Melbourne Red convertible with all the bells and whistles, I've already test driven the car twice.

Grace, the only female salesperson on the lot, has my number on speed dial.

"Money can't buy happiness, huh?" I lean both fists on the hood of the beautiful vehicle. "Pretty cliché, don't you think?"

I'm not sure if I'm imagining things, but I'd almost swear the Spirit shrugs.

"I'm Scrooge, the old miser. That's what you're trying to tell me?"

The slight inclination of the Spirit's dark hood does little to answer my question.

"But there's a difference. Scrooge was coming up on the end of his time, while I've got my whole life ahead of me, not to mention three million dollars dropping in my lap in two days. It's not too late to turn things around, is it?"

The Spirit turns and begins to glide away.

"It can be better than this." My voice drops to a mutter. "I can be better than this."

The Spirit stops. I try to take a step in her direction and find my feet frozen to the spot. The Spirit's gnarled hand appears from within her robe. Her bony finger, pointing at the ground, begins to twirl and like a marionette on a string, I begin to spin.

"Stop it." Her finger goes faster, as do my feet. "Stop it!"

Faster and faster I go, my stomach lurching like I'm about to lose my lunch. I clench my eyes shut to try to hold on. Then, just when I can't take another second, everything stops.

And a toilet flushes.

I open my eyes and find myself back in the bathroom at the sushi restaurant. A quick glance in the mirror reveals everything is fine. Hair, makeup, dress, all as flawless as when I left the house.

Except the twin trails of tears meandering down my face.

"You okay?" My head jerks to the left where Debbie/Denise from AP History is coming out of one of the stalls. "Carol, right?"

I grab a paper towel and dab at my cheeks. "I'm fine."

"You're crying."

A ball of ice forms in my gut. "Leave me alone."

"But you're—"

"I said, 'Leave me alone.' What? Are you deaf or something?"

"Okay, okay. Geez." She quickly washes her hands and heads for the door. "Just trying to help."

As the door closes behind her and I find myself again alone, I recall the old adage about biting the hand that feeds you.

Valerie. Mike. Christopher. Philippe. Roberta. Ryan.

And pretty much anyone else who crosses my path.

If I keep this up, I'm going to starve.

CHAPTER FORTY-FOUR

I take a moment to collect myself and head out into the restaurant. Debbie/Denise avoids my eyes as I make my way to my seat, which is probably for the best. Ryan sits with his back to me, our table covered with several plates of beautifully prepared sushi. Our bowl of dumplings rests empty, which isn't surprising. I forgot to check the clock on my phone before leaving the ladies' room, but I've got a good idea I've been gone a while.

I rest a hand on Ryan's shoulder. "Hi."

He looks up at me and suppresses a chuckle. "I was about to send a search party."

"Sorry. Had a girl thing," I blurt out before I can stop myself. "Didn't mean to take so long."

"It's all right." He waves a hand across the table at our assortment of *maki* rolls. "Not like sushi can get cold, right?"

I slide into the booth opposite Ryan and pick up my chopsticks without another word. My fingers still trembling, I attempt to grab a piece of sushi only to have the hunk of tuna and rice flip out of my grasp. Soy sauce and wasabi go everywhere and my only saving grace is that neither my dress nor Ryan's tux takes a hit.

"You're shaking." Ryan's eyes narrow. "Are you cold?"

"No."

He raises an eyebrow. "Nervous?"

"Maybe." Just the question serves to calm me. At least a little. "Rumor has it I'm out on a date with Ryan King."

"Ha." He looks down at his plate. "You know, I read an article that said in Japan people eat sushi with their fingers as much as they do with chopsticks."

"You read an article on sushi?"

"What's so surprising about that?"

"Not surprising. Impressive."

"Oh, really?" He takes a gulp of Coke. "In that case, I'm just getting started."

Over the next twenty minutes, we demolish three plates of *maki* and a couple additional orders of tempura before we're done. I'd planned to eat light tonight, knowing how much the rice in the rolls fills me up, but my little trip with the Spirit left me ravenous. I keep the conversation light, occasionally ribbing Ryan about this or that, but steer clear of any discussion of previous girlfriends and the like. Some things, I just don't want to know. Quip for quip, he keeps up with me, and by the end of dinner, I'm even more impressed than before.

He plays defense across a table of sushi almost as well as he does on the basketball court.

"Ready?" He hands me my wrap and then drops a generous tip on the table before sliding into his jacket. "It's only 7:30. Anything you want to do before we head to the dance?"

I consider for all of two seconds. "Can we swing by the boutique for a minute?"

"Where you work?" Ryan scratches his chin. "It's Christmas Eve. They're closed, right?"

"I think Philippe was planning on putting in some extra hours tonight." I stare pitifully into Ryan's electric blue eyes and channel my inner puppy dog. "Please? I'd love for him to see me all dressed up in the dress he put together for me." I slip my hand into the crook of Ryan's arm. "Not to mention I'd be walking in on the arm of the best-looking guy in school."

Ryan leans in and gives me a peck, his lips like warm velvet on my cheek, and whispers, "Well, when you put it that way..."

It's just a few minutes to the shop. Draped across my shoulders, Ryan's coat keeps me warm until the car heater kicks in. My little wrap is all right, but I find myself wishing I had my fleece.

And my boots.

And an enormous bonfire to stand by.

We pull into the shopping center parking lot, the whole place dead as eight o'clock Christmas Eve approaches and the downpour hits monsoon level. All the stores are dark, including Philippe's, but as we pull up out front, I can just make out a faint fluorescent glow coming through the glass. Ryan pulls in as close to the curb as possible before rushing around with Valerie's king-sized umbrella to let me out of the car. I somehow stay relatively dry despite the deluge, and in seconds, we're at the door. Remembering what the Spirit of Christmas Present showed me, I'm cautious as I unlock the door, half afraid of what I might find.

"Philippe?" The store dark except the light coming from the back, I quietly step inside with Ryan close behind. "Philippe? Are you here? It's Carol."

I hear a shuffling in the back. A moment later, a familiar silhouette pops around the corner.

"Carol?" comes Phillipe's voice. "You scared the Dickens out of me. What are you doing here?"

Dickens? Really?

"I could ask you the same thing, mister."

"I do own the place." Philippe flips on the store lights and steps up to the counter. "I can pretty much come and go as I please." His eyes shift past me. "The legendary Mr. King, I assume?"

"In the flesh." I can all but hear Ryan's smile. "And you must be Philippe. Carol can't stop talking about you."

Philippe's hand goes to his chest, his fingertips splayed across his heart. "I would certainly hope you two had more interesting things to discuss than me. I'm a good boss, but work is work."

Without another word, I circle the counter and give Philippe a hug, gladder than I could have imagined to find him sober and well.

"Now, Carol," Philippe says, "you're going to make me blush."

Ryan shakes Philippe's hand. "Carol was hoping you'd be here. She wanted you to see the final product."

Philippe gives me a quick up and down, his scrunched expression melting into a sentimental smile. "You look radiant, my dear. Even more beautiful than I imagined, though it's colder out tonight than the weatherman called for. Are you sure you're going to be warm enough out there?"

"Ryan let me borrow his jacket." I shoot Philippe a devious grin. "Plus, I seem to remember someone telling me once that couture beats comfortable every time."

Philippe puffs up his chest as if offended. "The rest of the world can catch their death tonight for all I care, but my little Carol? No."

"I'll be fine." I raise my hands before me, a bit embarrassed. "Ryan and I will be inside most of the night. Not to mention we've got an umbrella the size of Cleveland to keep us dry."

Philippe studies me for a moment before his gaze shifts back to Ryan. "You'll keep her safe tonight, Mr. King?"

Ryan steps up behind me. "Yes, sir."

"And warm?"

"Of course."

Philippe's eyes flip back to me, his eyebrow raised. "Not too warm, my dear."

Ryan's hand goes to his neck, his cheeks glowing a subtle crimson. "Don't worry, sir. I'll take very good care of Carol tonight."

"Yes, he will." If my eyes could shoot laser beams, nothing would be left of Philippe but a smoking pile of ashes. "Anything else?"

"Just one thing." Philippe stoops behind the counter and rummages through a couple drawers before reappearing with an old 35mm camera in his hands. "Do you two have time for a picture?"

CHAPTER FORTY-FIVE

Ryan pulls his car up to the civic center's main entrance and lets me out beneath the marquee. A violent shiver overtakes me as his Camaro disappears around the corner of the building. Though the tuxedo coat across my shoulders is more than enough to shield me from the wind and the rain, the weather isn't the only thing behind the chill working its way up my spine. I catch a glimpse of myself in the polished glass of the door and immediately steal around to the other side of the large column holding up the marquee.

No way I'm standing next to anything resembling a mirror till Ryan gets back.

A couple minutes later, he rejoins me at the door, the bottom of his pants and his shoes wet despite the umbrella. Draping an arm across my shoulders, Ryan pulls me into his chest.

"You didn't go inside?"

"What can I say?" I look up past his dimpled chin into those crystal blue eyes. "I'm tougher than I look."

Ryan holds open the door and we step into the carpeted

hall. The sound of music echoing through the corridor stops me in my tracks until I realize that Ryan can hear it, too.

Apparently, I got myself so worked up I forgot I was at a dance.

I return Ryan's coat and pull my wrap around me before we make our grand entrance. At the door, my math teacher from junior year is collecting tickets. A bit on the forty and frumpy side, she's dressed in a pair of mom jeans and one of those Christmas sweaters you don't believe actually exist until you see one in real life. I don't believe it at first, but there in the center of her chest, Rudolph's nose is blinking.

Honest to God blinking.

As we get closer, she catches my gaze and any friendliness in her face evaporates.

Surprise, surprise, we didn't exactly get along.

"Ms. Davis," she says with an appraising eye as we make the front of the line. "Mr. King."

"Mrs. Morrison." Ryan hands her the tickets, and she promptly tears them in half. "You look lovely this evening."

"Charmer." She gives Ryan an exhausted smile. "Any trouble getting here this evening?"

"The roads are still okay," Ryan says. "The temperature's dropping, but it's still mostly rain."

"And that's not stopping anytime soon." Mrs. Morrison glances up at the ceiling where the downpour pounds the roof like thousands of tiny feet. "More rain than any December on the books in the last fifty years."

Ryan nods. "When I saw the forecast a couple days ago, I was half-convinced they might cancel the whole thing."

"It was close, actually." Mrs. Morrison checks her watch. "It seems the powers that be really didn't want to cancel the dance two years running. Anyway, from what I understand, the temperature's not supposed to drop below freezing till some time tomorrow."

"Wow." I cross my arms. "Someone's been watching the Weather Channel."

Without batting an eye, Mrs. Morrison turns a withering glare on me. "While you, Ms. Davis, seem to be content keeping up with the Kardashians."

Clearly sensing both our claws coming out, Ryan steps between us and offers me his arm. "Shall we?"

"Of course." Ryan pulls me past Morrison, her presence forgotten a moment later as we step through the door and into a veritable winter wonderland.

It's my first time seeing the civic center all decorated up for the holidays. Couples from East and West Havisham fill the crowded room. As Ryan and I make our way through the sea of bodies, I recognize faces from both schools, some from my time on the cheerleading squad and others from my days on the swim team. The dance floor is packed as the speakers blare, "All I Want for Christmas is You."

Eight-foot trees decked out in Christmas lights and decorations fill the corners of the room, no doubt to keep all the students out in the middle where the teachers and administrators can keep an eye out for any "inappropriate" activities. In a bold move, however, a single sprig of mistletoe hangs at the center of the room beneath a beaming spotlight. In fact, as I look on, a couple takes full advantage of their moment at the center of the universe and don't come up for air for a good thirty seconds.

Everywhere you look, beautiful dresses and well-pressed suits. Trees clothed in light and ribbon. Wreaths hung with care. The mistletoe, dangling just out of reach like the ephemeral love it represents.

The whole thing is beautiful.

I hate it.

"Let's grab some seats." Ryan motions to a cluster of tables at the far end of the room where electric candles blink inside plastic wreath centerpieces. Coats and wraps occupy most of the empty seats, but a couple unoccupied chairs remain at the last table at the back. Ryan directs me over and pulls out my chair before heading for the refreshment table. I keep my eyes on him the entire time he's gone, hoping that just having him in my line of sight will prevent any further ghostly encroachments on my evening.

"Great." A strangely familiar voice grabs my attention. "You have got to be kidding me."

I turn and find a girl in a teal dress sitting at the next table, her sandy blond hair in a fancy updo.

"You don't even remember who I am, do you?" she asks at my purposefully blank expression.

Make no mistake. I know exactly who she is.

"Emily, right?"

"I swear." The red in her cheeks fills the spaces between her freckles, and her snarling grimace sparkles from the steel braces on her teeth. "First the rain, and now you at the next table?" Her head drops as she mutters, "I can't catch a break tonight."

She's about to disengage when a skinny boy in a matching blue vest and tie arrives at the table. "Hey, Em. Who's your friend?"

Emily shoots up from the table. "She's no friend of mine." She takes the boy's arm. "Come on, Jimmy. Let's dance." She turns and pulls him toward the dance floor.

And that's when I see it.

The teal dress from the boutique, every bit of two years out of date, is held up by spaghetti straps, or in this case, spaghetti *strap*. The one trailing across her right shoulder has torn loose in the back and is hanging on by no more than a couple of threads.

As Emily and Jimmy step onto the parquet wood of the dance floor, a techno beat fills the room. All but hypnotic, the crowd begins to jump in time with the song, and a cold certainty hits me. Though she may be relatively plain Jane from the neck up, Emily Stockton is anything but small-chested. My mind plays the situation out to its logical conclusion. Everything points to the poor girl having a wardrobe malfunction of the worst kind. Right there in front of pretty much every junior and senior in the county.

Good. Serves her right for getting me in trouble at the shop.

I lean back in my chair and wait for the show to start.

In an instant, the music shifts. The techno beat continues, but the DJ begins to mix in another tune.

A far too familiar tune.

The resounding tones of "Carol of the Bells," syncopated in time with the dance beat blaring from the speakers, bring the strange events of the last three days back into focus. Transported back an hour or so to the moment when Emily first showed her father the dress, I'm buffeted again by the cruelty of his words and the memory of Emily Stockton's tears. The spell is so powerful, I wonder if the DJ is, in fact, the one responsible for the tune.

My cheeks afire with conviction, I shoot out of my chair and rush to the dance floor, catching Emily's elbow before she can so much as give her groove thing the first shake.

"Come with me," I whisper in her ear.

She spins around, her eyes rolling when she realizes whose hand is clutching her arm.

"Let go of me," she grunts, "or I swear to God I'll knock you on your ass."

Jimmy pulls in close so he can be heard over the music. "Everything okay?"

"Stay out of this," Emily and I respond in unison.

"Fine," Jimmy mutters as he steps back, hands raised. "You two work it out."

Emily pulls her arm free and glares at me. "What do you want, Carol?"

"Trust me," I whisper, just loud enough to be heard above the music. "You want to hear what I have to say."

"What?" She pulls close to my ear. "That I look like crap in my dress? How sad it is that my family's too poor to afford any better? How pathetic I look standing next to you all Cinderella'd up in your pretty snowflake gown?"

At that moment, Ryan returns with a cup of pink liquid in each hand. "Hey. Got us some punch."

"Hang on to it." Praying she won't bite my hand off at the wrist, I grab Emily just below her shoulder and pull her from the dance floor. "Emily and I have some business in the ladies' room."

"Let me go." Emily pulls us to a stop and tries to jerk free from my hand again, but this time my grip holds firm.

"Look, Emily. I'll make you a deal." I pull close so only the two of us can hear. "Give me five minutes, and I swear to God I won't so much as look at you the rest of the night. Got it?"

Her lips form a straight line as she considers my words. "Five minutes."

I take her hand and lead her through the tables, heading straight for the ladies' room, hoping all the while that Philippe's stitching will hold. Once inside, she turns on me, her voice a whisper no longer.

"What the hell, Davis? Do you hate me or something?"

"Wait a minute, Emily. I'm just trying to—"

"No, *you* wait a minute. First, you piss all over me at the dress shop and make me feel like a piece of trash. Now you're doing your best to ruin my big night with Jimmy. I don't know where you get off being such a colossal bitch, but—"

My hand shoots out and smacks Emily square across the jaw before I even know what's happening. In the three seconds that follow, I half expect her to open up on me like a rabid orangutan. Instead, she simply glares at me, sullen and quiet.

Like the eerie calm just before a tornado takes down your house.

"You. Hit. Me."

"You were being a pain in the ass." My arms fold across my belly. "Trust me. On that front, I know what I'm talking about."

"What do you want?" she asks, seething.

"As hard as it is to believe, I'm trying to help you."

"You—Carol Davis—are trying to help me?"

"Look." I let out a quiet sigh. "I'm sorry for what I said at the shop. I was a total bitch, and I have no doubt I'm number one on the list of people you'd like to see dropped out of an airplane without a parachute."

"Maybe." Her head tilts to one side. "All right. I'm listening."

"Good." I pull in a deep breath. "Because no matter how much you hate my guts, if you don't let me fix the strap on your dress, you're going to be pulling a full-on Janet Jackson before the end of the night."

"Strap?" Momentarily defused, the unbridled anger in Emily's eyes shifts to confusion. "What are you talking about?"

"Your right spaghetti strap. It's hanging on by just a couple of threads." I circle her. "Hmm. Make that *thread*."

Her brow furrows in disbelief. "You're actually trying to do me a favor?"

"Look. I don't know what you and Jimmy have planned for later, but I have a feeling you'd prefer your dress to stay on at least till you get back to the car, right?"

She steps over to the sink and turns to check out her back in the mirror. "Shit. That thing is about to pop." She looks over at me. "Can you fix it?"

"I can try." If I just had a needle and thread, it would take all of a couple minutes to fix her up. God knows I've done my fair share of dress repairs over the last few months. "I just don't have anything with me to..."

Wait. I almost forgot.

"All right." I fiddle with my left shoulder strap and find what I'm looking for. "Come here."

"What've you got?"

"My left cap strap wasn't quite stitched right. Philippe put in a safety pin to make sure it would hold."

"And?" she asks.

"And..." I suck air through my teeth. "I want you to take it out so I can use it to fix your dress."

She stares at me dumbfounded. "But wouldn't that put you in exactly the same shape as me?"

"This strap will hold, and even if it doesn't, the other one should be more than enough to keep me covered." I motion to her ample chest and my comparatively modest upper body. "One of us is clearly a little better endowed than the other. We should probably concentrate our resources with you, don't you think?"

Her face a mask of utter disbelief, she peers at me from beneath furrowed eyebrows. "Why are you doing this?"

"Contrary to what you may believe, I'm not a completely horrible person." I peel up the strap to expose the steel safety pin. "More importantly, though, something tells me you've already taken more than your fair share of hits this week." I turn my left shoulder toward her. "Can we leave it at that?"

Emily doesn't say another word. She steps close to me and gingerly pulls the safety pin from the bodice of my dress. Handing it to me, she silently turns and lets me go to work. I tie a double knot in the end of the offending spaghetti strap and work the safety pin under the back of her dress to where it's barely visible. Not a repair that will last the ages, but it'll get her through the night.

"Is it fixed?"

"Done." I give the strap a couple tugs to let her know it's secure and give her a quick pat on the back. "And we're back to beautiful. All right. Jimmy's out there and ready to dance. Go get him, Emily Stockton."

She turns, dabbing at one eye with a loosened fist. "Thank you, Carol."

"No problem." I shoot her a quick salute. "All part of the excellent service at Philippe's Boutique."

She leaves the ladies' room without so much as a glance back, leaving me all alone, a state I've been dreading since Ryan and I left the restaurant earlier.

"All right, Spirit. I'm all alone. Come and get me."

I do a full lap of the space, inspecting the mirror, peeking under the sinks and checking every stall.

No one in here but me.

I am truly and completely alone.

And nothing is happening.

"What? All I had to do was fix that girl's dress and it's all good?" I step to the sink and peer at myself in the mirror, my face red with exasperation. "I don't believe that for a second."

Before I can take another breath, an invisible finger begins to write on the glass. A deep magenta, the letters run like blood from an open cut. Like the previous memo, the ghostly message is short and to the point, though this one is far more cryptic. The three words fill me with dread, and even worse, a certainty.

You must choose.

CHAPTER FORTY-SIX

"O. M. G." The high nasal voice, coupled with the creak of the bathroom door, raises the hair on my neck. "Did you see what Clarissa was wearing?"

"Slut alert, right?" A deeper voice, still feminine. "And that guy she's with..."

I jerk my head around and find two girls from East stumbling into the bathroom. The girl in pink gives me a quick smirk before heading to the other end of the counter with her friend in tow.

One thing's for certain: they've both been drinking something besides the punch.

Wait.

The writing on the glass.

Can't let them see.

I yank a wad of paper towels from the dispenser beside me and turn back to the mirror to wipe away the bloody letters only to find the glass clear.

Somehow, this still surprises me.

I get out of the bathroom as quick as my heels will take me. The two girls watch me out of the corner of their eyes like I should be in a straightjacket and carted away. I have no doubt who the target of their next OMG will be, but I really couldn't care less. I'm on a date with the best-looking guy in school, and for the first time since I woke up this morning, the Spirit has left me to my own devices.

I head back for the dance floor, eager to nuzzle back up to Ryan. Rushing between the tables as if the Devil is hot on my heels, I slow to a gentle glide when I start to catch some stares. Everybody already thinks I'm a bitch. Don't want them to think I'm crazy to boot.

Or worse, desperate.

I arrive back at our corner of the dance floor after narrowly avoiding two different encounters of the "Are you *the* Carol Davis?" type—at this point I can see it in their eyes—and scan the floor for Ryan. In the sea of tuxedos and taffeta, it's hard to make out anyone in particular, but at six-foot-seven, Ryan usually stands out in a crowd. It takes less than a minute to realize I'm looking in the wrong place. I'm his date, and while Ryan may not make valedictorian, I suspect he's smart enough to know the first dance is mine.

I skirt the parquet floor as an up-tempo dance song fades into a slow number and head for our table.

As I expected, it's not difficult at all to pick out Ryan King in a room.

What is difficult, however, is finding him with someone else.

For the second time this week, it seems Jamie Meadows has taken it upon herself to fill a vacancy left by yours truly. She's standing by my chair, her face far too close to Ryan's for my tastes. Chatting him up, she's all smiles in a little black dress cut both too low and too high for anything approaching respectability. And the worst part? He's responding to her. I stand frozen to the spot as Ryan listens to her every word and laughs at her jokes, unable to move a muscle or make a sound.

That is, till she touches his arm.

I'm by Ryan's side so quick, not even the Spirits could have gotten me there faster.

"Hello, Jamie." I rest a hand at Ryan's waist. "Where's your date? Surely you're not here by yourself."

Jamie shoots me a practiced smile. "Quentin Ridge asked me a couple weeks back and we were all set to come, but he's down with the flu as of Thursday. I already had the dress and a ticket, so I figured I'd come on out." She looks up at Ryan. "I just got here a few minutes ago and saw poor Ryan standing in the corner all alone. Figured I'd keep him company till you got finished taking care of whatever situation you had going on in the ladies' room."

"Thank you, Jamie." The nails of my free hand dig into my palm. "There was a bit of an emergency."

"That girl." Ryan looks on as if he's not sure if he's watching a conversation or a boxing match. "Is she okay?"

"Emily? She's fine." I lock gazes with Jamie. "Nothing I couldn't handle." I give Ryan's hip a gentle squeeze. "So, what were you two talking about?"

"Nothing big," Jamie intercepts before Ryan can say a word. "I was just seeing what you and Ryan had planned for later. They close this thing down around ten so everyone can go home and get ready for Santa Claus, but the main event is already kicking up at Benjamin Allen's lake house." She glances at Ryan. "Should be a good time."

Right up there with the wealthiest people in town, the Allen lake house was the site for the party two years ago as well when Benjamin's older brother was a senior. Last year's, of course, didn't end up going down after our homecoming queen was found floating dead in her own hot tub, but like most inconvenient tragedies, Marnie's death has been swept under the rug and all but forgotten.

The show must go on, right?

"Sounds good." I pull Jamie's attention back to me. "We'll try to make an appearance."

"Maybe we'll see you there," Ryan adds.

Jamie's smile grows wider. "Maybe you will."

The room lights up bright as midday as lightning strikes somewhere near the civic center. Two seconds pass and the inevitable peal of thunder shakes the entire building. I bury myself in Ryan's side.

"You okay?" he asks.

"Sorry." I extract my shoulder from his ribcage. "The lightning startled me."

Ryan stares up at the nearest skylight where the rain continues to pound. "Don't remember the last time I heard thunder in December."

Jamie cocks her head to one side and runs her top incisors over her bottom lip. "Grandma always said that thunder in winter means snow is on the way."

"Really?" I'm unable to keep the exasperation from my face any longer. "And what did she tell you about the optimal number of people on a date?"

"Sorry, Carol." Her gaze shifts to Ryan. "Three *is* a crowd." She peers past my shoulder as the DJ cranks up another tune. "Let's see if any of these boys want to dance." She strides away without a backward glance, barely making it ten steps before half the defensive line descends on her like a swarm of locusts.

Not much doubt as to who wants to be the next heir apparent to Marnie's crown at West Havisham High.

"Carol?"

Crap. Keep your eye on the prize, Carol.

"Yes, Ryan?"

He crooks his arm and smiles. "Care to dance?"

I flash Ryan a knowing look and take his arm. "Lead on, Mr. King."

We hit the dance floor just as the DJ shifts to a hip-hop song that was big back in the summer. In fact, I helped choreograph the squad's routine to this particular number. My hips start to move to the familiar beat, and Ryan pulls in close. I'm not sure what scent he's wearing, but it's clean and sharp and tickles my nose. Not to mention, the boy's got moves. Nothing as impressive as what he brings on the basketball court, but moves nonetheless. Our frequent bumps and brushes against each other bring heat to my face, and as the first song fades into the second, those chiseled cheekbones of his take on a healthy sheen.

"Ryan?" I half-shout into his ear as I run the back of my hand down his jawbone.

"Yeah?"

"The after party." I pull in closer. "You want to go, right?"

"Of course." He pulls back so I can see his smile. "We don't have to have you home till 1:30, right?"

"That's right. An hour and a half into my birthday, for what it's worth."

And with that, Ryan slips into the look I've seen ten thousand times. The "don't mention her dead parents" look.

Somehow, I keep myself from groaning and slip into a practiced smile of my own.

"It's okay, Ryan. Everybody knows what December 25th means to me. Not my favorite day of the year, but don't worry. I'll be all right."

And I will be.

After all, I've had ten years' practice.

"You know, we don't have to go to the party if you don't want to."

"Oh, we're going to the party." I take Ryan's hands in mine

and give them a gentle squeeze. "Tomorrow's a big day for me, and tonight we are going to celebrate."

So, here I am at the ball in a dress straight out of *Cinderella* and dancing with the closest thing to Prince Charming West Havisham High is likely to see for a while.

A fairy tale come true.

And all I can think about is one simple question...

What's coming for me at midnight?

CHAPTER FORTY-SEVEN

The next two hours are a blur of lights and sound, dancing and whispers, and even a little kissing beneath the spotlight at the center of the room.

Hey, mistletoe is mistletoe. It's the rules.

"You thirsty?" Ryan looks down at me, his skin aglow with a fine layer of sweat. "I'm going to grab a drink."

"Sure." I give his hand a gentle squeeze. "Thanks."

As Ryan makes his way across the crowded dance floor, I step to the edge of the mob and scan the crowd for the hundredth time tonight. Still no Roberta. Or Christopher, for that matter. I tell myself I just want to see how Roberta looks in her dress, but the truth of the matter is, I'm desperate to run into one person tonight besides Ryan who's genuinely glad to see me. Sure, there've been plenty of smiles and compliments exchanged with everyone in our crowd at school, but most have seemed more interested in talking to Ryan.

But even that's not quite it. People keeping a healthy distance has pretty much been the status quo since Marnie Jacobsen took me under her wing a year and a half ago.

So what *is* bothering me? I can't quite put my finger on it. Then, in a flash, it comes to me.

For the first time in a very long time, I care.

"Earth to Carol." The voice breaks me out of my reverie. "Come in, Carol."

I look up to find Christopher and Roberta all decked out in their formal duds and looking great. As expected, Roberta is a knockout in the purple velvet number I picked out for her while Christopher, surprisingly, fills out a tuxedo pretty well.

"Sorry, Roberta. I was somewhere else for a sec." I step in and give her the obligatory hug. "You look...great."

"And you look gorgeous." Roberta gives me the full up and down. "Mr. Delacroix told me he put something special together for you, but...wow. That dress is something."

"He did a great job." The nervousness behind Christopher's half-mumbled words is punctuated by his inability to meet my eyes. "You look really pretty in red, Carol."

"Thanks, Christopher." I adjust the lapel on his coat where a single white rose rests pinned to the black satin. "You look pretty sharp yourself."

Just a hint of color invades his cheeks as our gazes meet for half a second. "Thanks."

I turn back to Roberta. "I thought you guys were never going to get here."

She shakes her head. "Tonight's not going quite as planned. Christopher picked me up at seven, and we had planned to swing by the hospital for just a minute before heading this way. Tameka wanted to see me all dressed up."

I pull in a deep breath. "She okay?"

"She is now." Roberta rubs at her temple. "Poor thing spiked a temperature just before we arrived. They wouldn't let us back to see her for over half an hour, and when we finally were cleared to go back, she was all drenched in sweat and as weak as

I've seen her. It didn't feel right just taking off, so we stuck around and talked with her until Mom booted us out of there."

I let out a quiet laugh. "Your mom is hell-bent on you coming to this dance."

"You've been nothing but supportive of your little sister." Christopher rests a hand on Roberta's shoulder. And not nearly as awkwardly as I would expect. "Even you deserve a night off."

Roberta nods. "I suppose."

"Hey," Christopher says. "Before I forget, you wanted me to get a picture of you and Carol in your dresses." He fishes his phone out of his pocket. "Want to grab the picture now?"

Roberta puts her arm around my shoulder and pulls me tight. "The two hottest chicks at the dance, right?"

"Sure."

Not sure I could sound more noncommittal if I tried.

"All right." Christopher takes a moment to frame the shot. "Say 'fettuccine.'" He snaps our picture and starts to put his phone away.

"Not so fast, Kellerman." Roberta grabs his phone and motions for the two of us to get together. Christopher's cheeks flush as he steps toward me and drapes a cautious arm across my shoulders, almost like he's afraid to touch me.

"Come on, Christopher," Roberta says. "Carol doesn't have tuberculosis. Now, put your arm around her like you mean it."

Christopher lets out an audible sigh and allows his hand to trail down to my waist. Not sure what to do with my own hands, I fold them before me and try to keep any awkwardness from my expression.

"Now, you two. Give me a smile." She snaps half a dozen photos before handing Christopher back his phone. "See? That wasn't so bad."

"Sorry about that," Christopher mutters in my ear. "She's been kind of an unstoppable force all evening."

"Don't worry." I give his shoulder a light punch. "I've been caught up in Hurricane Roberta once or twice myself."

Without missing a beat, Roberta checks the clock on the far wall. "And now, Mr. Kellerman, it looks like there's still an hour or so before they turn out the lights." She takes Christopher's hand. "Care to spin me around while they're still playing something worth dancing to?"

"Sure." I catch the embarrassed glance Christopher sends my way. "See you around, Carol."

"Wait." I catch Roberta's arm. "You two going to the Allen place out at the lake later?"

"Ben's throwing the after party this year?" Roberta asks, chuckling. "I hadn't heard, but it figures."

"After party?" Christopher asks.

"We'll be there." Roberta grabs Christopher's arm. "And don't worry, Christopher. You show up with me, you're in. Ben and I go way back."

"Really?" I raise an eyebrow. "I didn't know you and Benjamin Allen were tight."

"You're not the only one with secrets, Carol." Roberta's hand goes to her lips as if she were wishing the words back into her mouth. Her eyes meet mine and flash with something between sadness and pity. "There's a brand new year around the corner. We'll catch up then." She turns back to Christopher. "But for now, it's time to step up, Kellerman. I've got fifty-eight minutes before they close this place down, and I came to dance."

As Roberta leads Christopher away, Ryan shows back up with drinks in hand.

"Miss me?" He hands me a glass of punch. "Here. Try this."

"Thanks." I take a sip, the cool liquid stinging my throat like I just took a slug of rubbing alcohol. "Wow," I ask, coughing. "What's in there?"

"Just a little shot of vodka. Might burn a little going down, but it'll feel good later." He pats at the breast of his coat. "Thought you might want a little more punch in your punch."

"I appreciate the thought, but I promised Valerie I wouldn't drink tonight."

"You do know that everyone at the party will be getting their drink on, right?"

"Not everyone." I hand him back the glass. "Can you get me another one? And just punch this time?"

Ryan peers at me quizzically for a moment, as if I'm speaking a foreign language.

"Sure." He takes the glass and heads back across the floor toward the refreshments table.

As he disappears behind the gyrating crowd on the dance floor, I catch sight of a few familiar faces. In one corner, I spot Emily, her arms around Jimmy's neck, the two of them oblivious to anyone else in the room. In the opposite corner, Jamie Meadows is grinding against one of our varsity linemen who I'm relatively sure was with a date earlier. And there, in the middle of it all, Christopher and Roberta, swaying in time with the music.

Talking. Joking. Laughing.

And here I stand alone.

"Not as alone as you might think, Care Bear."

Marnie's voice. Whispered in my ear. From directly behind me.

I spin around, expecting to see a drowned girl's dead lips grinning at me. Instead, the Spirit of Christmas Yet to Come stands there, her bony hand pointing at the center of my chest from beneath her voluminous cloak.

"No—"

Before I can utter another sound, she sweeps me into a cold embrace, and in an instant, we are somewhere else.

CHAPTER FORTY-EIGHT

A cubicle.

In a sea of cubicles.

A glowing computer monitor faces an empty chair, the error message at the center of the screen mocking in its gray insistence. Next to the keyboard rests a tear-off calendar showing a date of December 24th above a picture of some cartoon character I don't recognize seated on Santa's lap.

A December 24th nineteen years from the day I just left behind.

I inspect the pictures decorating the corner of the desk for any clue as to why I'm here or whose cubicle this might be. A middle-aged black woman seems to be the common element in all the photos, with various friends and family making guest appearances in the many locales pictured in this framed montage of her life.

A tropical beach with water like liquid turquoise. The Grand Canyon beneath a golden, cloudless sky at sunset. The Martin Luther King Memorial with her entire clan surrounding her.

Clearly someone who's lived a full life.

Funny thing? I have no idea who she is.

To my left in a space that was vacant a second ago, the Spirit of Christmas Yet to Come stands—or floats—immobile and silent. Sheathed within her mysterious shroud, not even her emaciated hand gives me the first indication of where we are or, more importantly, why we're here.

"The woman in the photographs," I ask. "Who is she?"

The Spirit raises her arm and extends her pale finger at the frozen screen.

"This is her computer, I'm guessing." I instinctively reach for the mouse, but my hand stops short. Something isn't right. I turn to the Spirit and bring myself nose to nose with her. Or at least where I think her nose ought to be. "It's not her I'm here for, is it?"

The Spirit doesn't move. Not a millimeter.

"Everything I've been shown. The shadows of my past, present, and future. They've all been people I've known, at their most private and intimate moments." I pass a hand over the collection of pictures. "I've never seen this woman before in my life."

I step out of the cubicle and scan the enormous room. The place is deserted, and if the clock on the wall is to be trusted, it's 9:03 in the morning. If I am to believe it's truly Christmas morning in this place the Spirit has brought me to, then this woman with her perfect family and perfect life won't be showing her face here today.

"There's someone else I'm here to see, isn't there?" I cross my arms and blow a stray strand of hair from my face. "Well, bring them on already. I haven't got all night."

The Spirit pauses at my words, extending her arm to the side as if beckoning a third to join our little party. Answering her silent summons, the click of a door echoes through the maze of cubicles, followed by quick footsteps that sound like they're headed our way. I start to duck under the desk till I remember how I came to be here, not to mention the company I'm keeping. Pulling myself up from the floor, I step to the rear of the cubicle and lean against the wall.

I'm not kept waiting long.

Rounding the corner in a faded t-shirt and jeans that have seen better days, a Christopher Kellerman that won't exist for a good twenty years steps past me and flops down in the mystery woman's swivel chair. The man before me is anything but the optimistic, awkward teenager I just spoke to at the dance. Carrying at least thirty extra pounds, he hasn't shaved in a couple days, and I get the feeling the scruff is less style than sloth. His shoes are the scuffed sneakers of a man who's given up trying to impress anyone. He looks older than he should, but it's not the strands of silver that highlight his temples nor the fine wrinkles around his face that age him beyond his years.

It's his eyes.

Even on Christopher Kellerman's worst day, a certain intelligence is always at play behind those green irises, a boundless energy that can't be extinguished by the mental exhaustion of an all-nighter, the taunts of bullies, or even the sometimes cruel remarks of an unrequited crush.

Compared to the boy I know, this man's eyes are as dead as Marnie Jacobsen's.

"Nora, Nora, Nora," he moans. "How many times do I have to tell you? Reboot your computer every couple of decades." He grasps the mouse, pulls up a menu at the bottom left corner of the screen, and restarts the system. The computer goes through a complete cycle, only to arrive at the same error message.

"Fantastic." Christopher cracks his knuckles and goes to work, his fingers flying over the keyboard as he attempts to undo whatever damage this "Nora" has left for him, undoubtedly an unwelcome Christmas gift. And that's when I see it. A detail I can't believe I missed before.

Christopher's platinum wedding band.

"Wait." I peel my eyes from this strange vision of my friend and peer at the Spirit, trying to discern any emotion from her hooded face. "If today is Christmas, what is Christopher doing at work? Shouldn't he be home with—I don't know—his family?"

The Spirit's finger trails downward and points at Christopher's front pocket, which sounds immediately with the first few bars of one of his favorite songs.

Funny, of all the worn-out rock anthems left over from the seventies that Christopher ever introduced me to, this was one of the few I'd let him play when I came over.

I always did like what Jimmy Page did with a classical guitar.

Christopher retrieves his phone, checks the screen, and answers. I get to hear one side of the terse conversation.

"Hey."

"Yeah."

"Um, I'm guessing a little after lunch."

"I know. It's just...today's the only day when no one is here and I can actually fix all the stuff they've—"

"Yeah. I know. I'm sorry."

"I know."

"I know."

"I know."

"Love you, too. See you around one."

Christopher ends the call and has the phone slid halfway back into his pocket before he pulls it back out and stares at the screen. He presses an icon that looks like a miniature camera and flips through hundreds of thumbnail photos until he comes to a picture that seems very familiar, though I know for a fact I've never seen it before.

The picture shows a tuxedo-clad Christopher standing by my side, his hand awkwardly resting at my hip, and me wearing the same red dress that currently hangs off my trembling form, my hands crossed just below my waist. Both of us are smiling, but neither of us looks particularly comfortable in the moment.

And that would be an accurate assessment.

It's the picture we took just minutes ago.

Christopher stares at the picture for a long moment before clicking off the screen and returning the phone to his pocket.

"Happy Birthday, Carol," he mutters before returning to work on Nora's computer.

A blink, and again, we're somewhere else. A well-kept apartment materializes around us, all decorated for the holidays, though only a few presents rest beneath the tree. A slender woman with hair dyed bright red sits on the couch sipping a cup of coffee. Her face is pretty, if a bit pinched. In the brief time I observe her, she checks her watch three times. The clock on the front of their entertainment center reads 1:18.

As she checks her watch a fourth time, a key turns in the lock. A moment later, the Christopher Kellerman I just left steps inside and kicks his shoes into a pile of footwear in the corner. The woman rises from the couch and meets him in the hallway.

"Hope you're hungry." She gives him a quick peck on the cheek. "I made you a sandwich."

"Thanks," he answers as he slips out of his coat. "I'm starving."

"How was your morning?"

"An empty office on Christmas Day. Pretty much what you'd expect."

Compassion flashes across her face before her features pinch again. "You get all caught up?"

"As much as I'm going to."

"You didn't have to go in, you know." She rests a hand on his forearm. "It is Christmas, after all."

Christopher glances over at the mostly bare floor around the Christmas tree. "We need the money, don't we?" he mutters as he walks past her and into what I'm guessing is the kitchen.

The woman waits for just a moment before following, hurt flashing across her features.

A blink, and the Spirit and I are standing in the kitchen. Christopher sits at the corner of the bar munching on a hoagie while this woman, who must be his wife, stands by the dishwasher watching him eat and gnawing at her knuckle. The silence becomes more and more uncomfortable until finally Christopher caves.

"Sorry, Becca. I didn't sleep well last night."

"I don't think either of us did. Whoever decided to call it morning sickness failed to mention the other eighteen hours of the day when you're puking up your guts."

"Is that medicine Dr. Birch gave you helping at all?"

"A little." Becca sits at the bar next to Christopher. "I'm doing everything right. Little sips. Sucking on lemon wedges. Eating my ginger. Taking my Zofran. Something's got to work."

Christopher wraps his arm around her and pulls her head in to rest on his shoulder. "Pharmacy's open till six. Let me know if you need me to go pick you up anything."

"Thanks." Becca pinches off a hunk of his sandwich and commences a slow chew. "You'd be proud of me. Got a lot done today in between sprints to the bathroom."

Christopher looks up from his plate. "Working on the nursery again?"

Becca grabs his hand and smiles wickedly. "You mean cleaning out your disaster room?"

Christopher returns her smile, a hint of defensiveness flashing across his face. "That was my office, thank you very much."

"Call it what you want." She points to a stack of magazines on the counter. "I stacked up a foot and a half of *Entertainment Weekly* alone. I know you like to flip through the old ones sometimes so I didn't throw any of them out."

His nose crinkles. "Thanks."

"Same for your Christmas cards." She crosses her arms. "You know, you hang on to everything. I even found a couple that went all the way back to high school."

Christopher's eyes go blank. "You didn't throw those out, did you?"

Becca laughs. "After the movie poster debacle two years ago? You know I don't touch your stuff anymore, but you're going to have to make some decisions. With the baby coming, we need the room, and unless we rent some storage space we can't afford, there's nowhere to put all this stuff."

A dreamy wistfulness overtakes Christopher's features. "We could always look at houses again."

Becca shakes her head. "We've been over this. The lady at the bank said we don't qualify for 100% financing, and unless you've been holding out on me, we don't have anything approaching a down payment. At least not for any house worth looking at."

Christopher puts down the sandwich and cranes his neck around to look Becca in the eye. "I could take a second job."

"No way." She rests her hands on his shoulders and kneads the muscles at the base of his neck. "I barely see you now, working six days a week."

"I know." Christopher spins in his chair and kisses Becca's belly. "But this baby is coming whether we're ready or not."

"We'll figure something out."

Christopher pulls her to him. "Yes, we will."

Becca and Christopher stand there wrapped in each other's arms for longer than I'm comfortable watching. Eventually, she disengages. "Back at it. I've still got a couple boxes to go through before I call it a day." She heads for the hall. "You want to open presents before dinner?"

"Sounds great," Christopher says before taking another bite of his sandwich.

Stepping through the doorway, Becca pokes her head back into the kitchen. "Oh, I found an old box of art supplies in the closet. The paints were all dried up, and the brushes look like they've seen better days. Is it okay if I throw them out?"

Christopher swallows. Hard. "Go ahead and trash the old paint, but do we really need to toss the brushes?"

"You haven't put paint to canvas in years, honey." She shrugs. "If you want to keep them, though, we'll find a spot. They won't take up much room."

Christopher stuffs the last bite of hoagie into his mouth and chews on the question as well as the sandwich. Taking a sip of soda, he washes it down and looks over at Becca. "No. You're right. Go ahead and throw them out." He looks off into space. "Won't be painting anything but the walls of the nursery for the next few months anyway." His gaze drops to his lap. "When it's time to start painting again, I'll just get a new set."

"Of course, honey." Becca disappears into the hall. "Of course."

Christopher pulls out his phone and stares at the blank screen for a moment before placing it face down on the counter and following his wife down the hall.

"He kept the brushes." My hand goes to my open mouth.

"All those years." I drop my arms and interlace my fingers to keep them from shaking and turn to the Spirit. "What happened to Christopher? Sure, he's married with a kid on the way, but he's meant for so much more than some dead end job. I saw his room. His work. His stuff is brilliant."

The Spirit looks on impassive as I silently wonder if Christopher ever finished the painting I found in his room.

"And it's not just him. According to you and the other Spirits, Philippe falls off the wagon, Roberta turns cold and bitter, and Valerie and Mike end up more miserable than I've ever seen them. And believe me, as the cause of their misery on more than one occasion, I know what I'm talking about. What happened to everybody?"

Though I can't see her face, I can feel the Spirit's eyes on me. The air grows cold as she raises her arm one last time, her gnarled finger pointing at the space between my eyes.

A blink, and I'm back at the dance. The crowd has dwindled by a good half. I scan the room. No Roberta or Christopher in sight. Just a bunch of kids I've never seen before. For a moment, I wonder if the Spirit has sent me to some future version of the Christmas Eve dance.

"Carol?"

I turn to find Ryan striding toward me, his steps clipped and fast. His face betrays a war of emotions. Anger. Concern. Confusion.

He grabs me by my shoulders as if he's afraid I might fall.

Or run.

"Where'd you go?" he asks.

My internal lie generator shifts into overdrive. "I was feeling a little out of it. Took a walk."

"Without a coat?" He lets his warm hands trail down my arms. "Aren't you freezing?"

Fantastic. I'm on a date with Sherlock Holmes. "I was just out in the hall checking out some of the artwork."

"For forty-five minutes?" He shoves his hands in his pockets and squints at me like some kind of interrogator on *Law & Order: Missing Date Unit*. "I've been looking everywhere for you."

"I've been right here the whole time. I swear."

"I didn't know if maybe you ditched me after that thing with the punch." Ryan shakes his head. "I was about to walk out the door a minute ago when I spotted you."

The tide of battle between me and my trembling lower lip begins to turn against me. "I'm...sorry." Unbidden tears start to well up in my eyes, and when I try to speak again, my voice abandons me.

"Oh man." Ryan takes a step back. "Didn't mean to make you cry." He envelops me in his muscular arms. A comforting gesture, though I have no doubt he's wondering right now what he's got himself into. "Are you...okay?"

"I thought I was," I croak. "Tonight was supposed to be, well, a whole lot better than this." I look away. "I've just got a lot going on. Nothing to do with you."

If only that were true.

"I understand." Ryan holds me away from him, his face breaking into a confident smile. "That being said, the night's not over yet, though. Think we can turn it around?"

"I'm not sure, but we can try."

He pulls me even tighter, and I feel the flask in his jacket press into my shoulder.

"I do know one thing, though." I look up into those glacier blue eyes of his. "I could sure use that drink right about now."

CHAPTER FORTY-NINE

Neither of us says much on the way to the after party. I sit shivering inside Ryan's coat despite the seat warmer cooking my backside and the heat blasting up from the floorboard.

Not to mention the quarter flask of vodka trying to burn its way out of my gut.

None of it dispels the growing chill at my core. In the space of a few hours, I've been shown the fate awaiting every last person in the world I give a crap about. Everyone's life turns out for shit, and without a doubt, I'm at the center of it all.

But it's more than that.

I've seen the movies. I know what's coming. The last thing Scrooge sees. I've known since Marnie Jacobsen's ghost first climbed out of my computer screen and sprawled on my bed. I've tried to push it down, banish it from my thoughts, but it's been there every waking minute of the last three days.

Gnawing at me.

Waiting.

The morbid revelation that will eclipse everything that's come before.

"You sure you're up for this?" Though Ryan's tone doesn't speak well for the rest of the evening, I'm grateful for the distraction. "We don't have to go, you know."

I stare out the window. "Can't stop now. We're almost there."

"Wow. That's enthusiasm."

His foot taps the brake, and I lurch forward.

"Hey. Easy over there."

"Sorry." Even in the dim light of the car, I can see Ryan's jaw clench. "Just doing my best to stay on the road in this downpour."

"No, I'm sorry. It's just all these curves are turning my stomach." I stare out the windshield as Ryan navigates another sharp bend of the lakeside road. Built to be picturesque with frequent views of the water, I'm pretty sure the engineers didn't take into account people driving this stretch of asphalt at night in a deluge. "Vodka isn't sitting too well, either."

"You all but pulled the flask out of my pocket, Carol." We come out of the curve, and Ryan hits the accelerator. "Wish you'd have told me you'd never tried hard liquor before."

"First time for everything, right?"

Taking his eyes off the road for all of a second, Ryan glances over at me, eyebrows raised. "Why tonight?"

"You wouldn't understand."

"Try me," he says as he takes another curve.

I consider for a moment. "The last few days, my life has spun about as far out of control as I think it can get." Against my better judgment, I grab the flask that rests on the seat between us and take another couple sips. Each goes down like battery acid. "What's another couple logs on the fire?"

"Careful, there." Ryan says. "I drop you off at your house drunk and your aunt's not going to be all smiley the next time I come around."

"Just get us to the party in one piece." A twinge of nausea rips through my midsection, but I keep my composure. "I'll deal with Valerie."

We come to the latest in what seems an endless succession of one lane bridges, this one a bit longer than the ones we've already crossed. The break in the trees coincides with a small gap in the clouds. A glimpse of the pale light cast by the full moon fires a series of images in my head.

Marnie's ashen smile in my bathroom mirror.

The silver luminescence cast by the Spirit of Christmas Past's platinum tresses.

The soft glow of the Spirit of Christmas Present's torch of plenty.

The moon is visible for but a second, and as the clouds and trees conspire to again mask its light, the resulting darkness summons but one image.

A dark shroud obscuring her terrible face, The Spirit of Christmas Yet to Come wheezing with somber laughter as she unveils her one remaining revelation, as horrible as it is inescapable.

"Almost there," Ryan breathes as we round another curve. "Last chance. You're sure this is what you want?" He rubs his dash like he's stroking a trusted steed. "We can still turn this thing around. Just say the word."

Wow. I never dreamed Ryan King would be the voice of reason in this story.

"I'll be fine," I whisper as we pass the first of a seemingly endless line of vehicles parked along the narrow two-lane road. "Anyway, we're here."

At least a quarter mile of cars go by before we find a place to park, metal ghosts barely visible in the torrential rain. Ryan pulls across the median, parking on the opposite side so I can step out onto the road, and goes to retrieve Valerie's king-sized umbrella from the trunk.

I flip down the visor and check myself in the mirror. The girl in the mirror looks back at me, albeit a little green around the gills, but otherwise none the worse for wear.

"Here goes everything," I mutter.

Huddled beneath the umbrella, Ryan and I rush through the rain. For the hundredth time that night, I wish I had worn my favorite pair of boots instead of the gorgeous shoes Philippe gave me. Nothing against fancy footwear, but I never knew till tonight how much I appreciated being able to feel my toes.

There's no question about which direction to go. Even through the trees an eighth of a mile away, the Allen lake house, all lit up inside and out, illuminates the surrounding forest like a fallen Christmas star.

"Wonder if we'll run into any wise men."

"What did you say?" Ryan asks.

"Nothing." My teeth chatter as the wind cuts through Ryan's coat like an ice-cold razor. "Let's just get inside."

Note to self: Dear Carol, If you ever leave the house in December in a sleeveless dress without a parka and a pair of mukluks again, I will kill you. Love, Carol.

As we draw close to the house, the thumping bass of a familiar hip-hop song fills the air, though the sound is barely audible over the sound of the rain.

"Careful," Ryan says as we head down the hill toward the house. "The concrete looks a little slippery."

The porch is littered with umbrellas, ponchos, and garbage bags. Ryan props our gear in the only empty spot remaining and shows me inside. We don't get very far past the door before we run into someone we know.

"Keys." Nate Murphy, the only sophomore on the varsity

basketball team, holds out his hand. "You get them back at the end of the evening when I'm convinced you're safe to drive."

Ryan eyes him quizzically. "Coach put you up to this, didn't he?"

Nate looks off into space. "He said if anybody on the team gets a DUI tonight, I get to trade in my jersey for a water boy uniform." He motions toward Ryan's pocket. "Now, hand them over."

Ryan hesitates for a moment before fishing his keys out of his pocket and placing them in Nate's outstretched palm.

"Fine," Ryan grunts.

"Appreciate it." Nate drops the wad of keys into a shoebox on a table by the door. "Catch you later."

Ryan takes my arm and leads me through the crowd. The wall-to-wall mob makes it difficult to breathe, much less move, but eventually we find our way to the kitchen where some variation of beer pong is happening.

And surprise, surprise, Jamie Meadows is right there in the middle of it all.

Spotting Ryan in the doorway, she takes a long slug from the proverbial Red Solo Cup and shoots him a smile that would light up the night sky, only backing down a couple of watts when she notices me in his wake.

"Up for a little Pong, King?" A linebacker from a rival school with no neck and a head like the pony keg resting on the counter waves for Ryan to come over. Ryan raises a hand, but No Neck is having none of it.

"Come on, Ryan," Jamie says, her lids half-closed as she props herself up on a barstool. "Let's see some of those legendary ball handling skills."

I appreciate that Ryan at least glances back to check with me. At my noncommittal shrug, he rolls up his sleeves. "All right. Let's do this."

Jamie, No Neck, Ryan, and some other jock with way too much product in his hair set up for another round. My stomach turns as Valerie's words trickle through my mind.

No drinking? That one's a bust. I feel like someone replaced my brain with a sponge, not to mention my feet don't seem to be working quite normally.

Home by 1:30? I'll still be tipsy if we do and grounded for a year if we don't. That's two strikes.

Then there's the part about not riding with anyone who's had alcohol.

I am so screwed.

May as well go for the hat trick and drag Ryan upstairs for a little fun.

Hey. I'd hate to lose my rep as an overachiever.

"Wake up, Carol." The half-shouted voice rips me out of my mental fog. "You've been zoning all night."

"Marnie?" My eyes shoot left and right. "Is that you?"

"*Marnie*?" Dripping with incredulity, the voice answers from behind me. "What are you talking about?"

I crane my neck around and curse under my breath. It's not Marnie, nor even one of the Spirits, but Roberta.

Who likely thinks her best friend could use a straitjacket and a padded room right about now.

She's not alone.

I turn as best I can in my dress, my fumbling feet rebelling against even the simplest commands, and find Roberta standing just inside the doorway leading back into the Allen's big den. Still a vision of perfection in velvet, her subtle frown carries equal amounts of worry and disapproval.

"Hi, Roberta." Not sure how you lisp a word like "Roberta," but I find a way.

She chuckles. "Carol Davis, have you been drinking?"

"Ryan let me try a sip or two of vodka on the way here."

Even saying the word makes me want to wretch. "How did you know?"

"You mean besides the bloodshot eyes, your two left feet, and the fact you can barely say my name?"

"Fine." I rest a hand on her shoulder. I try to make it seem a friendly gesture, but the truth is, I'm just steadying myself as the room pitches to one side. "Do me a favor and keep an eye on me. Don't let me do anything stupid."

Roberta lets out a quiet sigh. "A little late for that, but I'll do my best."

"Thanks." I peer past her, scanning the mob in the next room for one particular face in the ocean of people. A face I hope will help make sense of everything I've seen today, as hard as that is to admit. The TV on the far wall is running *Rudolph the Red-Nosed Reindeer* on mute as the hip-hop onslaught continues to ravage my poor eardrums. The mob of students pulses in time with the music, all apparently oblivious to the waves of heat rising from the floor. The flashing lights team with the smell of sweat and hormones filling the air, and a fresh wave of nausea rolls through my body. Leaning in the doorway, I let my eyes slide shut.

"Looking for someone?" Roberta asks, like she doesn't know exactly who I'm looking for.

"Maybe." I work up the courage to ask the simplest of questions. "Did Christopher come with you?"

I peer out through one half-opened eye. "Why do you want to know?"

And I'm pinned to the wall like a butterfly. The girl should take up fencing. "Just wondering how you convinced him to come. This isn't exactly his scene."

Roberta steps back through the doorway, craning her neck left and right, and smiles. "He's here, all right," she whispers, "and faring a little better than you are at the moment."

I hang in the doorway, peeking around the corner past Roberta, and finally catch a glimpse of Christopher through the undulating crowd. He's in the corner chatting up a cute blond girl I pass in the hall every day. A junior named Faith something-or-other. As I recall, she's on the tennis team and pretty smart. Just got her braces off too, it appears.

"There he is." I try to push past Roberta. "Be right back. I need to talk to Christopher."

Roberta raises her arm and blocks the door. "Sorry, chica. You just asked me to keep you from doing anything stupid."

"It's okay." I force her arm down and step into the room. "I just need to ask him a question. Real quick. I swear."

Roberta shoots me a motherly look I usually only get from Valerie. "Whatever." She lowers her arm and lets me pass. "It's your funeral."

CHAPTER FIFTY

I step past Roberta, my head swimming as I force one foot in front of the other. Countless elbows and hips block my path, but I plow through the crowd regardless, keeping my eyes on Christopher. His cheeks all flushed with the heat of the room, he's undone his bow tie and stowed his jacket somewhere. I wonder for a second if he's been drinking too, but dismiss the thought just as quickly.

No way he'd take so much as a sip with Roberta in tow.

Fidgeting with the charm at the end of my necklace, I step around a couple from East who seriously need to get a room. Christopher and Faith both look up as I approach. Despite a forced smile, Faith's nose crinkles as I make their duet a trio. Meanwhile, Christopher's already rosy cheeks go a couple shades darker.

"Hi, Carol." The surprise in Christopher's voice speaks volumes. "Didn't know if you were going to make it or not."

"I told you Ryan and I were coming." I wave my arm at the crowd, accidentally swatting a guy I dodged a moment before. "You think I'd miss all this?"

"You two have any trouble getting here?" Christopher asks,

a poor attempt at trying to change the subject. "Halfway here, the rain started coming down so hard, Roberta and I had to pull over for a couple minutes."

"You sure it was the rain?" I try to laugh. It comes out like a snort. "Roberta sure looks pretty tonight in that purple velvet dress I picked out for her." Met with the coldest gaze he's ever given me, I try to give Christopher a playful elbow to the ribs, but he's having none of it.

Faith takes a half step forward. "Can we help you with something?"

"Nope." I list to one side, but quickly right myself before getting friendly with the floor. "Just making the rounds." Suddenly thirsty, I grab a random cup off the end table by my knee and take a slug. Whatever it is tastes like lukewarm urine.

Must be beer.

"So, this is cozy. I didn't know you knew Faith."

"Funny." Faith raises an eyebrow. "I didn't know you knew me either."

My own cheeks grow hot. "She's funny, Christopher. A real keeper."

He wipes a few beads of sweat from his brow. "Faith and I are just talking, Carol. We're in the same AP Calculus class and are looking at some of the same schools for next year."

"Just talking, huh?" My gaze wanders back and forth from Faith to Christopher. "That's how it starts, I guess. First you're talking at a party, then you're going out, then you're taking a crappy job fixing computers and she's Becca and you're having a baby so you throw out my brushes and forget all about me." I cross my arms. "Just about sums it up, don't you think?"

"Is there a point to this conversation?" Faith keeps her voice even and her face placid, but her eyes are telling me to shove off.

Not a chance.

"Just saying. Christopher's here with Roberta and three's a

crowd." I lean in, my voice dropping to a conspiratorial whisper. "Unless you're into that sort of thing."

Her hands balling into fists, Faith's lips draw down to a narrow line. "Catch up with you later, Christopher." Her glare threatens to bore a hole between my eyes. "I need to get some air."

As she storms off, I lock eyes with Christopher and see something there I've never seen before. I've seen the poor boy happy, sad, twitterpated, disappointed, excited, hurt; pretty much the gamut of emotions.

I've never seen him pissed.

"What the hell, Carol?" he half-shouts, half-whispers.

"What?"

"Seriously?" Christopher stares at me incredulous for a moment before throwing his hands in the air. "You've gone and gotten yourself drunk."

"So?"

Christopher shakes his head. "You don't even drink."

I cross my arms and cock my head to one side. The room only spins a little.

"People change."

"I'll say. You've blown me off for well over a year, you don't answer emails or your phone, you can't even be bothered to pick up the TV I've had on hold for you for days, and now, all of a sudden, you want to talk?"

His eyes drift down to my chest. Any other day, I'd think he was just staring at the goods, but even in my somewhat fuzzy state, I know exactly what he's looking at.

"And you wore that? Tonight of all nights?"

"I haven't worn this necklace in years." Suddenly, I can't meet his eyes. "Don't you think it goes pretty with the dress?"

"Of course. Matches you and your dress perfectly, unlike the guy that gave it to you, I guess."

The air catches in my throat. "Christopher..."

"You know what? Forget about it." He scans the room. "I've got to go fix whatever it was you just broke."

"But..."

"But, but, but..." Christopher buries his face in his palm before running his fingers through his for once stylish hair. "Look, take some advice from someone who, for some reason, still gives a crap about you. Go get Ryan and have him take you home before you embarrass yourself more than you already have."

As if on cue, Roberta and Ryan pull up on either side of me.

"What's going on here?" Ryan asks.

"What's going on?" Christopher's eyes shoot from Ryan to Roberta and back. "Well, for starters, Carol here is drunk, and you've apparently been too busy being Ryan 'King of the World' to keep an eye on her."

"Hey." Ryan raises his hands, his fingers balling into fists. "She knew what she was doing. Nobody forced her to drink anything."

"Nobody forced her." Christopher's eyes narrow. "Just like last spring, right?"

My eyes shoot to Roberta's, and for once this evening I take a cue and keep my big mouth shut.

"What the hell is that supposed to mean?" Ryan steps into Christopher's airspace.

If I expect Christopher to back down, I am sorely disappointed.

"You know exactly what I'm talking about," he mutters, his face getting redder by the second.

Ryan bites his lip and half-smiles, his head bobbing with anger. "Please, then. Enlighten me."

"I heard you dumped your girlfriend the morning after

prom last spring. Any particular reason? Maybe you squeezed all the juice out of that lemon and were ready to move on?"

Ryan's face flushes a bright crimson. "You don't know the first thing about Bethany and me."

"Please, then." In a mocking tone, Christopher parrots Ryan's own words right back at him. "Enlighten me."

Ryan's gaze dances between Roberta and me before landing back on Christopher.

"Not that it's any of your business, but we just...didn't see eye to eye on certain things."

Roberta laughs. "From what I heard, your eyes weren't the problem."

"Shut it, Roberta." The words out of my mouth before I can stop them, Roberta steps back as if struck.

"Shut it?" she hisses between clenched teeth. "Did you just say that to me?"

Before Roberta can say another word, Ryan turns on her as well. "Stay out of this. I came over here to take care of Carol like you asked, but I'm not going to stand here and take a bunch of crap from some geek."

"Geek?" Showing a side of him I've never seen, Christopher pushes Ryan off him and raises his fists. "You'd best watch who you're calling names, Casanova."

"And you'd better watch your mouth."

"Just saying. Carol deserves a lot better than being another notch on your bedpost."

Before I can half-register what Christopher has said, Ryan's fist flies out like a striking cobra and sends Christopher's head rocking backward.

"Christopher!" Roberta and I scream in unison as our friend collapses to the floor like a marionette with its strings cut. The music screeches to a halt, and the entire room stops to stare.

Ryan surveys the crowd. Any momentary embarrassment on

his face fades quickly into practiced cool as he turns back to face me. "Your friend needs to watch his mouth."

"Leave him alone." My gaze flickers down in time to catch a glimpse of Christopher spitting up a mouthful of blood and drool and possibly part of a tooth. My stomach downshifts into fourth gear and I feel the half flask of vodka preparing for an encore appearance.

Not to mention the sushi.

And that wad of bubblegum I swallowed in fourth grade.

"I think I'm going to be sick."

I sprint for the bathroom, the crowd parting like I'm Charlton Heston's Moses leading the Israelites across the Red Sea.

Funny how fast people can move when they think someone's about to puke in their face.

I make it to the bathroom in the nick of time, and for the first time in my life, I'm glad to find the seat up. I grab the toilet with both hands and empty my stomach into the blue water at the bottom of the bowl.

Sushi. So good going down. Not so much on the return trip.

I puke till it hurts, till nothing comes but air, and then commence to dry heave as my intestines do their best impersonation of a pretzel. I half expect to see the red pumps Philippe gave me go flying from my mouth, but just when I think I can't take any more, my stomach takes a breather.

After flushing the toilet, I pull myself up from the floor and splash my face with cold water before dipping my head into the sink to rinse out my mouth.

One thing I know for a fact.

Nothing Valerie brings down on me when I get home will be worse than this.

I snag one of the fluffy hand towels laid out on the counter and bring it to my face. It's a little late to leave this party with anything approaching dignity, but I'll be damned if I'm going to let a roomful of strangers see me with tears in my eyes, much less puke in my hair.

The warm towel feels good on my skin, though the bizarre odor wafting off the soft terrycloth is a bit disconcerting. Rather than the fresh flowery scent left by most detergents, the towel smells musty, dank, earthy. I question whether I'm imagining the whole thing for but a moment before I realize the truth.

The smell is quite real, and it's not the towel.

CHAPTER FIFTY-ONE

The towel falls from my grasp as my eyes open on a scene I've dreaded since the moment this all began.

The chill, wet air surrounding me and filling my lungs.

The damp grass tickling my suddenly bare feet.

The gaping hole at my toes, barely visible in the dim light.

Lined up like soldiers going to war, the granite tombstones surrounding me are nearly imperceptible compared to their marble counterparts, which shine even in the low light of evening. The full moon tries in vain to pierce the veil of dark clouds that fill the sky from horizon to horizon. No more than a hundred yards away, a strangely familiar edifice shrouded in darkness and fog rests just beyond the boundaries of the cemetery. I cast my thoughts back to when Valerie and Mike would drag me along to worship on Sunday mornings, and everything becomes crystal clear.

This is our church, that is if I actually claimed any such association these days. Back in the Mesolithic Era, me and the other kids in my Sunday School class would play hide and seek in this very graveyard. I've likely run past this spot a hundred times.

"I've been waiting for this, you know." I try to sound brave, but the tremor in my voice betrays the truth. I peer through the dim fog, but no one, Spirit or otherwise, is to be seen.

"I've seen all the movies. I know what's coming. What you've brought me here to see."

Still nothing but silence.

"Ashes to ashes, right?" I take a fistful of earth and sprinkle it into the open grave at my feet. "Dust to dust?"

I step back from the grave and nearly fall.

Emptying my stomach may have been a sobering event, but I'm still a little tipsy.

"Is this all you have left? The last card up your sleeve to turn this Scrooge into a saint? Well, I've got news for you. Everybody dies." A blast of winter rushes past and threatens to leave the tears running down my cheeks icicles. "Everybody. Marnie. Mom. Dad."

I swallow away the emotion.

"Joy."

As if in answer, the Spirit materializes above the grave. Her pale hand indicts me as her cloaked gaze burns through my soul. Freezing rain begins to fall, and for the first time, it occurs to me what's different. Every other time one of the Spirits has taken me on walkabout, I've been sheltered. From the temperature. From the weather. From everything. A passive observer to all we encountered.

This time it's for real.

"So, Spirit." Still trying to pull off brave. Still failing. "This is my grave. Big deal. We all have to go sometime, right?"

The Spirit shifts to one side, her accusing finger drifting from me to the tombstone at the head of the grave.

"Carol Davis," I read. "Daughter, Sister, Niece." I glower at the Spirit. "Not very original."

The Spirit's head turns away, her pale hand still trained on the tombstone's inscription.

There. At the bottom. I can just make out the date.

"December 25th."

Before I can ask the obvious question, the high beams from an unseen car flash across the tombstone and I finally discover what the Spirit brought me here to see.

"Tomorrow?" Any vain attempt at keeping my cool flies out the window. "I die...tomorrow?"

The Spirit's arm slowly falls to her side, her invisible eyes again boring through me.

I step toward her, my bare foot leaving wet grass and coming to rest on cool, damp earth. "What happens to me?"

The Spirit's head tilts to one side.

I take another step. My foot comes down on a jagged piece of stone, but I ignore the pain. "Dammit, what happens to me? Do I buy the BMW and wreck it?"

As still as a painting, the Spirit merely stares.

I leap at her, clawing at the cloth hiding her face. "Tell me, damn you!" My tears begin anew. "Tell me!"

The thick veil comes away, and for the first time, I look on the Spirit's exposed face.

The eyes of Christmas Past seemed so alien and the eyes of Christmas Present all-knowing and wise beyond measure, but nothing could have prepared me for what I would experience looking into the eyes of Christmas Yet to Come.

Familiar eyes.

My eyes.

Like staring into one of those bizarre funhouse mirrors at the carnival, the Spirit's face is a cruelly rendered version of my own.

With one notable exception.

She has no mouth.

Where her lips should be, only smooth, pale flesh resides.

Silenced forever.

The freezing rain begins to pick up as the apparition and I stand and stare at each other. My teeth begin to chatter, and I summon the courage to speak again.

"You're...me."

The Spirit nods.

My lips tremble. "And it happens tomorrow."

Again, the Spirit nods.

"Do I want to know how it happens?"

The Spirit pulls one of the pine cones from her chest and crushes it in her hand, allowing the debris to drop into the grave, just before flinching in fear as the glow of phantom headlights glints across the tombstone a second time. Before I can so much as take a breath to ask another question, a pair of clammy hands close around my ankles. I cry out for my mother as the vise-like grip jerks me off my feet and flips me onto my back, only to scream anew when I see who it is pulling me toward the open grave.

Staring at me with sunken eyes from beneath her bedraggled hair, the girl, Apathy, tugs on my ankles with a strength far beyond that of her skeletal limbs. If she looked on me hungrily before, her expression now borders on ravenous.

"No!" My hands claw at the wet ground as the shriveled girl drags me toward the grave, but between the damp grass and loose earth, my fingers struggle to find purchase. Inch by chilly inch, I'm pulled on my back toward what seems my final resting place, the dress that Philippe spent an entire night perfecting bunching around my waist as first my calves, then my thighs, are pulled into the void.

"Stop!" I scream. "No!"

I flip onto my belly and grasp at clump after clump of freezing grass, but the girl's scrawny arms are too strong, and my inexorable march toward the grave continues. Without warning, my feet touch water. I may have spent half my life in the pool, but it's never felt like this. The icy water saps every bit of strength from me until I can no longer fight.

Past my knees, my hips, my breasts. As the water hits my chin, I take one last gulp of frigid air, though I have a nasty feeling the breath holding skills I've always taken for granted aren't going to do me much good this time.

Marnie drowned in her hot tub. And me? An inch below the ice-cold rainwater filling my own grave.

As the freezing water envelops me, I remember everything my old swim coach taught me.

Don't panic.

Conserve your energy.

Perfectly good air is just one kick away.

Truth is, it's just a matter of time. Even the best-conditioned swimmer in the world could only withstand such burning in their lungs for so long.

And I am far from my best these days.

As instinct forces my lips apart, I finally accept that the outcome of the fight was never in doubt. Silty water flows past my tongue, down my windpipe, and hits my lungs like frigid molten lead. Panic and peace, struggle and surrender, holding on for dear life and finally letting go—these all war in my mind until everything finally, mercifully, fades to black.

CHAPTER FIFTY-TWO

I awake in the Allen's garden tub, gasping as the faucet drips slowly on my upturned face. Unsure if I'm alone, I slide one hand and then the other up the side of the tub and pull my head just high enough to peer out.

"Hello?" I intone, barely above a whisper. "Anybody here?"

My question unanswered, I climb out of the tub and go to the bathroom mirror where, in a way, all of this started. When I see myself, I'm not sure whether to laugh or cry.

To say I look like crap would be an insult to crap.

"Tomorrow." The thought won't leave me alone. "Tomorrow."

I run my fingers through my damp locks, struggling to come up with a way to avoid my fate. I suppose I could stay in this bathroom for the next twenty-five hours, but I have no doubt that Death could find me here. Exploding gas line? Collapsed ceiling? Hell, I could burst a brain aneurysm as far as that goes.

Wait. Bathroom. Mirror. Near midnight.

I flip off the overhead lights, leaving only the lone night light on the opposite wall to illuminate the dim room, and turn to the mirror. With single-minded purpose, I take a deep breath and stare down my own reflection.

"Bloody Marnie. Bloody Marnie. Bloody Marnie."

I wait.

Nothing.

"Bloody Marnie." My nails dig into my palms. "Bloody Marnie." My fingertips begin to feel sticky. "Bloody Marnie."

Again, I wait.

In vain.

She did say I wouldn't be seeing her again.

"What the hell am I supposed to do now?" I pace the nearly dark room. "Scrooge woke up Christmas morning, bought the Cratchits a goose, and he was all good." No answer. "What about me, Marnie?"

I flip down the lid on the toilet and sit as the tears start to flow.

"This is all your fault, you know," I shout at my long dead friend. "I was perfectly happy till you popped out of my computer screen the other night."

Were you?

Before I can isolate the origin of this cryptic whisper, a barrage of knocks at the bathroom door nearly causes my heart to skip a beat.

"You coming out of there sometime tonight?" comes a rough voice, nothing like the mysterious murmur from seconds ago.

"Just a minute." I scramble to the door, flip on the lights, and turn the lock.

A junior on the tennis team whose name I forget rushes past me and heads for the toilet. "You have exactly three seconds to get out of here," he says. "Unless you want to get really familiar, really fast."

I pull the door closed behind me as I leave. The party is still going strong, but as with each of my ghostly abductions thus far,

I have no idea how long I've been gone. I know full well that my hair is a disaster, my face a mess, and the dress done.

The thing is, I don't care.

About looks or popularity or money or any of it.

I just want to go home.

I scan the room for Ryan, but he's nowhere to be found. Likewise, anybody I have any desire whatsoever to see. If I know Roberta, she's taken Christopher upstairs, no doubt, to tend to his fat lip—hope he's okay.

A few girls from the junior class saunter by, their faces all turned up in the same superior sneer that Marnie and I perfected back in what seems a lifetime ago. I give them a weary half smile and head back for the kitchen. The Allen living room is again an obstacle course of shoulders and hips and feet, one I could navigate a lot more easily if my own feet would follow basic commands, but eventually, I make it to the doorway.

I hear him before I see him.

"...girl's spent more time in the bathroom tonight than with me." The charm in Ryan King's voice replaced with sheer contempt, I have no doubt who he's talking to.

"Don't worry, Ryan," Jamie Meadows purrs, channeling her inner Marilyn Monroe. "I'm not going anywhere."

Neither says anything else for several seconds, and it doesn't take Kellerman-level IQ to figure out what that means. I peek around the corner, and my worst fears are confirmed. Seated on the kitchen island where the beer pong cups were arranged in a big triangle earlier, Jamie has Ryan by both lapels and appears to be doing her level best to climb inside his mouth tongue first. I tell my feet to move, to go back the way they came, but they don't listen. The display goes on for a good half a minute, the various spectators either attempting to ignore them or gawking incredulously. I'm about to step back into the next room and leave them be when Jamie opens her eyes.

Cold busted.

The corner of her mouth turns up in a vindictive smile and finally my feet become unfrozen from the spot.

I head straight for the front door without a shred of doubt as to my next course of action. I'm going home, right now, and since it would appear my date isn't ready to leave, the least he can do is provide the wheels.

Nate Murphy stands by the front door making out with that junior that joined the girl's swim team last year—What was her name? Zoe? Zelda?—about the same time I left.

I sidle up to the shoebox of keys and spot Ryan's near the top of the pile, the irony of his worn San Antonio Spurs keychain lost on the rest of the world. I wait till Nate and Miss Zippity-Doo-Da dive back in after a quick breather before fishing my hand into the box and coming out with my prize. I'm halfway to the front door when a familiar voice stops me dead in my tracks.

"Carol?"

Damn. Busted twice in two minutes. I turn and find Roberta, hands on her hips, looking at me like I'm a little girl with her hand in the cookie jar.

Not too far off, I suppose.

"Hey, Roberta." I hide the keys behind my back. "How's Christopher doing?"

"Upstairs with an icepack over his mouth." Her gaze drops to my waist. "How are you?"

"I'm fine." And that's at least half true. The adrenalin of being dragged into my own grave and then seeing Ryan with Jamie has at the very least given me a second wind.

"You look like shit."

Ah, Roberta. Girl never pulls any punches. "I think I'm ready to go. I know I have no right to ask, but would you and Christopher please take me home?"

"What about Ryan?"

My gaze flits in the direction of the kitchen. "He's a little busy right now playing tonsil tennis with Jamie Meadows."

"Oh, Carol." Roberta's brows knit together in a mix of confusion and irritation. "I'm so sorry."

"Just get me out of here. I can't stand to be in this place another minute."

She glances up at the second floor. "Let me go get Christopher. I have a sneaking suspicion he's ready to go, too." She lets out an annoyed laugh. "Poor thing's going to have to see a dentist next week."

My stomach churns. "Is it bad?"

"One of his front teeth is chipped, but I imagine they'll be able to fix it."

"Good." My eyes drop. "Before he comes down, can you tell him I'm sorry?"

"Of course, Carol." She shakes her head sadly. "Of course."

Roberta shoots up the stairs like a purple velvet cheetah and disappears down the upstairs hallway. No sooner is she out of my sight than Jamie Meadows steps into the room.

"Going home so soon?"

I give her my most withering glare. "My date seems to have come down with something nasty. Thought I'd give him some space."

"Nasty?" Jamie waltzes over and sniffs the air in my vicinity. "You stand there with puke in your hair, mascara running down your face, looking like you've spent the entire evening out in the rain and wonder why Ryan King is looking elsewhere for a little company?"

My stomach threatens to retch again. "Look, Jamie. I don't need this right—"

"Don't 'Look, Jamie' me, Davis. You may have been

something when you had Jacobsen around to watch your back, but now you're nothing but yesterday's news."

"But—"

Jamie raises a finger. "I know what tomorrow is. Your eighteenth birthday. The day when you get more money than God." A crowd starts to form around us. "You think that's going to change everything, don't you? Make everything all right?"

"Stop." Then more quietly. "Please."

Her arms cross before her. "No matter how much money you have, how pretty a dress you con out of your fairy of a boss, or how much you think you've got the wool pulled over Ryan King's eyes, you're still nothing but the same scared little girl you've been since the day I met you." The right side of her nose crinkles in distaste. "Three million or three billion isn't going to fix that."

The crowd surrounding us erupts into a mix of gasps and oohs. Jamie stands there triumphant, and I can't think of a single word to say.

After all, she's right. In ten years, what has changed?

Not a damn thing.

Raising a hand in defeat, I step onto the porch, collect Valerie's tent of an umbrella, and venture out into the rain as fast as Philippe's little red pumps can take me.

CHAPTER FIFTY-THREE

Ryan's Camaro roars to life as the torrential rain beats on the car roof like a thousand tiny tap dancers. I drop the transmission into drive, pull out onto the lonely two-lane road, and turn on the windshield wipers. For all the difference it makes. The asphalt barely visible through the pounding deluge, I step on the gas.

A glance at the passenger seat where I chucked the umbrella reveals a small lake forming in the nooks and crannies of the fine leather upholstery. God willing, it'll leak down into the seat and fry the electronics, seat warmers be damned.

I catch a flash of the car's front end crossing the center line and bring my full attention back to the road. One thing I'll say about sprinting a quarter mile through freezing rain. It clears the cobwebs from your head, vodka-induced and otherwise.

Still, this road nearly had me puking up my guts earlier, and that was when I'd just had a few sips from Ryan's flask.

All right, Carol. Sit up straight. Hands at ten and two. Check your mirrors every ten seconds. Straight home, straight to bed, avoid Valerie like the plague, and never touch a drop of alcohol again.

Between Spirits and spirits, I've had about all I can handle for one night.

I ride the brake as I coast down the first hill and barely touch the accelerator as I cruise up the other side.

Slow and steady is definitely the order of the evening.

Both sides of the road are still lined with cars, though on the return trip, I pass as many gaps as vehicles. The party may still be going strong, but at least half the crowd has headed for home. Unless I miss my guess, Roberta has just finished her sweep of the house and realized I've left.

Girl's going to kill me.

Though after what the Spirit showed me, I guess she'll have to get in line.

I cross the long bridge where the moon peeked down on me before, but this time there is no break in the clouds, no light from above, no glimmer of hope.

Just the dark and the rain. The never-ending rain.

As I round yet another curve, my thoughts wander back through the revelations of the last few days, particularly the things I learned while in the company of the second Spirit. I wonder how Philippe is faring all alone in his failing shop, nursing a glass of scotch with a photo of one long dead his only company. A flash of Marnie's mother, just as alone, flits across my memory, and I wonder again how much harder it must be to lose a child than to lose a parent. An unwelcome image of Mike and Valerie "celebrating" Christmas keeps creeping into the mix, and I make a mental note to—for once—make as much noise as possible when I get home.

The honking horn of a passing car with one headlight out jerks me back to the present. Only a few inches over the median, I drive all other thoughts from my head and focus on the road.

Slow.

Steady.

Deliberate.

Do not get pulled over.

Do not wreck a sports car belonging to a guy who dumped you on your first date.

And for God's sake, do not give Mike yet another reason to lecture you.

The chime of a text fills the car, causing my breath to catch in my throat.

Texting and driving, never a good combo, and definitely not on a night like this.

I ignore the first text. And the second. And the fifth.

The phone rings. None of the people who would be calling me at this moment are anyone I want to talk to. I let the first call go to voicemail, but when the phone rings a second time, I fish it from my clutch and hold it up in front of me so I can keep my eyes on the road.

No big surprise. It's Ryan.

I contemplate not answering, but a big part of me really wants to hear what he has to say for himself. Biting my lip, I press *Talk* and bring the phone to my ear.

"Hello?"

"Where are my keys, Carol?"

"Who is this?" I try to hold back a snort and fail.

"This isn't funny, Carol. You're in no shape to drive, and that engine has way more power than anything you're used to driving."

"So, you're only calling me because you're worried about your stupid car?"

All I hear for the next few seconds is the quiet sound of Ryan King breathing in and out. I can only imagine the words he isn't saying. "Just pull over, okay?" he whispers eventually. "I'll get some friends to give me a lift. We'll come pick you up."

"Not necessary." I pop my neck. "I'm doing just fine, and I'd hate to break up your and Jamie's romantic evening."

"Me and Jamie?" Ryan's momentary rise in volume is brief, his next words slow, calm, measured. "Look, Carol. Nothing's going on with me and Jamie. That was...a mistake." He pauses. "Everything's fine. I'm not mad. Just stop the car and we'll come get you. No questions asked."

The phone beeps in my ear. "Sorry, Ryan. Got another call coming in."

Before he can respond, I flip to the other caller.

"Hiya, Bobbisox."

"Carol?" Not Roberta.

Christopher.

"Hey."

"Where are you?" His voice sounds a little slurred, no doubt from the swollen lip.

"Why are you calling me on Roberta's phone?"

"We're using the GPS on mine."

As if to emphasize the point, Roberta's shouted "Curve! To the right!" comes through so loud I almost drop the phone. A few seconds pass before Christopher speaks again.

"Definitely not a night for driving," he says. "Now, where are you right now?"

"On the road."

Christopher lets out an exasperated sigh. "We kind of guessed that."

"Anything else?"

Another pause. He's mad.

Really mad.

"Look," he says eventually. "You shouldn't be behind the wheel in your condition. We're probably no more than a couple miles behind you. Just pull over. Please. We'll take you home and work all this out in the morning."

"Pull over. Pull over. Pull over." I groan into the phone. "It's like you all got together and rehearsed this crap."

"We're just trying to look out for you." Christopher takes a moment. "Not that you need to hear this, but Ryan is kind of pissed that you took his car."

"Ryan is pissed?" My foot presses the accelerator. "He can drop dead for all I care."

At that, a hiss of static comes across the line followed by a shouted voice that nearly sends me off the road.

"Girl, what the hell are you thinking?" Roberta shouts, as full of fire as I've ever heard her. "You trying to get yourself killed?"

"Well..." For the first time in my life, I really have no idea how to answer that question.

"Carol, listen. I know you're really upset right now, but everything is going to be fine. We'll get Ryan his car back and you can come stay with me tonight. We'll get you sobered up and I'll take you home in the morning."

"I'm fine, I'm fine, I'm fine. Look, I'm going straight home, okay?"

The road curves right and then a sharp turn back to the left. Ryan took this one a little too fast on the way in and I almost tossed my cookies. The tires squall. I grab the wheel with both hands, and my phone drops into the floorboard.

"Carol?" Barely audible above the purr of the Camaro's engine, what I can hear of Roberta's words comes across like the beginning of the world's worst haiku. "...careful...love you...dummy..."

The road straightens out before me as I pass the sign for the last bridge at the lake before the left turn back into town. I keep one hand on the wheel as the other feels around at my feet for the phone.

Want to lose something? Forget the Bermuda Triangle. Drop it in the floorboard at night when you're driving.

I'm almost to the bridge when I spot a hint of glow at my feet. My phone is underneath the emergency brake. I stretch my arm to grab it. Dammit. Just out of reach.

I kick off my left shoe so I can grab the phone with my toes. My feet are so numb I can barely feel it, but I get it out of the corner first try. I duck down to grab it.

That's when the whole world lights up around me.

Headlights careen toward me as the Camaro's front wheels hit the bridge a little across the center line. My foot slams on the brakes before I can so much as scream.

And then everything goes to shit.

The back end of Ryan's car fishtails across the median, completely blocking the other lane. The approaching car swerves left and into my lane as the sound of squalling tires fills the air. The two-lane bridge is plenty wide, but there's nowhere else for the car to go. The entire world slows to a crawl as the events play out like a movie being shown one frame at a time.

From inside the car, a woman stares out the passenger window at me, her mouth wide in a silent scream. An arm shoots across from the driver's side in a vain attempt to keep the woman from striking the dash. And then, a set of terrified eyes framed in the rear window of the car.

Her face just visible above the door frame, a pale little girl no more than six goggles out at me from beneath a full head of golden ringlets.

The green Subaru hatchback punches through the rails of the bridge like they're made of paper and disappears into the darkness.

The Camaro skids to a stop.

And I'm left alone in the rain.

STAVE V

THE END OF IT

Sunday, December 25th

CHAPTER FIFTY-FOUR

Shit.

Shit, shit, shit, shit, shit, shit, shit.

My breathing ragged, I run my hands down my torso searching for injuries, but other than some tenderness where the seatbelt tore across my collarbone, I'm fine. As if mocking me, the digital clock on Ryan's satellite radio flips from 11:59 to 12:00.

Fate, it seems, is right on time.

I check the Camaro's rearview mirror and look out every window. No headlights. No sign of life. Not a soul for as far as the eye can see, which in this weather isn't far. My heart pounding as images of jail cells from a hundred movies flash across my imagination, I take a deep breath and press the accelerator. The engine revs, but the car doesn't budge. Not an inch.

Must've knocked it into neutral when I slammed on the brakes.

I peer out of the car a second time. Still alone in the middle of nowhere, I can almost feel Roberta and Christopher flying up my tailpipe.

My brain shifts into overdrive.

I can leave now and no one will ever know I was here. That I was responsible for the accident. No one saw what happened.

No one, that is, but me.

And, I suppose, the three people I just sent careening off a bridge in the middle of the night.

Shit.

I punch the accelerator and make it all the way to the other side of the bridge before my foot hits the brake. A parade of faces marches across my mind's eye.

Valerie. Mike. Roberta.

Dad. Mom.

Joy.

I imagine each of them staring at me—no, through me—shaking their heads in disappointment as my foot hovers above the accelerator. More than just disapproval, though, I find something else in each of their gazes. A glimmer of hope that represents a simple fact my panicked brain is fighting to ignore.

I may be many things, but the girl who leaves the scene of an accident?

I pull the car onto the shoulder and aim the headlights down the hill. After almost a week of heavy rain, the previously stagnant creek has swollen to a rushing river. The little Subaru somehow landed sunny side up, but the water is slowly pushing it farther downstream and the car is sinking fast. Which leaves me with exactly two options: sit here and watch the car go under or do something stupid that all but guarantees the third Spirit's last vision will come true.

I climb from the warmth of Ryan's car and into the frigid rain and wind. No sooner am I off the shoulder than my heels sink into the muck. I abandon my shoes and rush barefoot to the water's edge. Square in the path of the Camaro's high beams, the Subaru has sunk almost to the level of the open driver's door window. Through it, I can just make out the woman's flailing arms.

"Help!" A shrill scream echoes across the rushing current. "Help us!"

I dip a toe into the frigid water and images of being dragged into a waterlogged grave flash across my memory.

"Daddy!" More piercing than the first scream, the girl's voice joins her mother's. "Daddy! Wake up!"

"Please!" comes the woman's scream again. "Help us!"

"I'm coming!" The shout out of my mouth before I can even think, instincts from the summer Roberta and I spent as lifeguards rush to the surface. Already shivering in the freezing rain, I look down at the perfect dress Philippe created just for me.

"Can't do much in this thing, I guess."

I reach behind my back to undo the zipper, but the freezing rain and whipping wind has left my fingers too numb to do much but ache and throb. Without another thought, I grab the damaged cap strap at my right shoulder and give it a tug, pulling it free before setting to work tearing my way out of the bodice. Like a butterfly shedding its chrysalis, I shimmy out of the dress, the silky fabric passing down my body till all that's left is the matching bra and panty set I'd half-wondered if I'd be modeling for Ryan tonight.

"Enough of that," I mutter, my bottom lip quivering in the cold. I peer around in the dark, half-expecting to find one of the Spirits or possibly even Marnie's ghost looking on to see what I'll do next.

But there's no one.

Other than the family in the car, I'm all alone.

Not sure why I'm surprised.

Before I have a chance to talk myself out of it, I mutter a quick prayer to a God I haven't spoken to in almost a decade and charge into the frigid water. Step by painful step, I push forward till I'm up to my waist, at which point I dive headfirst into the icy current. My specialty was always the freestyle, and it serves me well tonight. My head above water, I home in on the sinking Subaru like a torpedo, my arms and legs numb before I make it twenty feet. The current almost sweeps me past the car, but I catch the side mirror in my unfeeling fingers and hold on for dear life.

Almost out of the path of the Camaro's headlights, I use the remaining light to take inventory of the half-flooded car's occupants. Hunched over the wheel, the man appears unconscious, but a reflexive cough lets me know he's still breathing. Still belted in the passenger seat, the woman is conscious but hysterical, a trail of blood coursing down her face from an open gash above her eyebrow. The little girl, on the other hand, has unbuckled her belt and stands dazed on the back seat, whimpering even as she tries to keep her head above the rising water.

"Can you swim?" I shout at the woman.

"What?" she yells above the roar of the creek and falling rain.

"Can...you...swim?"

She nods.

"Then grab your daughter and get her to land." Stammering between chattering teeth, I point in the direction I hope is still the bank of the creek. "It's not far."

With all the strength I can summon, I force open the driver's door. Water floods the car, and the little girl lets out a bloodcurdling scream as the several tons of steel begins to sink even faster. I fumble with the man's seatbelt, a job apparently much easier when the nerve endings going to your fingertips are still functional. I finally find the latch as his lips dip beneath the current.

Pulling the man's mouth above water, I give the woman the most determined stare I can manage. "Don't panic. Just grab your daughter and follow me."

Her gaze shoots to her daughter, then to me, then back to her daughter.

"Come on, honey," she says after what seems an eternity. "Everything's okay. Just come to Mommy."

Fake bravado is better than no bravado.

"I can't," the girl gets out between sobs. "I'm scared."

"I'm scared too, honey, but we've got to get out of here."

The girl hesitates for another second before muttering a quick "Okay" and climbing across the seat and into her mother's outstretched arms.

"All right." I drape my arm around the man's chest and pull him out of the car. Though a pretty lean guy, his weight initially pulls me under. I push off the car's front quarter panel and, with a few scissor kicks, manage to get both our faces back above the surface. I cough, expelling a good mouthful of gritty water, and set to swimming. In seconds, the girl and her mother are lost to me as I exert every bit of brain and muscle power I have trying to get the man ashore. My lungs burn with every breath, every stroke, every kick. This would have been rough in my prime, and though cheering keeps me in reasonable shape, I'm nowhere near the athlete I used to be. Still, it's literal sink or swim time, and no matter how much it hurts, I keep going, the last bit of strength leaving my body when my hip finally scrapes across a jagged rock. I put my feet down, and my bare soles find silt and muck and stone.

We've made it to the edge.

I drag the man ashore and position him on his side, hoping he can cough out any water that's gone down the wrong pipe as I scan the poorly lit creek for any sign of the woman and her daughter. At first, I find nothing, and ice fills my veins.

And then, a miracle. A break in the clouds.

The moon shines down in all her glory and reveals an arm thrashing against the current.

My body responds before my brain can do anything to stop it. Back in the freezing water, my arms and legs hang like hunks of dead meat after getting the man's unconscious body back onto land. Every muscle screams in agony as I again force myself across the frigid current. By the time I get to them, it's almost too late.

Pushed farther and farther downstream with each passing second, the woman is treading water and holding her daughter's head above the icy flow. They're both sinking fast. I reach them as the woman's head finally dips beneath the surface and pull the girl from her clutching grasp. Little arms go around my neck in terror, forcing me beneath the icy flow where I take on a lungful of silty water. I kick and kick and kick and just make it back to the surface. Feeling around in the murky water, I find the woman's hair and pull her up as well.

"Go!" I shove her toward the shore, not sure if she's even still breathing. "I've got her."

Her eyes filled with the dreamy indifference of one half-frozen and half-drowned, the woman floats away from us, leaving me in her place, treading water as a panicked little girl chokes the life out of me.

"Not...so...tight..." I grunt and she relents.

At least a little.

Both easier and more difficult to manage than her father, I fight the current and get us just over halfway to shore when the sworn enemy of every swimmer rears its ugly head.

The cramp starts in my left quad and radiates around to my hamstring before jumping to the other leg. I order my legs to kick, to move, but as the muscle fibers in both thighs curl into tight knots, even straightening my legs becomes an impossibility.

That's when we start to sink.

I pull the girl around so I can look her in the face before we go under. In the low light she looks just like...

"Joy..."

The girl cries out, but I can't hear her as my head slips beneath the water.

CHAPTER FIFTY-FIVE

The full moon directly above fills my field of vision, it's circular contour blurred by the concentric ripples the rain leaves on the water above my eyes. Wiry arms and legs encircle my torso and waist like chains of icy steel, and my fading mind struggles to make one last connection.

Is it the little girl from the car, her weight dragging me to the bottom of a swollen creek normally too small to merit a name?

Or could it be Apathy, the creature from the Spirit of Christmas Present's robes disguised as a child? Has she returned to finish the job? Am I being dragged, bloated with water and sin to rest in the turned earth of my own grave?

Ah, the irony.

To be killed by indifference personified, and I couldn't care less.

I mean, everyone has to go sometime, right?

Everything goes dark. For a second? A century? I haven't a clue.

Then, a cascade of sensation.

Strong hands, pulling on my arms as if they mean to yank them from their sockets.

A gust of frigid air coursing across my face, my skin almost too numb to register the change.

Blow after blow to my chest and stomach, as if I stand defenseless in the fight of my life.

And finally, the warmth of a stranger's lips on mine. The heat of their breath. The urgency of their kiss.

Then nothing. Nothing at all.

CHAPTER FIFTY-SIX

I awake to the smell of coffee and antiseptic. Strong, dark-roasted goodness mixed with the sting of ammonia.

I welcome them both.

My eyes open on blinding fluorescence. For a moment, I wonder if it's the proverbial light at the end of the tunnel until I realize the source of the glare. One of those hospital lights on an arm like they always show on TV rests above my head with the beam pointed directly at my face. I try to convince either of my arms to rise and push it away, but they're having none of it. In fact, the only part of my body I can get to move is my eyes. I try to take a deep breath and even that seems an impossible task.

Good God.

I'm paralyzed.

Breathe, dammit. Breathe.

A beeping to my left grows faster and faster, but I don't need a machine to tell me my pulse is racing. Blood rushes in my ears, in time with a rhythmic throbbing behind my eyes, and a deep ache in my chest grows stronger with every heartbeat.

I try to cry out. My vocal cords have abandoned me.

So this is it. This is how I die. In a hospital bed, powerless to move or speak or even...

Breathe.

Suddenly back under my control, my fingers ball into fists, my toes curl under, and my head rises from the pillow as I suck in the deepest, sweetest breath of my entire life.

Who knew ordinary air could taste this good? Or that taking a simple breath could hurt so bad?

Surrounded by beeping machines, my body lies cocooned in some kind of inflatable blanket that feels hot enough to cook an egg.

Not that I'm complaining.

I try again to raise my free arm to move the light and feel a sharp pinch. Mummified with hospital tape to a board the length of my forearm, my right hand and wrist now sport a narrow plastic tube connected to an IV bag hanging beside the bed. The fluids, like the heated blanket, are warm and soothing as they flow into my vein.

Once my lungs and I come to something of an understanding, I try to call out.

"Hello?"

To call my first attempt a whisper would be a gross exaggeration. I clear my throat and try again.

"Hello?"

Several seconds pass before a brown-skinned woman wearing scrubs and a long white coat pops her head into the room. Her initial expression of concern fades quickly into a pleasant smile.

"Miss Davis." The slight squeak in her voice matches the kindness in her eyes. "Good morning."

"Where am—" My question is cut short by a bout of coughing that sends a wave of searing pain across my chest.

"Don't try to talk." The woman steps to the side of the bed and pulls a stethoscope from her pocket. "Just relax."

Though it takes every ounce of willpower I have, I force the coughing to stop and give her a quick nod as she places the cold metal instrument on my chest.

"I'm Dr. Patel." She wraps the stethoscope's tubing around her hand and returns it to her pocket. "I'm taking care of you." She surveys the various machines surrounding us before turning her attention back on me. "As for your question, you're in Emergency, and doing a whole lot better than anybody thought you'd be after your little swim last night." The look of concern returns to her face. "How are you feeling?"

I open my mouth to answer, then remembering that talking equals coughing and coughing equals bad, pull my free arm from beneath the warming blanket and rub my chest. Even my careful fingers find a few spots that hurt bad enough to make me wince.

The doctor shakes her head. "I'm sorry, but your chest is going to hurt for a few weeks. You took in a lot of water in that creek, not to mention your friends broke a couple of ribs reviving you."

"Friends?" The word sets off another bout of coughing, and my chest aches like a horse kicked me in the breastbone.

I'm thinking a Clydesdale.

And maybe a couple of his buddies.

"They came in with EMS last night," she answers once I'm done coughing. "Once we let them know you were out of the woods, they left to go see their families."

"How long have I...been out?"

"Since EMS brought you in around two, you've been in and out of consciousness. It was a little touch and go at the beginning, but you've stabilized over the last few hours."

"How...long?"

"It's still a little before three in the afternoon." That beaming smile of hers makes a reappearance. "Don't worry, Miss Davis. You didn't miss Christmas."

Christmas.

A stream of memory washes across my mind.

The family in the green Subaru.

The rushing water.

The unrelenting cold.

"The little girl," I croak out. "Is she—" Apparently I'm a slow learner. This spell of coughing hits me like someone jammed a bag of thumbtacks down my throat and chased it with rubbing alcohol.

"Please try not to talk." She takes a look at the chart in her hand. "Come to think of it, we haven't given you anything for pain yet. A shot of morphine might make your breathing a lot more comfortable. What do you think?"

Unwilling to give my throat and lungs another excuse to kick a girl when she's down, I answer with a simple nod.

"Good. My nurse will be in with the medicine in just a moment." Turning to leave, Dr. Patel glances back and gives me a reassuring nod. "Your aunt and uncle have barely left your side since you got here. They finally went down to the cafeteria about half an hour ago to get something to eat. You want me to send someone to find them?"

Despite the warmth coursing over me from the heated blanket, I shiver at the thought of facing Mike and Valerie. Mike's list of likely 'told-you-sos' run through my mind in rapid succession, though to be honest, it's the disappointment in Valerie's eyes I dread the most.

Tears well in my eyes, and my arms are too weak to even brush them away.

Dr. Patel grabs a tissue from the bedside table and dabs at my eyes. "It's okay, honey," she whispers. "We can wait."

"No. Let them come." I somehow get the words out without setting off another round of hacking. "Time to face the music."

Her smile shifts into a grim line as her soft fingers stroke my shoulder. "I'll send for them."

As Dr. Patel steps beyond the curtain, I'm left alone and realize she never answered my question about the family in the Subaru. I force myself back through every breathless moment at the bridge. I remember getting the man to shore, but have no idea if he was still breathing when I went back for his wife and child. The woman said she could swim, but so can I, and this is where I ended up. Then there's the little girl. She was counting on me, but when the cramps hit my legs, there was nothing I could do.

Another family dead, all thanks to me.

Fantastic.

My eyes well up anew, and since no one is here to brush them away, the tears simply flow, as unstoppable as the swollen creek that nearly took my life.

Minutes later, a nurse steps into the room and after a quick greeting injects something into my IV line. I start to ask her if she has any news on the family, but whatever is in that syringe—morphine, I think she said—acts quickly. Any question I might have had lost in the faint buzzing that overtakes my thoughts, I merely beam a dreamy smile in the nurse's direction as I make a failed attempt to keep my eyes open.

Time passes—A minute? An hour?—before the sound of familiar steps beyond the curtain brings me back to the present. I manage to raise one eyelid and attempt a smile when Valerie steps into the room.

"Carol," Valerie whispers. "Oh, thank God." She rushes to my side, her hand stopping just short of my face as if she thinks I might break if she touches me. "Are you okay?"

Afraid I'll either start coughing or bawling if I speak—and

not sure which of the two would be worse—I let my gaze wander around the room from one machine to another and give her a shrug as if to say, "You tell me."

Mike steps into the room, beaming from ear to ear, and joins Valerie by my bed.

"Hey there, slugger."

First time in years he's called me that. I used to hate it. I've even told him so on more than one occasion.

Today, it doesn't bother me. Not even a little.

"Doc says you have a few broken ribs." Mike circles the bed to inspect the machine that's monitoring my heart and lungs, his brow furrowed. "You breathing all right?"

I take a test breath and give Mike a quick nod. Though the pain in my chest hasn't gone anywhere, the medicine the nurse gave me has turned down the volume a bit. Braving another spell of coughing, I twist my face into the most ironic smile I can manage and get out two words in a gravelly whisper.

"Merry Christmas."

Mike and Valerie's eyes meet across the bed and then as one they look back at me, their disbelieving faces simultaneously breaking into wide grins.

"Merry Christmas, Carol." Valerie strokes my hair, her motherly eyes understanding and kind.

I take more comfort in that simple action than she will ever know.

"I'm so sorry, you two." I swallow. Hard. "This is all my fault."

"An issue for another day," Mike says. "We're just glad you're all right."

"Actually..." Valerie inclines her head, her eyebrow arching like it always does when she's about to let me in on a secret. "We're glad that *everyone* is all right."

I bite my lip, my eyes dancing back and forth from Valerie to Mike. "Everyone?"

"The Campbell family," Valerie says. "The ones from the bridge."

"They're okay?"

Mike takes my hand and gives my fingers a careful squeeze. "They're going to be fine."

"The little girl?"

"Her name is Jillian," Valerie says. "She's doing great. Her dad's going to be in the hospital a couple more days with a concussion and some broken bones, but she and her mom are being discharged this afternoon."

"Thanks to you." Mike looks on me with rare pride and even a hint of admiration. "You really stepped up last night."

"But the whole thing is my fault." My gaze shoots from Mike to Valerie and back. "I took my eyes off the road for just a second. Ran them off the bridge. I didn't mean to, but still..."

Mike holds up a hand. "We know. Still, it was an accident and everybody's fine." Mike shoots Valerie a worried glance. "But that's not the end of it, unfortunately."

"What is it?" When Mike won't answer, I turn on Valerie. "What aren't you two telling me?"

Valerie lets out a huge sigh. "A state trooper was here earlier. He was pretty interested in talking with you."

"A state trooper?" I'm not sure why I sound so surprised. I did nearly wipe out a family of three. "What did he want?"

"He wants to talk to you about what happened last night. About why you had Ryan's car." Valerie's gaze drops to the floor. "About what the doctors found in your blood."

A different pain roars to life in my chest. "Valerie, Mike, I can explain."

Valerie's palm goes to her right eye. "I asked you to follow three simple rules." She runs her fingers through her hair, refusing to look at me. "I didn't even know you drank."

"I don't." The tears start to flow anew. "You two have no idea what I've been through this week. It's been a nightmare."

Valerie looks up at me, her own eyes welling up. "So you got behind the wheel of someone else's car and drove intoxicated in the middle of a winter storm?"

I feel the indignant words that would have flown from my mouth three days ago fight their way to the tip of my tongue. I bury them. Deep. According to everything I've seen and heard the last three evenings, I wasn't supposed to survive last night. The fact that I'm still breathing has to mean something. Words I spoke to the third Spirit echo across my thoughts.

"I can be better."

"What?" Mike and Valerie say in unison, almost as if they rehearsed it.

"I can be better. Better than this. Better than I've been." Though it hurts like hell, I puff my chest with pride. "Better than either of you can imagine."

Valerie's eyebrows threaten to knot together. "Carol, are you feeling all right?"

"Never better." I free my left hand from the warmer blanket and take Valerie's while Mike rests his warm fingers on the other. "Things are going to be different. Starting now."

"I'm afraid that's truer than you know." A uniformed officer steps around the curtain, squat and sporting a graying mustache that hasn't been in style since the eighties. His pronounced southern drawl gives me a feeling he's not from around here. "Good afternoon, Miss Davis. So glad to see you're finally awake."

CHAPTER FIFTY-SEVEN

The trooper sidles closer, and Mike steps around the bed to intercept.

"Officer Chandler, can you give us a few minutes? Carol just woke up a little while ago."

"Of course." He veers past Mike and stops at the foot of the bed. "So, Miss Davis, how are you feeling?"

So much for a few minutes.

"Much better now that I have my family around me."

Valerie has on her game face, but I still catch the momentary flicker of her eyes at my words.

"That's nice." Chandler pulls a notepad out of his pocket and studies it for a moment before turning his attention back on me. His deliberate gaze, cool and calculated, lets me know one thing: he's here on business. "Mind if I ask you a few questions?"

"Why not? You've already asked me two."

"Fair enough." He rests a hand on the end of the bed. "Where were you last night around midnight?"

"Officer Chandler," Mike says. "Is this really necessary right now?"

"Mr. Fredericks." Chandler blinks as if he was just asked what color the sky is. "I've got a man downstairs with a broken arm and a severe concussion, a woman and her child admitted with minor injuries, and a three-month-old Subaru Outback at the bottom of a creek, not to mention a damaged bridge railing, and all from your niece's little Christmas Eve joy ride. At least five witnesses put your niece at the bridge after midnight last evening." He rests a hand on the end of the bed and meets my gaze. "That's a lot of unanswered questions, wouldn't you agree, Miss Davis?"

"Now, see here—" Mike begins.

"It's okay, Mike." I let go of Valerie's hand and push the button that raises the head of the bed. "So, tell me, Officer Chandler, what is it you want to know?"

"I'm just trying to put together the events of last evening." He glances over his pad once more, then narrows his eyes at me, as if trying to peer into my soul. "I understand you accompanied a Mr. Ryan King to the Christmas Eve Dance at the town civic center. Is that correct?"

I cock my head to one side and smile. "Pretty much the entire class was there."

Chandler rubs the top two pages of his notepad between his fingers, the sound like tree branches rubbing in a winter gale. "A simple yes or no will do, Miss Davis."

Fine.

"Yes, then."

"And afterward, you and Mr. King went to a party at the Allen family's lake house?"

"Yes."

"But you didn't leave with Mr. King."

"No, I didn't."

"Any particular reason?"

"I wasn't feeling well."

Mike's jaw clenches, and the color drains from Valerie's face as the entire room awaits the rest of my answer.

"When I went to ask him to take me home, he was busy, um...getting to know somebody else."

"Oh, honey." Valerie touches my shoulder. "I'm so sorry."

"It's okay, Valerie. I'm all right." I turn my attention back on Chandler. "I was upset and wanted to go home."

"So you took Mr. King's car without his permission."

"Like I said." My free hand balls into a fist. "I was upset."

"And back at the Allen house." Chandler's gaze drops to the floor. "Was alcohol being served there?"

"Some of the kids were drinking." I glance up at Valerie. "Some weren't."

"What about you, Miss Davis?" Like twin lasers, his calm, gray eyes burn into me. "Were you drinking?"

"That's enough." Mike signals for me to stop talking. "Don't say anything else, Carol. You have rights." He turns back to Chandler. "I believe my niece has been more than cooperative, but she's just come through a terrible trauma. If you have any more questions, you can direct them to our lawyer."

"Don't worry, Mr. Fredericks. I intend to." Chandler looks past Mike's shoulder. "And just to be clear, Miss Davis, I know who you are. What this particular Christmas means to you." He closes his notepad, shoves it in his pocket, and heads for the curtain. "Don't think for a minute that big fat check will change anything, understand?"

As Chandler leaves the room, I clench my eyes shut and wish the last twelve hours away. Neither Mike nor Valerie says a word for a while. The next thing I hear is the subtle squeak of Dr. Patel's voice.

"Ah, Mr. and Mrs. Fredericks. Didn't know you had made it back."

"It's all right, Doc," Mike says. "It looks pretty busy out there."

She shakes her head. "You have no idea."

"So," Valerie asks, "what's the verdict?"

"Well, let's see." Dr. Patel steps over to the bed, flashes a pen light in both my eyes, and takes another listen to my heart and lungs. "Other than three broken ribs and some residual hypothermia, Carol is doing quite well. All of her scans are okay, her blood work has normalized, and she seems neurologically intact. Other than some pain with breathing the next few weeks, she should have a full recovery. I think we'll keep her overnight for observation, but unless something unexpected happens, we should be able to let her go in the morning."

"Just in time to go to jail."

The room goes quiet at my whispered words. Dr. Patel brings the chart in her hand across her chest and quickly leaves, supposedly to finish the paperwork to get me upstairs. Mike says nothing, his silence conspicuous as Valerie's eyes slip closed.

I don't need to be a mind reader to know what she's thinking.

She's given up on me. They've all given up on me.

"No."

I look up into Mike's face, and where I usually see disappointment, I find only conviction.

"No?" I ask.

Mike shakes his head. "No niece of mine is going to jail."

"Mike," Valerie whispers. "Don't."

"Don't what?" Mike begins to pace. "Sure, Carol made some pretty bad decisions last night and we're all going to have a nice long talk about that, but I'll be damned before I let anyone forget she leaped into a freezing river last night and saved three lives."

A warmth blossoms in my chest. "Thanks, Mike, but the cop was right. None of it changes anything. Not the money. Not what I did. Actions have consequences, and it looks like ten years of being a complete pain in the ass has finally caught up to me."

"I don't know, slugger. You got a second chance last night." Mike sits on the bed next to me and pats my leg through the warming blanket. "I guess we're all going to have to wait and see what you do with it."

CHAPTER FIFTY-EIGHT

The next hour flies by as I catch Mike and Valerie up on the events of the night before in painstaking detail. My usual conversational evasive maneuvers left in the rear-view mirror, we run through an extensive play by play of the last few days, minus any reference, of course, to my various spectral visitors.

I've finally got my head on straight for what feels the first time in forever. Don't want to get sent back to my therapist now.

We end with a thorough review of what went down last night: the various goings on at the dance, the nauseating ride to the Allen house, my first unfortunate encounter with hard liquor, Ryan's fight with Christopher, me praying to the porcelain gods in the Allen's downstairs bathroom, and my unfortunate witnessing of Ryan's tongue hockey match with Jamie Meadows. I'd forgotten how good it felt to just get everything out and talk about it.

"I just wanted to go home, you know? I'd puked up my guts, my dress and hair were ruined, and I'd just found my date up to his tonsils in another girl's mouth."

Valerie squinches up her nose. "Honestly, honey, I would've

taken off, too." She cracks her neck like an action star in a movie. "Except I would've made sure it was Ryan's car that ended up at the bottom of a creek."

"Now, Valerie." Mike crosses his arms and tries to look all disapproving, though a subtle smile peeks between the cracks. "Is that what we're trying to communicate here?"

"What, Mike?" Valerie shoots me a wink. "We're all opening up a bit, and I'm just being honest with her."

Mike chuckles. "As long as we don't discuss calling a hit man, I guess it's all good."

The nurse who brought me the wondrous morphine steps around the curtain. "Miss Davis, your room is ready. Transport will be by in just a moment to take you upstairs."

As she disappears back into the ER, Mike stands and cracks his back. "Guess we're camping out here tonight."

"You know what?" I bite my lip, not sure what I'm going to say. "Why don't you two go on home?" My words come out stronger than I intend, and I start to backpedal. "I mean, all of us shouldn't have to spend Christmas at the hospital, right?"

Valerie and Mike look at each other in something like wonderment. Mike opens his mouth to speak, but Valerie heads him off at the pass.

"Carol." Valerie rests a finger across my lips. "I'm not sure what miracle has you suddenly appreciating the day of your birth for the first time in a decade, and frankly, I don't care. We almost lost you last night. Today is about you getting better so you can come home."

"But—"

"No buts. If you don't listen to anything else I say for the rest of your life, listen to the words that are about to come out of my mouth. You. Are. Family. Pretty much the only family I have left on the planet besides Mike, and that's not going to change any time soon." She grips my hand and gives it a not-so-gentle squeeze. "We're not going anywhere till you're better. Got it?"

"Got it." For the third time since awakening in the hospital, tears form at the corners of my eyes.

And for once, I couldn't care less.

The move upstairs takes a lot longer than I expect. It's nearly 5:30 before we're all settled in. My stomach starts to rumble a bit, so Valerie clears it with our nurse and sends Mike out for a pizza and dessert. This leaves Valerie and me alone for the first time since I awoke in the ER.

"So..." I pull Valerie's attention away from whatever variation of *Law & Order* is showing on the wall-mounted TV. "I've caught you up with everything I know, but there are still a few things I'm fuzzy on."

"Okay." Valerie leans back in the chair. "What do you want to know?"

"The creek." I take a deep breath and pain shoots through my chest like I inhaled a hive of yellow jackets. "Me and the little girl from the car. We were almost to shore when my legs cramped up and we went under."

Valerie doesn't blink an eye, though I can tell she's far more upset than she's letting on.

"I remember bits and pieces."

Memories start to flow.

"Being pulled from the water."

Strong arms.

"Someone pushing air into my lungs."

Warm breath.

"But I don't know who it was."

Soft lips.

"Do you know?"

"I do." Valerie looks past me, her mouth sliding into a

hesitant smile. "But I think you should ask someone who was actually there if you want the whole story."

I turn my head and find a familiar face in the doorway.

"Roberta."

My second oldest friend on the planet rushes across the room and pulls me into a tight hug. Though it hurts like I've been thrown into a medieval torture device, I let her.

"What are you doing here, Bobbisox?"

"Are you ever going to get tired of that stupid name?"

"Not in this lifetime."

Which according to the best sources on the matter is already eighteen hours longer than it was supposed to be.

Shaking her head, Roberta sits on the corner of the bed. "As for why I'm here, in case you've forgotten, I live here these days." She glances in the direction of the door, a sad cast descending on her face. "Tameka wanted to come, but her doctor won't let her leave her room right now. She's doing pretty well at the moment, but he says her immune system is too weak to risk her wandering the hospital." She gives me a quick up and down. "Speaking of which, you're looking a hell of a lot better than the last time I saw you."

"Sorry about that." I offer her an apologetic shrug. "If it makes you feel any better, I've sworn off vodka for life."

"Vodka?"

"Yeah. I was a little past tipsy at the party. Said some stupid things. Sorry."

Roberta's brows furrow. "I'm not talking about the party." She crosses her arms, her confused gaze shifting from me to Valerie. "She doesn't know?"

"Know?" I scan Roberta's face for the answer. "Know what?"

"The rest of the story." Valerie rests her hand on mine.

"Roberta?" She's got that "I've got something to tell you" look on her face. "What is it?"

Roberta lets out a weary sigh. "When we found you, you weren't breathing."

"I know, but—"

"No, Carol, you don't know," Roberta whispers. "We all thought you were gone. You were cold. Ice cold. Didn't even have a pulse."

"Well, looks like I've got one now." I jerk a thumb at the beeping machine to my right, the hair on my neck standing on end despite my poor attempt at putting on a brave front. "See?"

Roberta's head tilts to one side, her unamused gaze pinning me to the spot like no one else's can.

"All right, all right. I'm sorry. Just trying to lighten it up in here." A twinge of pain flares in my chest as I take a deep breath. "Now, will someone please tell me who I've got to thank for all these broken ribs?"

And with that, Roberta fills in the rest of the story. The missing pieces of the last twenty-four hours. I'm not sure if it's the morphine or a little ghostly intervention, but as Roberta speaks, the events play out in my head like a movie.

Christopher is driving his dad's Grand Cherokee with one hand while he pleads on the phone with me to pull over. Roberta starts yelling when they take a sharp curve too fast, and Christopher drops the phone in her lap to take the wheel with both hands. Roberta grabs the phone and starts yelling at me. When I stop answering, she hangs up the phone and tells Christopher to go faster. Christopher tells her they're the ones that are going to wreck if they're not careful. Before Roberta can answer, a black SUV roars past and disappears around the next curve.

"Quentin Young?" I ask.

"You know it," Roberta says. "With Ryan in tow."

Makes perfect sense. Quentin plays forward on the basketball team and is one of Ryan's best friends.

Christopher and Roberta catch up to Quentin's black Expedition a couple miles up the road. Across the narrow bridge that links the edge of town to the lakeshore properties, both Quentin's vehicle and Ryan's Camaro are parked on the shoulder, headlights beaming down at the raging water coursing under the bridge. Christopher notices the hole punched in the guardrail and whips their vehicle around as well to shed as much light as possible on the swollen creek. Ryan and Quentin have already made it to the bottom of the hill while Jamie is perched on the back seat of the SUV, her head craned out the window.

"I'll bet that little bitch was all smiles."

"I saw her, Carol." Roberta's eyes burn through me. "She was terrified."

"Truth is," Valerie adds, "Jamie stayed right here with Christopher, Roberta, and Ryan for most of the night and morning. Didn't leave till a couple hours before lunch when her parents came and picked her up."

"She...stayed?"

"Yeah." Roberta's shoulders rise in a puzzled shrug. "Who knew? Even Jamie Meadows has a soul."

"So, what happened next?"

Christopher is out of the car in a flash and sprinting down the hill in his tux and wingtips. Roberta drops a quick 911 call as she slides out of her heels and steps out into the rain and cold. She takes a moment to check in on Jamie, who appears to be going into shock herself, before hiking up her dress and heading down the hill after Ryan and Christopher.

"Those two didn't get into another fight did they?"

Roberta holds up a hand, silencing me. "Just let me tell the story, all right?"

At first, Roberta can't see or hear anything but rushing water. A peal of coughing brings her to the water's edge where she finds Quentin on the ground perched over a man so covered in mud she can barely make him out in the dim light. After she realizes Quentin has the man turned on his side like our swim coach used to bang into our heads every year in CPR class, she shouts, "Where's Ryan?"

Quentin glances up, wide-eyed and out of his depth. "What?"

"Ryan. Where is he?"

Quentin points downstream between firm slaps of the man's back, clearly the only thing he can think to do.

Roberta makes her way along the water's edge. Around one bend and then another, she comes upon a woman on all fours hacking up her lungs. The woman's haircut a pixie style and bleached bright blond, Roberta knows it isn't me, but checks on her all the same.

"Are you okay?"

The woman looks up at her, her eyes frantic. Between barking coughs, she asks, "My daughter? Have you seen my daughter?"

Roberta doesn't have the heart to answer and continues her trek downstream as the woman calls after her.

"Please...come back." Her croaked words bring on another peal of coughing. "My daughter..."

After feeling her way another fifty feet or so, Roberta catches up with Ryan and Christopher, though she hears them before she sees them.

"There!" echoes Christopher's voice.

"I see her!" Ryan's deep voice, fearful yet confident, followed by a splash barely audible above the coursing flood.

Roberta feels her way around a tree draped in vines and finds them. Christopher is shining that stupid pocket flashlight he carries everywhere out onto the water while Ryan charges out into the creek for what appears a bobbing melon in the current. The water gets as high as his waist before he stops and heads back for shore. In his arms, a little girl with long blond hair and a waterlogged dress hangs limp.

"That's not Carol," Christopher shouts.

"Really?" Ryan glares as he stumbles out of the water and lowers the girl to the ground. "I hadn't noticed."

Christopher shines his light on the little girl's chest. "Is she breathing?"

Before Ryan can answer, the girl coughs up what looks like half a gallon of water and raises her head. "The angel," she croaks. "Did you see her?"

"The angel?" Ryan and Christopher ask together.

"She saved us," the girl gets out between fits of coughing. "Where'd she go?"

"There!" Roberta rushes over to Ryan and Christopher, pointing frantically out across the water. "I see something!" Ryan and Christopher follow her outstretched finger and see it too: a pale arm draped across a dark branch at the center of the creek. Caught in the eddy currents of a fallen tree, a nearly naked form floats face down in the churning water.

"Carol!" Christopher screams and takes off for the creek's edge, stopped only by Ryan's firm hand on his collar.

"Don't do it." Ryan looks up, his face stricken with indecision. "If you go in there, we're just going to have two drowning victims on our hands."

"Then I hope somebody here besides me knows CPR." Christopher rips free of his jacket and rushes into the water. Roberta screams after him, for all the good it does. In seconds, he's up to his waist, his chest, his neck. He goes under a couple of times, each time longer than the one before, and just when Roberta doesn't think he can make it any farther, he surfaces by the fallen tree. Pulling himself along its dark mass, he inches his way to my motionless form and pulls my face from the water.

"She's really cold," he shouts, "and she's not breathing."

Sirens sound in the distance.

"What do I do?" Christopher yells.

"The EMTs are on the way," Roberta shouts. "Get her back here, and I'll help you."

"We'll help you," Ryan adds.

Christopher drapes my bare arm across his shoulder and begins the long walk back through the rushing water. Back on shore, Ryan rips a sturdy section of vine out of a tree, and he and Roberta form a human chain out into the water. Christopher stumbles more than once, but my head never dips below water again. He's almost out of juice when he reaches Roberta's outstretched hand.

"I've got you," she grunts as she and Ryan pull us ashore.

Exhausted, Christopher lays my pale form out on the ground. Ryan kneels beside me to help, but Christopher wards him off with an angry glare.

"Just Roberta," he spits in Ryan's direction. "You've already done enough tonight."

CHAPTER FIFTY-NINE

"You're kidding." I retrieve my jaw from my lap. "Christopher said that?"

Roberta grins. "Christopher may be a nice guy, but underneath it all, he's all boy, just like Ryan King."

"Boy?" Valerie asks. "After last night, I'd say Christopher Kellerman graduated to man." She squeezes my hand. "Not to mention he's got one thing going for him the illustrious Mr. King doesn't."

"And what's that?" I ask.

Raising an eyebrow, Valerie's lips spread in a devious grin. "He's the one who pulled you out of that creek."

"He was on a mission, that's for sure."

And with that, Roberta launches back into full on storyteller mode.

Standing there in shocked silence at Christopher's words, Roberta looks on helpless as Ryan pulls himself up to his full height and cracks his neck. Convinced that fists are about to start flying, she's relieved when Ryan raises his hands in surrender and humbly gets out of the way. Kneeling at my side,

Roberta checks my pulse, and not finding one, starts pumping on my chest.

"Now, Christopher," she whispers. "Give her a breath."

On his knees opposite Roberta, Christopher looks down on my nearly naked form and freezes. "I...I..."

"Chris, look at me." Roberta and Christopher lock gazes across my still chest. "It's now or never. Carol is dying. Maybe we can save her, maybe we can't, but right now she needs your help." Her eyes narrow as, yet again, she works my chest like a bellows. "Now, get in there and breathe."

Christopher pauses for another moment before taking a deep breath of frigid December air and lowering his mouth over mine. Pinching my nose shut, he fills my mouth, my throat, my lungs with warm, life-giving air. My chest rises and falls.

Roberta pumps at my ribcage with every bit of controlled strength she can muster. "Again."

And so it goes, the two of them alternating between forcing water from my lungs and pushing air down my throat. Roberta's stomach nearly rebels at the repeated snap of cracking ribs, a sentiment she finds mirrored in Christopher's nauseated gaze. An eternity passes before the EMTs arrive, though her watch shows the time as barely half past midnight when flood lamps light the creekside area as if it were midday. In a flurry of efficiency, the paramedics step in, strap me to a backboard, and insert a tube in my throat.

My chest rises unevenly with every squeeze of the resuscitator bag.

"That's when half the county showed up." Roberta gets up from the edge of my bed and paces the room excitedly. "There were police cars, fire trucks, ambulances..."

"And everybody did okay?"

"While Christopher and I were working on you, Ryan

collected up the little girl and helped her find her mother. Quentin stayed with the father till the paramedics arrived."

My lip trembles. "I wasn't even sure he was still breathing when I went back for the girl and her mother."

Valerie steps in. "His name's John Campbell, an accountant in town. They were on their way home later than expected from a Christmas party. He got the worst of it apparently. Got knocked out when the airbag punched him in the face and broke a couple bones in his arm trying to hold onto the wheel."

"But he's..."

Valerie pats my leg. "He's going to be fine."

"Fine..." My brain struggles to put it all together. Sounds like everyone's going to pull through, including yours truly.

But according to the last Spirit, I'm supposed to be dead.

Looks like I owe Christopher the apology of a lifetime.

Oh. My. God.

Christopher.

His hands on my bare chest. His lips on mine. His breath in my lungs.

"Wait." My hand snakes out of the protective cocoon of the warming blanket and goes to my neck, instinctively searching, though a part of me already knows what my fingers seek is lost forever. "No." My sigh fills the room. "No. No. No."

"What is it?" Roberta asks. "Carol?"

"Nothing." Again, my cheeks go hot. "It's stupid."

"Whatever it is has upset you." Valerie peers at me as if she has x-ray vision. "What is it?"

"I was just wondering. When Christopher pulled me out of the creek, did I still have on my necklace?"

"Necklace?" Roberta rolls her eyes. "Girl, you're lucky to be alive. We'll get you a new necklace."

"You don't understand." I look to Valerie and feel vindicated when understanding blossoms on her face.

"Was it...?"

"Yeah, Valerie. That's the one." I massage my neck. "You think it's...gone?"

"Probably." Valerie squeezes my fingers. "But you're still with us. I'll take that trade any day."

"Tell you what." Roberta touches my arm. "Soon as you're up to it, we'll go to the mall and find you something just as nice."

"Sounds great, but it's not the same." I close my eyes and take a breath. "That necklace was a gift. A special gift from a special friend. I'd give anything to have it back." My chin drops to my chest, and four muttered words make their way out of my mouth. "To have *him* back."

"Glad to hear it."

Distinctly male, the voice immediately sends a squadron of butterflies through my belly. All three of us look up to find Christopher Kellerman framed in the doorway. Dressed in jeans and what looks like a new sweater that is no doubt a gift from his mother, he studies me with an earnest half-grin.

"Christopher." I put on the best smile I can manage, though I'm pretty sure I left embarrassed in the rearview mirror a few miles back and am headed straight for mortified. "How long have you been standing there?"

"Just got here." He steps into the room, a little more confidence in his walk than I remember seeing before. "Promised Mom I'd stick around the house through dinner. Family's in from all over and they—"

"Merry Christmas." The words blurt out of my mouth before I can stop them. I hope they don't sound as foreign to everyone else's ears as they do to mine. "I mean, I hope your family has had a great day and everything..." My words trail away even as my brain entertains the various escape routes from the room.

"Umm...thanks." Christopher stops at the foot of the bed.

"It's been a pretty decent day, all things considered. Got Roberta's text that you woke up earlier and came back as soon as I could break away."

"I'm glad you did." I bite my lip, not sure what to say next. "There are some things we need to talk about."

"And that's our cue." Valerie rises from the bed and heads for the door. "Come on, Roberta. Let's go see what's keeping Mike and give these two some space."

"You all right?" Roberta asks. "I can stay if you want."

For half a second, I consider taking her up on her offer. "No, I think we'll be okay."

A nervous quiet falls across the room, a quiet that Valerie eventually breaks.

"We'll be back in twenty minutes or so, okay, honey?" She rests a hand on the door and glances back. "Coming, Roberta?"

Roberta follows, looking back with one last questioning glance before pulling the door closed behind them, leaving Christopher and me alone in the suddenly cramped hospital room.

"So, umm...hi." I search Christopher's face for any sign of what he's feeling.

"Hi," he mutters. "Looks like you're doing better."

"I am." We stare at each other for a long moment. "Thanks for dropping by."

"No problem." Christopher gestures to the foot of the bed, and at my nod sits in the spot Roberta just vacated. "How are you feeling?"

"Pretty well. It only hurts when I breathe." The slight chuckle that escapes my lips makes me wince. "Or laugh, or sneeze, or cough, or in any other way move my upper body."

Christopher inclines his head forward. "That's all on me and Roberta. We didn't know what else to do. We were just—"

"Saving my life?" And here come the tears again. "You have nothing to be sorry for. Believe me."

"We were scared." Head down like a whipped dog, he continues to apologize. His every word breaks my heart. "We just did what we had to—"

"Stop. Roberta told me. I know the whole story. What you did." I bite my lip. "What you risked."

Christopher chews on that for a moment, his expression inscrutable. "What else did you think I would do?"

"After I made an ass of myself at the party? I don't know."

"What are you talking about?"

"When you were talking to Faith. I was way out of line. I think I was...marking my territory or something." A single laugh comes from somewhere inside, the sound hollow and sad. "Fact is, you aren't my territory to mark."

Christopher rests his chin on his knuckles. "You know, Carol. That sounds suspiciously like an apology."

I lower my head, unable to look at him anymore. "Not even sure exactly what I'm supposed to be apologizing for."

"I don't know." It's Christopher's turn to let out a somber laugh. "We used to be best friends back in the day, but for the last couple years, you've pretty much blown me off at every turn. You only come around when you need something from me. And stupid me, I keep letting you." Crimson blossoms in his cheeks. "Guess I'm just a glutton for punishment."

"Well." All the sharp words that have rested at the tip of my tongue for months seem to have abandoned me as I stare into the eyes of a boy—or, as Valerie insists, man—who risked everything to pull me back from the edge and literally breathed life back into my body. "That pretty much sums it up, doesn't it?"

"More or less."

"So, I guess this is it, then."

Christopher shakes his head and quietly groans. "You still don't get it." His wheels spinning, he struggles for the next words. Christopher Kellerman may be one of the smartest kids in school, but snappy banter isn't exactly his thing. "Look, I'm not going to sit here and tell you everything's okay. It's not."

"I know that."

"There are things that have been said and done that can't be taken back."

"Agreed." My intestines tie themselves in knots. "So, what are you trying to say?"

"I've spent the last ten years chasing after you, as friends or maybe something more." He rises from the bed and jams his hands in his pockets. "I guess it took last night at the party to realize the person I was chasing doesn't exist anymore."

His words send a railroad spike through my navel. "She's right here."

"For the moment." Christopher goes to the window where a darkening yet clear sky greets him, the gray clouds and rain of the last week apparently having taken the day off. "But what happens tomorrow, or next week, or even next year?"

"Things are different now." I bring my forearm across my face to wipe away the tears brimming there. "Everything that's happened this week. Last night. All of it. I'm not the same person I was a week ago."

"Really?" Christopher asks, his voice deadpan, like he's heard all this before. "Just like that?"

"I've changed." I clench my fists so hard that blood flows back out into the IV line. "I can't explain how or why, but it's the truth."

His expression somewhere between amused and dubious, Christopher stares at me as if for the first time. "You expect me to believe that Carol Davis somehow found the Christmas spirit?"

I bury my face in my hands. "You have no idea." A bitter chuckle falls from my lips. "Not that it matters, it seems."

I hit Christopher with all the details of Officer Chandler's visit to my little corner of the ER, and the likely outcome once I'm released from the hospital.

"But, everyone's okay." His brow furrows. "You saved them. It's all over the news."

"They wouldn't have needed saving if it weren't for me."

"It was an accident." Christopher rejoins me at the bedside. "What you did last night? That took some serious guts."

"Yes." I reach for his hand before he can pull away again. "It did."

Staring at our intertwined fingers, he slips his free hand into his jacket pocket. "I have something for you." He pulls out a plastic bag folded in quarters.

"What is it?"

A sad smile fills his face. "Something that cost a certain seven-year-old all his birthday money and six straight months of allowance." He unzips the plastic bag and produces a newly cleaned chain of gold with a small garnet charm in the shape of a heart hanging at its apex.

My eyes grow wide. "You...saved it."

"It's yours." He undoes the clasp. "May I?"

I sit up in the bed and do my best to keep the pain from my face. His hands go to either side of my neck, and my face, chest, and belly grow warm.

"There." Christopher pulls away to his corner of the bed. "Back where it belongs."

"When?" I ask. "How?"

"Last night. Before the paramedics took you away." Christopher studies the blinking machine to my right. "I wasn't sure what was going to happen, but I promised myself that if you made it through, I'd get it back to you."

In that moment, I ponder how poorly equipped a seven-year-old girl is to realize when a boy is giving her his heart.

"Thank you, Christopher." My eyes slide closed, a cyclone of thoughts and emotions spinning in my head.

"Well, I'm glad you're okay." Christopher turns to leave. "See you around, I guess."

"Wait." I bring my hands to my face, afraid to speak. "I have something for you as well."

Christopher's brow furrows anew in puzzlement. "I...don't understand."

"Come here." I pat the bed next to my hip. "Sit."

Christopher lowers his head in exasperation. "Why?"

"Just. Sit." The third word comes out so quiet, even I can barely hear it. "Please."

Christopher pauses for a moment before sitting beside me atop the starched sheets of the hospital bed. Hip to hip, I feel the heat of his body against mine. The strength of his nearness.

And maybe—just maybe—a touch of electricity.

"All right, Carol. I'm here." He looks at me with the eyes of a puppy that's been kicked one too many times. "What is it?"

I take a deep breath. "In every fairy tale I've ever read, the hero always has one weapon in his arsenal that saves the day. One arrow in his quiver that always wins in the end."

Christopher doesn't say a word.

"When all else fails, it is the hero's kiss that awakens the sleeping princess. Brings her back to life."

His chest rises and falls once, twice, three times.

"So?" he says, finally.

"Last night, a kiss from you brought me back to life." I grab his sweater with both hands and pull him into me until our lips are a hairsbreadth apart. "I thought I'd return the favor."

CODA

TWELFTH NIGHT

Thursday, Jan 5th

CHAPTER SIXTY

"All rise." The bailiff's resounding bass echoes in the chamber. "The Honorable Calvin J. Rutledge presiding."

My lawyer, an old friend of Christopher's parents named Paul Blake, stands and assumes a practiced position of respect. I do my best to follow suit. Over breakfast this morning, Paul made it quite clear that making a good impression on the judge today was an important step toward our goal of me not spending the next few years in jail.

I glance back into the courtroom gallery and lock eyes with Mike. He shoots me a cautious smile. Though only a few feet separate us, the oak bar between us makes it feel like a mile. I wish Valerie were here, but she's sequestered in the next room with the rest of the witnesses.

I'll be seeing her soon enough.

"How are you doing?" Paul whispers in my ear.

"About as well as can be expected." I fight the urge to pour myself another glass of water from the pitcher on the table, the condensation on the cool metal reminiscent of the nervous sweat coursing from my every pore. "My heart's beating like I just swam fifty laps, and I feel like I'm about to puke. Otherwise, I'm great."

"Try not to worry, Carol." He rests a hand on my shoulder. "Like I told you before, this isn't my first time in court."

After a few seconds that seem to stretch into days, a door to the rear of the bench opens. The judge, an older Black man with more salt than pepper atop his head, enters the room and makes his way to his seat.

"Show time," Paul mutters under his breath.

"Be seated," the judge intones as he assumes his position at the bench. Paul and I take our seats as I do my best not to stare at the frowning man who is about to decide my fate. A glance back into the gallery reveals more than one familiar face, some friendlier than others.

The face I want to see most, however, remains notably absent.

Today of all days.

Where could Christopher be?

For the hundredth time, I check my pocket for my phone, my fingers trained to seek solace on its slick glass screen. And for the hundredth time, they come up empty.

Valerie didn't think it would be a good idea to bring a phone into court today.

A shuffling noise brings my attention back to the front of the room. A mousy woman dressed in a paisley top and pencil skirt and wearing horn-rimmed glasses that would qualify as hipster if she were twenty years younger rummages through a stack of folders. Finding the one she's looking for, she stands and opens the manila binder.

"Case number 19121843. State vs. Carol Davis." She hands the folder to the bailiff who, in turn, hands it to the judge. Over the next couple of minutes, he studies the contents like a hawk watching mice skitter across an open field. His frequent glances up send shivers up my spine as those raptor eyes behind his bifocal lenses dissect me to the core.

"Mr. Blake," he asks. "Is it true your client is pleading *nolo contendere*?"

Paul eases out of his chair and stands to address the judge. "Yes, Your Honor."

"And she has been made aware of the consequences of pleading no contest to the charges as listed?"

"Yes, Your Honor. We have reviewed all the pertinent information and that's how she wishes to plead. She does, however, ask for opportunity to speak in allocution before final sentencing, if it pleases the court."

The judge turns his attention back on me. "Ms. Davis. Will you please stand?"

"Yes, Your Honor." I rise from the hard wooden seat, willing my knees not to knock together in front of the entire court.

The judge closes the folder and sets it aside. "Carol Anne Davis. I must ask, are you aware of the charges to which you intend to plead no contest?"

"I am, Your Honor."

The judge lets out a quiet sigh. "Will the Clerk of Court please review those charges?"

The woman in the horn-rimmed glasses stands again. "Miss Davis, you have been charged with unauthorized use of a motor vehicle, reckless driving, and driving while impaired. How do you plead?"

I glance in Paul's direction and clear my throat. "I plead no contest, Your Honor."

"Miss Davis." The judge peers at me. "We're giving you every opportunity to reconsider. Are you certain you're completely aware of the consequences of such a plea?"

I swallow the acid building up at the back of my throat. "I am, Your Honor."

"These charges have the potential for heavy fines and possibly even jail time."

"Yes, Your Honor." Breathe in. Hold for five. Breathe out. "That's how Mr. Blake explained it to me."

"Your Honor," Paul breaks in, "while Miss Davis fully admits the facts of the case per the filed police report, she hopes the court will be merciful in sentence after hearing the testimony of her various character witnesses and her own allocution."

The judge shifts his gaze to the table to our right. "Does the prosecution have any objections to this course of action?"

The opposing counsel, a woman in her mid-thirties with strawberry blond hair cut in a short bob, comes to her feet. Obviously going for "intimidating" in her navy business suit, she looks over at me, her face somewhere between smirk and snarl.

I wonder if the rock on her left ring finger is visible from space.

"No objections, Your Honor." The prosecutor returns her attention to the bench. "Mr. Blake and I have already discussed the various character witnesses on Miss Davis' list, and the State has no objections to any of their testimonies."

"Thank you, Ms. White," the judge growls.

As my lawyer shifts through the papers before him, I glance over at the empty jury section. Twelve seats, all of them empty on this Twelfth day of Christmas. I think I'd be better off with twelve drummers drumming or lords a-leaping or whatever the hell the last verse of that stupid song says than trusting the next few years of my life to Judge McGrumpypants there.

Though I suppose he probably earned his title somewhere along the way.

The judge adjusts his glasses and peers at Paul. "Your first witness, Mr. Blake?"

"Valerie Fredericks, the defendant's aunt."

CHAPTER SIXTY-ONE

Valerie enters from a doorway to the left and proceeds to the stand where the bailiff swears her in. Then, in a move I've seen a thousand times, she turns to face the judge, her arms crossing before her as her pleasant expression downshifts into combat mode.

No doubt about it. My aunt has come ready to fight.

"Good morning, Your Honor."

"Mrs. Fredericks." The judge adjusts his glasses. "I've had opportunity to read the letter you and your husband wrote in regards to the defendant."

"Thank you, Your Honor."

"You've been a part of your niece's life since her birth and have even cared for her in your own home over the last ten years since the loss of your sister."

"Ten years." Valerie bites her lip.

"The court recognizes that you are uniquely qualified to speak to her character." The judge allows a subtle half-smile. "I'll start with a simple question. Imagine someone that had never met your niece before. They ask you to describe her. What would you say?"

Valerie looks out at me, then back at the judge. "I'd tell them it's like watching my sister grow up all over again." She glances out at Mike. "Holly was always a little different. 'Marched to her own beat' is what her teachers always said. She didn't follow all the rules. Wasn't the politest or most genteel. That saying about well-behaved women never making history? She might as well have had that tattooed across her forehead."

"With all due respect," the prosecutor interrupts, "we're here today to discuss Carol Davis, not her mother."

"But we *are* discussing Carol, Ms. White." Valerie turns her all-business gaze on the opposing counsel. "Coming up it was always me and Holly. I may have been four years younger than my only sister, but I watched her grow up as surely as I have Carol." She launches a broad smile in my direction. "Carol is every bit her mother's daughter. Stubborn. Sensitive. Tough. Vulnerable. Too smart for her own good at times, that's for sure. At her core, though? Gold." She turns to face the judge. "Your Honor, I'd be lying if I sat here and said Carol is all unicorns and rainbows. Anybody who knows her knows different. But for someone who's faced so much loss at such a young age, I think she's turned out pretty well. The last two weeks notwithstanding, her record speaks for itself."

"Indeed it does." The judge slips off his glasses and cleans the lenses. "I've reviewed the letters from her principal, teachers, and coaches as well as several from her classmates. While it is clear her wit may have a bit of bite, Miss Davis seems, for the most part, a model student." He slips his glasses back onto his face. "But what are your thoughts regarding the events of this past Christmas Eve? Her string of poor decisions that evening nearly led to four deaths, including her own."

Valerie looks out at me, her brave face threatening to crack for all of half a second. "To be honest, Your Honor, Carol broke nearly every rule of our household that evening. Our trust was violated, and though we couldn't be prouder of the bravery she showed when it truly mattered, she's got a long way to go to earn back that trust. We've spent hours upon hours the last two weeks taking a look at every aspect of our home life and have pretty much decided to start from scratch. A lot of good has come from this, but it hasn't been without its share of pain."

That's the truth. Other than school the last two days and an hour or two in the afternoon to drop by and visit Tameka, I've basically been on house arrest since I came home from the hospital. Have I rankled under the new rules? Sure. But can I really blame Mike and Valerie?

Someone in the gallery clears their throat. I peek across my shoulder and return a subtle nod from Jamie Meadows. We've made our peace since Christmas Eve, and though we're never going to be besties, our truce has made life at school the last two days way easier to handle. Ryan, on the other hand, didn't even bother to come today. I know he's still pissed about everything that went down, but the least he could have done was come out and show some support. I mean, he was the one playing tonsil hockey with Jamie when he was out with me.

On the other hand, you did steal his car and almost involve him in a triple homicide.

Note to self: Next time Roberta drops some truth on you, listen.

Back to Earth, Carol. There's a trial going on.

"...and I can assure you her uncle and I take this all very seriously and will abide by whatever verdict the court decides."

"Of course, Mrs. Fredericks."

"However, neither my husband nor I see what benefit jail time will bring to this situation. Carol is still in high school and—"

"And the charges against her are not insignificant." The

judge peers at Valerie. “Trust that I will take everything said in this court today under consideration before sentencing.”

“Of course, Your Honor.” Valerie’s eyes find me, her bottom lip trembling as she fights to maintain her composure before the judge. “Of course.”

CHAPTER SIXTY-TWO

"Mr. Delacroix," the judge says, "please state for the record your relationship with Miss Davis."

Philippe leans back in his chair. "Carol is an employee at my boutique."

"Your only employee?"

"At the moment." Philippe offers a slight shrug. "I have no need for other help."

"I understand you are an old friend of the family?"

"That is correct, Your Honor."

"And how would you describe Miss Davis' performance? Is she a good worker?"

Philippe smiles. "Overall, her performance is excellent. She's generally punctual, has a good work ethic, and a fantastic sense of style." His face falls as he fidgets in his chair. "To be honest, though, her attitude at times could use some work."

I glance back at Mike, who maintains his patented "just keep calm" stare.

"So," the judge asks Philippe, "you've had problems with her on the job?"

"From time to time. During the holiday season, it's been a

bit worse, but given Carol's history, I've given her a bit more leeway over the last month or so."

The judge rubs at his chin. "Can you please elaborate?"

Philippe glares out at me, a strange crossness in his gaze. "When it comes to issues of style and finding the right dress for a young lady, I have no doubts as to Miss Davis' expertise. It's her delivery that always seems to be the sticking point. Despite my best efforts, I've been unable to convince her to check her sarcastic streak at the door. This has led to no end to complaints from customers who have felt belittled and, at times, even insulted in my store."

My stomach knots and reknots itself. Why is Philippe doing this?

"And yet you kept Miss Davis on at your shop?"

Philippe looks out at me, his gaze unrepentant. "Her father and I were close in our younger years. I owe him more than I can ever repay."

"Even though her behavior has likely cost you business?"

"It has cost me business." Philippe sighs. "In fact, not three days before Christmas, I had to offer a young lady and her mother a steep discount on one of the nicer dresses in my shop to make up for Miss Davis' particular flavor of customer service." His gaze roves the gallery to my rear, his eyes widening as recognition blossoms on his features. "In fact, that lovely young woman is sitting in the courtroom today."

The entire courtroom follows Philippe's gaze to the far corner of the gallery. There, seated on a bench and keeping to herself is a particularly sullen Emily Stockton.

"Your Honor," Ms. White says, the slightest of grins on her lips, "it's a bit unorthodox, but would it be possible to hear this young woman's testimony?"

The judge's eyes narrow. "For what purpose, Ms. White?"

Her lips part in a shark's smile. "To get a flavor of how Miss Davis is seen by her peers."

Paul shoots to his feet. "Objection. This girl isn't on the witness list and—"

"With all due respect to opposing counsel, I've allowed Mr. Blake to cherry pick a selection of character witnesses to bring before the court in defense of his client and didn't bring a single one of my own. Though the facts of this case are sufficiently compelling, perhaps a more neutral point of view would provide additional insight to the case."

The judge contemplates this for a moment. "I'll allow it, but keep it brief."

Silence falls across the room, and my racing heart kicks it up another notch as Emily Stockton is brought forward. Philippe relinquishes his seat, moving to the periphery of the court while Emily sits and places her hand on the bailiff's Bible. Sworn in, she turns to address the judge and the courtroom at large.

"Thank you for coming forward, Ms. Stockton." The judge leans in. "Can you please tell us how you know the defendant?"

Emily takes a breath. "I was her last customer a few minutes prior to closing three nights before Christmas. I went into the store last minute to shop for a dress and shoes for the Christmas Eve dance. Five minutes with Miss Davis and I was left feeling worthless, an obstacle between her and the door." Her eyes drop. "A particularly unattractive obstacle, in fact."

The judge slips off his glasses and squints at Emily. "She hurt you."

Emily nods. "She ignored me. Made jokes at my expense. It's not something you forget very easily."

My toes curl in my shoes.

Emily fiddles with the buttons on her cardigan. "I've debated all morning what I'd say to Carol Davis if I had the opportunity to speak today."

"And what would you like to say to her?" Ms. White's question trails away as the judge shoots his hawkish glare in her direction.

Emily raises an eyebrow. "I'd like to say...thank you."

Gasps sound from the gallery.

"I'm sorry," the judge says. "Did you say 'thank you'?"

"I did, Your Honor."

The judge's brow knits. "You've come to testify on the behalf of someone who treated you so poorly?"

"No, sir." Her gaze finally trails in my direction, a smile blossoming on her face. "I've come to let you know the girl I spoke to that night isn't in the courtroom today. I don't know what happened to her, and quite frankly, I don't care. I never want to speak to her again."

The judge stares sternly at Emily. "It goes without saying that many see Miss Davis in a far more positive light given her heroic actions early Christmas morning."

"That may be true," Emily says, "but the change I'm referring to occurred long before that." Her gaze drops. "At the dance. Carol showed me a kindness. A kindness the girl I met two nights before would never have been capable of." She looks up from her lap and locks gazes with the judge. "This was hours before the accident. Before she would have had any reason to make a good impression on anyone. Before all of it. Something's different about Carol, Your Honor."

"Miss Stockton." The prosecutor rises from her table. "You strike me as a nice young woman. Still, while I appreciate your optimism regarding Miss Davis' apparent change in character, isn't it possible you're projecting a bit? Finding the best in someone rather than the worst?"

"You tell me, Ms. White," Emily says. "Two nights before the dance, I wouldn't have been particularly upset to hear that Carol Davis had jumped off a bridge. Imagine my surprise when

I heard she actually did, and all to save the lives of three complete strangers."

Emily answers a few more questions and then is dismissed to the gallery. She gives me a subtle nod as she passes the table, biting her lip as she passes the bar and exits the courtroom.

At the bailiff's motioning, Philippe takes back his seat on the stand.

"Mr. Delacroix," the judge intones. "Do you have anything else to say for or against Miss Davis before you are excused?"

Philippe allows a languid gaze to fall in the frustrated prosecutor's direction before shooting me a subtle wink. "Only that it appears I was...misinformed."

CHAPTER SIXTY-THREE

"Miss Oliver," the judge states, "I understand you and the defendant are close friends?"

"For years." Roberta, the only person from my school scheduled to speak today, looks out at the gallery at large, her expression calm, confident, resolved. "Between school, swim, and weekends hanging out, Carol is practically family."

Though the sentiment of Roberta's kind words warms me, a simple fact refuses to leave my mind.

Roberta's not the only one Paul asked to speak today.

I'm not supposed to know that, but Valerie and I have had a strict no-secrets understanding since our little heart-to-heart in the ER twelve days ago. Paul canvassed the school, but no one else came forward. Not one. No one from any of my classes, no one else from swim, no one from cheering.

When I burn bridges, I burn them good.

The judge studies Roberta. "What insight do you bring to these proceedings?"

"I'd like to share a story, if that's okay." She looks out at me without a hint of judgment, and the months we've spent barely speaking melt away like fog on a summer morning. "Carol has developed a reputation over the last couple of years as self-centered and unpleasant, far more concerned with being popular than with being liked. A lot of people, including more than a few people in this room, are surprised by her actions on Christmas Eve. Risking her life to save a family of strangers? Definitely different from the Carol we've known for the last year."

My fingers tremble beneath the table as I wait for Roberta to get to the point.

"I see it a different way," she says after a quiet pause. "Carol and I worked together one summer as lifeguards. We spent every minute we could by the pool, enjoying the sun and water and, of course, doing our jobs. Fortunately, we had a pretty easy time of it most of the season, but on that last day, a little boy no more than five accidentally fell into the deep end and started swatting at the water. Before I could even think, Carol was in the water, one arm around the child and the other pulling them through the water. The parents were understandably freaked, but the boy was fine." She catches my gaze, her lips turning up in a subtle smile. "Regardless of what has come since, I saw what Carol Davis was made of that day. When it comes down to the wire, you can count on her to do the right thing."

"Like stealing a car, driving while impaired, and nearly..." The prosecutor's rant is cut short by a withering stare from the judge.

"She saved an entire family from drowning." Roberta nods in my direction. "That's the Carol Davis I know."

A murmur of activity sounds from across my right shoulder. A glance back reveals that pretty much the entire gallery has turned to look at the Campbell family, the three of them seated together on the back row. I spotted them on the way in—it's impossible to miss the little girl's blond ringlets—but have been too embarrassed to make eye contact with any of them.

"The court appreciates your candor, Miss Oliver," the judge says. "Is there anything else you'd like to say?"

"Yes, Your Honor." Roberta glances again in my direction. "I'd like to tell you about my sister."

Roberta spends the next few moments regaling both judge and the gallery at large with tales of our twelve-year friendship with all of its ups and downs and how Tameka has always been there in the middle of it.

"These last few days since Christmas have been crazy for Carol, and yet she's been at Tameka's bedside at least two hours a day after school when she should have been studying or preparing for her day in court. But she knows how much it means. There's no one Tameka looks forward to seeing more." She shoots me a glance. "Like I said, she's family."

"Thank you, Miss Oliver." The judge clears his throat. "The court certainly wishes your sister well."

"Thank you, Your Honor."

Dismissed from the stand, the bailiff takes Roberta out the back of the courtroom instead of back to the witness room as he has with the others. She offers me a subtle nod as she walks past, but before my mind can begin to ponder on where she might be going, the judge catches my eye.

"Unless there are any further witnesses, Mr. Blake," he intones, "I think I'd like to hear from Miss Davis now."

CHAPTER SIXTY-FOUR

The judge motions me forward, and I comply. As I take my seat, I keep my eyes focused on Mike, the confidence in his smile only mildly tarnished by the unease in his gaze. The bailiff has me place my left hand on the Bible and raise my right hand as I swear to tell the truth, the whole truth, and nothing but the truth. I take the oath gladly, though I decide against making any mention of dead girls, ghosts, or my recent travels through time with the three Spirits.

Might get me locked up in a completely different kind of room.

"Miss Davis," the judge begins. "We've reviewed your list of charges. We've heard from your family, your employer, your friends. What do you have to say for yourself on this matter?"

I glance around the courtroom as I gather my wits. I find many friendly faces: Mike, Philippe, Emily, a few girls from swim, even the Campbells—though I still can't quite bring myself to meet their eyes. One face, however, is still missing.

Christopher's.

He said he'd be here today. The part of me that would so recently have bitten his head off for blowing off something so important wrestles with a growing part of me that hopes he's okay.

"Miss Davis?" the judge asks.

"Sorry, Your Honor." I let out a sigh. "I have a lot on my mind."

"The court is waiting to hear your allocution."

As am I. I tried all night to put thoughts to paper, to create some semblance of order from the chaos of the last three weeks, but every time I tried, the words just came out a colossal mess.

So, here I am, winging it in front of a judge with the potential for months to years behind bars hanging in the balance.

"Your Honor." I cast my gaze across the gallery. "And all of you. I haven't come here today to plead my innocence or even to ask forgiveness for my actions. I'm here for one purpose and one purpose alone." I take a breath. "To make a declaration."

The prosecutor's smile doubles in intensity, sending my heart racing.

"Thus far in my life, I've been two people. The first of those, a little girl, so sweet and so innocent, died on her eighth birthday along with the rest of her family. I miss her terribly, but she's not coming back. I've learned to accept that." I lock gazes with Mike. "The difficult person most of you have known for the last several years was the Carol Davis born that Christmas Day. I come today to declare before the law and all of you that ten years to the day later, that particular Carol Davis has died as well. I'm still getting to know this third Carol and hope that she gets the opportunity to prove herself to each and every person in this town."

Almost imperceptibly, Mike nods. I continue.

"I made many poor decisions the night of the Christmas Eve Dance—that goes without saying, I suppose—but that's just the tip of the iceberg of bad choices that have defined the last ten years of my life. I've turned my back on old friends, focused on the wrong things, and bitten the hand that feeds me at every turn. As of today, all of that stops." I turn to the judge. "I don't dispute a single charge from the police report from Christmas Eve. I've read it myself, and as best I understand it, that's pretty much the way it went down." My vocal cords finally give in to the moment as I barely choke out the next sentence. "Regardless of my actions in saving the Campbell family that night, it doesn't change the simple fact that none of them would have been in any danger in the first place if it wasn't for me."

"Don't cry." The small voice, from the back of the gallery, echoes through the room. Jillian Campbell, standing on the bench between her parents despite her father's repeated encouragement for her to sit down, stares at me, her little eyes fixed on mine like twin lasers. "Everybody's okay." She turns to her mother. "Right, Mommy?"

The mother pulls her daughter onto her lap and peers across the gallery at me. There is reproach in her gaze, and it's well deserved, but I find something in her eyes I never dreamed I'd find in a million years.

Gratitude.

Barely able to breathe, I force my way through the rest of my thought. "I'm not perfect, and never will be, but for the first time in a very long time, I care. After I lost my parents, I had to grow up fast, and it wasn't easy. The truth, though, is I had a lot more growing up to do." I swallow the emotion. "And still do."

I keep my eyes on Mike to keep myself from bursting into tears. A sincere admiration peeks through the trepidation that's been plastered across his face since we arrived at the courtroom this afternoon. I had forgotten how good it felt to have him be proud of me.

"So here it is," I continue, willing my lower lip to stop trembling. "I'll never catch up on all the apologies I owe, make up for all the wrongs I've done, or repair all the bridges I've burned in my life, but know this." I lock gazes with Mrs. Campbell. "I plan to spend the rest of my life making up for the things I've done and the people I've hurt along the way." My eyes fall on little Jillian Campbell, her face blossoming in an innocent smile. "I'm just glad I have the opportunity now to make things right."

CHAPTER SIXTY-FIVE

In his chambers for all of twenty minutes, the judge has returned to the bench and is carefully examining one of the many documents from my case folder. Just when I can't take it anymore, he looks up at me from behind his glasses, his hawkish expression somewhere between wise and world-weary.

"Miss Davis, you admit freely to drinking the better part of a flask of vodka, taking Mr. King's Camaro for a joyride, driving while distracted by your phone, and, in doing so, causing the accident in question this past 24th of December?"

"Yes, Your Honor."

"Even knowing that such charges could result in heavy fines and imprisonment?"

"Yes, Your Honor."

"And that since the fines corresponding to these charges are negligible compared to the amount of money you recently came into, any judge worth his salt would be pushing for jail time."

I shove my hands in my pockets to keep them from shaking. "Yes...Your Honor."

"One last question, then." He stares down at the document

in his hand. From what I can see from the light coming through the paper, it appears to be a list of some sort. "As you recall, your last call was cut short at the moment you caused the accident in question?"

Surprised by the question, my entire body stiffens. "As best as I can remember, yes."

He again studies the paper in his hand through his rectangular spectacles.

"You're quite certain of that fact, Miss Davis?"

"Yes." My eyes flick left at Paul. "Not a doubt in my mind."

The judge rests the paper on the bench and places his bifocals atop them. "Then it would appear this case is closed."

"Your Honor." My lawyer jumps out of his chair. "Please..."

"I wasn't finished, Mr. Blake. This case isn't just closed. It's sealed." The judge hands the paper to the bailiff.

"What's he talking about?" I whisper in Paul's ear. "What's happening?"

His fingers go white as he grips his silver Cross pen. "I have no idea."

The bailiff studies the document, a flash of understanding crossing his expression just before he takes the paper to Ms. White, the prosecutor. She scrutinizes the paper herself for all of five seconds before a quiet sigh escapes her lips. Her eyes slip closed as she leans back in her chair, arms crossed.

"That paper." My heart pounds in my chest. "What does it say?"

The bailiff retrieves the document from the prosecutor and hands it to my lawyer. Paul's confused expression quickly fades into one of wonder. He hands me the paper, a cellular phone record, and points to the end time of the final call on the list.

"11:58." I look up at the judge. "I...I don't get it."

The judge leans back in his chair and regards me with a mischievous not-quite grin.

"The law has many gray areas, Miss Davis, but times and dates are as black and white as it gets. According to this phone record, your last call on December 24th ended at 11:58 p.m."

I interlace my fingers to keep them from shaking. "And?"

"And..." The judge leans forward and rests his elbows on the bench. "That means you were still a minor at the time of the accident."

"Your Honor." The prosecutor rises from her chair. "Two minutes—"

"Is two minutes, Ms. White." As the prosecutor sits back down, the judge turns in the direction of our table. "As I see it, Miss Davis, you made several poor decisions on the night in question. These errors in judgment compounded on each other, leading to the various injuries sustained by the Campbell family, the loss of their vehicle, and destruction of public property."

"Your Honor—" My lawyer barely gets the words out before the judge quiets him with a stern glance.

"However, your quick thinking and unbelievable bravery saved the lives of the family in question as evidenced by the three of them sitting in this very courtroom." His stern eyes bore into me. "Miss Davis, I trust that your recent windfall is more than adequate to replace their vehicle and take care of any medical expenses they incurred from this incident?"

My heart races. "Of course, Your Honor."

"In that case, be it so ordered that Carol Anne Davis be responsible for all expenses incurred by the Campbell family as a result of the accident and that she be remanded to five years' probation and one thousand hours of community service to be carried out over the next three years."

"Your Honor..." Ms. White stands.

"One thousand hours..." Paul whispers.

"Further," the judge states, ignoring them both, "as I said

before, this case is sealed. Miss Davis has been tried today as a minor. Her adult record will remain unblemished." His bird-of-prey glare now falls upon the prosecutor. "Is that clear, Ms. White?"

Her eyes fall to the briefcase in her lap. "Crystal."

"One last comment." The judge's gaze again falls on me. "Miss Davis, today you are being given a second chance to get out there and do it right. Understand that such opportunities don't come along very often. I trust you won't squander it." The judge's stern expression shifts into a knowing smile he, no doubt, normally reserves for his grandchildren. "This court is adjourned."

His gavel strike still echoes through the chamber as the bailiff calls us all to rise. The prosecutor exits without so much as a glance in my direction. The judge returns to his chambers. The crowd files out of the courtroom.

It's over.

Valerie wraps me in a hug, quickly followed by Mike sweeping us both into his arms. Once my aunt and uncle are done suffocating me, I give Paul a quick handshake and thank him. He reluctantly admits that he had very little faith in my plan to plead no contest and can't believe our good fortune. I offer him a simple shrug and step around him to hug Philippe, who has come in from the witness room. The five of us stand there for a few minutes more, the adults all discussing adult things while I struggle to rein in my wandering eyes.

Still no Christopher.

The Carol Davis I was a week ago starts to get fired up until a twinge of pain in my still-healing chest reminds me of one simple fact.

Christopher Kellerman was there for me the day it really mattered.

As we file out of the courtroom, I glance over at the

previously unoccupied jury section. Empty no longer, the first three chairs now hold the only jury besides my friends and family that matters. The Spirits of Christmas Past, Present, and Yet to Come all look on intently as we walk past. Past's wan face for once is turned up in an open grin, Present can't seem to stop laughing, and Yet to Come looks on me with kind regard, her dark eyes just visible from beneath her hood. I peer around the room to see if anyone other than me can see them, but not a soul in the room reacts to the three apparitions in their midst.

When I look again, the Spirits are gone.

As if they were never there.

CHAPTER SIXTY-SIX

"I can't believe it." Valerie's arm encircles my waist as we stroll down the wide courthouse hallway. "It's all over."

"A brand new day." Mike beams from ear to ear, and for once I appreciate his unbridled enthusiasm. "What should we do first?"

A brand new day. A new start. That's what this was all about.

And yet, despite all the wonder and excitement before me, reality intrudes one last time, as a simple task I need to take care of before proceeding with the rest of my life becomes painfully clear.

In all the stress of the courtroom proceedings, I must have drunk ten glasses of water, and my bladder is letting me know it's had enough.

I tell Mike and Valerie to go bring the car around and scurry off to hit the ladies' room before we leave. An older woman I recognize from the gallery wishes me well as we pass in the doorway. I head for the nearest stall and take care of business quickly, not wanting to keep Mike and Valerie waiting. As I head to the sink to wash my hands, the girl that looks back from the mirror appears just as surprised as I feel.

A new start. A sealed record. Some money to the Campbell family that I would have gladly paid anyway.

And community service?

They have no idea what I have in mind.

Everything's turned out basically...okay.

Well, almost everything.

I glance down at my hands, the fine tremor present since I awoke this morning still going strong. Ever since I woke up in the Emergency Room on Christmas Day, there's one thing that has stayed at the forefront of my mind, and seeing the Spirit of Christmas Yet to Come again has done nothing but fan the flames of anxiety that have been eating at me for almost two weeks.

"I'm supposed to be dead."

"Not exactly, Care Bear." Coming from nowhere and everywhere at once, the familiar voice is both a surprise and yet strangely expected.

A glance up reveals a very different girl than was standing in the mirror a moment ago.

I raise an eyebrow. "I thought you said I wouldn't be seeing you again."

"Looks like both of us have exceeded expectations, then." Marnie's dead smile has a bit more life than the last time I saw it. "They decided it would be all right if I said goodbye, after a bit of pleading on my part, of course."

"They?"

"The Powers That Be. The Large and In Charge of the Afterlife." Her lips quirk to one side. "You'll understand someday."

"Someday?"

"A date far in the future, Carol. Don't worry."

"I'll do my best." I stare into the mirror, fascinated as much by the absence of my own reflection as I am by the image of my dead friend. "Still, there's one thing I don't understand."

"One thing?" Marnie chuckles, the sound nowhere near as ominous as the last time it hit my ears.

"The Spirits. Everything they showed me was right on target. Every moment of my past. Every aspect of the present. And yet, Christmas Yet to Come showed me my tombstone. My freaking tombstone." An army of spiders scales my back, taking up residence in my scalp. "I was supposed to die twelve days ago."

Marnie cocks her head to the right. "And?"

"And...I'm still alive and kicking. I was supposed to drown in the creek that night. That's why everyone's lives went to shit, right?"

"Perhaps."

"What changed, then? What happened?"

"What happened?" she asks. "You lived. That's what happened." She steps out of the mirror and stands beside me. "As for what changed..."

The reflection in the mirror goes black, replaced by a dark image that comes into focus like the opening sequence of a movie. Ryan's Camaro whips by on the rain-soaked asphalt. The bridge looms. The Subaru's lights hit the Camaro. Ryan's car fishtails. The Campbell's car swerves, flies from the bridge, and disappears into the darkness below.

My heart pounds in my throat. "Why are you showing me this? I lived it."

Marnie raises a hand. "Wait for it..."

Marnie's whispered words set my hair on end as the "camera" pans in. There, seated in the front seat of Ryan's road rocket, a frightened, hurt, and nauseated Carol stares at the hole in the bridge's rail.

And hits the accelerator. The engine revs, but the car's gear shift is stuck in neutral.

With tremulous hands, she slips the car back into drive and mutters, "I've got to get out of here..."

She punches the accelerator and peels away into the night, leaving the bridge, the Campbell family, and any responsibility for the accident in her rearview mirror.

"But I didn't leave..." I search Marnie's pale face. "I stayed."

"Yes." Her grin grows wider. "But you nearly didn't."

The Camaro rockets up the lonely road toward Havisham. Alone in the car, this Carol cries, her eyes flowing with tears of remorse, but she doesn't look back.

Not once.

She just drives.

She isn't alone for long.

Headlights flood the Camaro's rear window as this Carol's phone begins to ring.

"What?" she answers after letting the phone go to voicemail twice.

"Pull over, Carol."

Surprise, surprise. It's Ryan.

"Stop the car and pull over. Now."

"I just want to go home," this Carol gets out between broken sobs. "Leave me alone."

"Shut up, all right?" Ryan's voice ripples with cold anger. "Just pull the car over. I'll make sure you get home. I promise."

"You promise." This Carol runs a bare arm across her eyes, wiping away the tears even as she hits the accelerator. "Look, no matter what, I'm not stopping out here in the middle of nowhere. I'm going home. You can follow me and pick up your stupid car at my house since that's all you seem to care about."

"Stop the damn car!"

Ryan's shout, pumped by rage and hormones and alcohol,

echoes through the leather-upholstered interior of the Camaro. The Carol in the mirror drops the phone and puts the pedal to the floor, the engine roaring even as a lone deer, its eight-point rack gleaming in the glare of the headlights, leaps into the road.

"Shit." She jerks the wheel to the right, and the Camaro flies from the asphalt. It's over in half a second as the dark sports car hurtles down the rain-soaked embankment and flies into a tree half as wide as the car itself.

As dozens of pine cones rain down on the crumpled hood, everything becomes clear.

"The creek..."

"Was your salvation." Marnie's pale face returns to the mirror even as the image of Ryan's Camaro crushed like an aluminum can against a hundred-year-old pine begins its slow fade into memory. "Christopher Kellerman may have brought you back from the brink of death, but your decision to stay on that bridge and face the consequences of your actions is the reason you're still breathing."

"Christopher..." Even as icy fingers work their way up and down my spinal cord at having witnessed the moment of my forestalled death, I find myself wondering most of all what it was that kept him from the courtroom today.

Reappearing within the mirror, Marnie lets out another cool chuckle. "He's right outside, Care Bear. Why don't you go ask him yourself?"

My feet take two steps for the door before my mind even registers why they're moving.

"Wait." I stop in my tracks. "Is this it? No more visits from beyond the grave? No more Spirits?"

"No, on both counts." Marnie raises an eyebrow. "As I understand it, this was your big moment, and you passed by the skin of your teeth. From here on out, you're on your own."

"I think I've got it from here." I step back toward the mirror. "So, I'm never going to see you again?"

"I don't think so. I'm moving up and moving on. One less soul to wander aimless among the living, and I owe it all to you."

"To me?"

Marnie's brow knits together. "You weren't the only one on trial that night." She glances back across her shoulder for half a second before turning to face me again, her face wet with tears. "It's time. Oh, Carol. You have no idea how beautiful it is."

"Glad to hear it." My voice cracks as my own eyes begin to well up. "Any last requests?"

"Go see my mom every once in a while." Marnie's lower lip quivers. "She's lonely and doesn't have much family to call on these days."

I swallow the emotion of the moment. "She does now."

"Thank you." Marnie's image in the mirror begins to fade. "Now get out there. Christopher is waiting for you."

I raise a hand. "Goodbye, Marnie."

She brings two pale fingers to her lips and blows me a kiss. "Goodbye, Carol."

CHAPTER SIXTY-SEVEN

The mirror returns to normal just before a middle-aged woman enters the ladies' room and brushes past me. Through the open door, I catch a glimpse of Christopher. Dressed in a new jacket he got for Christmas and a pair of slacks I helped him pick out last week, he's staring at his smartphone, his eyes squinted in frustration. I reach for my purse to shoot him a text and am reminded for the four hundredth time today that my phone is out in the car.

Wiping away the tears, I head out into the hallway. I'm barely through the door when Christopher spots me. The irritation in his expression melts instantly to a beaming smile.

"Hi."

"You're late," I mutter, raising an eyebrow.

"And you haven't been answering texts."

Confident. Strong. I'm liking this new side of Christopher.

"Valerie made me leave my phone out in the car."

"Your aunt's a smart woman." He slides his own phone into his pocket. "I'm guessing you didn't get to talk to Roberta either, then?"

"She came and spoke for me, but we didn't have a chance to talk. Why?"

Christopher shoves his hands in his pockets. "Tameka took a bad turn last night—more fever, chills, and the like—and Roberta's mother isn't taking it well."

I take Christopher's arm. "Is she going to be okay?"

"They don't know." Christopher heads for the door with me in tow. "Roberta asked me to stay with her mother at the hospital so she could come and testify."

"She didn't have to do that." Ahead of us, the door leading out to the street opens. As two men in dark suits step around us, I get a glimpse of what awaits us outside.

Reporters. Cameramen. Trucks with satellite dishes.

Twice as many as this morning.

A part of me misses when it was merely Spirits that were chasing me around.

But if they want a sound bite, I'll give them one.

"Wait here."

"But—"

I slip on my coat and scarf and give his hand a quick squeeze. "There's something I've got to do."

I leave him standing there below the blindfolded statue of Lady Justice and step through the door. Immediately every eye, camera, and microphone are pointed in my direction.

"Miss Davis. How did you..."

"The Campbell family. What did you think of..."

"...three million dollars. What are your..."

I let them go on for a minute before raising a hand.

"If everyone will please hold your questions, I'd like to make a statement."

Something akin to a hush falls over the entire assembly. I motion the cameramen and reporters with their microphones to gather close, and they readily comply.

"First, I'd like to thank all of you for coming today. The outcome of this morning was beyond anything I could have hoped for. I have been ordered to take care of any expenditures, medical or otherwise, the Campbell family might have incurred secondary to the accident on Christmas Eve, and am more than happy to do so."

I take a breath.

"I've also been ordered to perform a thousand hours of community service over the next three years. That begins now."

I glance back at the courthouse. Christopher stands by the door leaning against the yellow brick. He's doing his hair a new way since the new year began.

A little bit of product and a little bit of effort.

Both go a long way.

Or maybe I just see him differently these days. Nearly two straight weeks of nightly Netflix binges on my new widescreen TV—Yes, I finally went and picked up the stupid thing—and we're back to being two peas in a pod, three on the nights Roberta's been free to join us. Those are the nights that feel the most like old times, though the one-on-one nights have been... well...interesting.

My cheeks burn as I turn to address the gathered reporters.

"Today is a new beginning for me, and in more ways than one." I wipe a tear from my cheek. "As anyone who's watched the news recently knows, I've just come through a life-changing couple of weeks. The events that led to my presence in court today notwithstanding, all of you know that I have recently come into possession of a large sum of money. More than I could ever need. More than I can even imagine." The corner of my mouth turns up in a half smile. "And I can imagine a lot."

A female reporter to my immediate left takes a step closer. "That begs the question, Miss Davis. What *do* you plan to do with the money?"

"I'm glad you asked." I look directly into the nearest camera. "Today, I'm proud to announce the formation of The Joy Foundation. Named for my beautiful sister who was taken from this life far too soon, this organization will exist to serve the needs of children who have nowhere else to turn. We have a long way to go, as even the millions from the settlement will only go so far, but I've already been in contact with advisors that will help us grow this seed of an idea into a tree that can shelter the young and helpless for generations."

The reporter's brow furrows. "And when do you anticipate beginning this ambitious new venture?"

"Effective immediately. And our work begins today." I direct their attention to the top floor of the hospital, just visible above the tree line in the distance. "On the fourth floor of Havisham Medical Center lies a little girl fighting for her life. Tameka Oliver, the little sister of the best friend I've ever had, is dying of leukemia. Cancer has ravaged her body, and the treatments the doctors are forced to use are little better than the disease. If she doesn't find a bone marrow donor soon, her chances of pulling through are pretty grim." I step closer to the nearest camera. "I'm heading to the hospital right now to get tested to see if I'm a match. I challenge each and every citizen of Havisham and anyone else watching this newscast to join me." I clench my fists to keep from crying. "God willing, if enough of us do the right thing, Tameka and who knows how many others will see next Christmas from somewhere besides a hospital bed." My voice cracks. "If they get to see next Christmas at all..."

Roberta cannot lose Tameka the way I lost Joy. She just can't...

I swallow in an attempt to regain my composure when a flash of movement catches my eye. Past all the reporters and microphones and cameras, the Spirit of Christmas Yet to Come stands alone on the sidewalk, her dark robe now a gown of shimmering white. Her full lips restored and turned up in a broad smile I've seen in the mirror a lot more often lately, she glances in the direction of the hospital and offers a single nod before dissipating like a dandelion head in a strong breeze.

For the hundredth time today, my eyes well with tears, but this time they are tears of joy.

If anyone knows what's going to happen to Tameka, it's the Spirit who knew exactly what would happen to me no matter which path I chose.

My heart about to burst, I turn back to the reporters. "Are there any other questions?"

A young reporter I recognize from one of the local affiliates raises his microphone. "Miss Davis, this all seems so...sudden. Can you tell us what exactly led you to this, shall we say, epiphany?"

I bite my lower lip, gathering my thoughts.

"For ten years, Christmas has been nothing but an annual reminder of everything I've lost. Of the pain I've endured. Of everything that can go wrong in life. I've waited years for that to change, but I don't think it ever will. Circumstances of the last few days, however, led me to a simple realization." I take a deep breath and stand as straight as I can. "I was the one who had to change."

I stay with the reporters until I've exhausted their questions. As I'm about to leave, an older woman whose press pass identifies her as a reporter from the Havisham paper hits me with one last query.

"Any last words, Miss Davis?"

"Yes." An image of Tameka's smile flashes across my mind's eye, and the words flow from my mouth as if from another time. "God bless us, everyone."

Christopher appears at my side, a welcome presence.

Taking my hand, he leads me through the crowd of reporters and down the sidewalk. Halfway down the block, I spy Valerie's car waiting for me at the corner. Another couple of steps and I pull Christopher into the shallow doorway of a shuttered furniture store.

Call me crazy, but I'm not quite ready to go yet.

Christopher inhales to speak, but I place a finger across his lips.

He doesn't say a word.

Boy's a fast learner.

We don't talk, per se, but we do communicate. And it's good.

Christopher Kellerman. Expert-level kisser. Who knew?

Lost in the moment, my mind wanders.

Throughout my life, my every experience has taught me there's no such thing as second chances, but here I am, living proof of how wrong I've been. Delivered from death by Spirits from beyond this world, granted a miracle reprieve from the stupidest night of my life, and now I stand here kissing a boy who has been in love with me since before either of us even knew what love was.

What do you know? The girl who has held her breath for ten years finally gets to come up for air.

Well, maybe in a minute.

THE END

AUTHOR'S NOTE

Just before Thanksgiving in 2012, I awoke from a dream around 3:00 in the morning, a few hours before I was supposed to be at the day job taking care of my panel of family medicine patients, and said aloud, "I'm going to write a young adult *A Christmas Carol*!" Having such nighttime epiphanies isn't all that rare for me, but this was an idea I didn't want to lose, so I rounded up my laptop, popped open an empty Word document, and wrote about a third of a page about the character you now know as Carol Davis and a few of the things that could transform someone so young into such a Scrooge.

The following morning, I was so excited about the project, I manically reviewed the basic plot ideas with my nurse, Linda Elder, and she caught the "spirit" as well. I was knee deep in working on my Fugue & Fable series at the time, but as I got to a good stopping point in that series of books, I got to work on the book you now hold in your hands, getting most of it written between mid 2013 and early 2015.

Once I got it in the best shape I could, my agent at the time and still my good friend, Stacey Donaghy, shopped it high and low, but we never found a home at any of the publishers we tried. "Too seasonal," most said, to which I wanted to ask why the bookstores fill with Christmas themed books at the front of the store for the last quarter of every single year if no one buys Christmas books. But I digress.

So, this not-so-little story of Carol Davis and her family, the ghost of Marnie Jacobsen, and my version of the three Spirits of

Dickens fame sat on my hard drive for a LONG time. I've dusted it off a few times, tried a publisher or two myself over the years, but never quite found it a home.

Then...2020 came. Pandemic. Cancellation of every single thing I'd planned to do for over a year including seventeen different events where I could meet readers and introduce them to my books. Week after week of sitting at home, often practicing the relatively new skill of telephonic medicine with which I continue to grow more proficient with each passing week, reinforced a truism that I've heard for my entire life.

Life is short.

And way too short to let a story that woke you from a dead sleep and demanded to be written remain unread.

So, like Carol, I decided to come up for air after holding my breath on this particular story for over half a decade. I certainly hope you've enjoyed it.

As always, a few acknowledgements:

To my critique partners back in the day, Matthew Saunders, Jay Requard, Caryn Sutorus, Traci Loudin, and Robyne Pomroy, thank you so much for your time and energy into helping me make this story as good as it could be.

To my friends in Charlotte Writers, thank you for all the years of sticking together as we've each worked toward our individual goals, all the while keeping Amelie's French Bakery in business on Wednesday nights.

To Mom, Dad, and Jilly, thanks for your constant support in my nearly half-century on this planet. You mean the world to me. (Yes, that was supposed to be a subtle pun.)

To Katelyn and Olivia, as it says up front, this one's for you and your mom. Hard to believe that when I started this thing, you were both in middle school and now one of you is in college with the other almost there. Man, time flies. I hope you both love this book.

To Melissa McArthur, and before her, Sharon Stogner, thanks for all the excellent editing on this manuscript. Between the both of you, I think we've polished this thing to a high sheen. Also, thank you to Melissa for such a beautifully formatted book. All the little flourishes are like the decorations on a Christmas tree.

To Natania Barron, all I can say is that judging a book by its cover is fine with me if that cover is one of yours. Thanks for yet another beautiful piece of art to introduce this book to potential readers.

My perennial shout out to all my teachers over the years, thanks for both instilling in me the desire to express myself and the teaching me skills to do so. One of you got a mention in this book; can you find yourself in these pages?

Lastly, what seems to be a constant part of my acknowledgments, my utter gratitude to a man long gone but who will likely never be forgotten.

Charles Dickens, in *A Christmas Carol*, didn't just write a book or craft a story. He reinvented Christmas. He created a legend, a myth, a piece of folklore that is so ingrained in Western Culture that just its barest mention sets imaginations alight. I think we all have our favorite Scrooge - I'm a tie between George C. Scott and Bill Murray, though Patrick Stewart is outstanding in the role as well. We all have our favorite version of the story (mine is the 1984 television classic with George C. Scott though Matthew Saunders swears by *The Muppet Christmas Carol*) and we all have our favorite moments in the story (When the boy with mutism in *Scrooged* says, "God bless us, everyone," I tear up every single time). *A Christmas Carol* has been adapted for theatre, film, television, radio, opera, comic books and strips, video games, and is still read publicly around the world in multiple languages every Christmas. It was a bit daunting to try to find something new to say with a field already so crowded with so many talented writers, actors, directors, etc., but this was a story that, as I said above, demanded to be told.

My final thanks, to you, the reader, for taking a chance on my take on a true classic. I hope it moved you, made you laugh, made you cry, and most importantly, made you think.

It was not a random story decision that led me to replace the Ignorance and Want usually found beneath Christmas Present's robes with the singular embodiment of Apathy. Looking out for number one in lieu of caring for your fellow man is the biggest problem underlying so many issues in our time. In this time of global pandemic and continued battle for true equality for everyone (hopefully, future readers will be able to look on this statement as historical), it is incumbent on each of us to strive to be the best person that we can be, to care for one another as best we can, and to always try to look past the "me" and try to focus on the "we." We're all together on this living spaceship we call Earth and other than the handful of us fortunate to venture beyond our atmosphere from time to time, we're all stuck together down here from our first day to our last. My final plea: care for this world, for it's all we've got, and care for each other, for we're all we've got.

ABOUT THE AUTHOR

Darin Kennedy, born and raised in Winston-Salem, North Carolina, is a graduate of Wake Forest University and Bowman Gray School of Medicine. After completing family medicine residency in the mountains of Virginia, he served eight years as a United States Army physician and wrote his first novel in the sands of northern Iraq.

His first published novel, *The Mussorgsky Riddle,* was born from a fusion of two of his lifelong loves: classical music and world mythology. *The Stravinsky Intrigue* continues those same themes, and his *Fugue & Fable* series culminates in *The Tchaikovsky Finale.* His *The Pawn Stratagem* contemporary fantasy series, *Pawn's Gambit, Queen's Peril,* and *King's Crisis* combines contemporary fantasy, superheroics, and the ancient game of chess. His short stories can be found in numerous anthologies and magazines, and the best, particularly those about a certain *Necromancer for Hire,* are collected for your reading pleasure.

Doctor by day and novelist by night, he writes and practices medicine in Charlotte, NC. When not engaged in either of the above activities, he has been known to strum the guitar, enjoy a bite of sushi, and rumor has it he even sleeps on occasion. Find him online at darinkennedy.com.

Printed in the USA
CPSIA information can be obtained
at www.ICGtesting.com
LVHW092125161223
766691LV00046B/663